Final Flight of the Ranegr

Other works by this author:

The Starlight Lancer
The Awakening
Path of a Hero
The Cursed Jewel
Metanoia
The Star Warriors

Find them online at
https://www.cscooper.com.au/books

In the rotations of the stars and planets, the duration of war and strife, came the decimation of the Antiqua kingdoms. Then Gorthol of the Golden Eyes that Terrify rained fire upon the Orda of Udhur. There was but one vessel that stood against her. It was named *Ranegr*.

Final Flight of the Ranegr

C. S. COOPER

Second Edition

Cover art by Tessa Eden

Edited by Maria Simms
Laurel Cohn Editing Services
www.laurelcohn.com.au

Paperback ISBN: 978-0-9876335-0-7
eBook ISBN: 978-0-9876335-1-4

Contents

Acknowledgements

It goes without saying that there are a lot of people to acknowledge in the creation and publication of this novel. It has been quite an endeavour, with more influences than I can possibly count. And it's not even the entire story I wish to tell.

Honestly, I haven't even started.

The first people I should thank are my Mum and Dad for letting me play *Commander Keen* on the old Windows 3.1 machine we used to own. I should also thank them for refusing to buy me the rest of the games in the series, since it was that impetus that drove me to create my own stories and worlds using scrap paper and pencils. It is that, combined with knowledge of physics, provided by the books they gave me, that has contributed to the creation of this universe. Thanks should also go to my siblings for letting me talk their ears off about my imaginary world.

I should also thank George Lucas for making *Star Wars*, germinating my love of science fiction and fantasy. I acknowledge J. R. R. Tolkien, C. S. Lewis, and also Don Bluth as influences as well, since their fantasy works showed me the value of creating languages and cultures in which to set my stories. Shigeru Miyamoto, the creator of *The Legend of Zelda*, should also receive a mention, since much of my idle fantasies that contributed to this invented world started while playing his games. Keiji Inafune receives a mention for creating *Mega Man X* – this invented world started as a story of me as the titular *X*. Hayao Miyazaki's visual style inspired many of the scenes in this novel, particularly those set on Ondyarii, as well as some of the characters. Hiromu Arakawa also deserves a special mention, since her manga, *Fullmetal Alchemist*, inspired me to learn more about alchemy and mysticism, which informed much of the invented mythos behind this novel.

Closer in each of the four dimensions, I thank the unnamed circus performers of the pirate-themed circus show I attended in 2011, from whence I received the inspiration for this story. I thank my girlfriend at the time for listening as I raved about the idea that had taken root in my mind.

I thank Holly, who was my first editor on this project.

I thank Tessa, who designed the cover art on this story – and all my other stories, by the way. She is super-genius!

An extra-special thanks goes to my friend, Abhinay, who was the first* to agree to read the novel without being paid for it. His input and encouragement had been invaluable.

I would like to also thank Mrs. Seaberg and Mrs. Faith, under whose tutelage I learned to perform in front of audiences, project my voice, articulate my speech, create and express my characters. Much of my skill with the spoken and written word wouldn't have been without their hard work.

I'd like to mention my kindergarten teacher, Mrs. Evans, of whom I have a fond memory: after a long time of writing one line stories about what I did on the weekend, I hand to her a handwritten page of writing, much to her delight. I recall her joyously screeching, "You only ever wrote little squibbly bits! Now you've written so much!" Well, as you can plainly see, this isn't a little squibbly bit, and the story isn't finished here either.

I would like to acknowledge Laurel Cohn, Helen Williams, and Maria Simms, whose appraisal and editing services have been invaluable.

There are probably people I haven't mentioned, because my head is already full of this story and what's to come. It is important to know, and often overlooked, that it is rarely one mind in a vacuum that brings a piece of art to fruition. Every piece of art, every invention, every discovery is merely a node of order in a swirling storm of noise, billowing up to the top to leave a tiny mark on the surface of our culture. It's probably one of the things that sucks about culture is how invisible so many of its contributors seem. To paraphrase Bernard of Chartres, I am a dwarf standing on the shoulders of giants.

I hope you enjoy the story.

Sincerely,
Craig

---

* I should probably mention Queenie, who stole Abhinay's Kindle so she could read the novel before him.

Notes on Pronunciation

A great deal of world building went into this novel, including the invention of two languages. I won't go into detail concerning the grammar and words of these languages. I will, however, go into some details on the sounds of these languages, so that you may better read the story.

The first language I invented is Ordang. This is mentioned in Chapter 5, and a written inscription is on the second page of this volume. Within the invented universe, this is the language spoken by my protagonists' ancient ancestors. The word *ranegr* is from this language. To pronounce these words, use the following guidelines: 'r' at the start of a word or after a vowel is pronounced as you would in English 'race' or 'roar', but is pronounced with a trill after a consonant; 'dh' is pronounced as a voiced 'th' as in 'they' or 'though'; and 'u' is pronounced as in 'pool'. All other sounds are as in English.

The second language is called Aimorein, spoken by natives of the planet Ondyarii. There are a considerable number of words used in this book. To pronounce these words, I provide the following guidelines: 'a' is pronounced as in 'cut'; 'i' is pronounced as in 'pit'; 'o' is pronounced as in 'not'; 'e' is pronounced as in 'net'; 'u' is pronounced as in 'sue'; all vowels are short, but are lengthened by doubling or, in the case of 'o', placing a 'u' afterward – e.g., *rii* "star" or *youkuro* "kindling basket"; 'y' always has the sounds as in 'you' even when following consonants – e.g., 'ky' as in 'cute'; 'u' is often not pronounced between consonants, such as *suke* "water" being pronounced as 'ske'; 'r' is pronounced as a tap against the ridge behind the teeth; repeated consonants indicate a short pause before pronunciation. All other sounds are as in English.

Prologue

A shower of mesmerising fireworks scattered the vaporised remains of fighters and their pilots across the star-speckled void. Photons from the blasts crashed against the hull of the warship as it awaited the enemy's full force. To say the bridge was tense would be an egregious understatement. Though they steeled their nerves, the crew was rank with the fear of impending inevitability. All prayed they would not see her face, her terrifying golden eyes.

All but one.

An admiral stood from the chair upon the dais, the seal of his beloved vessel and crew emblazoned upon his resplendent jacket. He called the attention of his bridge crew, who looked up nervously from their overflowing FOF monitors.

"I have left my fear in this chair," he said, pausing a moment before drawing his knife from his belt and thrusting it into the chair's padding. "Now, I have killed it!" he bellowed. "You must do the same if we are to survive!"

He sheathed his blade with a flourish and marched forward to stand by his first officer, who worked to regain her own composure.

"Losses?" she commanded.

"Half the vanguard is sunk," replied the tactical officer. "Enemy fleet advancing."

"Have the vanguard pull back and join us," said the Admiral. "Fear not! You watch. Today, at the end, we'll prevail."

Ethereal flashes of bright cyan filled the horizon, illuminating the galactic core beyond in a faint hue as more vessels appeared behind the retreating vanguard. The behemoths dwarfed the smaller vessels, which scrambled to the relative safety of the orbital defence fleet.

"Admiral, the enemy fleet has appeared in full force," exclaimed the sensors officer. He added with an ice-cold tremor, "Flagship vessel confirmed. She is here."

The admiral eyed the planet below, gritting his teeth with determination to protect his home world. Then his eyes turned to the fleet before him, and he scoffed, "Is this it? Is this all that witch can muster?" The crew thought he'd gone mad. He ordered, "Open a channel to all ships."

The communications officer handed him a microphone.

"Listen up, ladies and gentlemen!" he roared. "Look down, and remember what you're defending. Then look at our enemy, and see her for the pushover that she is. She's unworthy of being the opponent of the Orda! Arm yourselves! Put on your war paint! Let's show that beast just how good we are!"

Every arm hair rose in anticipation. The communications officer reported the fleet's response.

"Ready the main hadron cannons, and prepare for combat!" commanded the first officer.

The admiral's grin widened and he bellowed, "Let the *Ranegr* sortie!"

1 | Bioplant Crisis?

"You see," bellowed the geography teacher, "thanks to the bioplants, we can recycle matter much more efficiently than a planet can. We do this because we can't afford to lose anything on our voyage."

Neliya's eyes darted around the room, noting her classmates making a show of diligent work. It was just a show. Their hands were strategically positioned to hide the games they played on their tablets. Then she turned back to the window.

The clouds circled above: dark, billowing convections of vapour that rose out of sight, and reappeared minutes later elsewhere in the sky. The flow traced a circle in the air, carrying with it barely visible dots that Neliya was certain were garbage.

So much for our bioplants – We can't even keep something we built clean, she thought, bored, as she gazed at the flying trash heap. *If head maid can always remember to clean the filters on the laundry machine, why doesn't the Sidha remember to do it on our ship?*

Three loud chimes snapped Neliya out of her daydreaming. With Pavlovian symmetry, the students locked their tablets, packed their bags, and stood behind their desks. The teacher shouted last minute instructions and reading – which his students were certain to ignore – and scooped up an unmarked attendance sheet.

That one moment, when Neliya passed the source of drivel that was the junior high school teacher and said, "Present," was the most contact she had with most teachers.

No way would they fail someone in my position.

But today, the teacher stopped her before she could flee.

"Miss Dosag," muttered the teacher, barely moving his lips. "It's been brought to our attention that Mister Indra has not been present for several of his classes over the last few days. Do you know where he might be at this time?"

"He has a very weak constitution, and if he had to sit in one of these classes again, his skin would melt and his brain would ooze out his ears …" was what Neliya wanted to say to this particular teacher.

"He hasn't been feeling well lately," she said instead, and buttoned it with an expression of concern.

"Is he sick?" asked the teacher.

"Yes, he's come down with a case of intestinal *dershwaub*," replied Neliya, snickering slightly at the end. "Fyuren and I have been looking after him. Oh, would you look at the time! I need to get ready for practice."

The teacher pursed his lips, his eyes fixing on her.

"Miss Dosag," he said, more audible than before. "You do know that lying to a teacher earns you demerit points. Do you remember what that means?"

"Three demerits gets an hour of detention … cleaning toilets, usually," she said aloud.

"Indeed," said the teacher, who then drew close to her. "Don't lie again."

"Yes, teacher," said Neliya with an internal sigh.

"Mister Indra has skipped too many classes," said the teacher, turning away. "He may be held back again."

As the teacher walked down the corridor, Neliya held back a sneer of disgust. The man might well have clicked his heels while murmuring that tripe. She knew some teachers cared about her friend's issues, and one of them might have encouraged her to do something about his truancy. *That* teacher, she wanted to thump on the head with her tablet – or have him transferred to some politically unstable annexed system.

Never mind him, she thought. *Run a few laps at track club, and you'll feel better.*

She clambered up the stairs from the social sciences classroom and turned right. A great rumble echoed through the open plaza, reverberating through the windows of teaching rooms and the staff room in the corner. Given what Neliya could see swirling in those clouds, not just water was about to fall.

I hope that doesn't fall for a while, or they might cancel practice.

She heard another ruckus rising above the ebbing thunder. The dismay centres of her brain caught fire, and told her exactly what the sound was and from where it came.

She raced through the nearest passageway toward the toilets between the math and language classrooms. A congregation had gathered around the entrance to the boys' bathroom like flies fighting over garbage. She pushed through it to reach the door and entered without a moment's hesitation.

The whole crowd (at least those who could fit into the bathroom) watched a fight between three boys, and cheered as if enjoying a favourite past-time.

Two of the combatants were big, stocky, and red faced either from exertion or sheer amusement at the appearance of the third, who was shorter, fuming with anger, with tears rolling down his face, and a red, sticky stain smattered across his dishevelled hair. His hands were clenched so hard his knuckles were white.

He swung savagely at the two boys, a burning hatred in his eyes. He growled louder and threw a punch at the nearest bully, but missed and fell flat on his face. Laughter resounded like a dash of salt on the boy's wounds; he pulled himself to his feet and charged at the bullies again. They dodged nimbly, chortling as they did so, and then laughed even harder as the boy tumbled headfirst into Neliya.

"Ha ha! Teary-Zeery!" taunted the bullies, chanting it until the whole bathroom resounded with it.

"Zeers, stop it!" cried Neliya, holding onto the boy.

"I'll rip 'em!" grumbled Zeers, his cheeks flushed with anger.

"You will, huh?" said the nearest bully. "Yeah right! You're fourteen and still in Year Six. You want to pick a fight? Fight the kindergarten girls. Heh, your girlfriend'll probably still have to rescue you."

The crowd dispersed when a teacher appeared at the entrance. Upon pushing her way through the rabble, her attention fell entirely on a flailing, screaming Zeers. At that, the bullies nonchalantly blended into the crowd, leaving Zeers to receive a scolding and demerit points for starting yet another fight.

Neliya tried to explain to the teacher, who wasn't listening. Her frustration built until she barked, "Would you bother to ask him what happened?"

The teacher was flabbergasted. "I beg your pardon, Miss Dosag?"

"Why don't you ask who did *this* to him?" she pointed out the red goo tangled through his hair.

The teacher sniffed the muck tentatively. "It's egg. Did you make a mistake in your home-economics class again, Mister Indra?"

"Tayure threw it at me!" shouted Zeers. "He and Finsti did it!"

"Why don't you stop dishing out demerits and find those big fat arses?" snapped Neliya.

The teacher's face went redder than the drying yolk on Zeers' shirt. "Two demerits for speaking back to a teacher!" she screeched. "Two more demerits for falsely accusing other students! And *two more* for foul language!"

With six demerits each, Neliya and Zeers spent the next two hours after school cleaning the toilets. There they stood, blazers aside, sleeves rolled up, aprons on, rubber-gloved, with buckets of sponges and chemicals. They started with the outermost cubicles and working their way inward. The first toilet Neliya picked issued a stench from which she withdrew in disgust. She hastily flushed the offending matter away.

"You shouldn't have been mouthing off to teachers," murmured Zeers.

"That way you wouldn't be doing this."

She lowered her sleeve from her nose and said breathlessly, "Totally worth it."

Zeers responded with a chuckle.

"Was it worth it for you?" asked Neliya, coughing as the bleach vapours stung her throat and eyes. "I mean, working yourself up into a froth and embarrassing yourself in front of most of the kids in the school, *again?*"

"If I could land a hit, that'd be worth cleaning all the toilets in the Commonwealth," replied Zeers, punctuating his words with a thrust of his sponge. "And one day I'll get 'em!"

Neliya shook her head in dismay. The geography teacher's warning came to mind, and she sternly said, "You can't wag class forever."

"Yeah, I know," sighed Zeers. "The term's not over yet. I'll have more than enough attendance hours."

Neliya shook her head, unable to contend with her friend's stubbornness. "Only if you actually come to class. You know the Guild doesn't look kindly on a lack of commitment to education."

"Hey, if the Guild doesn't want me, I'll at least get to keep my arm," replied Zeers.

Neliya's face turned pale both at the sight of her next cubicle and the repressed thought Zeers just revived. Goosebumps prickled along her right arm.

"I'd never let them lop my arm off," she murmured. "I don't care how much mind powers I'd get from their robot arms."

"I would!" said Zeers. "I'd get those powers, then use them on Tayure and Finsti. I'll show them just how good I am."

He said it with such certainty and enthusiasm that Neliya liked the idea. Then of course her mind immediately reminded her of the mechanical arm, and the chopping off of a real arm to provide said mechanical arm. She gulped back her concern and went back to her cleaning. A while later another teacher entered the bathroom.

"I think that's fine for your detention," he said, holding his mouth. "Leave this to the groundskeepers. You can go." Then he promptly fled.

Zeers hastily shoved his head under a faucet and scrubbed the gunk out of his hair. Then he turned to Neliya, "Didn't you have track club today?"

Neliya checked her watch dejectedly, "Yep, but it'd be over now. Plus it looks like rain soon."

Zeers smirked apologetically, and shrugged, "Want to go see Fyuren?"

Points of light spread out across the corners of the room, illuminating the floor like a tiny city skyline. In the centre of the room stood a small boy, not much younger than Neliya, who waved his arms around the air in front of him. Though it seemed like a game of imagination, the child was hard at work, and so wrapped up in it that, even when he looked directly at the new arrivals, he didn't even acknowledge their existence. That was, until Zeers called out, "Hey! Fyuren!" for the tenth time.

"Oh! Hi, guys," said Fyuren. "Umm ..." he mused a moment, nibbling his lower lip as he studied some invisible object before him. Then he swiped the air in front of him. "Saved," he mumbled.

"Whatcha working on?" asked Neliya. Zeers shot her a glare, to which Neliya replied with a look that said, "Sorry, force of habit."

"Here, have a look," said Fyuren, handing them pairs of spectacles. They reluctantly placed them over their eyes, and saw what Fyuren saw: a cornucopia of mathematical symbols and complicated graphs floating throughout the room. The equations sat patiently, honestly displaying their contents to the viewers, but the only one who understood them was Fyuren. He navigated through the lines of math with his hands as an explorer would the dense shrubbery of a forest, until he found the crux of his work.

"This here," he said, holding up a rendering of a bizarre machine neither Neliya nor Zeers recognised. "It's the core of a tunneller, the Tharenian Induction Module, or TIM for short."

His friends understood straight away.

"Oh, so that's how we travel between stars?" asked Neliya.

"Oh Gods, when'll I get to go on the CTN?" said Zeers.

"Seriously, Zeers, it's *not* fun," said Neliya, her face paling when she thought of the rush that made the scariest rollercoaster feel like a breezy bike ride.

"Anyway, all this is my work on the tunnelling theory," explained Fyuren. With a flick of his fingers, a jumble of equations leapt from their peaceful place in the corner and came to him like a diligent servant. "This is the tunnelling formula. Generally, you can't solve it with a tensor size larger than the Kratzi Radius, since that would violate the Second Law of Relativistic Dynamo-Alchemics–"

"Yes, Fyuren, we get it, you're smart," blurted Neliya and Zeers, already beyond their capacity for their friend's babble. "Please, speak Myddish."

"Fine," exclaimed a disappointed Fyuren. "What I mean is, you can't have a tunneller bigger than about five metres. It just won't work."

"Hence the cramped ride," mumbled Neliya.

"It's that bad?" asked Zeers.

"Worse!" said Neliya.

"*But!* I'm trying to find a solution that doesn't involve the Kratzi Radius," said Fyuren. "If I can, you could possibly modify the CTN to carry a ship even the size of the *Othala!*"

Fyuren's work suddenly became more interesting than anything else in the world. Normally he'd prattle off some confusing, long-winded, seemingly pointless rant about his ideas. But now, although the math hanging in front of them still looked like gibberish, it was also a ticket to one of their longest-held wishes.

"The problem is, there're plenty of solutions without this size limit," said Fyuren. "But they have problems as well. There's one that can have a ship as big as you liked, but causes backwards time travel. I'm trying a different approach ... which I'm not going to explain in case I get yelled at by you two. Anyway, I'm almost finished, so give me a second."

Neliya and Zeers took a seat, and watched intently while Fyuren rearranged his equations, most of the work going on in his little head. While anticipating the results, they marvelled at the child researcher who, not too long ago, was a precocious know-it-all in their class.

"I think I got it," he said excitedly. He scanned his math one last time, and then another last time, before finally stating, "Yep, I got it. It should work now."

Neliya jumped up and clapped her hands.

"So, will we be able to use tunnelling on the *Othala*?" asked Zeers.

"I'm getting the computers to simulate the solution now," replied Fyuren, his breath shaky as he awaited the results. His hands clasped together as he watched a dizzying stream of numbers and plots whip through the air in front of him. He bit down hard on his lower lip, waiting for the results to finally come in, proving him right. Neliya and Zeers stared intently at the results as well, as if waiting for the climax for a film that for months had promised to be amazing.

The numbers stopped. Fyuren growled in frustration, smacking his hands in a painful clap and screaming, "Damn it!"

"What's the matter?" asked Neliya.

"It doesn't work, obviously! Even after I spent a month getting rid of the infinite summations on the time-like curves and accounted for the resultant instabilities of perturbation!"

"Calm down," barked Neliya as Fyuren began kicking over boxes of equipment. He shouted and kicked some more, before slumping against the wall and wiping his glistening brow.

"Sorry, it's just ..."

"We get it," said Neliya gently. "Explain to us what's wrong with your solution."

Fyuren sighed, running his hand through his hair, and as calmly as possible, said, "I simulated my solution, and it works. It allows a ship to travel through the CTN just like a tunneller. The power requirements are just within modern capabilities. But ..." he punctuated the word with a contemptuous clench of his fists. "But, the solution causes the ship, and all it's occupants, to be flipped."

"Flipped?" repeated his friends. "As in, they come out upside-down?"

"No, I mean as in the whole ship is flipped, so that people's hearts are on the wrong side in their chest. Their left hands would be their right hands. That sort of thing."

Neliya and Zeers pulled away from the equations as they would the sneezes and used tissues of a sick classmate.

"Yeah, Fyuren, don't use that solution," pleaded Zeers.

Fyuren just glared resignedly at the equations and the results.

"Stuff it all! I want ice cream, and I want stars … Now!"

That was all the convincing they needed. In a flash, the equations were saved to Fyuren's tablet, and the three friends were out the door.

A quick jaunt on the maglev brought them to Sector Seventeen: a modestly busy street, lined with shops and peppered with afternoon traffic. The rain hadn't reached this part of the city yet, but the rumbling Neliya heard earlier grew nearer.

They power-walked across roads, earning horn beeps from drivers, but they paid it no mind, and marched into an ice-cream store at the corner of two busy streets. Coins were turned to satisfied smiles. With skips in their steps, they scooted around a closing newsstand, where Fyuren lost a few more coins for a copy of the day's paper, and headed back to the maglev station.

An elevator ride took them down into a completely different area. They entered a long high-roofed corridor. One side lined with sitting areas, small cafés, and vending machines; the other housed a huge window, overlooking a mural of innumerable stars and nebulae painted on an ocean of darkness.

The friends took a seat on the bench they usually picked when they came to this spot, as close to the glass as possible. There, the stars filled their entire field of view, allowing them to forget for a moment that they were on a ship.

They quietly enjoyed the view, except for Fyuren, who instead read the paper he'd bought. He and Neliya ate their ice cream slowly, savouring each spoonful, while Zeers wolfed his down not long after taking a seat. The beautiful view of the stars could only keep his attention for a short time before his eyes were inexorably driven to Fyuren's half-full cup. He eyed the melting mixture lustfully. He checked Fyuren's gaze. Making sure Fyuren was fixed on reading the newspaper, Zeers slowly edged his spoon toward the cup.

"Do and die," said Fyuren, his eyes glued to the newspaper.

Zeers growled wistfully.

"That's what you get, you big glutton," jibed Neliya. Before Zeers could even open his mouth, she pulled away from him. "Not a chance," she snapped, clutching her ice cream like a precious treasure.

"You're both eating so slow," complained Zeers. "You're staring at the view, and Fyuren's too busy reading. What are you reading, anyway?"

Fyuren held the newspaper up to his friends. Neliya and Zeers studied the headline and the first few lines, not bothering much to read the details.

"Bioplant crisis?" they repeated.

"Remember the other day when I was talking about those food poisoning cases and those roaches infesting the third through to sixteenth sectors of the city?"

"How could we forget?" said Zeers sarcastically.

"You droned on for hours about it," said Neliya. "I was losing the will to live."

"Well, I was right," said Fyuren, unfazed by their jokes. "It was a bioplant problem. I even wrote a letter to the government! But did anyone listen?"

"Yes, Fyuren, we get it, you're smart," Neliya sounded off. "So you're right. Maybe that's why Mum hasn't been around that much." As she prodded her ice cream, her thoughts drifted to the worried looks her mother had worn recently. "Now that I think about it, she's been really busy lately. And agitated, too."

"So what?" asked Zeers, eyes still on Fyuren's ice cream.

Neliya glared at him. "If you'd bother to show up to class, you'd know that if there's a problem with the bioplant, then food and water would be affected."

"Hence the food poisoning," added Fyuren.

The word *food* suddenly wedged an unpleasant thought in their heads. Fyuren and Neliya looked to their ice cream cups, pursing their lips thoughtfully as they wondered just how bad the crisis was. Without a word, they tossed the cups into the nearby bin, much to Zeers' horror.

"So, what are they going to do about it?" asked Neliya, reading the paper with Fyuren while Zeers mourned the lost ice cream.

"Looks like the Sidha is considering evacuation," replied Fyuren. "See here: 'The Sidha has convened an emergency session to discuss remedial measures. Projections for the repair time suggest level six conservation measures will be enforced, and an evacuation through the Commonwealth Tunnelling Network is to be expected.' They're not sure how long it'll take though … At least a month."

"That'd be all summer holidays," said Zeers. "Where're we going to go?"

"Why don't we go stay with my Dad on Lethanis?" Neliya suggested. "There's camping and festivals. Maybe we can take a trip to the beach too. We can spend the whole summer there. On an actual planet!"

Zeers was wide-eyed and agape with excitement, as if he'd been offered a fortune of gold and silver. He grabbed Neliya's hands and agreed ecstatically. Fyuren watched both of them dance like a pair of sweepstakes winners. A grin lingered on his lips.

"Don't get your hopes up," he warned. "We might not evacuate."

His warning fell on deaf ears, and rightly so. The next morning, an edict was delivered to each household in the city, detailing the time and order of evacuation. Among the evacuees were three very excited children.

2 | Who're the stowaways I'll note in my log?

After the announcement, school days were halved, and much of them were dedicated to preparation for the evacuation. Both Zeers and Neliya were glad to have no more homework, but dismayed for different reasons. Neliya was very put out that track club was cancelled, though not as much as Zeers was annoyed by the school's boring evacuation drills. Fyuren spent the days leading up to the evacuation backing up his tunnelling solution to continue his work during their holiday.

Neliya's mother, Orune, arranged for her daughter and friends to leave on the same tunneller. Thanks to her connections as manager of the company that maintained the *Othala*'s bioplants, they were assigned a tunneller on the first day of the evacuation.

The day of departure came: the weather was dismal, and winds carried all kinds of muck throughout the city, clanging against light poles and buildings. The skies grumbled with the portent of a downpour. That was hardly the worst of it. When Neliya and Orune exited their house, they shuddered at the unsightly roaches and blowflies eating away at the once well-kept gardens of the Dosag mansion. Neliya looked down at her clean dress and polished shoes, and wondered whether it was worth it.

She sighed, trying to hide the excitement about her imminent departure from her mother and the house staff. But everyone could see it, even the chauffeur holding the car's passenger door open for her.

"Is everything alright?" asked Orune. She was dressed as if she was going to a formal occasion, and poised as much. But Neliya was sure that beneath her mother's self-control she was very worried.

"Yes, Mother, just a little tired," replied Neliya. She turned the backs of her hands inward to her hips, which piqued her mother's gaze. The older woman grabbed her daughter's hands and examined the red blotches marring her skin.

"Are these burns?" she asked fretfully.

"I just spilled some wax," Neliya blurted as she pulled away. "I couldn't sleep last night, so I fiddled with the candles in my drawer."

Orune glared at her daughter, before her gaze darted down to the burn marks. They did indeed resemble droplets. She let her concerns dissipate in preparation for the more important matters at hand.

"Do you have everything?" she asked.

"Yes, Mother," said the girl curtly.

"Well then, say good-bye to the staff."

Neliya wore a cheerful smile and gave the head maid a hug.

"Goodbye everyone," she said. "I'll see you in a few months."

"Don't worry, Neliya, dear," said the head maid. "They'll have this bioplant problem fixed in no time. You'll be back before you realise you left."

With a smile, Neliya thought, *Gods! I hope not.*

The passengers waved kindly to the staff as the car drove down the driveway. Eventually all Neliya could see was the mansion.

Good riddance, she silently cursed. *I hope the roaches eat the place.*

As the car drove through a few residential districts, the rain started. The whine of the car engine was completely drowned out by the loud, dull drum of heavy water drops smacking the roof. Neliya turned up the volume on her music player and gazed out the window. Every single street was the same: families struggling to load their children into cars, buses, and taxis. Orune fretted, ticking and tapping and fiddling in vain effort to relieve the stress that would not go away. Meanwhile, Neliya listened to her music player, and ticked and tapped to suppress the excitement that she was going away.

The car soon left the residential districts and joined a long stream of vehicles, ferrying evacuees to a huge metallic tower that reached into the clouds above. At its base was an entrance into a brightly lit tunnel. The road in front of them changed from asphalt to glowing tracks that took over the job of the car's wheels.

The car continued down the tunnel, following its various contours, until it entered a dock full of people. The chauffeur pulled into a stop near a hatch marked Express Passengers, some distance away from the bulk of travellers.

"I'll have to say goodbye here, Neliya," said Orune regretfully, with one foot still inside the car.

"Alright, Mother," said Neliya. "You no doubt have to help with the repairs."

"Give my love to your father when you see him," she said. Then she kissed her daughter on the cheek and said, "Be safe, my child."

"And you too, mother," replied the girl. They embraced momentarily, and her mother shed a tear. Then she re-entered the car and it drove away. Neliya felt a sharp twinge in her throat.

I suppose it's not all good that I'm leaving.

She put her homesickness aside and pulled her itinerary pages from her pocket. The instructions read Gate 5C, which she saw after a quick glance across the bustling dock. She pushed through arriving passengers, toward Fyuren and Zeers, who waited for her outside the gate.

"Excited for your first CTN trip?" Neliya asked Zeers.

Zeers wore a grin that answered for her. A dark-skinned hand rested on his shoulder, and its owner said, "Well, we better hurry up so you don't miss it." Though she spoke Myddish with an authentic Lethanis accent, she was nothing like the yellow-skinned four-fingered Mydian boy she guarded. The leathery skin, longer arms, *five* fingers, and colour-speckled vine-like curls protruding from her scalp set the Earthen woman out in a crowd that hardly noticed her difference.

A Mydian woman put an arm around a recalcitrant Fyuren and said, "I'd rather they miss it. I'd like to go *with* my boy."

"Too bad, Mum," murmured Fyuren, trying to pull away from his mother who relished his flushed face when she gripped him in an even tighter hug.

"Oh, but my boy will be going on a tunneller all on his own! What will I do?"

"Gah, knock it off, Mum!"

The Earthen woman joined in the fun and hugged Zeers from behind. "What will *I* do without my best friend's little baby boy?"

"Boggima, it's only a few months," droned Zeers.

Neliya allowed herself a brief chuckle, and then made for the door. "Janice, Boggima, we'd better hurry or our shuttle will leave."

The women let go of the flailing boys and herded them through the gate.

The cabin of a small transit craft lay beyond the gate. When the five passengers were seated, the pilot moved the ship out of the dock. All of a sudden, the windows were filled with a breathtaking view of space as the ship pulled away. A massive, slow-spinning cylinder of metal and blinking lights drifted away behind them. It was so long in both directions that the passengers could not see the ends.

"I never get sick of seeing the *Othala* from outside," intoned Fyuren.

Zeers' attention gravitated to a fleet of smaller (but still enormous) ships surrounding the mega-vessel; their arrays of weapons would have been conspicuous from twice the distance. He pointed out one on the vanguard. "Boggima, Dad's supposed to be on that one, right?"

"Yep," replied his Earthen guardian. "He wanted to be here to see you off."

"I know," he droned.

Not fast enough, thought a fidgeting Neliya

"There's the CTN Terminal up ahead," said the pilot.

There were so many transports zooming to and from the ship ahead, it looked more like a flying insect's nest. Some smaller ships broke away from it and vanished into the void in vibrant flashes of pink and yellow.

"Hey, Fyuren, are those tunnellers?" asked Zeers, who had only ever heard second hand about those strange plumes of light. "They're so small."

"That's why I want to get that solution working. Damn quasi-spatial interaction curves ..." He went on to mumble a tirade of technical terms. Janice wore a proud smile.

The transport reversed into a docking port on the Terminal Ship, and deposited the passengers into a mostly empty corridor.

"Where is everyone?" asked Zeers. "I thought it'd be packed."

"It's an express tunnel. Mother organised it so we could cut the queue," said Neliya.

A short walk and an elevator ride up two levels, and the friends entered a larger corridor. This one had wide viewports, offering a spectacular view of the *Othala* on one side, and the dust bands of the galaxy on the other. Those viewports were separated by hatches leading into the tunnellers.

Pushing through the crowd, the friends and their escorts reached hatch thirty, and found a small area out of the way of the flow of people. Now it was Fyuren and Zeers' turn for goodbyes. Janice clutched her son tightly, squeezing her eyes closed to hold back tears. Boggima assaulted Zeers with a less-than-reciprocated hug, and ordered him to be safe. The three friends said one last farewell, and then followed the attendant through the hatch.

Three spacesuits were set out for them in the change room, and a partition set up for privacy. Zeers was the only one confused.

"The tunnellers don't have life support," said Fyuren. "They only have enough space for the CTN device. So we have to wear these suits."

Zeers shrugged and stepped up to one of the spacesuits.

"It's embarrassing that they're skin tight and revealing," complained Neliya.

Fyuren chuckled, "Seriously, you'd prefer these to the big canvas bag suits they had back in the day?"

They suited up and stowed their clothes in the bags provided. The attendant then led them into the very cramped tunneller. The seats were packed together tightly, and could barely fit them. Neliya went in first, and had to twist around at first to put her bag under the seat, and then sit in the chair. Zeers was equally challenged.

"Fyuren, you'd better get that solution working for next time!" he groaned as he pulled the belts over his body.

"I'll ... try ..." replied the boy as he edged into his seat, bumping his helmet on the ceiling.

When they were painfully strapped in, the attendant said, "Alright, closing hatch. You'll know what is happening over the intercom. When the countdown gets to zero, exhale. It won't hurt as much that way. Ready?"

Zeers' face went pale, "Umm ... No."

The ship's hatch slammed shut on the trio, and sealed itself with a puff of steam. "Venting atmosphere in cabin," said the attendant over the intercom. Another rush of air, and the children's ears popped a little.

The eerie silence of the tunneller, the shudder and loud clang of its detachment from the *Othala*, and the sudden weightlessness that came with it, were all quite unnerving.

"Tunneller One, we have you in stable grav-lock," said the attendant. "Begin CTN Node Sweep, destination Lethanis."

A brief moment of silence ensued, during which the only things the children could hear came through the radio or the vibrations of the ship travelling through their bodies to their ears.

"Node detected, synchronisation complete. Control, release grav-lock."

The ship began to tumble, only slightly. But the children's nerves heightened their senses, and their stomachs churned at the subtle motion. It was like a notoriously scary theme park ride.

"CTN Node Lock established," announced the attendant. "Alright kids, get ready! Initiating CTN Jump in three ... two ... one ... Exhale!"

The children's every nerve buckled with a sensation of pressure, and their brains seemed to confuse their ears for their eyes, which simmered with a kaleidoscope of colours.

A high pitched screech suddenly reverberated over the radio, and sparks and flashes of light burst from every seam in the tunneller's cabin as the passengers were thrown to and fro. Their tight seatbelts snapped under the strain and they flew about the cabin. The ship tumbled sickeningly, and dragged them with it.

They cried, screamed, and begged the attendant for help, but received no reply. They were sickeningly thrown against the walls of the cabin, and their senses went blank.

The children took some time to regain their senses. Fyuren activated the lights on his helmet, and showed the others how to do it.

Zeers was the first to panic. "Is this what a CTN jump is like?"

"No, something has gone really wrong," replied Fyuren.

"Can we use the radio? Call for help?" asked Neliya. Fyuren pushed past Neliya, and felt across the front-most walls for a concealed control panel. He found one and prised it open, receiving only jets of smoke and sparks.

"Controls are fried," he said. "And I don't think we're in range of the *Othala*, anyway."

"How?" exclaimed Zeers. "We didn't even start moving. How can we not be able to contact the ship?"

"A trip on the CTN should feel like no time at all!" yelled Fyuren. "Since the attendant definitely engaged the TIM device, we were probably hit by something mid-flight."

Zeers took a moment to process the information, then he murmured, "Does that mean ... We could be anywhere in space?"

"That's exactly what it means," said Fyuren.

Zeers and Neliya were flabbergasted to the point of breathlessness. It took a while before they asked themselves, "How will we get home?"

Fyuren, on the other hand, remained in his musings: *We must have hit something, or we'd have continued tumbling forever. If we're not near the Othala, then there must be something outside. Something close ...*

Before he could voice his conclusion, the children were again thrown against the wall of the cabin. They felt themselves growing heavier and heavier, until whatever pulled them stopped and they flew into the opposite wall.

A rush of air accompanied a sharp metal object loudly piercing the ship's hull, and a stream of white light flooded the cabin. Neliya squealed as a fat, dirty-nailed hand reached through the hole, and hauled her out of the ship. The man to whom the hand belonged was a brute twice her height, with pierced lips, a sneer full of yellow, chipped teeth, and only one eye. The one who grabbed Fyuren and Zeers was equally fearsome, with facial tattoos contorting whenever he smiled.

"Oi, lookie 'ere, Kajil," roared the cyclops as he pulled off Neliya's helmet. "Kiddies!"

"Heh, heh, heh!" chortled the tattooed man. "We're gonna have a feast ter-nite, Jugga!"

A troupe of thugs, not all Mydian, drew near. Some were short, others tall. Some were burly and heavily tattooed, while a few others were lanky. All of them were tickled by the children's flailing.

"Let me go! How dare you!" shouted Neliya.

"Wet me go, how dare you!" mimicked Jugga. "Ain' she a cutie."

"Yes ... She cute ..." mumbled a strident, ill-favoured voice. A hunched creature poked its head from behind one of the larger men and eyed the trio. "You play with Borig? We have fun ... I show you fun ..."

The man nearest the thing gave it a hard kick. "Oi, Borig, you keep eye 'n' pervy hand off, hear?"

Borig snarled at the brute and skulked away.

"Been hungry a while, eh! These'll be good and tasty," exclaimed Kajil, leering at the game in his hands. Frustrated, Zeers gave a spirited kick toward Kajil's face, but missed.

"Where are we?" shouted Zeers.

Kajil leered at him, "Heh! Ya dun need in ya know. Ya'll go roast kid soon enough!"

Neliya's panic hit a zenith. She swung once, and hit Jugga's good eye.

"Me eye! Me only eye!" screeched Jugga, dropping Neliya to the rusted steel floor. Fyuren and Zeers wriggled out of Kajil's hold and the trio fled. They didn't get far before they saw there was no escape. They stood in a metal chamber that reeked of rust and sewerage. Any door they saw was an opening to admit more brutes. Then they noticed a huge window set against a backdrop of stars, and realised they were on another ship.

A spotlight assaulted them from above. The hangar fell silent as a disembodied voice issued from within the blinding light.

> *Fizzle and drizzle!*
> *Bibbledy bog!*
> *Who're the stowaways I'll note in my log?*
>
> *See this one? Take a good look.*
> *A runt, a nerd!*
> *You sit all day with your nose in a book?*
> *You must eat nothing but curd,*
> *Or else you'd be fat! All blown-up!*
>
> *This one's a feisty fighter,*
> *A vessel of igneous rage.*
> *Loaded with dynamite, just needs a lighter.*
> *To seek vengeance at this age,*
> *A parent must not have shown-up.*
>
> *See this? The crew's new bliss!*
> *A girl. Give us a twirl.*
> *A dancer at heart, but something's amiss.*
> *A dream that may not unfurl,*
> *Lost forever when she's all grown-up.*
>
> *Oh, yes, a normal day,*
> *To capture and snare*
> *A few new crew members. They pray*
> *We don't send 'em down there!*
> *To the reactor core.*

The crew chortled with each improvised verse.

A concerned voice spoke up, "Captain, I should remind you that we are short on time, and supplies."

The first voice exclaimed in agreement.

Right, no, 'tis not a normal day!
Too many mouths to feed!
Too important plans to heed!
We take new crewmen no more!
So throw them away!
Strip their ship, take up what's useful,
Shake 'em down till we get what's useful,
Then out the airlock, their corpses soar.

The children stared at the silhouette, their mouths agape with horror. The brutes came at them with murderous countenances. They reached for Fyuren first, but Zeers came to the rescue with a small wrench he found on the floor. He swung it at Kajil's tattooed face, stunning him. Other crewmembers charged at him. He dodged one attacker, and clobbered him over the head with his weapon. Then he rolled between the legs of another brute and delivered a crippling blow to his privates.

"This limber little's a good grappler," bellowed the captain. Zeers pointed his weapon at the captain and roared, "Hop off your high-place, you circus clown. I'll show you just how good I am."

Every eyebrow in the hangar went skyward at the boy's boast. Even those cradling fresh bruises from the boy's weapon gave cheers of admiration.

A growl bursting from Jugga's mouth betrayed his rear attack, and Zeers leapt out of the way. He landed in front of Kajil, who swiped his hand like a fishing net to catch him. The brute hoisted him into the air with a murderous glare, and squeezed Zeers' wrist until the wrench fell from it. Then he threw the boy to the ground.

Neliya and Fyuren ran forward to help him, but Jugga and another hangar worker scooped them up.

"Ya wrigglin' bits o' space muck!" bellowed Kajil.

"Off to the resomators with 'em!" roared Jugga.

"Wait," the captain roared. All eyes turned to him. He descended a flight of stairs and walked into the light. He was a Mydian, like them, but his skin had lost its yellow colour in favour of a pale appearance, contrasting with the red cape flowing about his tall form. A smile striving to conceal schemes sat on a face crowned by wide, manic eyes, unaware of their own exhaustion as they pierced the children before him. A glyph stained the skin about his left eye, and it wrinkled when he grinned.

He motioned his crew to release the children, and when they stood up he said, "You worked well to avoid my crafty crew. No doubt you are friends with a strong bond. Your names?"

"Neliya Dosag," said the girl.

"Fyuren Orthos," said the youngest boy.

"Zeers Indra," rasped the elder boy.

"Ah, from my youth, I remember the name Indra," said the captain. "It belonged to an accomplished alchemist, it did. You are perhaps related, Littles?"

"My family has always been in the Military Alchemists' Guild," replied Zeers with a twinge of pride in his voice.

"And perhaps you one day hope to spend your arm for the potent power of your patriarch?"

Zeers gave no reply, absentmindedly clutching his right arm. The captain smirked, before turning to Neliya and Fyuren.

"From what I have heard from the Commonwealth worlds, the Dosags are quite the entrepreneurs. Surely, Femie's perturbed parents will petition her procurement?"

"Definitely," replied Neliya. Her mind suddenly filled with inklings of dread, the source or meaning of which she couldn't understand, and they made her tremble.

"Well, I know *my* parents will look for me," said Fyuren.

The captain laughed at the boy. "Says the scrawny scree that screamed behind his cronies. I can't recall the name Orthos on any ship I've shattered. You're hardly anything, are you, Shorts?"

Neliya gripped Fyuren's hand to silence him.

The captain studied the children, who felt like they were awaiting a verdict on their lives. He gave a hum part way between a sigh and a giggle, and then swivelled on his feet, his cape swishing about him. "Normally, if we can't take new crew, we either devour them or dispel them. That is the way. But! If I can help it, I would like to keep these on board. So I say, if no job can be found for them now, gone they go! If use anyone has for them, speak now."

A moment passed, during which the children's blood ran cold. Then out of the gathered crowd stepped a man in a soiled, black suit. His ethnicity was hidden beneath the dirt and grime of years of work in some dark place.

"I'll use 'em. The coolant pipes for the tokamak ain't go' scrubb'd in yonks. These're midgety and they'll fit."

The captain swivelled and smiled at the children. "There you go! For now, today, you get to not die. Work hard, and that won't change. Vice-chief engineer Allo, you're in charge of these kiddies. Put 'em to work." To his crew he shouted, "That goes for the rest of you useless puke-drinking scab hackers! We've got a cunning coup to plan."

The crew moved purposefully out of the hangar. The captain turned back to the children and loomed over them. "I found a reason to keep you. But don't be complaining about wanting to go home. Here's your home now! You want to stay among the living, you work.

"Littles, Shorts, Femie! I am Gelfri! Welcome aboard the *Ranegr*!"

3 | Why can't we be friends?

Neliya had thought the *Othala* evacuation was crazy and disorganised. When she saw the *Ranegr*, she took it all back. The ship was filled with gruesome faces much like Kajil's and Jugga's. Yet each had their own features that set them apart in the rabble.

"Over 'ere!" rasped Allo as he herded the trio down the left path at an intersection. The children narrowly dodged a low-hanging cable, electricity arcing between the frayed wires.

"You realise that could electrocute someone?" exclaimed Fyuren.

Allo scoffed, "Yep, so keep ya eyes up with ya toes. No-Eyes dunn't paid gaze, 'n' drop'd 'is face in a puddle o' waste."

"What happened to him?" asked Neliya.

"He go' his nickname," quipped Allo with a grin.

The blood drained from their faces, and their eyes became a great deal more watchful.

After walking down a few more corridors, Allo shoved the children into a small alcove with one bed that looked vile, to put it lightly. The furry mattress sported manifold colours and textures, which made the children dry retch. The faintest sound of dripping water emanated from an even smaller adjacent room that, the children suspected from the faint odours, was the remains of an en-suite bathroom. Neither had a sufficiently strong stomach to find out.

"'Ere's ya sleepin' spot," said Allo.

"For all of us?" murmured Zeers. Allo nodded.

"You can't be serious!" exclaimed Neliya. "This room isn't fit for farm animals, much less us."

"Farm beasts're more use than you," spat Allo. "Eff-wye-eye, this is our primo-accomo – check that, *my* primo-accomo. And *I* jus' spare'd ya bein' chow'd or made void garnish. How 'bout ya say 'thanks, Allo?'"

"But just one bed for all of us?" replied Fyuren.

"The fungus on this bed might eat me in my sleep," Neliya protested.

Allo glared at them for a moment, before letting his eyes wander to Zeers. "How 'bout you, Littles?"

Zeers shifted a little on his feet, still gripping his right arm. "It's fine. We'll deal," he muttered.

Fyuren and Neliya exploded, "*We'll deal?* Who's the *we* here?"

"Sounds good," said Allo jovially. "We go' one okay. Now, if the snobbos dun't like it, snooze in the hall!"

Neliya and Fyuren were tongue-tied at the idea of being stuck outside. More and more, the bed looked like an appealing option. Finally, they gave in and accepted the room. Satisfied, Allo moved onto laying out ground rules.

"We go' 'bout thirty-four-hour days, 'n' right now we're at half-point. We go' six hours til shift end, then night-chow, then lights-out. The resomators're no-go, 'n' the secondary hangar bay down on the lower deck just past the farms."

"What's there?" asked Zeers.

"The Nightshift quarters," said Allo with a sneer. "They ain't Mydian, them things. Ain't too civilised either. Cross them, get chow'd. Got it?" The children nodded. The engineer clapped his hands together. "Great! Now, get outta 'em spacesuits."

The children quickly changed into the only other clothes they had: their school uniforms. As they followed Allo toward the reactor room, Fyuren intoned despairingly, "This isn't going to end well, I just know it!"

"By now, our parents're looking for us," said Neliya. "They'll find us and we'll be fine."

"Only if we survive cleaning these coolant tanks," replied Fyuren.

An unusually calm Zeers just shrugged, "How bad can it be? We just go in and scrub. Easy!"

Allo turned a corner, and the children followed him into a chamber bigger than the hangar, filled with sweat-drenched workers, most of whom had deep dark skin and wielded giant spanners and screwdrivers. In the centre of the room stood the focus of their labour: a gigantic, doughnut-shaped machine. The conduits, wires, and leaky pipes extending from its top and base made for a visceral contraption.

"Fyuren, what is it?" asked a very nervous Neliya, gripping her friend's hand as they followed Allo cautiously down the stairs.

"Go on one of your spiels," added Zeers, for the first time betraying some unease.

"It's a tokamak – a sun in a bottle," he replied, unsettled by the decrepit state of the machine.

"And we have to clean it?" murmured Zeers, averting his eyes from the bright, purple light that shone from gaps in the machine's housing.

"Nup, jus' the coolant pipes runnin' in it," said Allo, dodging the tumult of workers scurrying to and fro. "Ain't go' none but this tokamak workin' prop'ly, 'n' it ain't too smooth-goin'."

"Properly?" exclaimed Fyuren. "It's about to fall apart! What idiot lets a vital system get so rickety?"

Allo shot a smirk over his shoulder, "Malse 'eard ya say that, 'e'll smack ya."

"Who's Malse?" asked Zeers.

"Me!" belched a hunchbacked man. The haggard core worker hobbled toward them. His face was riddled with scars, blisters, and tumours from years working with the reactor. "Ah, Allo, I 'erd we'd snagged some pipe-cleaners."

"Yep, they're plenty midgety, 'n'll fit the pipes good," replied Allo.

Malse compared his height to theirs, and studied them with a rough hand. The children couldn't stomach to look at him for long.

"Humph, I s'pose they'll do a while," the hunchback said, sounding almost disappointed. "I'm Malse. I'm Allo's boss. Allo's your boss. That makes me double your boss. We go' one decree 'ere in this crew: do your job. Got it?"

"Yes sir," replied Zeers.

Malse gave a black-gummed grin, and said, "Spare 'sir' for Gelfri, if ever ya break word with him again in life. Let's get 'em to work, Allo." Then he left to bellow orders to the rest of his crew who flinched at the tiny invalid's barking.

Allo turned to the friends and handed them a duffel bag each.

"What're these?" asked Fyuren.

"Protective Suits," replied Allo. "Gonna be steamy in 'em pipes, 'n' ya'll sizzle without 'em."

Neliya gulped. Fyuren's face grew paler than it had ever been. Zeers opened the duffel bag without a word and pulled the protective suit over his head.

"Littles' volunteerin'!" exclaimed Allo.

Zeers headed over to where a pipe was ready for cleaning. Neliya and Fyuren put themselves in front of him.

"The suit won't protect you!" exclaimed Fyuren. Feeling the material between his fingers, he added, "It's flimsy and it has holes too!"

Zeers straightened to his full height and glared at the boy, "Fyuren, right now, we've got no way out of this. I don't want to try breathing in space, so get out of my way."

He said it with such conviction that he frightened his friends, who stood aside wide-eyed. Zeers approached the hatch, and Allo handed him an overused brush.

"Pu' some elbow in it, 'kay? Ya think them sticky arms're able?"

Zeers shot the engineer a glare. Then he threw on the protective mask and motioned for the crew to open the hatch. Steam blasted out of the opening, hissing like a strangled snake gasping for breath. Neliya and Fyuren were certain more than water vapour gushed out of the metallic orifice – the smell was worse than a ripe bowel movement.

"You're not seriously going in there!" exclaimed Neliya.

"It'll be like cleaning the toilets for detention," said Zeers, his voice muffled by the headgear, before he crawled into the pipe.

Allo leaned down, gripping his nose. "Wriggle upway to the end, 'n' bang the door. If it stuffies up in there, turn up your oh-two." He slammed the hatch shut.

"This is insane!" cried Fyuren. "Tokamak coolant is supposed to be liquid lithium! How can it smell so bad in there?"

"The *Ranegr*'s on the up-years," said Malse, muscling them along. "We cross-link'd systems, keeps it workin'. Back-before, 'ad a plumbing failure. They link'd the core to the water system."

"Are you serious?" exclaimed Fyuren. "You might as well use this place as one big toilet. If you fix the problem, you wouldn't need us to clean the pipes and we could go home."

Malse gave a chuckle that evolved into a wretched cough. "We did that, ya'd be meetin' your granddaddies and grandmummies on the firmament."

Fyuren moved to protest further, oblivious to Malse's meaning. Neliya held her hand over his mouth and whispered in his ear, "This job is the only thing keeping us alive. Let's just stay out of their way. Okay?"

Allo grabbed their shoulders and pushed them along. "Ya go' them pipes 'ere, drain'd 'n' ready. For you," he said to Fyuren, crouching to his level in a condescending manner, "we pick'd one that ain't link'd up with the reso's or the bioplant, so ya won't crawl in squat-ploppin's. Howzat sound, hmm?"

The boy slumped his shoulders and begrudgingly followed the engineer. He pulled on the protective suit and crawled into his pipe.

Malse and a duo of bulky workers awaited Neliya impatiently. She took the cleaning tools and donned her suit, praying it didn't leak and let a month's worth of faeces on her.

A chill raced down her spine, and she looked around fretfully. She was certain that she saw that strange Borig, watching her insidiously from behind a large tank next to the core. In the next instant, the mirage was gone.

"What's issuin' ya?" asked Malse.

"Nothing." She put her mask on and crawled into the hatch.

The children walked into their quarters and retreated into the corners. Despite the success of the protective suits and their relatively clean clothes, they still felt the crusty oxides and poo that had dribbled through their fingers.

Fyuren frantically brushed himself down with his bare hands, as if it would shoo the feeling away. Zeers winced and groaned, massaging his very sore arms. Neliya tried in vain to forget that tomorrow she'd have to repeat the job.

Allo appeared in the doorway with a smirk.

"Howzat for ya intro to real labourin'?" he asked. When no reply came, he held out a large plate, "I got dinner: bitter-pot and sausage!"

A rumble through their stomachs drove them toward the man, but hit an invisible wall when they saw his offering. The filthy plate carried a pile of red stuff and three tubes of green matter.

Neliya's stomach turned to rock. "Tell me that's sweet potato mash and green beans."

"We call it bitter-pot," said Allo. "Sausages're kerect†. What? Don't like the colour?"

"It's fine, I'm starving," said Zeers. He sampled one of the sausages, his upper lip sneering slightly. He chewed it thoroughly and swallowed, then promptly gulped the rest of the sausage and some potato. "It's not that tasty, but edible."

Neliya and Fyuren picked up some mash and tentatively licked it. Fyuren recognised a bitter taste and turned to Allo in horror.

Allo saw his cries coming, and threw up a hand. "Shorts, we go' none but it. Deal!" And he marched out of the room.

Fyuren snatched a sausage and sat down near the bed, scowling as he nibbled it. Neliya forewent the mash and took the last sausage. She chewed it tentatively, but found something malleable in the mouthful. She pulled the culprit out of her mouth and gagged at its crescent-moon shape.

"A finger nail!" she screamed, throwing the offending item and the sausage away.

Fyuren found something worse in his, and similarly disposed of it. "This is terrible! We're eating goddess-knows-what, having to clean pipes that shouldn't need to be cleaned. If these people weren't so lazy, this rust bucket wouldn't be falling apart."

Zeers spoke up, "They're making do with what they have."

"Who are they anyway?" asked Neliya.

Zeers rolled his sore shoulders. "I heard that escaped convicts and refugees set up ships and societies in interstellar space. They're called Drifters. This might be them."

Fyuren growled, "I don't care who they are! I want to go home. I say we steal a shuttle and escape."

---

† A lizard-like creature similar in taste to chicken.

"Try that, and we die," retorted Zeers.

"Oh yeah, and what about what you said to Gelfri? 'Show him just how good you are!' Like always, you're just bluster, you mummy-boy!"

Zeers charged at the boy. "Say that again, Fyuren. See what happens! You're just whiny 'cause it's the first time you've done any actual work in your life."

The boys' argument could be heard through the corridor, rousing tired crew who wanted to knock them out of their misery. Eventually Allo returned and broke up the fight, while Neliya remained motionless. Intrusive thoughts pounded at the inner walls of her head and drew her attention inward from anything going on around her – even her friends baying for each other's blood.

I want to go home ... But I hate home ...

Her body trembled irately and fearfully.

I don't like this place either. Isn't that what head maid said? Beggars can't be choosers?

Neliya slept that night with that one despair-soaked thought drenching her consciousness.

Without a sun (real or artificial) to rouse them in the morning, the days aboard the *Ranegr* were less days and more time periods. The children lost count of the days before they turned into weeks, until the periods between waking and sleeping merged into a blurry lump of indiscriminate events in their memories.

For a long while, Fyuren rocked at the foot of the bed, chanting, "Mum and Dad're looking for me." When that stopped working, he found a piece of old chalk under a film of dust in the corner, and took to scribbling his tunnelling theory on the walls. "It keeps my mind off things," he said when asked.

Zeers often found himself restless after work, and took to push-ups and other exercises. His periodic grunting annoyed his already troubled friends-turned-roommates, though they admitted he looked fitter.

Neliya spent her nights watching her music player's battery indicator drain. A soft-spoken part of her mind suggested she ask Allo to charge the battery, but it fell silent long after the device crackled away its last tune. Too much of her mind was overrun with a single thought.

You wanted off the Othala.

"Not here," she would growl deliriously.

You want to go back?

"No!"

You're stuck ... Like always.

The cycle repeated for hours until she returned to sleep and dreamed of a pipe shrinking around her. Somehow, she managed to clean the real pipes every day.

The crew paid them little mind in those first months.

The only thing Allo said to them, except which pipes to clean, was, "Mind the Nightshift."

It was that consistent warning, among other things, that put nightmares in their heads. Every now and then, Neliya or Fyuren would point out shadows at the end of a rusty corridor. Zeers was always quiet, however, and brushed off their sightings as, "Just seein' things."

One night, as they trudged back to their room with sore shoulders once more, Neliya looked down a corridor, the lights of which had been replaced recently. At the end of the corridor was an intersection, the walls of which were bathed in shimmering red light. Then, slowly and sinisterly, a silhouette crept into the light: a burly creature, seemingly multi-armed, with a pair of sharp horns. Neliya's whole body trembled with horror, absolutely certain that the thing's eyes were glowing at her.

Fyuren believed her, and went into another spiral of panic that lasted the entire night. When the children asked Allo for a weapon in case something came after them, he just laughed.

In sets of three, the conduits feeding the reactor were cleaned and flushed out, until inside smelt slightly less rank than before.

"And that's what matters," Allo had said.

The last day of the job finally came. The maintenance crew finished repairing the pipes, and filled the clean coolant vessels with water. The pipes made a noise like a relieved sigh after overcoming an awful stomach-ache.

Captain Gelfri watched from the observation deck. "Well done, my creative crew. Our giant generators are back to maximum magnitude. We can now accelerate our plicate plans!"

The crew punched the air above their heads. Malse yelled over the jubilation, "Captain Gelfri! If I'd find boldness, we'd not 'ave 'ere results if we'd not 'ad these kiddies!"

"I agree," replied Gelfri. "You three have been instrumental. My commendations."

The three friends, their faces blank with exhaustion, were nearly pounded through the floor by fervent pats and hair tussling. Then they were hoisted into the air and carried out of the room.

All about them the crew chanted, "Chow Party! Chow Party! Chow Party!"

Bewildered, Neliya looked around for her friends, who were a short distance behind her.

The crowd marched toward a doorway, above which hung a sign: Food Hall. Memories of cannibalism threats loomed in their heads, but their minds drew a blank on what to do – most likely thanks to their fatigue.

Their carriers dropped them at a wooden table, an oil-lamp burning quietly in the middle. Allo and a bunch of core workers stood next to the table, while others found seats at adjacent ones.

Kajil sat next to Neliya, "Ya lot did solid scrubbin', so we're throwin' a knees-up for ya!"

The children relaxed a little, and gave cautious smiles of gratitude. The crew jovially formed a queue, starting at a buffet table in front of the galley and snaking its way through the maze of tables and out the door. When the children's turn came, they saw an array of variously coloured vegetables, steamed, fried, or baked with aromatic herbs. A keg of beer sat at the end, surrounded by a rabble of crewmen eagerly filling cups. Then their eyes fell on the spit roast.

Zeers let out a relieved sigh, "Oh, roast *kogruk*. Finally, some proper food!"

Neliya and Fyuren were similarly delighted by the food, which was a stark contrast to the fingernail sausages they'd been served heretofore.

"Come to think about it, why haven't we eaten anything like this until now?" said Neliya.

"Them's rations. Been chow'n 'em for yonks too," said Allo as he handed Malse a plate.

Jugga plonked down next to Neliya with his plate and a pint of sickly orange beer. "Yeah, Murraloohaa 'ere says livestock's in the wars of late. Now the tokamak's workin', they go' more juice in the farms, so we chow prop'ly now, eh!" He and Kajil clinked mugs with the Earthen fellow referred to as Murraloohaa. Unlike Boggima, there was a lot more green of varied and wild shades to his hair, and his skin sported many more marks and grazes.

"Capt'n was on the ups with our work," exclaimed Allo over the din that the party had become.

"An' ain't these kiddies handy, eh!" said Kajil, wiping a dribble of beer from his lips. "Honestly, the god's droppin' the kissies with the kiddies."

"Too right," exclaimed another crewman. "First that EMP, then the kiddies. Now the tokamak's goin' max."

"Can't mem'ry last it did that! Must've been before I go' here," said Allo.

"How long ago was that?" asked Fyuren.

"Oooh …" intoned Allo as he scratched his chin. He winced as if digging through his memories was a painful act, and finally ground out, "I'd say 'bout ten … fifteen years prob'ly."

"Try twenty," growled Malse with a mouthful of food. "I know, 'cause you were whinier than these three."

"But I adjusted, hey!" returned Allo.

"Too right," interjected Kajil. "Me 'n' Jugga was stok'd to get 'board the *Ranegr*! It's the chief-est 'mong Pebhorda ships."

"What's *Pebhorda*?" repeated Fyuren.

"That's us. Means *Free People*."

"Yeah, but we ain't free, really," said another crewman. "The work's pish, 'n' the captain's bonkers."

"Hey, bridge crew 'ears that, ya'll be reso'ed before ya hiccup," warned Malse, pointing his fork fixedly at the man.

"But he *is* a little crazy," interjected Neliya. "Seriously, what's with all the alliteration?"

"*Allo turn nation?* What's meanin'?" said Jugga.

"Spewin' tons o' words with the same startin' sound, dummy," snapped Kajil.

"That's just captain talk," replied Malse. "Same as all the captains of the *Ranegr* do. Ya'll ge' used soon."

"I reckon it's funny," said Allo as he polished his plate with his tongue. "All I mem'ryin' of me first here is tryin' not to laugh my head off at the last captain. No mem'ryin' much o' how I go' aboard, but I 'member that."

"I 'member," said Malse. "Not diff'd from these kiddies. 'Cept yours was a 'scape pod."

Allo shrugged disinterestedly when he couldn't recall anything. But the children were interested.

"So, how do people come to be here?" asked Neliya.

A few of the crew shared their stories. Most had grown up on the *Ranegr*, others came by the same way as the children. A few even told dark stories of attacks on their home ships by the malevolent Zej. Others were sceptical of their high-talk of such space monsters.

"Urh, yeah right," yelled one drunk crewman. "Zej zippin' in outta thin-space 'n' suckin' ships away into hell. Yeah, heard them stories all the time. Pish, it is."

"The Zej are real," said Zeers. "My dad works in the Military Alchemists' Guild. He's stationed on our ship in case the Zej attack us."

"Wow, you're dad's a soldier, eh?" asked Kajil.

Their interest piqued, the crew prodded the friends about how they came to be on the *Ranegr*. Each of them, interjecting at various points in each other's stories, gave an account of the bioplant crisis, and their plans to stay with Neliya's father on Lethanis. The crew, most of whom remained rowdy in their own conversations, slowly tuned in to the story of the friends, until the food hall was quiet save for their recounting. Neliya answered interrogatories about her interests and her family's work; Fyuren boasted his intelligence, while heeding his friends' chides not to point out the ship's problems. Soon it was Zeers' turn to talk about his family.

"I haven't much to say really," he droned.

"Oh c'mon!" exclaimed an increasingly inebriated Jugga. "Sayz ya daddie's a soldier. A Military Alchemist, eh?"

"Yeah, he's stationed with the *Othala*," said Zeers. "He's part of the defence fleet. He's really busy all the time."

"What 'bout ya mum?"

"My mum died when I was little, and a friend of hers looks after me."

The crew nodded understandingly, followed by silent pats on Zeers' shoulder.

"Enough with your whining and sentimentality," roared the captain's voice, blaring from the ships intercom. "Get your wart-ridden backsides to your quarters before the Nightshift gets out!"

The crew collided with each other and with bystanders at the door, climbing over each other and leaping down the corridor.

"That captain has some way with his crew," Zeers thought aloud.

"That he does," said Allo. "Now you three, go get some snooze. T'morrow, ya'll get more int'restin' work."

"Yes sir!" exclaimed the three, Zeers more enthusiastic than his friends.

"Oh, an' clear from the Nightshift's way," added the supervisor.

Neliya, Fyuren, and Zeers were diligent on their way back to their quarters, carefully checking corners and over their shoulders for any glow-eyed shadows. When they had time they talked about the food hall, the atmosphere of which seemed a world away from the rest of the ship. The friendliness of the crew, though unexpected, was a welcome change.

"It's like an initiation," said Zeers. "When Dad joined the Guild, they were really mean to him until they all got together. Then they accepted him, and were friendly. So we must have been initiated. We're part of the crew!"

"Hold on," said Fyuren. "Shouldn't we be trying to get back home? Sure, it's been good fun tonight, but we can't stay here."

"Why not?" exclaimed Zeers, more excited than his friends had ever seen him. "Neliya, you've been desperate to get off the *Othala*. Fyuren, you have a whole ship you can tinker with! We got what we wanted, didn't we?"

Before his friends could respond, a strident cackle echoed through the hallway, "Do they get what they want on this ship?"

Then Borig appeared in front of them. He cocked his head as he studied the three children, and grinned a black, oily grin.

"You heard not my story, how Borig got here, no," he said with an animalistic rasp. "I am here longest, I am here always. But, no, I not get fun. All the" – he shot an ill-favoured glare into the air in front of him – "*fun* went away. *Fun* came not a long time. Borig, me, got many a kicksie-wicksie." As he spoke he drew closer to the children, advancing faster as they moved away, until there was less than a breath between them. He intoned slowly, hissing through his throat as he did so, "Not any more."

Zeers decided on a pre-emptive strike. But he found Borig to be quite strong despite his hunched and feeble stature. The maniac struck Zeers savagely, sending him onto his back in a daze. Then he floored Fyuren.

Borig burst into tears, "You meanies! All I want is fun!" His eyes fell on Neliya, who stood against the wall petrified. "You'll be nice to me, won't you?

Let's play and be friends!"

"No!" returned Neliya.

Then Borig lunged for her, gritting his vile teeth as he pinned her to the wall by the shoulders. She clamped hard upon his arm with her teeth. Borig squealed in pain, but strengthened his grip. Zeers appeared behind him, and leaped onto his back. Fyuren gripped Borig around the waist.

"Neliya, go get Allo!"

She didn't give it a second thought, and bolted down the corridor. She focused on looking for Allo, but she hadn't had time to explore the ship, and soon found herself lost. Her lungs burned and her legs weakened. Yet she pressed on, putting as much distance between herself and Borig as she could, very unwilling to find out what *fun* meant to that thing. She spat as well, feeling the taste of his clammy skin in her mouth from where she bit him.

She ran and ran, until she could move no more and collapsed against a wall.

Just let me breathe for a minute, she pleaded to whatever gods or spirits were listening. *Don't let that thing catch up to me.*

It seemed there were no higher beings listening. She heard the same eerie chuckles that gave her goosebumps. Her fear escaped her in a series of jittery coughs as the voice uttered:

> *Runs away … Ran away …*
> *Oh, for me what a sad day.*
> *Me wanted happy, me wanted fun.*
> *I want a friend, just a little one.*
> *I ask to play, but I get left out,*
> *Poor Borig, him no one cares about.*

Neliya forced her body to move, and she tiptoed down the corridor. The voice shadowed her like a lingering curse.

> *Why can't we be friends?*
> *Lil' brother likes you.*
> *I'll bring some toys, you can too,*
> *I have dolls, cards, lots of odds and ends.*

She checked every corner in what appeared to be a deserted part of the ship. Not a sound could be heard except the wretched voice of Borig.

> *Why not a game of hide and seek?*
> *I'll count first and I won't peek.*
> *Easy to play, just have to sneak,*
> *But make sure you don't squeak!*

Then he was in front of her, a face blazing with insane glee. Neliya narrowly avoided his lunge, and sprinted with whatever energy was left. But

Borig seemed to be lurking at every corner, taunting his prey and waiting for her to tire. She saw a doorway through which green light flooded. She charged for it, and prayed there were people beyond.

The floor was a gantry suspended over a green-glowing fog. Along the gantry, workers of strange races cast piles of bones and oozy effluent into the fog. Some had many eyes, others had none; some of them were tall and skinny, others were fat. They all blended into a fearsome mosaic that made Neliya's skin crawl.

The Nightshift, she thought, recalling Allo's warning. But her horror-scrambled brain couldn't be bothered with past warnings.

She burst forward, screaming, "Help me! Please get him away from me!" But all that did was annoy the labourers, who irately shooed her away. Borig darted acrobatically through the moving forest of limbs and overweight bodies, gaining on his quarry. On a point where the floor was rusted and looked ready to give way, he caught her and pinned her down.

"I win! I caught you!" he spluttered with glee that seemed far from playful. He squeezed her shoulders and she screeched in pain. "Don't scream! It's your turn to count and I'll hide!"

"Hey sicko!" shouted a voice. Zeers and Fyuren stood on the gantry, their faces bruised from Borig's attack.

Borig fumed with insane fury.

"Meanies … why … can't … I … have … FUN!" he boomed, rising to his full height, greater than the captain's. He advanced on the boys with murder on his mind. Neliya quickly gripped his left ankle and tripped him. Borig fell to his knees and put his face at a perfect height for Zeers' to punch, followed briskly by Fyuren's foot. The wretch staggered around the gantry in a daze, long enough for the trio to regain their own footing.

"Guys, over the edge," barked Fyuren.

They raced forward and triple-kicked him in the chest. The wretch flew wailing over the ledge, and into the fog below.

Out of breath with relief, Neliya slung her arms around the boys in gratitude. "How did you find me? I must have run all the way to the other side of the ship!"

"We just followed the screams," said Fyuren.

"He'll be real mad next time," said Zeers. Neliya's face drained of blood.

"No, he won't," interjected Fyuren. "That's the resomator down there. The only way he'll come out of that is as fertiliser."

Zeers and Neliya looked down to the fog below, gazing at the flowing eddies of glowing mist. All they could say was, "Eww!"

As if their troubles weren't over for the night, one of the labourers marched on them.

"Your little chase game nearly knocked us over!" the fat thing bellowed. "You get outta 'ere or we'll throw you in there!"

Zeers straggled to throw a pile of crates in the beasts' path, while Fyuren and Neliya raced onwards, finding a deep pit at the end of the corridor. Zeers sprinted after them, and collided with them.

Together, they fell into the pit.

4 | Things ain't always how you s'pose 'em

The children did not fall far before they hit a derelict sheet of steel and began to roll. The giant slippery-dip landed them on a squishy pile, which smelled much like their school grounds on the first day of a new year. The heap was so tall and steep, the children continued to roll and tumble toward a cold metal floor. They stood up, covered in the brown stuff.

"Gah, blood and bone," snorted Zeers.

"No it's not, it's resomate," said Fyuren as he brushed it out of his clothes.

"Yes, I know. The gardeners at school call it blood and bone."

Fyuren couldn't help himself. "Actually, blood and bone is–"

"Don't care, Fyuren," snapped Zeers.

Neliya could only give a dismayed sigh. So far, she'd kept her dress mostly clean. Now it was absolutely filthy.

"Where are we?" she asked as she wiped her face on her already dirty sleeve.

Fyuren eyed the pile of muck, "Well, considering where we fell, this could be the outlet of the resomators."

The compartment appeared five times the size of their school's assembly hall, and filled with a dense forest. For a moment, they wondered if they were in fact on Lethanis and just lost.

"It must be a greenhouse," said Neliya, eyeing a red-flowering plant. "I bet that flower over there is that bitter-pot they feed us."

Fyuren was again amazed and irritated at the same time.

"They even let their agriculture department go insane? This is why we have to eat that junk all the time. Who knows what mutants are here."

As if the word *mutant* was a cue, the bushes rustled. Neliya and Zeers shuddered, worried that *mutant* meant ferocious claws. The creature pushed past the last curtain of branches. The woman was Earthen, like Boggima, but much thinner, her muscles more toned, and her hair much thinner and less colourful. Her skin, far lighter than any Earthen they knew, hid beneath little more than a pair of tattered shorts and a brown tee shirt. She looked at them expectantly, and the children grew more anxious.

She finally blurted, "Well? Gonna tell me what you're doing here?"

The startled children squeaked at her exclamation, and feebly stammered out introductions and explanations.

"So, that wretch has been at work again," she murmured half to herself.

"Any chance you could show us back to the food hall?" Neliya asked.

The woman yanked an orange pyramid-shaped fruit from a tree next to her, and dropped it in the woven-reed bag hanging from her shoulder. "I could, but I wouldn't with the Nightshift out."

"Yeah, we've been warned of that," said Zeers sardonically.

"Perhaps there are shortcuts or ways around the Nightshift?" asked Neliya. "We'd really like to get back ho … I mean, to our quarters."

The woman shot Neliya a grin, which made her feel threatened. "You'll have to put your feet up elsewhere tonight. I'm almost finished with the harvesting here. I'll take you back to my camp and we'll find a spare sleeping mat, or three." The woman checked a few more trees nearby, finding no more ripe produce. Then she beckoned the children to follow.

Once they passed beyond the trees, it was as if they'd gone through a portal and appeared on a world Boggima had described in her many stories. Everywhere they went on the *Othala* – in Neliya's manor garden, to the parks, even on bush walks – the soil was hard as a rock, or dust.

Consistent, homogeneous, boring …

Here, there were slimy bits, cold and warm areas, rocks and pebbles. The air was pungent and soothing at the same time, and free of suffocating fumes of industry or civilisation. Neliya took a deep breath. The sights and sounds of rustling bushes and the odour around her shooed away the nagging thoughts that had kept her awake at night, and she took the moment to enjoy the terra incognita.

She barely heard Fyuren's complaining, or Zeers' questions about the woman. Luckily, the woman gave no response, or Neliya might have missed an interesting recount. When she detected the faint aroma of smoke, Neliya looked forward and saw a red light trickling through the trees. The group entered a clearing in the artificial forest. A fire crackled humbly in a shrine-like circle of stones, and filled their noses with a sweet and spicy smell.

About the fire were a number of huts, chimeras of dried wood and metal. Sleeping mats were laid out on the ground, cosily nestled around the fire. People were interspersed between the tents, huts, and sleeping mats. One man leapt to his feet and embraced the woman warmly.

"Deloorie! I waited ages for you," exclaimed the man.

"Welcome home, Murraloohaa," replied the woman. "I was a bit behind on my harvesting. But you can't have been waiting that long."

"Why do you say that?" asked Murraloohaa.

Deloorie shot him a sly expression, and patted his stomach. "Because there was some kind of big party at the food hall, wasn't there?"

Murraloohaa smiled gauchely, especially when the rest of the tribe chuckled at his wife's accusations. "How did you know?"

Deloorie beckoned the trio forward, "I picked up these three near the output of the resomators."

Murraloohaa was shocked. "How did you get here?"

The children recounted Borig's chase, and his fate in the resomator. When Murraloohaa heard that, he made a sound part way between a gasp and an incredulous laugh.

"I knew you kids wouldn't go down without a fight." He eyed Zeers. "'Specially you, Littles."

"Oh yeah!" exclaimed Zeers. "You were the one I got with the spanner!"

Murraloohaa winced, recalling the lightning-like agony of Zeers' blow, and clutched his lower stomach.

Deloorie chided her husband, "You should know better! We hope to have a baby someday, don't we? And you shouldn't be with a gang that bullies kids."

One of the onlooking people, an elderly lady, ignored the lovers' spat and rose to her feet to approach them. She looked on them with a kindly face, though her brow was so heavy that it weighed over her eyes, reducing them to tired slits.

"Ya know," she murmured in a sweetly raspy voice. "Deeze kiddiez been havin' a rough night, I thinkz. Maybe dey should get ta bed now, huh?"

The mention of sleep made the children yawn hard. Some sleeping mats were set out for them near Deloorie and Murraloohaa. The kind old lady, who introduced herself as Kagoolie, went into one of the huts and returned to the children with a basin and three washcloths. Those washcloths looked to their facial grime like a salve to an infectious wound.

Deloorie took one of the washcloths and approached Neliya, while Kagoolie approached the boys.

Zeers took one bluntly, "I'd like to wash my own face, thanks." Kagoolie replied with a smile, which, her aged visage notwithstanding, was overwhelmingly warm.

"Y'all look real bushed. Ya must be in da middle ov a big adventure, eh?" She gently scrubbed Fyuren's scowling face. "What's da matter, boy?"

"It's all wrong! The tokamak is a mess, the ship falling apart, and now this greenhouse has gone haywire. Where are the proper controls to prevent runaway forests? You realise those plants could be poisonous?"

The old lady was silent and pensive for a moment. Neliya palmed her face, never more annoyed with her friend.

Oh, why can't you just let it go? Now you've offended her and we're going to get kicked out of here!

The old lady began making a sound that resembled coughing. It slowly evolved into a raucous cackle, as if Fyuren made the most hilarious joke she'd heard in her long life. She wiped a single tear drizzling down her cheek, as she said, "Oh, dat a real cack-up! Boy, you sound like me ol' Dad. He waz a worker back 'fore da *Ranegr* got us. He'd pound the supper table shoutin', 'Oh they ain't got dis or dat! Dey shoulda doin' dis'n'dat! Dis ain't da way it's s'posed ta be!' Den our ship got took by da *Ranegr*, 'n' we put ta work here. 'N' ya know what he learn'd? Things ain't always what *you* s'pose 'em. Dey's da way dey are. Ya have ta hack it, or ya end up losin'."

Fyuren was quiet a while – a simply incredible sight for Neliya and Zeers. For years, this boy was the self-proclaimed brain of the world. And this old lady shut him up in a sentence!

That night, the three friends slept better than they had in a long while. When they awoke the next day, it was well into the morning. Deloorie and Kagoolie made them a breakfast of the vegetables picked from the forest. Fyuren had a chance to witness the preparation of a poisonous berry into a lovely jam on a slice of vegetable with the same consistency as bread.

"Ya see, eh?" said Kagoolie as she sipped some tea from an egg-shaped cup. "If ya want everythin' your way, ya never learn anythin' new."

"Well, speaking of new things," said Neliya as she swallowed a mouthful of vegie-bread. "I was wondering how you figure out which plants are okay to eat?"

"Oh, itz not dat hard at all," said Kagoolie. "Deyz just the ones the animalz don't like. Deyz all look at 'em and move on. We learn how to get rid of the poison by watchin' doze dat do like 'em. See, animalz learn quick when deyz left alone and not made pets, and ya can learn lots from dem too instead of teachin' 'em to rollover or sit or anything silly."

"That's why I don't like pets," muttered Zeers.

Fyuren was far from convinced, and argued, "But if you don't keep controls on the animals, they might develop some kind of disease, or become really vicious, and people would get sick or hurt. It's negligent to not try and prevent that."

"Ah, me Dad come from da dead," chortled the old lady. "Sickness is part of life, gettin' attacked by animals is too. Goin' through doze things is how ya learn. Ya find out amazin' new things when ya pushed to it, eh?"

"I wouldn't learn how to fly if someone pushed me from a plane," retorted Fyuren.

"But someone else would learn something by watching you fall," interjected Neliya. "That's what Kagoolie is saying. If a person is hurt or sick, they'll still learn something, and so will everyone who watched them."

Fyuren snorted, "Well, I don't think anyone should have to go through bad things so that other people can learn something."

For once, Neliya and Zeers didn't sense an argument coming, even though Fyuren looked like he wanted to debate his point to the bitter end. They finished breakfast just as Murraloohaa appeared with an angry Allo in tow.

"What did I say about the Nightshift!?" barked the engineer. "I was looking everywhere for you. I spent a day's food rations having the galley cook up some breakfast for you. And then I find your quarters empty and you're gone!"

"We're sorry!" cried Zeers.

"It was Borig!" cried Neliya. They both made like they were about to cry.

It obviously hit Allo's soft spot, because he huffed, "Come on! We've got work to do."

The children stood and thanked their new friends for the lovely food.

"Dat's no problem, sweetie," said Kagoolie.

"Come around any time," said Deloorie.

Urged by Allo's impatient chiding, the children departed and followed their supervisor to the reactor core.

The following days saw a renewed enthusiasm in the children. They felt increasingly familiar with and comfortable around the crew. Neliya in particular could set her mind at ease knowing she wouldn't feel the stare of that crazed Borig on her back.

The friends remained at the posts in the reactor core, but found different jobs that were much better than cleaning.

Fyuren was appointed Malse's personal assistant, and helped refine calculations and perfect core functions. He still preached a determined message of the ship's state of disrepair, but Malse welcomed it and channelled his energy into improving the *Ranegr* one issue at a time. After some tutoring from Kajil, Zeers and Neliya learned how to weld, manage the electronics, and repair broken heat exchangers.

The crew, especially the core workers, were quite taken with the children. Jugga and Kajil often invited them to play in a makeshift sport hall they'd built by cutting through some bulkheads in an unused part of the ship. Murraloohaa took to teaching the children some fighting skills. With every day of exercise and work in the reactor core, the children grew stronger and better at their jobs.

Even though they had settled in surprisingly well aboard the *Ranegr*, the topic of a return to the *Othala* remained on their minds, and popped up in conversation every night. Neliya was silent whenever it arose, while Fyuren and Zeers grew divided on the issue. One night in particular, their quarrel reached an uncharacteristic level of hostility.

"How can you not like it here?" asked Zeers. "We didn't have it good the first few weeks, yeah, but that's changing now. We get good meals, get plenty of exercise, and actually do real work. Landing on the *Ranegr* is the best thing that's ever happened to us, I reckon."

"You're such an idiot, Zeers!" retorted Fyuren.

"Why? Because I don't agree with you?"

"No, because you keep asking that same question, 'How can we not like it here?' I think I tell you the same thing every night: my Mum and Dad aren't here. I can hardly sleep sometimes when I think about how worried they are right now. But I guess that doesn't really matter to a problem child like you."

"Why don't we ditch the talking and take this to the training hall?" said Zeers, his voice lowering into a deep growl. Fyuren's eyes betrayed an ounce of startled fear. "What's the matter, Shorts? Afraid to go a few rounds?"

"Why would I want to fight someone who can't even keep his cool when two bullies mention his Mum's name?" spat Fyuren. Neliya's ears perked, and she glared at the boys with worry and alarm.

"At least I've been in a fight," exclaimed Zeers.

Fyuren pushed against Zeers, his face exhibiting a blend of emotion Neliya usually expected from the older boy. Sensing actual fisticuffs approaching, she put herself between the boys.

"Okay, this is getting too rowdy," she urged. "Let's just call it a night, alright?"

Fyuren tried to push his way toward Zeers, barely noticing her. The older boy was not finished with his taunting.

"Yeah, Shorts," he said. "You miss the cushy life you had on the *Othala*. You want to run back to your little cubby house where you won't have to deal with the hard life here."

"You just want to stay here because, on the *Othala*, you were a mum-less loser!" barked Fyuren.

Neliya froze with shock, so horrified by Fyuren's words she didn't notice Zeers push past her. The older boy grabbed the younger by the shirt collar and threw him out of the room.

"Don't come back," he snarled.

Fyuren stormed down the corridor, gritting his teeth audibly. He barked over his shoulder, "I'm going to Deloorie's place. I'll live with them from now on."

Zeers turned around with a triumphant smirk plastered on his face. When Neliya saw his expression, she let out one of her rare bursts of wrath. She grabbed Zeers, caught him off-guard, and drove him to the floor, looking him dead in the eye.

"What do you think you're doing? Throwing him out with such a smug look?"

"He asked for it," protested Zeers.

"You taunted him, just like you taunt Tayure and Finsti … Oh yeah, don't think I don't know how it's usually *you* who looks for a fight with those two."

"Do I look for eggs getting thrown in my face?" returned Zeers, his indignant voice riddled with guilt.

Neliya's stamina was already dimming, and she moved away from the boy. She ran her hand through her hair and sighed as she tried to gather her thoughts.

"Zeers, we need to be together if we want to survive here, and get back home," she said calmly.

Zeers looked fixedly at her in disbelief, "Do you even *want* to go home?"

Neliya avoided eye contact while she tried to find an answer. She could only say, "I don't know." As she rubbed her tired eyes she thought, *Well, maybe Kagoolie can work her magic and make Fyuren feel better.*

Whether Fyuren actually spoke with Kagoolie, Neliya didn't know. But, if he had, obviously it didn't work. The following day, the boys avoided each other where they could and shot each other deadly glares where they couldn't. Since Gelfri had warned them not to complain about going home, they couldn't recount their fight, although most of the crew were already talking about it. It bothered Fyuren so much that he grew sloppy with his work.

"C'mon, Shorts!" chided Malse, thrusting a fistful of papers in his face. "This math sucks. Ya wanna see a leak-sprung tokamak? Wanna get reso'd?"

"Whatever," droned the boy. Malse's short temper broke, and he slapped Fyuren's head.

"Knock it off, you stupid little boy! Just 'cos you had a fight doesn't mean ya get sobby. You make one mistake 'ere and you'll wreck the whole reactor!" The boy glared at the scarred man but found no power to retort. "Never mind. Go take a break."

Fyuren marched away, pushing past core workers who responded with indignant curses. Neliya walked in to see him pacing toward the door, and quickly put the gas refill for her welder on the floor to stop him. The distraught child threw his arms around her and buried his face in her chest.

"I hate it here," he moaned.

"I know." She looked around the reactor room, eyeing the onlooking workers with some disdain. *This isn't a show, guys,* she nonverbally chided.

The friends went to the food hall, which was empty during the day, save for the lone kitchen hand who usually did the dishes after dinner. The woman sat silently at one of the tables, cradling her head on her palm and staring off into space. When she saw Neliya appear in the door, her arm slung around a scowling Fyuren, it was like an oasis of social activity in a monotonous desert.

"Femie, Shorts! Come on in!" she exclaimed.

"Hi … umm … Dennie, right?" asked Neliya, a little intimidated by the woman's spiked coloured hair and pierced nose and lips. The piercings moved with her expressions as she warmly welcomed them.

"Slackin' off work today?" she asked.

"Just this once," said Neliya. "Not feeling in a good mood. Any chance of two mugs of ginger beer?"

"Coming right up!" said Dennie ecstatically, racing toward the galley. She quickly reappeared with the drinks. When she placed one in front of Fyuren, she saw his disenchanted face, and grew concerned. "Oh, what's the matter, darl?"

"He's homesick," said Neliya.

Dennie covered her mouth in shock, gazing wide-eyed at Fyuren like he was a lost puppy.

"Not just that," intoned Fyuren. "I've been arguing with Zeers ... Littles." He recounted the events of the previous night, up to the point where he hit one of Zeers' nerves.

"Don't you think it'd be better if you stuck together?" asked Dennie, eyeing Neliya mysteriously as she spoke. "If someone's a loner here, they end up like Borig. That's why you three need each other. And if a chance comes that you three can get home, he can make his choice to stay or go."

"So I can stay friends until he makes a stupid mistake?" snapped Fyuren. "He's a moron to stay here."

Neliya placed a hand on his shoulder. "Fyuren, that's your view. But here on the *Ranegr*, he's a completely different person. If he's found a place that he likes, then it's his right to stay."

"It's not for you to decide how he lives," added Dennie.

Fyuren was pensive for a moment, even though his eyes were filled with the determination of his own righteousness. But slowly that emotional shell was melting away as he remembered one of Kagoolie's teachings: *Things ain't always what you s'pose 'em.*

Damn authority figures ... Gotta do as the oldies tell me, even though I'm smarter, he growled internally. The thought made his insides twist into knots of frustration, which eventually snapped and released their tension in a long, exhausted sigh.

"Alright," he grumbled. "I'll go apologise."

The two finished their ginger beers and thanked Dennie before departing. They went back to the reactor room, which was still busy as ever. The reluctant Fyuren needed a gentle shove from Neliya before he trudged toward a ladder and climbed to where Zeers sat finishing a weld.

"Uh ... Zeers?" he shouted over the screech of the arc-welding torch. Zeers stopped his work and turned around, eyes widening in an expression of displeasure.

"What now?" he barked.

"Umm ... I wanted to say," Fyuren stammered. *Honestly,* he thought, *why is it so hard to say two words?*

He lost his chance. The boys heard a squelching sound, then a soft squeal like a teakettle singing. It sent horrifying chills down their spine. Zeers' weld sprang a leak, and before he could stop it, the pipe ripped open as if it were tissue paper.

Zeers tackled his friend. They narrowly dodged the rush of mortally scalding steam, rolling in mid-air and falling to the hard metal floor. The failed pipe buckled in more places until it shattered. Sparks flurried from the tokamak's support modules, and the reactor rocked violently, its purple ambience devolving into an icy blue glow.

"Beta spike!" barked Malse. He pulled the boys out of danger and yelled orders to the crew. Hands flew at computer terminals, workers swivelled valve wheels and flicked switches on the damaged electrical module, trying to wrangle the out-of-control tokamak. The core rumbled with such power that it shook the entire chassis of the *Ranegr*. A dark look of resignation fell over Malse's face.

"Everyone scram!" he roared. "Lock down the reactor chamber and prep for purge."

The workers flooded out of the room, dropping their tools willy-nilly. Neliya tried desperately to push through the stampede, looking for her friends, but the sheer force of the cascade of terrified workers was too much for her. The blast doors began to descend, the men diving and ducking as they passed until it slammed shut. Neliya pushed through the crowd and found Zeers, pale-faced and worried.

"Zeers!" she cried, throwing her arms around him. "What happened? Where's Fyuren?"

"I don't know!" replied a breathless Zeers. "The seal I was working on blew up. We got separated in the rush."

Neliya's heart stopped. She grabbed Zeers by the hand and pulled him through the crowd toward the observation viewport. They frantically scanned the room, and saw him face down on the floor.

"Preparin' purge, on ya go, Captain," they heard Malse state into an intercom.

"Fyuren's still in there!" shouted Zeers.

"What?" exclaimed Malse.

"Malse, you gotta let him out!" cried Allo.

"Radiation shieldin's started to ooze. We don't purge now and we all die," returned Malse.

By now Fyuren had come to his senses, and confusion gripped him. He sprinted for the door, begging to be let out. Neliya and Zeers could only watch while the crew bickered. He pressed his back to the blast door, regarding the tokamak as a feral beast.

What is this? Tokamaks can't explode! They're not even proper stars! This isn't how it should be! I shouldn't be here, vaporized by some bizarre machine! I'm not supposed to die here! This isn't how it's supposed to be!

Then it came to him again, *Things ain't always how you s'pose 'em.*

Fyuren growled furiously, "Damn authority figures! I'm not gonna die here!"

He scanned the machine for a way to prevent the imminent explosion. Then a vague inkling rose in his mind as he recalled things the core workers had said when he was barely listening.

"A clench," he mumbled, as if witnessing some cryptid he'd only heard described in passing.

He sprinted toward the electrical module and yanked closed all the breakers. His fingers flew at the keyboard, entering commands faster than his eyes could see them. Then he bolted across the room and sealed the coolant intake valves.

Outside, and through security monitors on the bridge, the crew and captain watched the small boy at work. Malse held off on ejecting the core, watching in amazement to figure out what he was doing.

Fyuren finished his preparations, and tried to open the outlet valves. But they were locked down too tightly for his short arms, and wouldn't budge.

Gelfri's voice screamed over the intercom, "What are you waiting for, you pee-drinking sissy pants! Get your petticoats in there and help him!"

The blast doors flew open, Neliya and Zeers leading the charge into the room. Fyuren welcomed the help, barking instructions with enough resolve to put Malse to shame.

"When I give the order, hit the reboot command on the main control board," he commanded Malse. Neliya, Zeers, Allo and a few more core workers lodged crowbars into the outlet valve wheels, and pulled.

"Heave!" they chanted. And the bridge crew joined in, and the hangar crew, even Kagoolie and the agriculture team watched through a broadcast sent through the ship. Enjoying the very welcome entertainment, Dennie bellowed along too.

The valves suddenly gave way with a clang, and the reactor roared.

"Malse!" shouted Fyuren.

Malse slapped the switch, and the rumbling grew worse. A flash of sparks and a loud clamping noise echoed through the room. The crew scrambled away from the machine, which growled like a rowdy beast reluctant to lose its freedom. One last plume of sparks burst from the shielding manifold and sent everyone face down to the floor.

Lights flickered, and though the room was filled with smoke and debris, a familiar purple light permeated the fog. Malse climbed to his feet and rubbed a prominent bump on his head as he bellowed, "If you're dead, give us a shout."

"I ain't dead," said Allo.

"I'm fine," said another crewmember. Other crewmembers gathered their senses and chimed in. Those who could move found the emergency fire extinguishers and snuffed the embers from damaged equipment. Malse felt his way past his scrambling crew and found the intercom system, from which Gelfri's voice bellowed demands for a report.

"We're still twitchin', Captain," he said though a series of coughs and splutters.

"What's the status of the tokamak?" said the captain.

Malse roared out, "Oi, anyone near a diagnostic 'splay?"

Fyuren finished coughing the remainder of his lung capacity and found a station near the heat exchanger. He let out a spluttering laugh and yelled, "All tokamak read-outs returning to normal!"

The ovation on the bridge was just as fervent as it was in every part of the ship. Gelfri gave a relieved sigh, wiping his brow and chuckling to himself.

"The problem started with a pipe that they broke. But they stopped it. So they get to live?" asked the man standing beside the captain.

Gelfri smiled. "No, that precarious pipe had been welded so many times it was nothing but flux and slag. Instead …" His smile became a wide grin. "I'm going to have those kids for dinner."

5 | Don't say it's impossible

There was still much work to be done before anyone could relax. The crew reassembled the control systems, and grew calmer as the tokamak was brought under control. After triple checking the read-outs, Malse announced the reactor was in working order once again. The crew let their fatigue overtake them, some falling onto their backsides on the metal floor and wiping their glistening brows. Almost straight away, there were talks of drinks all round.

The children walked in tow behind Malse and Allo, and as they made their way to the food hall, Murraloohaa, Jugga, and Kajil joined them.

"You guy's did great, eh!" roared Kajil, patting the boys on the shoulders. "Ooh, you're gettin' strong, you are! When you first got 'ere, you were all sticks for arms! Thought I might flatten ya if I whacked ya too 'ard, eh? Now you're walkin' real tall!"

"And ya saved us too!" exclaimed Jugga, enthusiastically bear-hugging Neliya from behind.

The food-hall was more rowdy than usual. Normally, most of the crew would skip dinner and head straight for their barracks, their tiredness drawing them there as the scent of cheese lures a mouse to a trap. But after the brush with imminent death and Fyuren's amazing feat, even some bridge crewmembers were in attendance.

The children were propped up on a table in the centre of the room and handed mugs of ginger beer. Malse led the crew in a toast: "To Littles! 'E's more stand-up than kiddie'd be near a tokamak! To Shorts! Brainier 'n me! To Femie! Way stronger than any gal I know! We ain't 'ad none like 'em! 'N' they saved our bums!"

"Our bums!" the crew roared, and downed their drinks in one gulp. Then came the stampede toward the beer kegs at each table. The friends could only smile at the crew and each other, and clinked their glasses in cheers.

The lights started to flicker just as people started drinking. A lot of them started to choke on their ale. Malse and Allo made a quick run down to the tokamak chamber, and came back with relieved faces.

"It's alright," they said to a nervous crowd. "Just the Nightshift gettin' settled into things. Keep partyin'!"

Everyone sighed with relief and went back to their drinks.

Neliya looked down at her ginger ale apprehensively. She recalled the shadow down the corridor, and the monstrous beasts that had accosted her near the resomators. Jugga noticed her face and popped down next to her.

"What's happenin'?" he asked.

"Oh, umm … I'm just thinking about the Nightshift," said Neliya. "We'd run into them weeks back. I … just … I don't get why they're here. Why would you have such wild animals maintaining the systems while you're asleep?"

"They're not so bad," said Kajil with a burp. "Was a wrangler for a bit, 'n' I figured they're pretty smart. Not really fans o' Mydians though. But when ya get ta know 'em, some're real nice."

Neliya's insides shuddered, and she gripped her cup tighter. Jugga and Kajil took her mind off it with interrogatories about what happened in the tokamak chamber. The conversation soon gave way to songs and dance. Even Zeers sang along with Jugga and Kajil, as they danced along the length of the tables.

Smish, smash, soot and ash,
Burned off skin and singed moustache!
So off we go where the booze'll flow,
A hard day's work when a tokamak blow.

Not a day goes by, 'ere in the expanse,
We don't brush with death or a Nightshift wight.
A fair reward, we near in a trance,
Some food, some drink, and a bed tonight.

What spirit or god do we give our dues
For the three lucky charms here in our mid?
Another room for them to snooze?
Or a drink that's fit for a kid?

Slob, sloth, rot and broth,
Ferment on the top, or the bottom, or both,
Makes for a lager, an ale, or a klup
Drink to our health 'fore we all blow up.

Neliya and Fyuren chuckled and laughed as they clapped in time with the singing. Zeers dancing with two brutes more than twice his height made for a hilarious sight. And Jugga and Kajil's drunken stumbling just amplified the comedy.

Though the dancing and song drew to a close (at least for the time being) another group grew more rowdy. That rabble of core workers and farmers stood near the wall and expelled sharp bursts of cheer or disappointed jeers following the sound of metal on cork. The sounds drew Neliya's attention and she drifted toward it.

"Oi! Seems alike got 'ere us a challenger!" said the first of the group that saw her approach. "Go on 'ere, Femie, 'ave a look."

A hand pulled her through the crowd to the front, where she saw a dartboard hung up on the wall beside a growing pile of empty beer kegs. Allo, who had been playing until she appeared, pulled his darts from the board and faced her.

"Ya seen this, eh?" he asked.

"In movies, I guess," said Neliya, though she tried to edge away lest she be dragged into the game.

Allo read her mind and said, "'Ave a go, then."

Every eye turned to see the potential hilarity of a child *trying* to play darts. That child was then lifted onto a chair and given a handful of the sharp toys. The crowd simmered with "Go on, then, Femie!"

Fine then, she thought. *I've always wanted to play this anyway.*

She lined up the dart with the board and threw with a flick of her wrist. Her perfect bullseye was met with a simmer of whistles and hums.

Jugga scoffed, "First-time luck. Go again!"

Neliya threw the next one. Another bullseye. Now the crowd chuckled with excitement.

"I must be a natural," Neliya jibed with a smirk. Jugga's folded arms tightened around his chest. Neliya shrugged in reply, "I guess it's hard having no depth perception."

Jugga's only eye glared, while the scarred pit next to it twitched in response to the, "Oooh," that flooded the crowd. He drew near to the girl and said, "Betcha can't do three in a row."

Neliya's confidence was so bloated, her mouth asked "How much?" before her brain knew it. Jugga laughed at her boldness.

"Week's ration of ginger ale," he said. "That somethin' kiddies can drink, eh?"

"Deal," said Neliya. She held her hand out to shake his, which he took with a grin of respect for the girl's brashness.

The room fell quiet, and Neliya threw the last dart. The crowd exploded with flabbergasted cheers at the third bullseye. Jugga yelled, "Oi! That was one! Jus' one! Femie still go' two more!" But his protests lost against the roar of cheering for the girl, whose nerves finally caught up with her. As she screamed "I did it! I won!" Jugga acquiesced to the will of the crew, and poured out a mug of the brown liquid.

"Week's ration o' ginger ale," he announced, before dumping the mug's contents on the victor's head. The crowd fell silent. Neliya glared up at the man, who, behind the mischievous grin, began to panic. She started to move before he could get really nervous, grabbed a mug and filled it with beer. Then she locked her eyes onto him.

"You are *so* dead, Jugga!" she bellowed.

The beer flew from the mug and over the hangar worker's face. The food hall screamed with laughter as Jugga rubbed the liquid out of his good eye. Then he looked back at Neliya.

"We gotta fight now," he proclaimed.

Neliya grinned cockily, "Bring it!"

The brawl was clearly a jest, and the crew pretended to goad them along with the typical *fight* chant. Jugga lifted Neliya into the air and twirled her around, and when the dizzy girl found her footing, he let her tackle him to the ground, and she proceeded to tickle him.

"Gah! Tickles! Me weak bit!" he wailed.

As they roughhoused to the crew's inebriated delight, a guest entered the room. Eventually people caught on to his presence, and the rowdiness died down. Neliya and Jugga noticed the quiet, and looked up to see the figure. His uniform was a similar blue and red colour scheme to Gelfri's, though he seemed a little younger and a lot more composed. That said, the evident wrinkles growing from the corner of his eyes indicated a life of extreme stress, or extreme boredom. He shot a glare at the children, which made them shoot to their feet.

"The captain was greatly impressed by your efforts, young ones," said the man in a business-like manner. "He extends an invitation to dinner in his quarters."

The crowd crackled with astounded whispers and impressed whistles. The children, taken aback as much as the crew, stammered as they exchanged glances with each other. Silently, they agreed.

The man hurried them out of the food hall and toward the elevator, like a farmer desperate to be done with his herding work.

"So, what do we call you?" asked Zeers as the elevator started to climb.

"You may refer to me as the Quartermaster," replied the man in a monotone.

"Umm … Don't you have a name?" asked Neliya.

"Not to be known by you," said the Quartermaster. His tone was no different, yet it clearly carried disdain, and the children piped down.

The elevator moved sluggishly, and not just Fyuren trembled at the thought that the rickety carriage could fall at any moment. But the elevator was strong for its age, and valiantly delivered them to the bridge deck.

The doors slid open, and what the children saw reminded them of their look-out spot on the *Othala*: a feeling that they'd teleported to another world. Rather than rusting bulkheads and fraying wires, the walls shone with the ambient glow of well-kept light fixtures, the floor made of varnished hardwood too precious to sully with their feet. There were no odours of sewerage or sweat either.

"Dinner is being prepared," said the Quartermaster, who now resembled one of the butlers in Neliya's house. "The captain has arranged some washing facilities and clothes for you."

A bath and new clothes, they thought delightedly. The children regressed to half their age, jumping and skipping behind the Quartermaster, who took far too much time to reach the baths for their liking.

The boys entered a small but luxurious room with two beds that *weren't* mouldy. The window afforded a view of the galaxy, spectacular if smaller than their view on the *Othala*. Then they saw Deloorie and Dennie, holding some towels and bags of soap.

"We were asked to help you get ready for dinner with the captain," said Deloorie.

Dennie opened a door in the wall, leading into a beautiful, white-tiled bathroom. Both boys thought they'd died and gone to paradise. They gladly threw off their dirty, torn clothes and charged into the bathroom.

Neliya's room was much the same as the boys', and she was no less thankful for it. Kagoolie was waiting for her, but unlike her friends, she stopped the lady when she followed her into the bathroom.

"I don't really need help washing," she murmured.

"I think we'd chat," said the lady warmly. "We ain't done a privy talk yet, 'ave we? 'N' I wash ya back."

Neliya's face burned, and she backed away.

"Dun't be shy," said Kagoolie, shutting the door behind her.

Neliya sat rigidly on a small stool in front of the mirror, and in between her embarrassed shivers noted how brown with dirt and grime she'd become. Thanks to cleaning the pipes, sleeping on a dirty floor, and the mulch-pile in the greenhouse, she was absolutely filthy.

"I look awful," she droned.

Kagoolie readied a small showerhead and warned, "Get ready, water's chilly." Neliya suppressed a shriek as the water fell on her back. "When you're oldie like me, ya won't be worryin' 'bout looks," Kagoolie went on. "Ya'll be too busy lookin' after ya grandkiddies, who'll get ya nice presents and give ya hugs."

Neliya chuckled, relaxing a little as the water grew warmer. Kagoolie held the water over her head and soaked her hair with it.

"Not if I'm stuck here forever," said the girl.

Kagoolie chuckled, "Don't ya worry, eh. Ya'll find a way home." Neliya grunted unenthusiastically. "Ya don't want to go home?"

Neliya held legs close to her body and avoided the mirror, where a reflection of her caretaker's eyes fixed on her.

"I don't know," she mumbled. "For the longest time, I hated the *Othala*. My Mum was always working, and my Dad was never around. But that wasn't the least of it. It was only ever that cramped colony ship, that big spinning tube that held me in place. Every breath was recycled air. I looked up and saw a simulated sun. Nothing ever changed. And I got sick of drinking the same glass of water every day. I wanted so badly to get out of there.

"Every now and then I'd get to go see Dad on Lethanis. Most of the time he'd need to work, but other times he'd play with me, especially when I was little. He once showed me a movie about dancing, and it was so beautiful and looked fun. So Mum signed me up for lessons. But it was all horrid ladies teaching strict rules. So I quit and tried the track club, but that only ever relieved exam stress; it didn't make me happy. Eventually my Mum stopped listening when I tried to ask her about leaving. They had to focus on the bioplants on the *Othala*. I was stuck.

"But then I got my wish … I ended up here. And almost straight away, I wanted to go back home. Even after I got used to the place, and the crew – Jugga and Kajil have been so kind to me – I wake up in the middle of the night, and I still wish I were on the *Othala*, in my house, with both my Mum *and* my Dad! But I'm still stuck!"

Tears leaked from her eyes at first, and as she continued her story they gushed. She sobbed and heaved, not noticing Kagoolie spinning her around. Pulling her hands away from her face, the old lady took a washcloth to it.

As she wiped away the streaks of dirt, she said, "Maybe now, ya know just 'ow important ya home was to ya?" Neliya's eyes filled with disgust at the idea of seeing the *Othala* again. Then Kagoolie said, "Or ya just miss ya Mum and Dad, eh? Wish ya could just go to some planet, and live all together, eh?"

Neliya grimaced. "I hate having my parents separated by goddess-knows how many light-years. I hate being on a ship where you could explore the whole place just by walking down the street, or the only animals you can see are in cages. I wish I could go on trips with both my Mum and Dad, and see animals in the wild. And go to a real dance school."

"Then think, Neliya," Kagoolie urged. "Maybe ya parents miss ya as much. Dey on the *Othala* right now, thinkin' a way to find ya. And if ya just sit wishin', ya'll never get home to tell them what you feel, eh. Why not go back home, and tell 'em straight out ya wanna live some other place, eh?"

The old lady gave the girl a warm smile, and spun her around to look in the mirror. Her face was clean, exposing the pretty girl beneath that Neliya hardly recognised. It had been so long since she'd seen herself.

Kagoolie embraced her from behind. "Set ya mind to what you want, and decide."

Neliya sighed, as if to excise the final shreds of malaise from her body, and leaned back into the old lady's embrace.

"Thank you, Kagoolie," she murmured.

Neliya finished her bath and, while she dried herself, Kagoolie procured a blue dress from a wardrobe in the main room. It wasn't extravagant like the ones she often wore on the *Othala*. Nevertheless, it was beautiful in its own right.

Kagoolie beamed, "Dunnit suit ya?"

Neliya smiled, twirling around in front of the mirror. Her skin was clean and unblemished, her hair shone brighter than she'd ever seen it. It felt like a rebirth. She reunited with the boys, who stood pristine and well dressed. Their blue button-up shirts suited them, and they looked quite handsome. They stood in the corridor gauchely, and Neliya giggled as their faces reddened at her appearance. Although Fyuren found words to complement her, Zeers was tongue-tied.

Neliya leaned over to the boys and whispered, "Did you two make up?"

The boys replied in nonchalant unison, "Yep."

Neliya sighed, knowing their talk was nowhere near as open or expressive as her chat with Kagoolie.

Boy's can never just express their thoughts honestly, she inwardly bemoaned.

The butler-like Quartermaster ushered them into the captain's quarters. What lay beyond was more a museum than someone's home. Shelves full of figurines from numerous cultures and tapestries of equally innumerable and contrasting styles lined the walls of the chamber. The captain sat at the head of a table, bare except for the place settings for three additional guests and illuminated by a finely kept chandelier chained to the roof above.

He stood from the table with a smile. "Welcome, my feisty friends, please sit."

"Thank you for the invitation," said Neliya, minding her upper-class manners.

The captain withdrew toward a cabinet nearby and procured a glass water bottle and filled the cups at each place setting.

"I lack drink that children may have, unfortunately. I hope water will do."

"It will be fine, Captain," replied Zeers, taking a seat at his right hand. Fyuren sat at the left, and took a large gulp of the drink before thanking his host for it. Neliya sat to face the captain across the table.

"It will be a few minutes before dinner is ready, so please make yourselves completely comfortable," said Gelfri. "To think I'd charm children in my chateau, but it's the least a hostile host such as myself can do as thanks. That tortuous tokamak is the only reactor remaining. A purge would have been perilous."

Fyuren grinned proudly.

"My curiosity defeats me," Gelfri went on. "How did you fix the reactor?"

Zeers warned, "Oh, you don't want to ask him that."

"Littles, a moment for the lucid lad," replied Gelfri.

Fyuren scratched his temple as he recalled the amazing epiphany that saved the crew. "I'm not really sure. I'd thought damage to the power regulators'd just quench the magnets and shut down the reactor. Obviously not. Then I remembered the outflow couplers were a tad corroded. So when the regulators were damaged by … umm, *our* accident, the couplers failed. Instead of power going out to the ship, it was diverted inward to the coils. The magnetic field got stronger, the plasma pressure spiked, increased the reaction rate and generated more power that went straight back into the coils. It's called a *clench*, but I only ever thought it was theoretical. I had to find another outlet for the power, and drain the field coils quickly … The rest is a bit of a haze."

The captain's grin widened. "Truly, my encephalitic epiphany to spare you was a good one. Without you three, we would not have made such arduous advances so quickly."

"We didn't think the crew would take so kindly to us," said Neliya.

Zeers nodded in agreement. "I always imagined Drifters – or Pebhorda – were more, I dunno, brutal? But, everyone seems so friendly with each other."

"Funny how far from fact rumours roam?" intoned Gelfri. "That said, not all on this ship functions favourably. Crewmen, especially. I can think of one right now."

The friends exchanged glances, knowing whom he was talking about.

"What was Borig's story?" asked Neliya, her shoulders quivering where the maniac had gripped her.

The captain paced about the room, absentmindedly eyeing his varied treasures. Caressing the head of a feline figurine, he said, "He came aboard long ago, ignorantly innocent. The crew bullied him, taunted him, called him names, and were quite cruel. But that's how it is here. You have to become one of the group and be accepted. Borig couldn't. Eventually he became so isolated, he was as a spooky sprite upon the ship, haunting the dark areas where nobody else went."

Neliya and Fyuren sensed something strange about Gelfri's behaviour as he told the story. Yet they couldn't put their finger on it. It was Zeers who noticed the captain's eyes darting to and from a framed photo on the mantelpiece.

"Was Borig related to you, Captain?" he asked, failing to be nonchalant.

"You're a sharp shooter, aren't you?" the captain chuckled. He held up the photo to the children, and his smile widened at their shocked expressions.

"Your son?" asked Zeers nervously.

Neliya pre-empted the captain. "No, this photo is way too old. I'd say it's almost as old as you are, Captain. And the woman has your grin." She compared the photo with the smiling captain before her, "No, this is a picture of you, your mother, and your brother. The shorter one is your brother, Borig?"

"Wrongo!" chirped the captain. "I'm the slouchy sloth. Borig's the one smiling in the photo. That was taken aboard the *Khajulgr*, during its maiden voyage from Lethanis. Our first-rate father had died, and we were off for a new life. We were attacked, by none other than the *Ranegr*! Our mother was killed in the raid, but we survived. I was determined not to die like my father and mother, and I chose to work on the ship and survive. My broken brother didn't. He was much closer to our monotonous mother than I, and her death downed him to desolate dismay. He refused to recognise the reality of the *Ranegr*, coercing him to craziness."

Neliya felt a knot form in her chest, and she clasped her hands to it.

"Captain, I am terribly sorry that we caused your brother's death!" she said, the boys joining her in a show of condolence.

The captain held up his hand and shook his head. "Please, don't grieve for me. My brainless brother was gone long before you met him. I am at least grateful that he was finally able to make some contribution to us."

Neliya and Zeers' faces turned green at the remark, recalling what the resomator does and its relation to food. With timing so awful it was comedic, the Quartermaster announced dinner.

The dishes were exotic to say the least, and on a considerably higher level than the buffet from the food hall. Still, despite their artistic design, the dishes did not appear very appetising.

"What's the matter?" asked the captain.

"Umm, after remembering Borig in the resomators, I'm a bit …" said Neliya as she edged away from the food.

"Don't worry about him, Femie," said the captain after swallowing a spoonful of soup. "Whether you're on a planet or a bioplant ship, your family will eventually end up on your plate. Eat up."

She saw her friends sampling the meal. Fyuren and Zeers' expressions became surprised and amazed, which gave her a little more confidence to try the food. It was delicious.

"Food really is a deceptively delicious discipline, isn't it?" mused the captain. "In the beginning days, it was just food to live. Now, it has become food for tantalising tastes and exquisite expression!"

The meal was accompanied by more polite conversation as the topic drifted away from Gelfri's past to that of the children. Yet, the food made the topic of home roll off their tongues like reminiscence of a past long gone and no longer meaningful. The children also found Gelfri to be quite an agreeable host, much like a neighbour long rumoured to be cruel until you personally find him to be polite and funny. He was particularly relatable when, as Fyuren civilly objected to the decrepit state of the *Ranegr*, he said, "Shorts, you needn't make a better case for your intelligence."

Zeers laughed so hard his mouthful of water flew out his nose. Fyuren's glare alternated between the captain and his chuckling friend, and he retorted, "Shut up Zeers! Seriously, this ship has to be at least sixty years old!"

"Older," said the captain with a mysterious grin.

"A hundred?" asked Fyuren, his tone unchanged.

"Older still."

"Two hundred?" asked Neliya after a surprised pause. The captain's widening grin said it was even older.

"How old then?" asked Zeers.

"Legend says it's a thousand years old," said the captain. "Others say even older – millions even."

Fyuren scoffed, "You're just making this up. For a ship to be this old and yet still function, it would have to be more advanced than anything the Commonwealth has!"

The captain snickered mysteriously as he filled a cup of liquor from the nearby cabinet. With a look reminiscent of a bard withholding legendary stories, he returned to the table, and began his tale.

"Before the Mydians, there lived an ancient adamant assembly of aliens. They built an enormous empire more amazing than the Commonwealth. Thanks to their nonpareil knowledge, they needed no mass colonisation fleets, resomators or bioplants, or the CTN, for they could control things with their magnificent minds. They could move objects at will, boil water by waving a hand, transform matter into any form they needed."

"I know this," said Neliya. "You're talking about the Antiqua."

"An old fairy tale," scoffed Fyuren. "Next you're going to say that the Military Alchemists try to impersonate them, eh?"

"Exactly!" exclaimed Gelfri. "It is believed the Antiqua mentored our ancestors, the Orda, in the ways of space travel."

"And the *Ranegr* was theirs?" asked an intrigued Neliya.

"No, but the old Orda couldn't have built it without their help," said Gelfri. "You see, the Antiqua were nought without enemies. And their most flagitious, most ferocious, *most feared* enemy was the Zej: vermin voraciously violating the void. Yet, the astonishing Antiqua found and obliterated the Zej home world.

"Then, after millennia of peace, the Zej returned. Leading the way was their queen: a winsome, wicked witch with a gaze gilded gold. Our ancestors called her Gorthol the Terrifying. With her malevolent magic, which surpassed the power of the Antiqua, she overran the galaxy, until only a few worlds remained.

"One world was Udhur, our ancestral world and the last Antiqua stronghold. During their last stand, the defence fleet tried to hold its ground.

But these burgeoning battleships were barely a boy's bobbing boat against a big bang, and they were annihilated, save for one: the *Ranegr* ... it means 'steadfast' in the Ordang language.

"The adamant admiral challenged Gorthol to show herself, and lead the final charge against Udhur. She did, her golden gawkers petrifying anyone who looked into them. But she was fooled, and the Antiqua used their wiliest weapon, and destroyed her beastly body. The Zej minions, without their leader, fled into the deepest, darkest, most desolate dimension.

"Udhur was scorched in the battle, so the sedulous survivors searched for salvation amongst the stars. Some ships made the perilous peregrination, others didn't. The *Ranegr* lost its way and was adrift. The crafty crew decided it would combine the resources and manpower of the other ships that chose to follow it. So was born the Pebhorda, the Free People. From those times, few great ships remain. This is one of them. And it is mine."

The children were speechless, and were happy to remain so while the story congealed into epic visions in their minds: battles waged between good and evil, the gilded stare of the witch as she commanded her troops, the courage of the crew opposing her.

Zeers was the first to speak, "What happened to the other survivors?"

"They became the Mydians," interjected Neliya. "Our ancestors colonised Mydia long ago."

"How do you know that?" retorted Fyuren with a smirk.

"I paid attention in history class," retorted Neliya. She ignored her friend's scoff, and returned to Gelfri, "I like how the *Ranegr* was the one to survive the war! That admiral must have been brave."

"Well, where you either fight or perish, you might as well be brave," said Gelfri. "A good leader knows nothing comes of fretting and fleeing."

"How did you become captain?" asked Neliya.

"Ah, that's a stimulating story," replied the captain. "Like I said, I was young when I came aboard. Like you, I was put to cleaning work. After, I went through several jobs including resomator maintenance (which was *not* my most pleasant position, I'll say).

"One day, I am drafted into a secret syndicate of saboteurs plotting a mutiny. They planned to cut power to the bridge, and then storm in and cut down the languid leadership. Initially I was inhibited, then I identified that I could integrate with the introduced initiative and improve my influence.

"We almost made it, but our clever captain had made some changes to the ship. When we tried to cut the power, a sly circuit tripped an alarm. I managed to escape when the remaining rabble was caught, and I went around a confidential course-way through the ventilation system. I got to the captain's quarters – right here, where you sit. I tried for the captain's thrilling throne, but he defeated me.

"Lo, he let me live, and levied my loyalty. I learned so many things in his care. The most precious precept I procured was to persistently progress to more prestigious prizes. So after I became captain, I set my sight on another goal: to become the leader of the Pebhorda, the Pebhasid."

"Is that the coup we've heard so much about?" asked Fyuren.

Gelfri's eyes radiated an ambitious flame. "Indeed it is. The Pebhasid leads a large legion located in an asteroid field about a week's travel from here. Whoever sits there is king of the county. And I want it. With the lauded loyalty I command from my crew, I have developed a wad of weapons and widgets. One weapon was an electro-magnetic pulse generator, a tantalising tribute, thought I."

"An EMP? Wow!" said Fyuren. "I'd love to have a look at it."

"Don't be so hasty, Shorts," said Gelfri. "Tempting, it is. Yet, you tender a tariff of tastier tier."

He was silent a moment, gauging the children's expectant faces. Then he continued, "I must confess, I planned to summon you a week ago, being so impressed by your confounding capacity for cooperation. I want your help.

"The Pebhasid palace is too powerful to penetrate. I want to impress the Pebhasid with an opulent offering, so that he will grant me an audience. When he does, I will swiftly strike him down. I have honed my skills in combat, and can assassinate the Pebhasid within twenty metres."

Zeers leaned back in his chair and grinned, "Really? You're that good?"

The captain harrumphed. In the next instant, he had outstretched an empty hand. The children followed his pointing finger to the opposite wall, where his dessert fork was embedded in a cork dartboard – a perfect bulls-eye!

"Once a man comes within twenty metres of me, he might as well be dead," he proclaimed. The children trembled at his skill.

No wonder the crew is so loyal, thought Zeers.

"But it's not enough," he said. "Of all the contrivances and contraptions we have created or copied, none are certain to impress the Pebhasid … But a TIM device would."

Fyuren instantly caught his meaning and moaned, "It's imposs–"

"Don't say it's impossible!" barked the captain. "Mere hours ago, you alone diverted the destruction of my ship. Malse said it was impossible to stop it, yet you did. Like the Antiqua, you can do impossible things. I know you can make the *Ranegr* into a tunneller. If you do, all three of you shall receive grand rewards when I become the Pebhasid!"

"Rewards?" murmured Zeers.

"You can have whatever you want," Gelfri exclaimed. "I shall bestow upon you any luxury or laurel."

Neliya and Zeers' mouths watered at the idea. But Fyuren, despite the allure of the offer, could not accept.

"I can't," he mumbled. "I really appreciate your kindness. But I want to go home."

Gelfri's smile widened, "Then you shall! If that is the credit you crave, I shall take you wherever you want."

"Didn't you say 'No complaining about wanting to go home?'" Neliya asked.

Gelfri waved the comment off. "I changed my mind. Adapt the tunneller to the *Ranegr*, and I will take you home." With a low bow, he concluded, "On the *Ranegr* and it's crew, I swear it will be done."

That night, they were invited to stay in quarters prepared for them. With the dinner, the story, and the captain's deal still fresh in their minds, not one of them could sleep. Through most of the night, they gazed out into the star-speckled void, pondering the bargain they had made.

6 | We want ya to be happy

Fyuren worked tirelessly to complete his task. First, he went over every solution he'd tried, attempting to address each of its problems. But each new idea put up more baffling paradoxes, with names of increasing strangeness.

The engineering crew wasn't much help. When they met Fyuren, they trembled at his presence or sneered at his age. Fyuren paid this no mind. The vision of returning home was so strong in his mind that nothing swayed him.

Months passed with little progress.

Malse and Allo chipped in with ideas when they could find the time. Neliya and Zeers offered support as well, but were careful about when to visit his lab. Luckily, whenever they entered, he was in need of a break.

One such night, Fyuren and Neliya sat quietly on the observation deck, surveying the stars.

"The stars look the same as on the *Othala*," mumbled Neliya. "It's like we never left."

"Except we can't call our parents," replied Fyuren. The months of fruitless work put a very dispirited look on his tired face.

"Don't worry, Fyuren. You'll figure it out," said Neliya.

"I'm sure I will," he said with a long yawn. While gazing at the constellations, he asked, "Where's Zeers?"

"Gym with the others," said Neliya.

Fyuren grimaced. "You think he'll decide to stay?"

"Why not ask him?" said Neliya.

At that moment, Zeers walked onto the observation deck, panting and covered in sweat. As he sat, Neliya leaned away from his billowing musk.

"You look like you've been having fun," noted Fyuren. "Running or weight lifting?"

"Fighting," panted Zeers. "Gelfri had one of his fighters train me. He says I'm a natural."

Neliya grinned. "I remember you fighting off Kajil's gang, and doing a good job too. It was weird, since when you got into fights at school, you were always crying and thrashing about like a little–"

"Kid?" interjected Zeers. "Yeah, I told my master the same thing. He said that anger gets in my way if I fight to satisfy it. He's been teaching me to fight calmly, even when angry. It's been helpful, really."

"Next time you see those bullies, they'll be too scared to throw eggs at you," said Fyuren with a grin.

"I'm not so sure," Zeers muttered. "I've never had a chance to try it. Whenever my master tries to make me mad, I just shrug it off."

"It's not the same when it's someone you know," said Neliya.

"Anyway, who do you want to ask what?" asked Zeers.

Neliya swallowed nervously, trying to find a way to avoid their earlier topic. Things were going so well on the ship, the last thing she wanted was to reignite past fights. Luckily the sound of rustling of paper and scratching from Fyuren's direction interrupted her. The boy scrawled equations and diagrams at an unusually frantic rate, his eyes shimmering with thought. Then he leaped from his chair and vanished through the door.

"Okay … That was a little weird, even for *him*," mumbled Zeers. "Think he might have worked it out?"

"Let's hope," said Neliya.

There was a brief pause, during which Neliya thanked her brainy friend for the distraction. But Zeers read her thoughts.

"Ask who what?" he repeated.

"Just leave it alone, will you?" snapped Neliya.

"But I'm curious now," said Zeers playfully.

It took a little more repetition and nagging, but Neliya finally gave in.

"We wanted to ask you what your thoughts were about going home," she said.

"Oh," he stammered. He gazed at his feet, fiddling with his sweat towel. Then his eyes wandered about the stars in front of them. He stayed like that a moment, frustration growing evident in his furrowed brow.

"I don't know!" he blurted. "It's great here. Back on the *Othala*, my dad spends all his time working, I have no mum, I have to repeat school grades, those bullies – what *were* their names? Here is just … Good! But …"

"But what?" asked Neliya.

Zeers flushed cheeks grew redder as he diverted his eyes. "Never mind."

"Come on!" said Neliya.

"You're going home, and you wouldn't be with me," he blurted. "If you were with me, the *Othala* didn't matter. But now that Gelfri is offering us a chance to leave … I just don't like the idea of being on the *Ranegr* without you."

"I'm glad for that," said Neliya. "We'd miss you too, Fyuren and I."

Zeers silently stammered, "I … w-wasn't talking about the both of you."

Neliya frowned. "What do you mean?"

Zeers gulped loudly and hoarsely, as if he were trudging through a desert. He shuffled fretfully. Neliya edged toward him worriedly. His eyes locked onto hers, and then, as if something had suddenly snapped in his head, he leaned over and pushed his lips to hers.

Neliya jumped as her skin broke out in burning goosebumps. She leaned away breathlessly and stared right back at the boy. He had a look of utter terror in his eyes, his cheeks glowing deeper red than the stars around them. When he started stammering an apology, Neliya realised she hadn't been breathing for at least a minute, and gasped in surprise. Without a command from her brain, her hand reached out and grabbed his before he could escape.

Their eyes locked as their fingers intertwined. Neliya's heart fluttered and she smiled warmly. Slowly, as if stepping onto foreign soil, she slid her arm around her friend.

"I don't want to be somewhere without you, either," she replied, resting her head on his shoulder.

Zeers shuffled a little. "I'm a bit smelly, so maybe you shouldn't."

"I'm fine," Neliya replied. She let the feeling of his shoulder against her temple, the coarseness of his shirt on her cheek, and the faint drumming of his heart drain away her concerns like a sponge. Zeers' own nervousness faded, and he put his arms around her.

For both of them, it was a novel feeling. They had hugged before, even tightly held each other when one of them was in an angry fit. While part of their present embrace felt familiar, it was alien at the same time. And neither saw a reason to end it. So they stayed there all night.

The following morning, Fyuren danced through the corridors of the bridge deck, like an impoverished writer receiving his first royalty cheque. Completely uncontrollable, any inquiries as to his ecstasy fell on deaf ears. Gelfri picked the ecstatic boy up by the shoulders and said, "What have you done, my prancing prodigy?"

"I have a design for a TIM device that will work on the *Ranegr!*" screamed Fyuren.

Neliya and Zeers sat in the corner of the captain's quarters while their friend explained his design in the simplest terms possible. The captain was delighted to find his ship already had most of the necessities. The only missing ingredient was a quantity of a strange mineral.

"Temellut," said Fyuren. "It's a porous mineral that produces gravito-photon pairs when exposed to high-frequency magnetic oscillations. We'll need it for the drive housing."

"But we don't have anything like this!" exclaimed the Quartermaster.

"Don't worry," said Fyuren. "I asked the sensors officer to scan for traces of temellut, and they hit pay dirt." He opened his tablet computer and brought up a star map to show the captain. "The scans show a rogue planet two weeks away, and it has a large vein we can mine."

"Have the helmsman set course," ordered the captain. To Fyuren, he gave his compliments and thanks.

"Don't thank me," said Fyuren in an unusually highfalutin manner. "It was Neliya who gave me the idea."

"Me?" choked Neliya when the attention fell on her.

"You were talking last night, and when you said, 'it's not the same when you know it,' ... it just struck me!" said Fyuren, wide-eyed with excitement.

Neliya met the questioning glances of Gelfri and Zeers with a confused one, and shrugged.

The *Ranegr* took much longer than two weeks to reach the planet. With his labours done, Fyuren spent most of the trip on the observation deck, gazing toward the *Ranegr*'s destination: a dark blue speck against the manifold colours of the galaxy. He would occasionally search space for the *Othala* with his eyes and his memory. Even though he was certain he was looking in the right direction, he saw not even a dot.

Other people hadn't as much free time or favour with Gelfri. Neliya and Zeers, though better dressed and accommodated than most, went back to their posts in the tokamak core. When they weren't replacing old components with older ones, they were together, and it wasn't long before people started gossiping. That led to hoots when people saw them holding hands and subsequent blushing on their part. But they were content to just enjoy their time.

Months passed. The *Ranegr* pulled into orbit above the rogue planet. Even the small view out of the bridge windows was breathtaking. Bathed only in faded light from the vibrant galactic core, the vast, lonely orb glistened in shades of blue. A silvery-white sea girdled continents carpeted by forests of monolithic crystals that diffracted the starlight.

"The planet is covered in copper sulphate, hence the blue," said the sensors officer. "The ocean's a frozen mix of toxic compounds."

"What about atmosphere?" asked the Quartermaster.

"Thin. Some Oh-two, but mostly chlorine," said the sensors officer.

"If only we had a swimming pool aboard," quipped the captain. "What about temellut deposits?"

"There is a large lode halfway between the north pole and the equator," replied the sensors officer. "It looks like we can get the mineral by open-cut mining. But we'll need space suits."

The captain grinned at Fyuren. "It's good we kept the sleek space suits you three arrived in."

"I had my team set up our suits, and I've made arrangements to run the operation," said the boy.

The captain blinked, a little disappointed that there was not even a stammer or stutter of surprise in Fyuren's voice. "Well, I'll leave the mining management to you, Shorts."

Fyuren promptly left the bridge deck, called the hangar crew over the intercom, and then found Neliya and Zeers in the food hall. He dragged them into the spacesuit storage room, and announced, "You're helping us with the mining."

"I don't know the first thing about mining!" exclaimed Neliya.

"Neither do I," said Zeers.

Fyuren replied, "I know, but we need more muscle and helping hands to get the job done faster. That's why I'm also taking the hangar crew."

"Reportin' for duty, Shorts," Kajil sarcastically announced. His friends had a good chortle at his pompous, wrong-handed salute.

"You guys aren't going to complain, are you?" asked Fyuren.

"Nah, seriously, we're glad ta help ya out, bud!" said Jugga.

"Thanks," said Fyuren. "We launch in half an hour."

"Yes sir," said the troupe, charging for the lockers. Zeers and Fyuren headed toward a locker that contained the spacesuits they wore on the tunneller. Neliya rolled her eyes and followed.

Fyuren showed them the modified spacesuits. "That planet is going to be pretty cold and those crystals are going to be sharp as. So I had these suits upgraded. See?" He held up one of the suits to show them the new features. "We'll be working in these suits for a while, so they've got some new systems in them. They'll keep you warm and dry while you work." Then he added, pointing to Neliya, "Plus, I had the chest on yours made a bit bigger to accommodate your ... umm ..." His voice trailed off as his cheeks reddened. Zeers caught his meaning, and his jaw dropped awkwardly. Then the rest of the gang clued in and diverted their eyes. Finally Neliya realised the meaning, and growled indignantly, "Fyuren!"

He held up his hands defensively. "I didn't mean it like that. It's just been a while since we wore these. And you've—"

"Fyuren, lie down before you hurt yourself," Zeers warned.

"You didn't ... measure me in my sleep, did you?" Neliya asked nervously, crossing her arms and holding them high on her chest.

"No, I figured it out by sight," said Fyuren, this time nonchalantly. Neliya just slapped him on the head and snatched the spacesuit away. Behind them, Kajil and Jugga worked hard to stifle their laughter, lest they suffer Neliya's wrath.

"How long is this mining trip going to be?" she asked, still shooting evil eyes at Fyuren.

"Not long, a few days," stammered Fyuren.

Neliya sighed and packed the spacesuits onto the trolley. She and Zeers started to push the cargo out of the room. Fyuren's face was still deep red with embarrassment. He chased after Neliya, whose scowl had turned to a smirk.

"Neliya, I'm sorry, I wasn't perving or anything," he babbled.

"It's alright, Fyuren," said Neliya. "Just remember for the next time you talk to a girl."

The mining shuttle floated above the floor, held in place by humming white rays that girdled its long fuselage. It resembled a perched bird, with folded metal wings nestled into its back, protecting the rear thruster nozzles. As they ascended the ramp into the ship, one of the mining crew met them. They were led through the corridors of the shuttle, far less spacious or high-roofed than the *Ranegr*, to three rusted metal portals that were their quarters. Zeers took the middle door, and had to shove it open with his shoulder. The inside had barely enough space to stand, with a tiny cot beside a circular viewport.

"At least the bed is better than the one in our first quarters," said Zeers.

Neliya and Fyuren agreed, but prayed the trip wouldn't last longer than a few days. They stowed their bags, then headed for the upper deck.

There they found arrays of seats, not unlike the ferries on the *Othala*. The hangar and mining crews had strapped themselves in, and the friends did the same. Even Dennie was along for the trip to serve as cook. Neliya took up a seat next to her.

"Everyone, we're heading out," said the pilot over the cabin intercom.

The ship shuddered as its mooring disappeared and it floated free. Outside, the maintenance crews scurried as if fleeing a stampede. The pilot edged the shuttle toward the hangar exit, and then punched the accelerator. The passengers' insides lurched at the force, which then jerked them to the sides as the shuttle banked hard and headed for the planet.

As they regained their senses and forced their breakfast back down into their stomachs, the children overheard a few voices riddled with wonder.

"Oi, Littles, Shorts, Femie, look 'ere!" shouted Jugga from near one of the windows. When the trio looked through the window, they saw the *Ranegr* for the first time. They'd seen renderings on computer displays around the ship, and a painting in the captain's quarters. But beholding the real thing was infinitely more breathtaking. The ship was much bigger than the children had yet explored. There were at least four hangars, only one alight with activity. The main engines were enormous, bulging at the rear; the bridge deck perched like a streak of gold on the head of a red bird of prey. Across its rusted but sturdy hull, a great seal had been painted – the one tattooed about the captain's eye.

The children could not help but grin, finding it much more appealing and satisfying to behold than the grey, cylindrical *Othala*.

"It'll be sad to say goodbye to it, eh?" asked Murraloohaa. The children turned around, wearing the same surprised expression. "Everyone already knows about your deal with the captain," he added with a grin tinged with a hint of sadness.

"It'll be sad for us to say goodbye too, eh?" said Kajil, patting the boys on the shoulder.

"So you know we're trying to leave," asked Zeers.

"That's why we're helpin', eh," said Jugga.

The children could only stammer in response, "Why?"

Most of them shrugged or scratched themselves awkwardly. Only Dennie could step forward and speak for all of them.

"'Cause we like ya," she said. "And we want ya to be happy."

"Yeah, what she said," interjected Kajil. "You guys helped us tons when ya ain't even s'posed to be 'ere."

"And you got your mums and dads waiting at home for you," said Murraloohaa.

The children replied with smiles. But before their emotions could get the better of them, the crew laughed the touching moment away, bellowing merrily, "No need to get all teary!" The children joined in with the laughter, and it continued throughout their descent to the planet.

From orbit, the crystal forests carpeting the planet's surface resembled fur. As the shuttle drew closer, the forests filled the windows. Massive structures stood proudly on the horizon, glistening in the starlight, more intricate and complex than the imagination of a three-year-old.

The temellut lode drew near, and the shuttle set down in a clearing some distance from it. The shuttle settled on a prairie of crystal grass, crushing it to dust. The leader of the mining team rose and addressed the passengers.

"Alright, surveyors check out the lode. Shorts, you're coming along too. Who's on the suit maintenance team?" Dennie, Neliya, and a few others raised their hands. "You're coming along too. Get down to the airlock with the survey team and suit up. The rest of you, start prepping the diggers. Move it!"

Dennie grabbed Neliya's hand and led her down to the airlock. At first, the lack of a ladies' change room concerned her. But when she stepped up to her suit locker, it closed around her and became a small change cubicle. The modified suit was also much easier to put on than before, and more comfortable to wear.

Dennie helped fit and seal her helmet, and she returned the favour before they proceeded to help others. The crew then walked her through the maintenance process. Finally the survey team was ready and exited the shuttle onto the planet's surface.

Neither Neliya nor Fyuren had ever been on a rogue planet. Just feeling gravity without air was enough to confuse their senses. As they came out of the shadow of the shuttle, they looked up and their jaws dropped. The galactic core glimmered even more brightly and more spectacularly than they had ever seen.

"This is better than when we went camping on Lethanis," said Neliya.

That earned a wistful chuckle from Fyuren. "That should be first on our list when we get back."

Once the survey team had disembarked, they began their trek to the lode. Fyuren found himself busy with his scanner readouts and his conversations with the other members of the survey, so Neliya and Dennie shared their stories.

"My first time on a planet," said Dennie.

"Really?" exclaimed Neliya. "You've been on the *Ranegr* your whole life?"

"Yep," Dennie chuckled. "My dad used to tell stories about what it's like being on a planet. Where instead of machines making the air it was living plants and animals. He once told me about quakes, times when the ground itself shakes."

"Quakes're bad, but seasons're nice," mused Neliya.

"Seasons!" exclaimed Dennie. "I can't imagine it getting cold then hot every year."

"Summer on Lethanis is great," replied Neliya. "I don't know how anyone could live on a ship their whole life."

"Well, don't get me wrong," began Dennie. "I like being on a ship. I just would like the chance to see summer change to autumn. And see snow as well. I don't think I'd mind living on a colony ship then."

Neliya shook her head. "Not me. When I get home, I'm going to ask my parents to move to Lethanis. I want a real sky above my head."

The conversation continued as they followed the survey team. Their topics went from ships to a comparison of the rogue planet's landscape with that of Lethanis, to Neliya's plans for home, and finally to her growing closeness to Zeers. Their feet marked out a trail of blue dust on the crystal prairie. It led downwards from the shuttle's perch toward a cliff wall, where the dull temellut stood out as conspicuously as graffiti on the side of a building.

The surveyors studied the lode and discussed the best places to drill. They eventually reported back to the shuttle with a mining plan. Then the digger was launched. It was a large machine, with spiked wheels and several arms. Neliya and Fyuren looked up to the cockpit and saw Zeers, smiling smugly at them and waving as the digger reached the lode and revved its drills.

The following days were more strenuous than cleaning the tokamak coolant pipes, but the friends enjoyed them much more. Fyuren and Zeers were allowed, more than once, to detonate charges. But they always fought over it like brothers bickering over the top bunk. These squabbles were a source of endless entertainment for the miners, and stories over dinner back in the shuttle. Every meal the children shared with the crew marked another day closer to their return home. Though it excited each of them, there was a bittersweet air above the dinner table. A point came when even Fyuren, the most excited of the three, pondered the pain of leaving their friends aboard the *Ranegr*.

Then came the fifth day of the job. By then, Neliya had grown tired of her friends arguing over the detonator, so she pushed past them and hit it herself. Clods of blue sand washed over the dig site, leaving a gaping hole that, the miners hoped, would give better access to the remaining lode. While there was a hole, with just the right access they wanted, it had no end. One of the surveyors did a scan and found it led deep into the mountain.

"So there's an ongoing orifice in your ore," Gelfri mumbled over the radio. "So what?"

"Captain, if we try to mine more, we'll lose most of it down that hole," said one of the miners.

As the radio conversation went on, Zeers peered down the tunnel. Curiously, he shone a torch into the passageway. He waved it back and forth to see the walls. Then, just as he began to lose interest, a glimmer reached him from within the pit. He shone his light back down, and saw that same glimmer. When everyone else looked, they confirmed it.

"A fleeting flicker, eh?" murmured Gelfri. "Another one of those callous crystals of copper carbonate?"

"Sulphate, Captain," said Fyuren. "And we don't know what it is. But it could be something worth checking."

The channel was silent as Gelfri pondered. Then he said, "Send Shorts down. It's nicely narrow, so he'll fit."

7 | We will teach you

On one side of Fyuren's head, Jugga notched a torch lamp. Behind him, Murraloohaa locked a karabiner clip to his suit's harness. He wore his nerves plainly on his face.

"I'm sure that harness was designed for abseiling," he murmured.

"Ah, ya dun need worry ya self, Shorts," said Kajil with a slap on the back.

That only amplified Fyuren's already high anxiety, and he shrieked. As he eyed the hole, it seemed to grow larger and more menacing, like a carnivorous plant evilly aware of an innocent fly veering toward its maw. He wished he'd installed a wastewater recycler into his spacesuit.

"All ready," said one of the surveyors.

Nearby, Neliya's fingers pressed against the viewport of her helmet. Had it not been there, she'd have been biting her nails.

"I don't think this is safe for him," she said, her fear blatant on her face.

"Nope, it's not safe at all," snapped the terrified boy. "Listen to the smart girl."

At that, everyone's eyes widened with surprise. Jugga was the first to ask, "Ya sayin' Nel's smart then? Smarter than ya?"

"Sure!" exclaimed Fyuren. "Tunnelling solution was her idea. She's always been smarter. Especially *now*."

Neliya cracked a smile, "I'm flattered, Fyuren." Her interest was slightly piqued at Jugga's earlier comment and she said, "Also, Nel?"

"Short for ya real name," said Jugga. "Femie's startin' ta get silly."

Zeers was still quite concerned for Fyuren, and he added, "Seriously, though, what if he gets stuck and can't get out?"

"What if the suit breaches?" added Neliya.

"We done scan'd, *Ranegr* too," said one of the miners. "Goes down a hundred metres, then a sorta … chamber. Whatever's 'flectin' ya torch is in that chamber. Ya should can stand 'n' turn. So, ya'll be fine."

Fyuren's lips trembled as the dark hole stared back at him, still uninviting. Just as he seemed on the verge of screaming, he felt a hand on his shoulder. He looked up to see Jugga, a grin on his one-eyed face. "Ya'll be fine. That hole there's bigger 'n 'em tokamak pipes ya clean'd back when. Ya did that, no prob!"

Murraloohaa stepped forward, his hands cradling the cable that linked Fyuren to the digger. He said, "Plus, we can just yank ya out when ya done."

Nearby, Zeers opened his mouth to speak, earning his helmet a slap from Neliya. She kept a nervous but encouraging smile.

"The sooner we find out what's down there, sooner we leave, get the tunneller working, and go home," she said.

Fyuren's heart lifted at that sentiment, and the image of a roast dinner with his parents shooed away at least some of his nerves. With a huff, he clapped his gloved hands, and approached the hole. His intercom buzzed with encouragement as he edged his feet into the hole and began his descent. Very soon, his lungs learned Jugga lied about the width of the tunnel, which squeezed a little too tightly in some places. Yet he pressed on, edging around the sharper protrusions in the rock surface. The light from above grew dimmer and smaller, though he could still see the outlines of Neliya and Zeers' helmets when he looked up. Words of encouragement crackled through the channel, which grew noisier as he descended. It reached a dull crackle by the time he dropped into the dip at the bottom with a surprised grunt.

"I'm at the bottom," he said.

"What's down there?" came Neliya's broken voice.

A thick layer of sand girdled his boots as they sank to the bedrock just below, and he had to work hard to wade through the mess. He shone his torch around the room. At first, all he saw were walls of powdery stone. With every laboured step, some of the powder dropped like an eerie waterfall that twinkled in the dull beige light of his torch.

Some parts of the walls weren't jagged or completely covered in sand, and he brushed them down to reveal indentations that resembled writing – of what language was anyone's guess. Much of it had eroded so as to be indistinguishable, but there was one segment that stood out as the least degraded.

Not a single stroke stood out as familiar. However, the larger symbol's prominence told Fyuren that he was in some kind of shrine.

Into his crackly radio he said, "Just a single room down here. There's writing on the walls. May be an ancient temple."

"Who'd build temples 'ere?" asked a voice that sounded like Jugga.

"I dunno," replied Fyuren. "Some aliens that lived here before the planet

went rogue?"

"Underground?" asked Zeers.

As Fyuren pondered a moment, another idea crept into his mind. "Either that, or it's a tomb," he thought aloud.

"That so, ya'd best get up 'ere," said Kajil.

At that, Fyuren decided he'd seen enough and turned to leave. As he waded back to the tunnel opening, his foot kicked against something solid but lighter than rock. He bent down and found a metal chalice. Initially, he thought it was made of silver, but the metal changed to gold as he tilted it in the torchlight.

"Think I found what Zeers saw," he said. "A shiny cup."

"If that's a temple or a tomb, then the cup'd probably be important," said Neliya. "You should leave it."

"I don't think anyone'd care if we kept a nice souvenir, Neliya," said Zeers.

Neliya argued with him and everyone tuned into the channel heard it. Fyuren, however, couldn't be bothered with the debate. Something had caught his eye: another glimmer, slightly submerged in the dust and debris. He edged his hands over, and pulled from the dirt a sapphire, about half the size of his fist, cut into a perfect polyhedral shape. Each surface appeared so smooth and beautiful, Fyuren's breath caught in his throat. He tore his eyes away from it to the chalice, in which were a quartet of inward pins that would have held the sapphire in place.

He opened his mouth to announce his discovery, but his tongue froze. A soft, high-pitched ring filled his ears, and it grew in volume as the sapphire hypnotised him. The buzz grew louder and louder until his ears seared, yet he couldn't scream or cry. His brain was locked to the internal symmetry of the sapphire's lattice, which sang with manifold colours.

Suddenly, another set of hands gripped his own. They were as bare as the person who owned them. Fyuren looked up and saw deep fluorescent green eyes crowning a spitting image of his own face. His ears rang with an absolutely raucous noise as the doppelganger screeched, "We will teach you!"

His face hit the front of his helmet as he fell forward into the thick dirt. He floundered around, confused and dazed, as flashes of false colour and black holes whizzed about before his eyes. He couldn't shut them out, even with his eyelids clamped down. His heart racing and his breathing shallow, he pressed his back to a wall and focused his eyes forward.

"Go away!" he repeatedly mouthed, the blurry afterimages slowly obeying his silent orders and fading. Then his eyes looked about for the other 'him.'

Another yell permeated his consciousness, this one from the radio. "Fyuren! Respond already," snapped Neliya.

"I'm here!" he blurted.

"What's the matter? We heard you breathing really heavily," said Zeers.

Fyuren thought up a quick lie. "I just slipped over and got my foot stuck in a crevice. Don't worry, I'm fine. I'll be up in a minute."

It took a while before a more lucid part of his mind, which tended to sleep when adrenaline kicked in, woke and convinced him he must have imagined the doppelganger.

You're just tired and you've had a long trip, he thought as his breathing slowed. *No one was there. You're alright.*

Finally, his mind settled. The last part of his body to relax was the hand that gripped the sapphire tightly. He held it up again.

Maybe this thing made me see things, he thought. The idea spurred him to leave it behind. And yet, he couldn't let it go. There was just something so fascinating about the gem that he had to keep it. A swell of curiosity and intrigue gripped his heart, and he shoved it in his belt pouch. His mind stayed on the jewel even as he climbed up the tunnel, and he thought, *If nothing else, it'll make a good souvenir.*

When he reported back to Gelfri what he'd found, there was less than interested reception.

"So there was a cup, and that's it?" asked Gelfri.

"And an inscription I couldn't read," added Fyuren, his lips pursed. "But no, nothing worth noting."

"Well then, I suppose that settles the situation," said Gelfri over the radio. "Maintain your meticulous mining."

"Gelfri, wait a minute," snapped Neliya. Her remark earned quite a few raised eyebrows. "If it's something important, we shouldn't be mining here."

"Oh, furious Femie, this curious cairn couldn't have persisting patrons," replied Gelfri. "The messy monument was buried deep, was it not? And desperately decrepit too. I doubt dead denizens would demur."

Neliya looked to Zeers for support.

"He's got a point," he said with a shrug.

Jugga patted the girl on the back. "Never mind, Nel. Let's just get the job done."

They went back to their various jobs. The digger hacked out a few more chunks of the ore, which made its way back to the shuttle's hold. The miners managed to procure a few more tonnes of the stuff, which made Gelfri very happy. Two days later, Fyuren announced to Gelfri that they had enough.

"Sure, Shorts?" he returned. "I don't want to pack up only to find you mistakenly misinformed me."

"We got exactly what my calculations require," replied Fyuren confidently.

"Then get more," snapped Gelfri.

Fyuren's heart sank in his chest. "My math isn't wrong here. We only needed a certain amount for the device."

One of the miners leaned into the radio microphone and said, "Captain, we can hold at least another ten tonnes of this stuff. We should make sure we got margin for errors."

"I agree, perspicacious prospector," replied Gelfri. "Ten tonnes more. Just in case."

Fyuren spent the next few hours in an irate state. He took a seat on a rock beside the road the ore loaders had etched over the last few days. From there, he watched the miners prepare for another round of detonations. As Neliya rode in on one of the trucks ferrying oxygen, she noticed him slumped on the rock and hopped off and waved the driver to move on.

"Seriously, you're annoyed because they want more ore?" she asked, able to read his thoughts from the scowl on his face.

"I calculated what we need, so we shouldn't need more," snapped Fyuren.

Neliya patted his helmet, which he shooed off. "Relax, Fyuren. Staying here an extra day or so won't be too bad."

"An extra day I'm away from Mum and Dad," growled Fyuren.

Neliya's expression softened and she put her arm around him.

"Gelfri's making a sensible decision," she said calmly. "Think about it. It took days to set everything up here. If we pack up, leave, then you realise you need more temellut ..."

Fyuren grumbled more, though he clearly had no counterargument. He eventually shook his head and said, "Fine. I'll wait."

Neliya wanted to stay with him a little longer, curious about the interesting writing he found in the pit. A signal from another channel stopped her, and when she switched she heard the high-pitched snapping of her fellow maintenance worker. She reluctantly rose with a huff and hopped on the next transport down into the mine.

Fyuren sat, his ire replaced with boredom. He cursed the design of his helmet, for he couldn't find a more comfortable position for his head within it. He shuffled around a little to find a comfy spot. He switched off his radio to blot out the sneers from miners for his laziness or his wasting oxygen, and watched the workers go.

It looked like they were ready for another blast, but Fyuren declined the offer to trigger the charges. That made Zeers grin excitedly, and he slapped his palm on the button. The charges threw gravel and dust into the air, just like they'd always done. However, from Fyuren's vantage point atop the bluff, he felt the ground beneath him shudder. On the shuttle, a dozen sensors went haywire with alarming readings.

Fyuren saw blasts of dust launch from the ground to the north of the mine. The blasts grew closer to the mine as the tremors reached a zenith. The whole valley started to split and heave as countless centuries of pent-up pressure released itself. Half the site tilted eastward and threw frenzied workers off balance.

The lead miner's voice roared over the emergency channel, "Fault-line split! Evacuate, now!"

Without a second thought, Fyuren raced down the hill into the chaotic site. He dodged the fleeing miners and workers, searching for Neliya and Zeers. He found them trying to help workers onto the trucks.

"We're fine, Fyuren," yelled Zeers.

"We need to get onto a truck now!" snapped Fyuren.

"Once we help everyone else," said Neliya.

The boy opened his mouth to protest, but felt a crash through his feet. The whole rock bed lurched, throwing them to the ground. Zeers looked up to see Neliya tumbling head over heels over a precipice. She skidded down a steep hill that grew steeper with every tremor, but didn't fall far before Zeers and Fyuren caught her. Searing pain coursed up her leg as she tried to climb back up. She saw Fyuren and Zeers' horrified gazes, before looking down to see a sharp rock, bathed in a crystallising red substance that gushed from a tear in her spacesuit leg.

The boys threw Neliya's arms over their shoulders and fled from the encroaching precipice. They reached the digger, loaded to the brim with panicked workers, and with Jugga and Murraloohaa's help, hauled themselves onto the back deck. The digger's wheels spewed blue gravel and dust out behind them as it sped away.

The fault continued to split, its edges charging after the digger like a predator determined to have them for its dinner. Most passengers demanded the driver speed up, while others were concerned with injured friends. Jugga caught sight of Neliya's wound and paling face, and he knelt down to help. He cringed at the gash along her calf.

"There's a shard stuck in bone," he said. "Turn off her radio 'n' hold her hard, 'cause this is gonna cane."

If Neliya heard what he said, she was far too dazed to understand it. Her friends held her limbs while Jugga opened the wound with his hands, took hold of the debris and yanked. They couldn't hear her shrieks of agony but the expression on her face was enough to hurt them. When Jugga was finished he grabbed a bandage from the first aid kit and wrapped it tightly around her leg. By then, she was unconscious.

"Gotta ge' her to the docs on the shuttle," said Jugga, standing up and closing the kit.

"Watch out!" cried out a voice from the front of the speeding digger. Suddenly every passenger felt weightless, and tumbled over each other. Fyuren and Zeers grabbed the rails of the deck, holding themselves over Neliya to protect her. When the crew regained their senses, they looked behind to see a bump in the path they'd crossed.

Then Kajil let out a horrified yawp, "Man overboard!"

Two bodies tumbled and rolled on the ground behind the digger, becoming more distant with every second. Jugga and Murraloohaa stood up to see the vehicle speeding away from them. Panicked, they scrambled to their feet and charged after the digger. The crumbling precipice seemed to accelerate, as if delighted to claim their lives. The ground beneath their feet buckled as they sprinted for more solid footing, but there was none to be had. The rock disintegrated and they toppled backwards.

Zeers and Fyuren stared, horrified, at the sight, while Kajil let out a desperate wail for his friends. Their terrified, panicked faces kept eyes locked on them as they fell out of sight.

Satisfied, the fault slowed to a crawl before it finally stopped. The edge of the precipice fell behind the digger, which stopped near the shuttle. Kajil and Fyuren leapt off the back of the vehicle and scrambled to the edge. All they saw was the edge of a steep valley that extended far and deep, beyond the light of their torches or the starlight above. They saw neither bodies, nor movement.

"Jugga! Murraloohaa! Can you hear me?" Kajil said into his radio.

No response.

"*Ranegr!*" Fyuren bellowed. "Any life-signs?"

There was a brief pause, after which Gelfri mumbled, "None."

Fyuren fell onto his back and his eyes started to sting with grief. Kajil's eyes remained fixed on the chasm below, until his viewport blurred with his tears.

8 | Where is my son?

Neliya drifted aimlessly through many different dreams. One minute, she was walking on technicolour clouds; the next she flailed in an endless sea of viscous water. Her sensations went from pain she was too groggy to act upon, to warm bubbles of bittersweetness bursting in her chest.

A voice reached her ears from beyond the tumult. Her feet moved toward it without permission from her brain. Her leg itched, so she scratched it, but it worsened as she neared the voice calling her name.

The itch bothered her terribly, but she could not stop moving. The voice was like a lasso. It pulled, and she scratched, and the voice grew louder.

Then Fyuren stood before her. He looked as if every reason he had to live was snatched away from him.

Neliya's leg itched agonisingly now. She put her hand to it, feeling a warm slimy substance on it. Her confusion turned to horror at the red stain upon her fingers.

Fyuren roared with all his desperation, "Neliya! Please wake up!"

There was no scream, not even a gasp. Neliya just opened her eyes, and saw around her the *Ranegr*'s infirmary. Then her eyes fell upon Fyuren, sitting by her bedside, eyes ready to overflow with pent up anxiety.

"How long have I been out?" she grumbled as she rubbed her eyes.

"Nearly a month," said Fyuren.

"You're joking!" exclaimed Neliya. "What happened to me?"

"You don't remember?" asked Fyuren.

"I remember the planet, and the quake … I slipped … and … my leg!"

Fearing the worst, Neliya threw off the covers. Her calf, from her knee to her ankle, was wrapped in thick bandages, tinted with slight blotches of red.

The vision of blood on her fingertips sent chills down her spine. She pulled the covers over herself and gazed around the infirmary. She soon noticed an absence that rang more clearly in her mind than the pain in her leg.

"Where's Zeers?" Fyuren's dismayed countenance worried her more, and she pressed.

The boy's head hung from his shoulders in defeat. With a series of long breaths that seemed bred from sighs and sobs, he began his story.

"Jugga spotted the crystal shards still in your leg and pulled them out. He bandaged your leg as best as he could, but you'd lost a lot of blood and you were really bad when we finally got you here. The doctors kept you under for a few weeks to let your body heal. If it hadn't been for Jugga, best case you'd have lost your leg. Worst …

"But as soon as he was finished, we hit a bump in the road. Jugga and Murraloohaa were thrown off the digger, and we couldn't save them before the fault got them. They fell into the crevasse … they died. We couldn't even find their bodies.

"Deloorie was a wreck! We were too scared to tell her. She came up, hearing that you were injured. Then she asked about Murraloohaa.

"'Where is he?' she shouted at us. It reminded me a little of Boggima that one time when Zeers got lost in that shopping centre … That was a very bad comparison! Ugh, I'm such an idiot.

"When we finally told her … I can't even think of a word. I've never seen anyone act like it. She punched Kajil when he broke the news. And she shook him by the neck, shouting over and over again, 'Liar! You bloody liar!' Then she ran away screaming and crying, and we didn't see her for days.

"Gelfri," Fyuren belched the word with distain, "held a nice funeral for them. I don't think I ever cried so hard in my life."

"After that, I decided I had to finish the TIM device, so that they'd not've died for nothing. Gelfri, of course, went on one of his spiels and *assured* us he'd take us anywhere once I'd finished the drive. So I got to work.

"That said, it was a very tiring and glum few weeks … Glum? Why glum! That's such a stupid way of saying it! Damn it, Fyuren, you're supposed to be smart, right?

"Sorry, I haven't slept for days.

"Anyway, we had the temellut and Allo whipped up a refinery for it. We finished the job in a week. Everyone pitched in. Kajil and the hangar crew helped on the hull, but they had a hard time pulling Zeers from your bedside. Dennie made extra food for us. The miners dropped their work repairing the shuttle and moorings. Allo and Malse checked my calculations for mistakes – even though I was … my brain's not working anymore … sad, glum, whatever! I didn't make any mistakes. I really badly wanted off this ship. Everyone worked so much harder for us. I guess they were determined to make Jugga and Murraloohaa proud.

"Gelfri was determined enough, that's for sure. So determined he'd lie, cheat, steal, and discard anything to get it.

"Finally, we were ready for a CTN jump. Zeers and I went out to the observation deck, so we could see the *Othala* the moment the jump finished.

"The ship shuddered like nothing I'd ever felt before. Might've been because the *Ranegr*'s so big. But it worked! The star positions had changed, and we were on the outskirts of a small nebula somewhere. But I thought I we'd miscalculated because the *Othala* wasn't there!

"Gelfri'd lied to us. He'd reprogrammed the drive to take us somewhere else.

"He told us, 'When you make a deal, get it in writing, my inexperienced innocents. Why, when I take the Pebhasid, I'll have enemies galore! Those rebellious rodents will try to do what I did, and I'll need new tech to fend them off. Why would I release the genius that gave me my winning wozzle?'

"Zeers said, 'We're not working for you anymore. Throw us into the resomators if you like. We don't care!' We were seriously ready for our trip to the next world. We thought Gelfri wouldn't have power over us anymore. But we were wrong.

"'Do you care about what happens to your dear friend, Femie? That poor person, that vulnerable vixen, that defenceless dame. You'd happily join her in the resomators. But would you care if I gave her as a toy to one of the flagitious phantoms of the Nightshift?'

"So that was it! He had us in his hand. We'd never escape as long as he was captain of the *Ranegr*. We had to take him down.

"We spent days sitting in the old quarters, trying think of a plan to beat Gelfri. But we had no ideas. Then Kajil showed up, along with Deloorie, Kagoolie, Allo, Malse, and Dennie. They all said they'd help.

"They were so mad at Gelfri for going back on his word – basically spitting on Jugga and Murraloohaa's graves.

"'It ain't becomin' of captain of the *Ranegr*,' they'd said.

"So we put a plan together to release the livestock to create a distraction. Then me, Zeers, and Kajil's gang steal weapons from the armoury, storm the bridge and take over. Once the ship was ours, we'd take it back to the *Othala*.

"But something went wrong. It gets to the time when the livestock were to start rampaging around, but we heard nothing. After a few minutes, we started to get worried. Then Kajil noticed the bullets in our guns were blanks!

"Gelfri had anticipated even this.

"Next thing I knew, Zeers was bolting down the corridor, toward one of the ventilation ducts that lead to the bridge deck. I tried to follow him, but Gelfri's goons caught us!

"We were left in the brig for three days. We were all worried, angry, and confused about why it didn't work. Most of all I was worried about Zeers and you. I kept thinking you'd woken up and Zeers and I weren't there. Or that as soon as you were up, the captain was going to feed you to the Nightshift. It took a lot of begging the captain's aide, before he let me come here. That was yesterday, and I haven't moved from here since."

Neliya did not speak at all during Fyuren's story, not for wanting the tale to finish, though. She could only stare dumbstruck, sorrow growing on her face with every word her friend spoke. Her hands drifted up to hide her gaping mouth, tears dribbling down her cheeks. Part of her silently begged the gods that her friend was joking; another part of her openly demanded he admit it.

"It's true, Neliya," stammered Fyuren.

Neliya grabbed him by the shirt and shouted, "You're lying! You're making up some sick joke! You're just doing this to have a laugh, you damned sicko!" It took two medics to lift the screaming girl off her friend. Neliya continued to flail as the medics tried to restrain her, but the pain in her leg overcame her, and her energy left her. Even still she cried, "Fyuren, where is Zeers? Gelfri would have told *you*, at least!"

Then she caught a glimpse, through the tumult of the grief and the pain in her leg, of a new emotion Fyuren was trying to conceal: his teeth gritted, ever-so-slightly, with bubbling anger. Neliya was about to repeat her question, when she saw a caped figure at the door.

At first, she thought the captain had come to visit. Indeed the garb matched Gelfri's, right down to the eye tattoo. But this one was shorter than Gelfri by far, appearing as a little dwarf in the doorway. Fyuren turned around to see the figure, and his mental floodgates opened.

"You!" He charged ferociously toward the figure. In the next instant he was on his back, the figure countering his attack with a blow so powerful it hurt the onlookers to witness it.

Neliya tried to sit up, despite the commands of the medics to relax. As the figure marched forward, his face became clearer, shaking Neliya more than anything Fyuren had yet told her.

"*Fizzle and drizzle, Debbledy dam. You wanted Zeers, so here I am,*" His grin sickened Neliya. Zeers turned to Fyuren, who nursed a swelling cheek, and exclaimed, "Hey, Shorts! You didn't tell her? What a cowardly kid!"

Shorts? Cowardly Kid? The words reverberated in Neliya's mind. "Tell me what?"

"You haven't heard the news, Femie? The captain has taken me under his wing. When he becomes the Pebhasid, I'll be the new captain of the *Ranegr*. Isn't it devilishly delightful?"

Neliya had never been more confused in her life.

"You didn't tell her anything?" Zeers shouted at Fyuren. Frustrated, he kicked the boy. "Answer me, you mumbling moaning mog-flogger!"

Neliya grasped his cape. "Zeers, stop it! Why are you acting like this?" It was futile.

Zeers turned to Neliya, walking calmly to her bedside and taking her hand in his. He looked at her with a smile more maniacal than kind.

"I hope Shorts has at least told you about our shot at a mutiny?" asked Zeers. "Well obviously it failed. 'Cause I planned it that way. And the grateful Gelfri made me his new second in command. I, now, will be captain of the *Ranegr*."

"Why?" mouthed Neliya, no longer with the breath to use her voice.

"'Cause I'm not going back to the *Othala*. But since you confounded companions wouldn't shut up about that cursed craft, if Gelfri kept his word, you wouldn't leave without me. So I tricked Shorts into the mutiny, along with all the other annoying acquaintances you have. It was the only way I could prove my loyalty to the captain."

"And what about us?" asked Fyuren as he pulled himself to his feet.

"Once we take the Pebhasid, you will go with Gelfri," said Zeers. "You will run his new research division, and design new ways to make sure he stays in power."

"Like I'd do that!" barked Fyuren.

Zeers smirked most condescendingly, and Neliya yelped in surprise when he squeezed her hand.

"You *will*," snarled Zeers. "Because you, Femie, will be coming with me. We'll live together on the *Ranegr*. But if Shorts doesn't be the good little nerd," He squeezed Neliya's hand harder, gazing fixedly at her.

Neliya was petrified. She yanked her hand out of Zeers' hold, and began slapping herself. She tried to convince herself it was all a dream. She cried, "Zeers, what about our families on the *Othala*?"

The boy sneered, "Might've mattered to *Zeers*, but not to Littles. Zeers is gone!"

"What about me?" Neliya sobbed.

"What *about* you?" rasped Littles. "Chances are you'd ditch me for some rancid richie. Then what? Spend all my time alone hoping my delinquent dad will show up? Seeing pictures of a dead mum I never got to know? Get stalked and attacked by bullies? I'm not going back there! I don't care who I have to hurt, cheat, betray, or kill! If you get in my way, I'll purge you."

He stood up, his cape swishing about him as he turned toward the medics working to fix Neliya's stitches.

"When she's well enough to walk, take her to my quarters," he ordered. Then he turned to his former friends. "Don't be complaining about wanting to go home. Here's your home now. You want to stay among the living, you work!"

Despite the overwhelming blow to her psyche, Neliya recovered quickly and was able to walk comfortably with crutches after a few days. Even though the medics were less than enthused by the captain's actions, they obeyed orders and took her to Littles' quarters on the bridge deck. She shivered upon recalling the time she shared with him, the memories far away and more real than a present she still couldn't accept.

Littles appeared in the doorway. She had a good chance to study his new features. His hair was longer, tied into a ponytail. With that, the tattoo, and the bags under his perpetually unblinking eyes, Neliya could barely recognise him.

"Yeah, the tattoo hurt a lot," said Littles. "Worried gawky Gelfri might miss and take me eye. But he's a crafty creator, that captain."

The strange speech made Neliya's skin crawl. "Zeers, stop talking like that! I can't accept you'd team up with Gelfri!"

The boy bellowed, "I am *not* Zeers! My name is Littles!" Then, as if it were a conversation stopper, the boy went onto other matters. "It's a little late, I'd say," he said with a welcoming smile. "You and I can share quarters now. The bath is in there, and the bed is over there."

"I'll sleep on the couch," said Neliya flatly.

Littles gave an ill-favoured grin. He left her alone, but she knew that if she didn't find some way through to him, and escape the ship, it was only a matter of time before something bad happened.

Just relax, she thought, though it helped little. *Knowing Fyuren, he and the others are putting together some kind of plan.*

Fyuren peered through the slits of his heavy eyelids at the small sliver of window the brig afforded. He saw the inky black void, speckled with stars. He naïvely sought a glimpse of the *Othala,* but found none.

Kajil and Deloorie looked through the same window, and wondered whether their friends were still out there in space somewhere. They wished those distant lights could simply tell them with comprehensible words the truth they sought, and cursed them for not doing so. Their eyes turned to Fyuren.

"Come on, Shorts," grumbled Kajil. "There's gotta be a way!"

Fyuren grunted negatively.

"Fyuren!" barked the man, saying the boy's real name for the first time. "Get off ya backside and think! Neliya is depending on ya. Even if she's able to get away from Littles and get down here to let us out, we'll still need ya!"

"That's right!" said Deloorie. "Only you'll be able to get us out of this. So come on, get going!"

Fyuren sighed, his fogging breath carrying the last of his intellect. "I'm done. I've had enough of being the only one. Someone else can be smart now."

Then came another voice, one that no one recognised at first. It uttered, rather sardonically, "Did I really raise you to give up so easily, Fyuren?"

Fyuren's eyes first widened in surprise, then narrowed in suspicion that his ears were paying tricks on him. The guards outside were knocked out cold. Fyuren leaped to the bars of his cage to see two men in Mydian uniforms at the door.

The first he recognised with greater joy than he'd ever felt in his life.

"Dad!" he screamed, though his amazed voice was barely audible.

The other man stepped forward. His thin hair was the same jet-black colour, and his eyes gave the same fixed gaze as Zeers. Clenching the mechanical gripper that was his right hand, he looked at Fyuren and demanded, "Where is Zeers? Where is my son?"

9 | It is my ambition, and I shall achieve it!

When his cage opened, Fyuren leaped like a frog into his father's arms, never having been so happy in his life.

"How did you find me?" he cried.

"Long story! What's important is that you're alright," said his father, his voice trembling with relief and joy.

After a moment of silence and another embrace, a cough resounded from Kajil's cell. "Um, not to split the nice moment, Shorts Senior, but how 'bout lettin' *us* out?"

The man raised a confused eyebrow at the name. Fyuren said, "Shorts is my nickname here." To his fellow prisoners, he said, "This is my dad, Fenk. And yes, we should let them out. We'll need their help finding Zeers and Neliya."

The man with the mechanical limb shot Fenk a look. Then they both looked to Fyuren and nodded. The cybernetic soldier rolled up his sleeve, revealing the full extent of his mechanised arm. "Everyone, move as far away as possible from the doors of your cells." They did. The man waved his hand, the insides of its mechanisms glowing an ethereal red, and the locks shattered.

One by one, Fyuren's friends climbed from their cells and introduced themselves. Fenk studied the crowd that gathered before them, and anticipated a long and entertaining story when they got home. His comrade hid both his amazement and his worry beneath a very stern and businesslike expression.

"Thanks for lettin' us out, hey," said Kajil to the overbearing soldier. "So you're Littles' dad?"

"Littles is Zeers' nickname," interjected Fyuren. "And yeah, Kajil, this is–"

"Gast Indra, Military Alchemists' Guild, Third Class," blurted Gast. He paused a moment to study the much larger man, who shuffled nervously. "You've been looking after my son and his friends?"

"Yeah, everyone else too," replied Kajil. He squeaked as Gast thrust his hand into the air between them and said, "Speaking for all parents concerned, I thank you, sir."

With a very confused and bewildered smile, Kajil shook the cybernetic hand.

Gast then looked to Fyuren. "If you're here, where are Neliya and Zeers?"

Fyuren's smile disappeared, and he knew the man would not like the tale he was about to tell. Nevertheless he had to tell it.

"First, I think we should talk somewhere else. It's going to be a long story."

"I agree," said Fenk.

Gast and Fenk led the group from the brig through the corridors of the ship. They soon found themselves in a very dark corridor, illuminated only by glow rods and filled with air that smelled a thousand years stale. Gast continued walking down the path of glow rods, which grew dimmer as they progressed into the lonely parts of the *Ranegr*.

They stopped at a hole in the bulkhead. Smoke rose from its melted edges where the ancient hull had been cut away. The interior of a small military shuttle lay beyond.

"This is how we got here," said Fenk. "When you and your friends didn't get to Lethanis, Mister Dosag called us up. But the CTN Interlink was slow, so we didn't find out until a while after. When other parents found out kids had gone missing, it was uproar! Everyone's sending IMSes to make sure *their* kids were safe. That got in the way of us finding you. Finally, the Evelyns got on the case, and found that some weird blast had interfered with your CTN route."

"Who're the Evelyns?" asked Dennie with a scratch of her yin-yang coloured head.

"They're what built them tunnellers," replied Kajil, surprising everyone – especially Fyuren, who for the first time in a while was ready to give an astute explanation.

"Anyway, they found the ship," Fenk went on. "But we weren't able to mount a rescue mission, since a rogue comet's path interfered with our sensors and we lost the trace! Needless to say, we were devastated. Your mother is worried sick, so are Neliya's mum and dad. Boggima too. But then, about a week and a bit ago," Fenk added with an incredulous grin. "The Evelyns' tracking system picked up the darnedest thing."

"A jump by this ship?" interjected Allo.

Fyuren glared at him, "Hey, I'm the smart sentence finisher here!"

Fenk could have collapsed with laughter but restrained himself. "Yeah, not even the Evelyns could figure it out, but this huge ship had used the CTN to cover a good two and a half light years. And now we had a lock on where it was, and it was nicely within range of a jaunt from the *Othala*. So we found the smallest shuttle we could, rigged it with a TIM device and came to pick you up. Only took a bloody year and a half."

Fyuren shook his head in amazement. "Felt like a decade."

Fenk and Gast regarded him expectantly.

His father asked, "So? What's your story?"

Fyuren's mood became sombre. He abridged his tale as much as he could. He recounted how he, Neliya, and Zeers had come to be accepted by the crew, and the deal they made with Gelfri to be returned home. Fenk was particularly proud to hear about his son's success at solving the tunnelling equations. Then Fyuren went onto the mutiny, and reluctantly recounted Zeers' change. It was a great deal easier to deliver the news to Gast than to Neliya, since the man's expression remained unchanged. But as soon as Fyuren mentioned 'alliteration spiels,' Gast's eyes widened in shock.

"Was there a lesion on the back of his neck?" he asked curtly.

"I'm not sure, I haven't really had a chance to look," replied Fyuren.

"There was, I think," Dennie spoke up. "First time he bragged at us, I saw it. An egg shaped mark. Looked real painful too."

Gast inhaled sharply, and shook with alarm. His eyes turned to Fenk. "Pilot Orthos, you and your son stay with the ship. I'll go and find Zeers and Neliya." To Kajil, he barked, "You! Be my guide!" Kajil nodded meekly.

Fyuren stepped forward. "What's this scar on Zeers' neck?"

"He's been brainwashed," said Gast. "This *Gelfri* used an illegal device on him. Terrorist factions use it to convert people to their cause. Strange speech habits are a side effect."

"So, it wasn't really Zeers who did those horrible things?" asked Fyuren, tentative hope in his voice.

"No, it was not. He can be helped," said Gast.

The ship began to shudder, as if it heard Gast's plan and had other things in mind. The company grew nervous, and that feeling turned to terrible dread as Fyuren realised what was happening. "He's starting the TIM device."

"He's goin' after the Pebhasid!" cried Allo and Malse as they fell off balance against a wall.

Fenk looked to the hole in the hull, and a realisation struck him with panic. "Won't our ship be ripped off?"

"I'd bet it would," said Fyuren.

"Orthos, go!" exclaimed Gast. "Get back to the *Othala*. I'll go after Zeers."

Fenk scooped Fyuren up in his arms and made for the shuttle. But it was too late.

The high-pitched whirr of the TIM device reverberated throughout the chassis of the *Ranegr*, reaching an ear-piercing zenith. In the next infinitesimal moment, Fyuren felt time stop, his weight vanish, and his mind go blank.

Never before had he felt a CTN jump with no restraints. Just as he recognized how dangerous and deadly that could be, time resumed, and his weight came back with a vengeance. He fell, face first, against the ground, and tumbled back down the corridor. An unrelenting blast of wind then grabbed at him. He looked up in dread to see the hole in the bulkhead racing toward him. The shuttle was gone, and only the vacuum of space lay beyond. Panicked, he grasped futilely at the floor and the side of the corridor, until Fenk caught him. His father's teeth gritted with all the painful tension coursing through his chest, from the arm that held Fyuren to the arm that gripped an outcropping pipe on the wall.

The wind stopped as suddenly as it had started. As everyone regained their senses, they saw an ethereal film of light plugging a hole in the hull. The attached ship was gone, along with their escape outlet. Gast glared at the group, his outstretched mechanical arm trembling and glowing, and his brow furrowed in intense concentration.

"Move!" he growled.

Everyone ran back down the hall. Most of them stopped at an open blast door a short distance from the hull breach, and waited for Gast, who moved slowly.

Allo lagged, and asked, "Where's Malse?" People stopped to look for the scarred and calloused visage of the reactor worker. Their eyes finally fell on the hole, the only other outlet through which Malse could've fallen. Speechless, the group moved behind the blast door.

Gast released the hole, and then with his mind quickly closed the doors. He fell to his knees, panting and sighing. "We have no other choice. We must take the ship."

"Really? Jus' stroll onto the bridge and plant a flag?" retorted Allo irreverently, his respect for the alchemist lost along with his mentor.

"Obviously this Gelfri will leave the ship," said Gast. "He'll go to this Pebhasid, if that is indeed where we are now. When he leaves, we steal the ship, and use the TIM device to get back to the *Othala*."

"I guess that's as good a plan as any," said Fenk.

Deloorie palmed her fists, "It's a brilli' plan! I'm a get that two-timer."

"I'm in too," said Dennie.

Fyuren glanced around the group, finding expressions of resolve and confidence. Fenk and Gast saw the same, and nodded in agreement.

The bridge crew were silent as they, after recovering from their second CTN test, came in view of the Pebhasid's station. To the crew looking out the forward viewport, it looked like a botched hodgepodge of different ships welded to a massive external chassis. Within each compartment the ships formed, vast patches of green, indigo, and even deep magenta were visible. The very sight stole the warmth from the blood of those who had not yet beheld the seat of Pebhorda power. It sat in the middle of its asteroid field like a jewel girdled by gritty tidbits of dirt.

"The Pebhasid has been expanding," thought the Quartermaster aloud.

"He's been harvesting metals and materials from asteroids across the sector for decades," said Gelfri. "Of course it'd get bigger, you badly-informed baboon."

The Quartermaster clenched his teeth. Littles grinned at him from the corner of the bridge, and imagined how satisfying it would be to strangle the man.

"Littles, my furious friend," said Gelfri, slinging his arm around the boy. "Today will be a great day for you … and an even greater day for me. Today, we'll prevail at last."

A small klaxon sounded from the communications console. The whole bridge fell silent, and Gelfri broke out in goosebumps. He took a brief second to calm his excited nerves, and then activated the display on the arm of his chair. The perturbed visage of the Pebhasid viceroy filled the screen.

"Captain of the *Ranegr*, Gelfri," she said.

"Linoua! Lovely to see you again," exclaimed Gelfri.

"Our sources indicate that you were in the Flukh sector not three days ago," said Linoua, her expression rigid and unchanging. "What would your explanation be?"

Gelfri grinned like a little girl standing before her mother with a surprise behind her back. "The *Ranegr* can now travel using the Commonwealth Tunnelling Network."

Linoua's eyes narrowed suspiciously. She bowed her head to listen to her earpiece a moment, and then said, "The Pebhasid would like to meet with you in person. A shuttle will come to collect you."

The screen went blank with little more than a nod from the captain. He glanced around the room, truly satisfied with himself.

"How will we know if you have succeeded?" asked the Quartermaster.

"Oh, you faithless fool," moaned the captain. "I'll of course succeed. And *when* I do, I'll simply contact you."

"If he fails, the signal might be in the form of us all blowing up," interjected Littles. Gelfri spluttered with unexpected laughter, while the rest of the bridge crew looked very concerned.

"Captain, should we keep defences on?" asked the weapons officer.

"No! We keep no defences up and weapons down! Understand?" barked Gelfri.

"But how about just in case?" asked another crewman.

Gelfri glared at the man. "Don't you know my policy? Succeed, 'cause you won't get a second chance! And I *will* succeed! It is my ambition, and I shall achieve it!"

The crew regarded him incredulously as the stench of cold feet filled the room. Littles looked at them with disgust, and asked flatly, "Is this your resolve? You followed this generous gent thus far. And now that it's real and raunchy, you're too cowardly to see it through? *This* is what Pebhorda loyalty is like?"

The crew pensively darted their eyes around the room, to their shipmates, to the captain, to the Pebhasid's station. Some surreptitiously stole glances at the Quartermaster, who moved forward and saluted Gelfri.

"We have faith in the captain of the *Ranegr*," he proclaimed. Everyone followed suit.

Gelfri grinned, "That's the courageous crew I know. Helm, take us in. Littles, you will be my backup."

"Yes, Captain," said Littles with a bow.

"Oh, and make sure Femie doesn't interfere," added Gelfri.

In a very Gelfri-esque manner, Littles swirled around and marched out of the room toward his quarters. He opened the door and savagely thrust the door into the head of the assailant lurking behind. He shut the door, picked up a dazed Neliya, and violently shoved her into a chair.

"Damn it, Femie," rasped Littles as he tied her to the chair with bedsheets. "You've made me injure you."

Neliya struggled furiously against his bindings. She winced when the knots tightened enough to bruise her wrists and ankles.

"All you have to do is sit and be nice," growled Littles. "You just have to let me do what I want, and I wouldn't have to hurt you." Littles caressed her face in a maniacal manner that reminded her of Borig.

"What did he do to you, Zeers?" asked Neliya, her gaze doing everything it could to pierce him.

"Nothing! Littles is as I should be," barked Littles.

"No, you're not the Zeers I love." Neliya remorsefully swallowed back her grief, and putting as much contempt into her voice as she could find, she said, "You're just *Littles* ... a whiny *little* cry-baby, thrashing around just to get attention. And when Zeers gets back, he'll kick your arse to the other side of the universe. I'll bet any money."

Littles glared at her with a smirk that barely concealed his terror of her. "I'm so scared."

"You should be, you puny petulant punk!" barked Neliya.

Littles might as well have run away screaming. As quietly and as quickly as possible, he marched out of the room, slammed the door shut and leaned against it, clutching the back of his neck and panting profusely. A nodule of flesh quivered on the back of his neck. It burned as if allergic to the thought of Neliya and her hot-headed diatribe, and he growled to bear the pain.

Stay out of my head, he screamed inwardly. *Gelfri put out the wedge but it wants back, where it burns cold. I'll wedge it in her, she'll crack and do what she's told.*

"Littles," snapped Gelfri, slapping him to get his attention. "What's the matter, boy?"

Littles' eyes were blank a moment as he tried to shake his mind free of the clouds inside his head.

"I don't know, Captain," he said, standing up and shaking the wrinkles out of his uniform. He opened the door to his quarters, finding Neliya still in her flight chair, tied down and gagged with tape. Her eyes burned holes into their faces.

"Still no luck with the little lady?" asked Gelfri.

Littles didn't reply.

I don't remember gagging her, he thought.

"Are you alright, my pensive partner?" asked Gelfri. "Perhaps you can sit this out."

"No," exclaimed Littles. "I'll come. I must come. This is my chance … and yours."

Gelfri enthusiastically patted the boy on the back, his eyes beaming a light of resolve. "Then come, my courageous colleague!"

Together they walked down the hall, marching with determination and trepidation. Littles looked over his shoulder, resentfully glaring back at the door to his quarters.

10 | Your loyalty is truly iron-clad

Cheered on by the crew and with Littles and a small guard detail in tow, Gelfri strode into the hangar and toward the shuttle the Pebhasid had sent for them. Littles stole a glance downward. There was a small patch of white-tinted scrapes and scratches on the ancient metal floor, where a tunneller had once hit the surface.

The most elating event that ever emerged, he thought

As if able to read his mind, Gelfri intoned, "A flight of nostalgia, eh?"

"Yes sir," muttered Littles.

"Rest assured, Lucid Littles, you have many more elating experiences ahead of you."

The interior of the craft smelled like the limousines Neliya's family used on the *Othala*. The seats were of soft cushion, and the bulkheads hadn't a scratch. The systems were in excellent shape as well, as evidenced by a take-off Littles would not have noticed had he been admiring the upholstery instead of looking eagerly out the window.

The shuttle wasted no time and sped toward the waiting maw of an open dock port on the Pebhasid station. It entered the new hangar as fast as it had exited the *Ranegr*, and the hatch whined open to reveal Linoua and two security personnel waiting to welcome them. Their gazes fell to the dagger fastened to Gelfri's waist.

"You will meet the Pebhasid without weapons," said Linoua.

Gelfri and Littles surrendered the handguns and daggers concealed beneath their capes and placed them in the tray the Pebhasid's aide presented. She beckoned them to follow.

A short walk across the hangar brought them to an elevator, which was transparent on the side opposite the door. As it ascended the shaft, the hangar passed out of sight and was replaced by a view of the outside of the Pebhasid station. The *Ranegr* loomed against the backdrop of stars, reflecting radiance from the galactic core. Littles' ears tickled with Gelfri's barely audible sigh, and stealing a glance in the captain's direction, he saw the briefest glimmer of homesickness. In the next instant it was gone, and his typical air of determination and ambition replaced it.

The shaft led into the nucleus of the station. The trusses and levels of shielding grew denser, until they reached the Pebhasid's innermost sanctum. The doors slid open, shuddering slightly under a subtle rush of air. The chamber beyond seemed carved from a material that appeared more alien than any creature comprising the Nightshift. But the most surprising aspect of the room, dwarfing its artful construction in significance, was the abundance of green ferns and flowerbeds. They were wild and tame at the same time, like pets with freedom to spend time as they wished within the confines of a well-furnished environment.

A five-petal flower sporting flamboyant colours drew Littles' attention, and he felt a temptation to touch it before an overbearing voice stopped him.

"You'd best leave that be, boy," said the dark-skinned figure seated on the far side of the room. "Those flowers are like beautiful women: they enjoy the attention, but you must treat them with respect, and never touch without their permission."

Gelfri straightened when he saw the person, who stood from his dining table and faced them, his black silken robe glimmering as it waved about his stout physique. Linoua stepped forward.

"I present his excellency, the Pebhasid." She turned around and reported, "My master, Captain Gelfri of the *Ranegr*."

"Welcome to my home, Gelfri Dagelastr," said the Pebhasid.

Gelfri bent reverently, "I am humbled, Pebhasid."

The Pebhasid returned to his seat to continue sipping at a small bowl of soup before him.

"You have quite an interesting piece of technology, Dagelastr. And no doubt," he meticulously slurped another mouthful, "a less than interesting story to go with it?"

"Both would be interesting equally, my precious Pebhasid," said Gelfri. "Perhaps if I could come closer, I could tell you without straining my voice."

The Pebhasid let out a droning sigh, evolving into a slow chuckle. He beckoned them nearer. When they closed to within a few metres, a very strange sensation struck Gelfri and Littles' faces, as if they'd just run head first into an invisible wall. Linoua continued onwards, until she stood behind the Pebhasid.

"What is this?" asked a flabbergasted Littles.

"Oh, that little thing," the Pebhasid began, his chortles sounding more like chesty coughs. "I promoted one of my lieutenants in exchange for a device among his plunder." Then he sighed, taking a mouthful of clear pink drink from a glass nearby. "Dismally unfortunate, though, we cannot yet reverse engineer it. I have only one. It's a good method to keep assassins away, I must say. Now I can enjoy my garden without fear of untimely death."

"Congratulations, Pebhasid," cried Gelfri. "With more technology, your territories will grow and your enterprises prosper."

"It helps to have loyal underlings," added the Pebhasid. "With them patrolling the frontiers of the surrounding sectors, it is inevitable that they happen upon new technologies. I must admit, though, the ability to appear without forewarning would accelerate my enterprise tenfold. I may even be able to challenge the leaders of our neighbouring space."

"My thoughts exactly," said Gelfri.

"How then did you come across this ability?" asked the Pebhasid.

"Some years ago, we found a tunneller adrift," explained Gelfri. "Naturally, salvaged it, finding three cowering kiddies inside. One of them had a brilliant brain, and taught us how to attach the TIM device to the *Ranegr*. And so, here we are."

The Pebhasid finished his bowl of soup, and his hand shakily gravitated toward a plate of marinated meat and vegetables. He sampled a cut of meat and some purple tuber mash, scrupulously chewing the food.

"You can sit," said the Pebhasid.

Cautiously, Gelfri held out a hand to confirm the invisible wall's absence. He then took a seat, facing the Pebhasid. At a wave of the monarch's hand, Linoua set out a plate and cutlery for Gelfri, and brought some of the dishes to him.

Littles stood behind him, and studied the individual the crew had worked their way toward. A dark-skinned person, though he looked more Mydian, having a yellow tinge to his complexion and gloved four-fingered hands. His hair was also a faint reddish-grey. His slow movements and lack of coordination when reaching for his food made it obvious that he was blind.

We've won, thought Littles excitedly as he tried not to laugh.

"I assume the genius of which you speak is this young one here?" groaned the Pebhasid, as if half asleep.

"You are incorrect, my lord," said Gelfri, taking a small bundle of pale green beans from the serving dish.

"I was one of the three occupants of the tunneller when the *Ranegr* found it," interjected Littles. "The one who was able to engineer the solution was a friend."

The Pebhasid sighed again, scratching the underside of his chin. He said, "So the *Ranegr* is not only legendary amongst the Pebhorda, but is now the most advanced? More so than even Commonwealth ships. Suppose a fleet equipped with these devices. The Mydians could annex an entire star system in one fell swoop. Truly amazing … and terrifying."

"As I believe," said Gelfri, his obsequiousness sending chills down Littles' spine.

Just kill him already, he growled inwardly.

"And you would trade this genius boy, for the same reward as is reserved for my lieutenants?" asked the Pebhasid slyly.

"Of course! I live to serve you," said Gelfri.

The Pebhasid grinned, every inch of his face crinkling as if the action would disintegrate his skin. Littles was now suspicious, and started to wonder, *Was this just a ploy to get in the Pebhasid's pocket? Do you really mean to sell the Ranegr? Give away my prize?*

"Tell me, Dagelastr," said the Pebhasid. "The *Ranegr* is more heavily armed, and its crew the best. Now it has the power of the CTN! I ask then, why give it to me? You could have simply taken it anywhere in the Commonwealth territory, ransacked whatever vessels you could find. Build up enough armaments to take my home by force, and I'd have not been a match for you. Your loyalty is truly iron-clad."

"It is, my lord," said Gelfri, his hand surreptitiously edging toward his fork.

"Is it?" retorted the Pebhasid. "I keep tight security. And I only invite someone if they've interested me." He looked fixedly at Gelfri, as if heretofore he only feigned blindness. "Until now, you have not. You are a boring, bizarre, old codger, Dagelastr, and I would not in a million years have invited you. You are not loyal. You performed a trick to draw my attention, so that you could come here, within reach of my throat to slash it."

Littles' mouth fell agape, and his eyes widened in panic. He leaned away from the table, stealing a glance at Gelfri who remained motionless and expressionless.

"How did you discover my plot?" asked Gelfri.

"I didn't," muttered the Pebhasid. At his silent command, Linoua activated a large display in the wall. On it was a face that Gelfri or Littles would never have expected to see.

"Hello, Captain," said the Quartermaster with triumphant smile. Most of the bridge crew stood behind him brandishing weapons. The others lay lifeless on the floor. "I hope you don't mind, but I'll be taking this ship."

Gelfri glared maniacally at the screen. He pounded the table with his fists and roared, "You won't get far with *my* ship, you deceptive, daring, devious, devilish, defective deserter!"

"He shall," interjected the Pebhasid. "That is his payment for warning me. Did you really think that your duplicity would not cost the loyalty of those in your circle? Did you really think you could obtain the power of the Pebhasid so easily on your own?"

Gelfri rose from the table, a fork in his hand, and proclaimed, "Of course!" And he let loose the projectile.

The Pebhasid did not fall; he arose, his gloved hand outstretched and pulsating with heat. The fork hung in mid-air, held there by nothing. Littles' heart jumped into his mouth at the sight.

"A Megin Device!" he cried.

The Pebhasid shot them a grin, and then with a flick of his wrist sent the fork into the wall.

"Didn't you wonder what generated that invisible wall?" roared the Pebhasid, throwing off his silk robe. His body was little more than a growth of frail flesh clinging like mould to the mechanisms of a robotic arm. His arm pulsated green, and his wrinkled grin glimmered freakishly in its light. "With this, Dagelastr, I can live eternally as the Pebhasid. No matter what trickery you bring to bear, I will crush you!"

The Pebhasid upended the table with one hand, and knocked Gelfri across the room like a rag doll. Before Littles could help his mentor, Linoua drew a rapier from her sleeve. He blocked the sharp blade with a chair, stunning the woman long enough for him to catch her in a neck-choke. Linoua responded with an elbow to his ribs. He lost his hold on her, and she swivelled around and punched him. Her blade aimed for his heart. Though she was much older than Littles, his strength kept her blade at bay.

The Pebhasid hauled Gelfri into the air with his real arm while readying his mechanical one. The limb grew bright with heat, and the Pebhasid said, "This tattoo doesn't suit you really. Let's take it off!"

Gelfri thrashed as the scorching hand approached his face. He squeezed hard on the Pebhasid's arm, but the grip didn't loosen. Thinking quickly, Gelfri took a nearby hanging pot-plant and smashed it on the Pebhasid's face.

Gelfri hit the floor and staggered away, coughing and clutching his throat. He turned around and saw the Pebhasid rubbing his bruising head. He quickly scanned the mechanical limb for a weak spot.

"That was a Lohwana Flower, you damned herbicide!" spat the Pebhasid between moans of pain. "Have you any idea how difficult it was to cultivate that plant?"

"Nope," replied Gelfri breathlessly. He picked up another pot plant nearby. "But they make brilliant bolas, eh?"

The Pebhasid frothed at the mouth. The captain dodged his assailant and smashed the pot on his head, incapacitating him further.

"Tell me, how long did it take to master this … Megin Device?" he asked as the Pebhasid struggled to his feet, a second bump blooming on his skull. The Pebhasid threw a punch toward Gelfri's chest, but the captain spryly stepped to the side, caught the arm, and used his opponent's momentum to hurl him across the room. The man landed hard, shattering the pristine stone floor.

"I just want to know how much pain you went through," asked Gelfri as he dusted his hands off. "As in, how much did it hurt, compared to being beaten by a boring, bizarre, old codger?"

"Beaten?" retorted the Pebhasid. Suddenly, Gelfri was pulled as if falling sideways toward the Pebhasid's outstretched mechanical arm. Then he stopped mid-air. The Pebhasid laughed sadistically as he hit some switches on the arm and elicited an agonised screech from his prey. "I'll show you *beaten,* you worthless little maggot! The last thing you'll see is your skeleton leaking out your backside!"

Littles heard Gelfri's cries, and turned to see his mentor thrashing above the floor. Linoua saw his distraction, stabbed him through the hand, and pinned him to the wall.

"Looks like your captain is going to be mashed into mulch," Linoua cooed into his ear. "And that girlfriend of yours ... you'll watch her get hers, right before you get yours."

Littles' lesion burned as rage filled him. He closed his fingers around the hilt of the rapier and pushed. His manic fury escaped him in a low growl that matured into a fierce roar. With a swift move of his arms, he shattered hers. He pulled the rapier out of his hand and plunged it upwards into her stomach.

"Yours first," he growled at her stunned face.

He withdrew the blade and threw her into the wall. Without a second thought, he charged toward the Pebhasid. He let out a barbaric yawp as he leaped through the air, the bloodied rapier ready to strike. The Pebhasid noticed and released Gelfri to knock the airborne boy unconscious.

Gelfri hit the ground. With barely a scrap of lucidity left, he saw the rapier clatter nearby. He scooped it up, and decisively jammed it beneath the Pebhasid's jaw.

The Pebhasid's eyes were radiant with surprise and uncertainty; Gelfri's shot back two rays of victorious determination. The bionic man fell backward, impacting the ground with a tremendous thud. The dust cleared, and all was silent.

Gelfri rubbed his sore joints and winced as he hobbled over to the Pebhasid's upturned dinner table. He sifted through the mess, found a hand-held communications terminal, and activated it.

"Attention, subjects of the Pebhasid." Throughout the station, everyone stopped what they were doing and listened. Even aboard the *Ranegr*, the announcement was heard. "I am Gelfri, former captain of the *Ranegr*. I have killed the Pebhasid. This station, this throne, this sector, is now mine. I want a team sent to the *Ranegr* to reclaim my ship from that mutated, mutinous, moronic maggot!"

He shut off the communications, and fell silently on a chair with a yawn.

11 | If we take the bridge, we win

Neliya tugged as hard as she could on her bindings, but her struggling only darkened her already bruised wrists. Even still, she persevered, using whatever thoughts came to mind as a distraction.

It's like he's gone insane, she mused. *Of course he's crazy. Gelfri must have done something to him. I have to get out of here, find Fyuren, and then find a way to get Zeers.*

Over the moans of pain echoing through her nerves, she heard movement outside the room: footsteps, shouting voices, and then gunshots. All aversion to pain went out the window, and she pulled as hard as she could.

"Oi, Femie," barked a voice from behind the door. She knew it wasn't Zeers. "Think you could open the door? Ya know, so we can shoot ya."

Before she could react, the vent in the ceiling came clattering down, and a familiar creature dropped through it. Despite his facial burns and different clothes, his identity was unmistakable.

"Borig!" Neliya would have cried were she not gagged.

The thing's dirty-coloured eyes paralysed her with fear. Borig turned away from her, snarled at the banging on the door, and procured a knife from his pocket. Neliya started thrashing in her seat, trying everything she could to break the knots. She squeezed her eyes shut as Borig raised the knife. She waited for that fatal blow.

Neliya felt the binding around her arms fall away. She opened her eyes. Her arms were free, and her wrists were almost black with bruises and rope-burn. Borig cut the ropes around her legs as well, and tore away the tape over her mouth.

"Come on!" he growled.

He pulled her off the chair. He rose to his full height, which Neliya remembered being much taller, and lifted her into the hole in the roof. Just as he leaped after her, gunshots blasted through the locked door.

Neliya tried to crawl faster, unnerved by Borig behind her. But the cramped duct made it difficult to move quickly. The wretch grabbed her ankle and yanked her back.

"This way, idiot!" he snapped, pointing to the right and thrusting her down the passage.

"Where are you taking me?" she asked, unsure if she wanted to hear the answer.

"Safe place," rasped Borig. "Li'l Brother lost the plot, took Big Meanie's plot too. Now Pee-Pants Quartermaster thinks he can take the cake while Li'l Brother's away, gonna scratch them who won't let him have his party. Pee-Pants told on Li'l Brother to the boss, and gets the cake for being a dibber-dob. But Li'l Brother is smart and strong, and Big Meanie is too. They'll win."

He grabbed her ankles again and threw her down another passage, which led into the elevator shaft. Borig motioned Neliya onto his back, and whispered, "Don't scream, girlie."

Before Neliya could ask for clarification, Borig leaped down the shaft. Neliya gritted her teeth to stifle her cry of terror, as Borig danced a dizzying jig with gravity down the vertical catwalk. He leapt from side to side, using the walls to slow his descent, until they stopped close to the bottom. Neliya was shaking, having barely a thought in her head. Borig shoved her into a nearby duct and pushed her along.

"How did you do that?" exclaimed Neliya.

"Lot o' practice," said Borig.

"Come to think of it, how are you still alive?" wondered Neliya. "We knocked you into the resomators."

The thing harrumphed, "It burned a lot, but Borig is still Borig, and I just climbed out. But you made me sad, and hurt me, and I don't like friends who give me kicksy-wicksy."

"Maybe if you weren't so weird, people wouldn't kick you," mumbled Neliya.

"Weird, she says," Borig grumbled rolling his eyes. "Her little friend knows it all, and gets yelled at by her. Her boyfriend joy and fun, and hurts what he loves. And she is rich, but wishes she wasn't, and now that she isn't, she wishes she was. And she calls me weird. You hurt each other, love to do it. You're mean and cruel and call names. And you call me weird?"

"At least I don't attack people like a maniac," retorted Neliya.

Borig caught her leg again to stop her as she passed over a vent, through which light seeped. He lowered her through the opening and into a dimly lit corridor, then beckoned her to follow.

"Maniac," he mumbled resentfully. "Starving makes a maniac for food. Making lonely makes a maniac for a friend."

Neliya pursed her lips, her gaze shifting to the floor.

Who was the little girl on the Othala who would do anything to get out of there?

"Where are Fyuren and the others?" she asked after they walked further.

"Were in cages, 'til two sneakies got 'em out," replied Borig.

"What do you mean, *Sneakies*?" repeated Neliya.

"Sneakies!" blurted Borig. "They cut a hole in the ship, got in. Watched 'em do it too. One had robot's arm. Li'l Meanie called the other 'Dad!'"

Robot's arm?

Neliya grabbed him by the shoulders. Borig tried to shrug her off. "Can't play tag now, girlie!"

Neliya gripped him tighter. "Wait a second. These sneakies, what were they wearing?"

"Purple suits, I think," replied Borig. "And it said words on the back. But can't remember words said. I think it started with … O … maybe?"

"*Othala*?" asked Neliya.

"That's the one!"

In the next instant, Neliya's arms were around Borig's neck, hugging him tighter than she'd ever hugged a person before.

"That's Fyuren and Zeers' dads!" she said elatedly. "We have to go find them."

Borig pushed her away. "No way! Big Meanie and Li'l Meanie's dads, they'd be even meaner. I'm not going anywhere near them."

"Fine," said Neliya, pivoting on her heel and marching down the hall. "I'm going. You can stay here."

Borig followed her. "Pee-Pants is going to kill them. If you go, you'll get shot."

"You don't know Zeers' dad," said Neliya confidently. "He's a Military Alchemist."

"Even he gets tired," retorted Borig, stopping Neliya. "I watched. He got really tired just getting Little Meanie out of a cage. Lots o' guns'll beat him good."

Neliya paused a moment, chewing her lip slightly while she thought hard. It didn't take her long to come up with an idea.

"Take me to the Nightshift cages," she ordered.

Neliya had imagined the Nightshift cages as big prisons to hold the monsters, with heavy chains to bind them. But just when she thought she understood the Pebhorda, they surprised her. The Nightshift crew were holed-up in one of the out-of-service hangars, which had been divided into cubicles. The single beds therein looked quite comfortable for the creatures lounging on them, chatting amicably amongst themselves or sleeping off the previous night's work.

When Neliya and Borig appeared at the chamber entrance, the hangar fell silent and everyone stared at them.

"What's this slack-jawed silver-spoonie doin' here wit' that pet of hers?"

roared a stout swine – the very same that attacked them in the resomators long ago.

"I came to say hello," Neliya stammered.

She gave a startled squeak when some of the Nightshift responded with a garbled chorus of, "Hello to you."

Borig barked, "Girlie wants help with stuff. But she thought you'd get with the kicksy-wicksy. But you lot don't kick me, do ya?" Some of the creatures replied with shrug-like gestures. "So will ya maybe help her?"

"Depends on what it wants," slurred a long-necked creature as it inserted a bookmark into its novel.

All eyes fell expectantly on Neliya, who felt as if she was in a school assembly full of students waiting for a performance she hadn't rehearsed.

Borig nudged her ribs, and she blurted, "My friends are about to fight the Quartermaster and his men who have staged a mutiny and I want them to win so that I can get my boyfriend back and I want to go home and so will you please help me by fighting the Quartermaster and his men!?" She gasped for breath, her face a bluish hue, and then exclaimed at the top of her lungs, "Please!"

The Nightshift looked at her a moment. Then one of them murmured past sharp fangs, "So Gelfri's dead?"

Neliya was so befuddled by the response she couldn't reply. Before she could correct them, the entire hangar erupted, "Woohoo! Gelfri's dead!"

Neliya's jaw dropped in shock as the Nightshift thrust their fists into the air in joyous celebration. Beside her, Borig chuckled and mumbled, "Them's thinks anyone better than Li'l Brother. They's'n't wrong."

The girl broke through her flummoxed fugue and yelled, "The Quartermaster's not better! He's killing my friends."

"So what?" cried the swine, merry tears seeping from his eyelids. "Gelfri's run us ragg'd 'n' his wranglers're brutal! Ol' Q'll be a change. Might good what them *other crews* get comin' their way!"

With that, the Nightshift went about cheering the change in management, as if their favourite team had just won the Commonwealth competition in some sport.

Some of them started clicking their heels, eliciting memories of a teacher from a distant corner of Neliya's mind.

Suddenly, a pipe hit the ground, the clanging sound echoing through the hangar. Neliya held the pipe, gripping it so hard she almost squashed it. She issued a glare with the power to incinerate anyone who received it.

"You ... damned ... uncivilised ... monsters!" The Nightshift sneered at her insult, some advancing with clenched fists. Borig withdrew, almost trying to stop Neliya as she slowly marched into the crowd. "You're happy the others are getting killed, just 'cause you didn't like Gelfri? What an utter load of crap!" Those near her flinched, while others punched their palms, ready for a fight. "You're the scum of the universe, disgusting monsters! How can you be able to speak, think, even read, and yet not care about others? Why would anyone even consider you sapient beings?"

"If you're not careful, missy, you'll get hurt!" warned a nearby fanged beast.

"What're you going to do, sharp-teeth?" asked Neliya. "You look so dumb, you couldn't land a punch on me if I helped you!"

That was the last straw. The beast came at her, its claw clenched. Neliya parried the blow with the pipe in her hands, jabbed it painfully into the creature's thorax, and then bashed the creature's face with it. She turned around to see the long-necked bookworm staring at her. She grabbed the book and brought it down on the thing's head.

Then the swine came at her roaring, upending bunks and pushing fellow labourers aside. Neliya picked up the pipe and tripped her attacker, giving a swift and spirited blow to the back of the swine's head. When the swine hit the ground with a thump, everyone else backed away.

"Look at you, a bunch of sewer workers," she barked disgustedly. Pointing at the subdued swine moaning on the floor, she said, "You won't even come to help up one of your own! I've wasted my time asking for your help."

One of the meeker-looking creatures spoke up with an ire-filled voice, "Bein' pretty, planet gal, shan't callin' *uncivilised*."

"You are uncivilised, damn it!" she screamed, hurling the pipe in their general direction. "Being civilised doesn't mean you come from a planet. It doesn't mean you're smart, pretty, or strong. *You're* uncivilized because you don't care!"

She gazed at them a moment longer, her face flushed and her eyes glistening. The creatures stared right back at her, but if they meant to express remorse she couldn't see it.

"Why'd we help you, if ya jus' gonna shout and bash us?" spat the swine as he pulled himself up.

The long-necked bookworm rubbed his head and intoned, "Ya same as Gelfri ... Don't get ya wants so ya yell and hit."

Neliya tried to find a retort, but came up empty, and it made her heart tingle with fury. It wasn't just for the Nightshift, scowling at her. She felt anger for herself as well; that for all her shouting and wrestling, she was powerless.

With a sigh, she slumped, red-faced, against one of the bunks. That she was right upwind of the maw of a fanged beast didn't bother her in the slightest. She tried to sniff back her tears and murmured, "My boyfriend ... Zeers. I know Gelfri's done something to him ... Made him a horrible person. But, it wasn't just Gelfri that did it." Her eyes scanned the crowd that glanced tentatively in her direction, perturbed by her behaviour. She continued, "Before we were on the *Ranegr*, people were horrible to him before. Not just kids in school … Sometimes even the adults couldn't give less of a crap."

Her gaze fixated upon the swine, whose face softened with intrigue.

"When you all started celebrating before, it reminded me of a teacher who seemed *happy* that Zeers was failing school," she said. "And I just lost the plot." Neliya looked at all of them, lingering especially on the people she'd attacked. "I'm sorry for hitting you. I was just upset, and I won't do it again."

The words rammed their way into every mind in the hangar, and stuck there hard. The words were so foreign to their ears they couldn't find a response. But that only gave Neliya the floor even longer. She rose to her feet and proclaimed, "If you help me beat the Quartermaster, no one will ever beat you up again. Kajil will take over as captain. You all know him, right? He's a good man who knows how to care. And I promise, he'll be the best captain you'll ever have!" She offered a hand to the swine, who was so perplexed by her words he didn't realise he'd accepted the help. She hefted him to his feet and asked earnestly, "Will you help me?"

With Gast in front, the mutineers crept through the corridors of the *Ranegr*. They moved slowly, Gast and Fenk glancing around each corner and listening carefully before moving on. A klaxon suddenly echoed through the halls.

The voice of the Quartermaster resounded through the ancient speaker system. "Hello, crew of the *Ranegr*. This is a mutiny. I have informed the Pebhasid of Gelfri's plan, and he will be dealt with appropriately."

"This is not good," Fyuren mouthed to Kajil, filled with horror and amazement, topped with a fresh serving of the rage present in everyone's eyes.

The Quartermaster continued, "Oh, it's just been brought to my attention that those mutineers from a few days ago have escaped the brig. If anyone sees them, please shoot them. Thank you."

The communication ended.

"What do we do now?" asked Deloorie.

"Ya should can fight 'em off with that arm, eh?" asked Kagoolie, pointing to Gast's bionic weapon.

"Not if there's too many of them," replied Gast. There was sudden movement just outside his field of vision and his head whipped around to see a crewman in the corridor. His mechanical hand instinctively rose.

Kajil quickly caught Gast's hand, and didn't return the man's glance for fear that the sight would bring death. He locked eyes with the crewman, whom he recognised as one of the miners.

The miner said, "Corridor Nine, Subjunction Twelve. Go' a weapons stockpile there. I'll 'stract 'em." Then he ran back down the corridor and out of sight.

"Where do you think you're going?" asked the Military Alchemist as the group followed Kajil's lead. "That smells to me like a trap. A nice piece of info the enemy would feed us."

"Sir, Alchemist, whatever, we need more weapons," said Kajil.

"He's right," interjected Allo. "You jus' said ya can't fight a bunch o' 'em on ya own."

"I can do it," said Gast. "Fenk, if you lay down cover fire, I'll be able to disarm all of them. I'll be enough."

"That ain't whatcha just said, Gast," said Kagoolie. "Let us all help."

Fyuren ended the argument by racing down the passage. Just like that, everyone followed the boy. Gast acquiesced with a frustrated growl. The boy darted through the corridor, stopping only a moment to let the group catch up. Then he scrambled up the ladder tube in the side of the wall, climbing into corridor nine. A small group of people waited outside subjunction twelve, armed with weapons procured from a concealed compartment. They cocked their pistols like startled prey.

"Hold off!" shouted Kajil, recognising the miners. He slowly beckoned the company up the ladder.

"For everyone," they murmured in unison. The miners then handed them arms from the locker. When Fyuren picked up a small handgun and loaded it, Fenk reflexively moved to take it from him.

"Don't worry, Dad," said the boy as he holstered the symbol of adulthood. "I learned how to use this for our mutiny. Speaking of which, make sure the bullets aren't duds." Everyone nodded enthusiastically.

Fenk choked. When last he saw his son, the boy barely reached his waist; now, he held a weapon, ready to fight for his friends. The man was both proud of his son and disappointed with himself for missing the transformation. However, deep within him, the sight of his son with that gun terrified him.

Gast grew impatient. "The enemy will no doubt know we're here."

"Do we have a plan?" asked Fenk.

Some discussion went back and forth, while Fyuren's mind silently went to full power.

If we take the bridge, we win. What's the Quartermaster's hand? He doesn't have eyes all over the ship, or he'd have found us already. The only eyes he's got are the security cameras I fixed in the tokamak chamber, the main corridor, and the food hall. He'll also have one team guarding the bridge ... probably the most heavily fortified – he's waited ages to take the Ranegr, he's not about to lose it to anyone ...

Then an idea struck his brain like an arc from a plasma torch.

12 | Did you really think this would work?

The Quartermaster paced irately, waiting for news on the mutineers from his crew or a reply from the Pebhasid announcing Gelfri's demise. Neither had come yet, and it made him very nervous. He stole a glance at the captain's chair, marvelling at the headaches and humiliation he'd had to endure to claim it, what he still endured to keep it. He gazed down his nose at it.

Being captain of the Ranegr is indeed a curse, he mused.

He tore his mind away to the present, and turned to the communications officer. "Show me the security feeds."

The images appeared on the screens at the communications terminal. The Quartermaster first looked at the feed from the tokamak chamber, and the blood drained from his face. There stood the escaped mutineers with a tall Mydian he'd never seen before, their weapons cocked as they stood over his defeated loyalists. Before he could order his men into action, the food hall feed caught his attention.

Fyuren stood alone in the food hall, grinning triumphantly. His voice crackled through the speaker. "Quartermaster! See the mob in the tokamak chamber? I taught them how to initiate a clench – just like the one I fixed months ago. Meet me, unarmed, in the food hall to negotiate your surrender. Bring Neliya with you or I'll destroy this ship."

The Quartermaster gritted his teeth so hard that they nearly shattered. "Order the teams to the tokamak chamber, and destroy that scum."

He then burst from the bridge, snatching a firearm from one of the guards. Blistering ruminations pierced through his subconscious in the form of incoherent mumbles.

Negotiate? Surrender? I've already won! I'm going to kill that little twerp!

The elevator finally reached the lower deck. In a bout of frustrated strength, the Quartermaster pushed the sluggish doors open and raced down the corridor. When the food hall came into view, he cocked his pistol, and scanned the room for Fyuren.

The boy sat facing out from behind the buffet, gazing at the door with a grin. The Quartermaster tapped the headset clinging to his ear and said, "Status on the tokamak chamber?"

"Teams are on their way, three minutes out," replied the communications officer.

The Quartermaster marched into the room with a smirk, and raised his gun.

"I really wouldn't," warned Fyuren.

"Why? Because you're a poor defenceless child?" retorted the Quartermaster.

The boy smiled, and picked up a handheld radio. "I'm still here, so hold off."

"Roger that," replied the radio.

"That was Kajil," said Fyuren. "I don't check in every three minutes, they start the clench."

The Quartermaster's entire body trembled with anger as he lowered the gun. Fyuren's smile grew smug, which almost overwhelmed the Quartermaster's judgement. He flatly asked, "Now then, where's Neliya?"

"I just shot her," snapped the Quartermaster.

"Your gun-barrel isn't smoking," said the boy shrewdly. "Did she escape?"

The Quartermaster's lip tightened and he diverted his gaze.

Fyuren chuckled, "Did you really think it would work? This whole take-over business. I mean, you helped Gelfri all the way to get to the Pebhasid. Not just you. The whole crew pitched in, expecting to be in the new Pebhasid's favour – some even died for it. Then along you come, betray their captain. Now, no favour. Kajil and the others saw Gelfri for what he was when he doublecrossed my friends and me. And now the crew's gonna see you for the same thing: just another treacherous captain. You stuffed their chances, and they're out for blood." Fyuren gave it a moment to sink into the Quartermaster's mind, and then asked, "So, did you really think this would work?"

The Quartermaster's pale face drooped and he slumped with a sigh. Fyuren relished the sensation of control that consumed him as he stared the adult down.

"You will tell all your men to stand-down," Fyuren commanded. "You will report to the brig and stay there, until Captain Kajil decides what to do with you."

There was a long pause, after which the Quartermaster sighed with relief.

"I don't think so, Shorts." He pulled himself out of his hunch and stood tall over Fyuren. "You see, my men have secured the tokamak chamber, and you are no longer in a bargaining position." He pointed his gun fixedly at Fyuren's head. "So, did you really think this would work?"

He squeezed the trigger. The gun clicked, but there was no ignition and no blast. The Quartermaster shook the gun and tried again. A click, but no boom. He was suddenly thrown back by an invisible force. Gast stepped out from his hiding place behind the bar, his mechanical arm outstretched and pulsating.

"Allow me to introduce Gast Indra, Zeers' father," said Fyuren with a smile.

"Stay away," screeched the Quartermaster as Gast approached him. "I have eliminated your group. I've beaten you."

"Oh, you mean this?" roared the voice of Kajil. All the Quartermaster's allies were pushed into the room and prostrated on the floor. Following them were Kajil, Deloorie, Kagoolie, Dennie, Allo, Fenk, the miners, farmers, and hangar workers. They stood victoriously, their vengeful gazes directed squarely at the Quartermaster.

The Quartermaster teetered on the verge of crying. "But my teams had taken the tokamak room."

"I should probably mention how good I really am," said Fyuren. He showed his tablet to the Quartermaster, who was horrified to see the same camera feed as was shown to him on the bridge.

The Quatermaster's jaw dropped. "A faux video feed?"

"Well, I s'pose we win," said Kajil.

The food hall erupted into cheers. Gast dragged the Quartermaster to his feet and thrust him into Kajil and Deloorie's waiting arms. The rest of the crew pulled the Quartermaster's men into seats and encouraged them to join the new command. Most swore allegiance straightaway. Those that didn't followed the Quartermaster to the brig.

The Quartermaster didn't go so quietly, and began shouting, "Wait! You have to go to the bridge!"

Kajil and Deloorie were quite happy to ignore him. Fyuren stopped them and took the earpiece from the Quartermaster.

"This is Fyuren. The Quartermaster is defeated. I'm in charge now."

"Never mind that!" barked the officer on the other end of the link. "Gelfri defeated the Pebhasid! He found out about the Quartermaster's involvement, and he's sent soldiers to take the ship back!"

Fyuren's heart froze with shock, but he didn't have a chance to warn anyone. Footsteps resounded through the nearby corridors: heavy boots, falling to a synchronised drumbeat.

"Take cover!" screamed Kajil.

Around each corner appeared several troops, armoured in dark blue and heavily armed. They opened fire, felling several of the crew. Those who still lived scrambled back into the food hall. Gast held up his hand, and a glowing barrier appeared over the door. The Pebhasid's troops cautiously approached, like predators sniffing out their next meal. The leaders edged toward the glow, but withdrew when the material of their gloves fizzled. Those within safe range fired, but the bullets flattened against the barrier.

"I can't hold this forever," Gast growled. Smoke billowed from his mechanical arm as it burned through his uniform. A group of men dragged the heavy fridge from its place behind the bar and placed it over the doorway. The moment Gast released his mental control, the soldiers on the other side immediately pushed against the fridge. Every crewmember pushed against the barricade to hold it.

"Have any ideas for this, Shorts?" yelled Kajil half-jokingly.

Fyuren sighed a moment as he gathered his thoughts.

"Bridge, are you there?" he said into the earpiece.

"Not for long," replied the officer frantically. Gunshots punctuated the feed.

Panicked and annoyed, Fyuren threw his arms up. "Anyone else have an idea?"

"I do!" a voice resounded from beneath them. An explosion behind the bar blew a hole in the wall. Two very welcome figures climbed out of it.

"Neliya!" screamed Fyuren, sprinting towards her and embracing her.

"It's good to see you, Fyuren," she said, returning his hug. "Hi, Mister Orthos and Mister Indra. Thanks for coming to pick us up."

"I figured you'd escaped," said Fyuren.

"Thanks to Borig here," said Neliya with a giggle.

Fyuren's eyes widened in shock at the scarred wretch. "How are you not dead?"

"I think ya plans matters more!" shouted Kajil over the din of the troops. "Nel! That hole'll fit us?"

Neliya glanced down at the hole. "Nope. Don't think so."

"Then what? You come 'n' get mow'd over too?" asked Allo.

The girl smiled cockily. As if that were the cue, the Pebhasid's troops lost interest in the barricade, and opened fire on an unexpected foe. Strangled screams and crashes reverberated through the corridors. The crew cautiously stepped away from the barricade, just as it toppled over to reveal the battle taking place beyond.

Nightshift creatures hurled Pebhasid troops like sacks of foam balls. Anyone who managed to aim his weapon was caught unaware from behind and flew headfirst into a bulkhead. The beasts pummelled anyone who stood in their way. One of the monsters noticed the open passageway to the food hall, and with a growl galloped toward the prey within.

Neliya sprinted forward, leapt onto the fallen fridge, and proclaimed,

"Stop!"

The beast halted on command, coming to a complete stop barely an inch from Neliya's upturned hand.

"Anyone in here is your friend," she said.

"Yes, m'lady." The creature turned and rallied the others to follow. They made short work of the remaining troops, until the corridors were strewn with unconscious Pebhasid soldiers.

All eyes turned speechlessly to Neliya, who grinned. "Maybe I should be a Nightshift wrangler."

13 | Zeers is coming with us

Gelfri, with a few small bandages and bruises, strolled with a flourish onto the bridge of his new battle cruiser. Moored in the Pebhasid's shipyards, its crew hurried to ready it for a sortie against the fleeing *Ranegr*. It was a good deal cleaner than the rusted bulkheads and the lacquered wood décor of his previous ship.

"I don't like it," he said.

"Is the vessel unsuitable, Pebhasid?" queried the first officer. She had a pronounced sneer when she regarded Gelfri, who met her gaze with a pensive smirk.

"It has no story," complained Gelfri. "It hasn't yet been wrangled."

The woman suppressed a growl. She saluted him. "I am Fedya, your first officer."

"Nice to meet you, Fedya," said Gelfri. "I'd shake your hand were it not for fear I'd lose it."

Fedya tightened her lips. "You have killed a man to whom I was loyal. I was promised territory and titles, which I will not now receive."

Gelfri teetered into the command chair. "Ah, pause on the pessimism, Fedya. If you are as loyal to me as you were to that weakling wart, then I will grant you more than he promised."

"And how does the new Pebhasid judge loyalty?" asked Fedya.

"Like this," said Gelfri, drawing his sidearm and pointing it at her head. In the next instant, his arm was restrained behind the chair and his weapon was in her hand. The bridge fell silent in anticipation – it wasn't often that two Pebhasida were succeeded in one day. Gelfri began to laugh.

"Interesting response for someone staring down the barrel of a gun," said Fedya.

"Those rewards you were promised, you shall have," said the Pebhasid.

"You bribe from beneath my foot? Disgusting!" barked Fedya.

"The gun's not loaded," replied Gelfri.

"But this one is," said another voice. At the bridge entrance stood Littles, his own weapon aimed at Fedya's head.

"Don't let his age or appearance fool you," Gelfri warned. "Littles is a fantastic shot."

Fedya quickly surrendered. She returned Gelfri's weapon, dropped to her knees, and proclaimed, "Forgive me, my Lord Pebhasid. I accept any punishment for threatening you."

Gelfri rolled his eyes. "Get up, you spurious pseudo-sycophant. It was a test." The first officer regarded him with a confused glance. "I wanted to make sure you weren't a cowardly coxcomb like my last aide who betrayed me. Now I know. You have earned my respect, Fedya, and you will have your reward."

Fedya rose, straightening out her uniform, and said with an air of genuine reverence, "Thank you, My Lord Pebhasid."

Gelfri smiled, and then settled into his chair as Littles came to his side. The boy leaned over to his mentor's ear. "I like her much better than that treacherous trilobite."

"Speaking of which," Gelfri continued, his tone becoming determined and vengeful, "Shall we go visit that virulent vomit-stain of a villain?"

"Yes, my lord!" said Littles and Fedya.

"Well then, let the *Shar-Ranegr* sortie!" proclaimed the Pebhasid.

Popping sounds reverberated along the hull as the shipyard's tethers burst and fell away. The ship filled with the echoes of nascent whirrs and whines as the engines roared to life.

The *Shar-Ranegr* accelerated from the moorings toward Gelfri's beloved ship. Flashes and sparks lit up the screen, and Littles' brow tightened for fear of losing his prize. Yet he remained silent as the Pebhasid ordered full-speed-ahead. The station and the troopships zipped out of view, and their quarry grew larger ahead.

"Open a communications link," said Gelfri. "I want to see that sodding scallywag's face."

The communications officer brought up a link, and Fedya directed Gelfri to a folding screen built into his armrest. Gelfri giggled delightfully at the immediate retrieval of an image and sound feed.

"Well, you pompous, pus-ridden puke!" he barked to the screen. "How do you feel now about your mutiny?"

He'd expected to see the Quartermaster, tearfully pleading for his life at the mercy of his new army. Instead he saw his old crew, armed to the teeth with his soldier's weapons. On the centre of the screen, in the captain's chair, sat Neliya, with Fyuren at her side.

"Well, erm," stammered Gelfri. "I was not expecting you two. Were you, Littles?"

Littles' breathing quickened and his lesion burned at the sight of Neliya's victorious grin.

"Gelfri," said the girl. "We have the Quartermaster in the brig. Your troops were beaten by the Nightshift, which is loyal to me. I will be taking the *Ranegr* now."

"We'll use the tunneller to go back to the *Othala*," said Fyuren. "Once we're home, Kajil will take over command."

"Give us rank 'n' rewards for done beatin' the Quartermaster, I'll turn over the tunneller," said Kajil.

Gelfri's smile widened and he narrowed his eyes. "I'll have to decline. I already promised Littles he'd be captain."

"Zeers is coming with us!" barked Gast, who marched out of the ranks. The moment Littles saw his father he pushed in front of Gelfri, grabbed hold of the display and glared at the image. "I'm not going anywhere with you!"

"Zeers, snap out of it," cried Neliya. "Gelfri's put something in your head, and you need to fight it!"

"I don't need help," returned Littles, his lesion burning an expression of agony onto his face. "This thing made me strong, took the wedge out, but you'll just put it back in! I won't let you!"

Gelfri added with a chuckle, "As you can see, the boy has decided."

"That's just your control," Gast fumed. "Turn him over to us. Now."

"Or what? I doubt your prodigious powers work over a comm-link," taunted Gelfri.

Gast gritted his teeth, while Neliya and Fyuren grew nervous.

"Gelfri," Fyuren began. "All we want is to go home. Why can't you let us?"

"Shorts," Gelfri replied. "All I want is to keep my throne. I'll need your immense intellect for that. Why can't you give me that?"

Fyuren and Gelfri held each other's gaze. Neliya and Gast tried to make eye contact with Zeers, but Littles refused to meet either gaze.

Finally, Kagoolie spoke up, "I think we're stuck, eh? Ya want what ya not gonna give up. Sad, eh? 'Cause now we gonna fight."

Kajil, Fyuren, and Neliya looked to each other, and nodded.

"Then fight it is!" exclaimed Gelfri. "You kiddies think you're ready for war?"

"We survived on the *Ranegr*," retorted Fyuren. "What's a little space battle?"

Gelfri cut the link with a childish giggle. Next to him, Littles gripped the back of his neck. "What ... about ... *my* ... ship?"

"Be calm, Littles, you panicking pubescent panter. I'll just put holes in it to vent the life support. Then we patch it up all good as new ... Unless you want

Femie back?"

Littles' teeth chattered as he looked out the forward viewport to the *Ranegr*, as it turned to meet them. He was certain he could see into the bridge's viewport, right into Neliya's eyes. He pursed his lips and heaved resolutely.

"No, she's nothing now," he said. "I want the *Ranegr*."

Neliya released all the fear and anxiety she'd bottled up during their exchange, and collapsed into Deloorie's arms. If she and Littles had been in the same room, an onlooker would have thought they suffered the same affliction.

"Fyuren, can we beat 'em?" asked Kajil.

Fyuren huffed. "That ship's got more weapons, it's bigger than us, and its armour is stronger."

"Then we run," said Fenk.

"That's the best idea," said Kagoolie. "We go' no chance. Gelfri'll blow us up."

"No!" snapped Gast. "We have to fight!"

"And die," retorted Fyuren. Gast glared at him, but the boy had seen far worse. "I want Zeers back too, Mister Indra. But now, we have to get out of here."

"If we run, he'll just chase us," Gast insisted.

"But we have something he doesn't," said Neliya. Her eyes were riddled with an air of determination the crew had come to expect of her. "The TIM device should still work, right?"

Fyuren nodded excitedly.

"We get back to the *Othala*, then come back with reinforcements to rescue Zeers," said Fenk.

"Let's do it," said Kajil. To his new crew, the man bellowed, "Allo, keep that tokamak a runnin'. Fyuren, make sure that tunneller's workin'. Everyone, get to the aft tactics station. Got it?" The crew roared in the affirmative. "Charge the EMP! Let's show that Gelfri the true Pebhorda spirit!"

Gelfri chuckled excitedly as the weapons locked on target.

"Weapons at the ready, Pebhasid," said Fedya.

"Fire!"

Before the order could be carried out, the underside of the *Ranegr* began to glow with a blue hue. Gelfri recognised the glow too late, and an electrical discharge burst from the ship, and struck his cruiser. Every crewmember flew through the air, like beans in a shaking jar, as the vessel pitched in space.

"EMP blast!" cried Gelfri, nursing a bruising forehead. "Gelfri, you pitiful puerile patriarch! You should have seen this coming! Damage?"

"Minimal," replied the first officer as she studied the readouts on a terminal. "The engine control systems are rebooting after the blast. It'll take some time to restart them."

Gelfri's dazed focus turned to the viewport. The *Ranegr* started to swivel away, and he roared, "They're trying to escape!"

The helmsman complained that the engines were unresponsive. Gelfri moved to retort, but his head injury overcame him and he collapsed. Littles looked at him, and then to the *Ranegr* slowly drifting away. He snarled furiously, "That treacherous trollop is taking my prize!" He threw the bewildered helmsman over his shoulder. He jerked the controls forward. The engines squealed like an exhausted slave being whipped back to work. Yet despite the damage, the vessel bent to Littles' overbearing will and lurched forward.

"Femie's not getting away this time!" he roared.

Biting his nails, Kajil looked at the video feed from the rear cameras. The *Ranegr* had a head start, and was gaining some headway. The Pebhasid's ship sputtered and bled gas from breaches in its hull. Then it pitched purposefully and gave chase.

Whoever's helming that thing must be insane, he thought. He tapped the intercom and said, "Arm the aft weapons. They revved up from the EMP quicker than we figur'd."

Accompanied by Nightshift creatures, the farmers raced toward the rear weapons station. They burst into the room and set to work, just as Allo shunted power to that part of the ancient ship. Lights, consoles, and ammunition storage lockers came to life, emitting sounds like electronic yawns.

Allo took Dennie, a dozen Nightshift and a few defected Pebhasid soldiers, and together they pushed the tokamak to its limits. Allo got a surprise when, upon asking Fyuren for advice, the boy replied over the intercom, "Shunt water from the sewerage system, get hydrogen from the farm run-off. Do everything you have to. I'll need as much power as I can get."

Neliya and Fyuren, followed by Fenk, Gast, Borig, Swine and the rest of the Nightshift, found the TIM device chamber. Neliya was dumbstruck. Entire decks had been cut through and hollowed out to make room for the massive contraption, which hung from the roof and was held in place by massive struts. Cables and conduits grew outwards from it like tentacles.

"So you strapped your tunneller to the ship?" asked Fenk as he navigated the tumult of cables and hacked secondary systems.

"A bit more complicated," said Fyuren. "The infrastructure surrounding the central module is like an amplifier."

"Like a gear box in a car?" asked Fenk.

Fyuren actually stopped in his tracks to explain, "No, it's more like–"

"Not the time, Fyuren!" interjected Neliya.

"I get it, I'm smart," jibed the boy.

He hopped over a few pipes and piles of wire toward a messy desk, where he attached his tablet into an interface. Everyone stood by patiently while Fyuren tried to initialise the device. But the interface didn't respond. Confused, he tried again. Nothing. He punched in an escape code. Still nothing. He held down the power button, but his tablet remained on, displaying the same blinking widget. Cautiously he tapped it, and a video screen popped up.

"Hallo, you slimy slithering sloppy slogbogger!" said a recording of Littles. Everyone heard it and raced to the terminals. There he was, a vindictive grin plastered on his face. "I suspected you'd try to escape and use the TIM device, so before I killed the engineers," – the camera pointed to the floor, where the team lay in a heap. Everyone winced. "See? Yep, so before I dispatched them to the happy hereafter, I had them hack together this little trap." Everyone's brow furrowed in confusion. "Goodbye, Shorts."

Suddenly, something came loose from above.

"Look out!" barked Swine.

Fenk and Gast pulled Neliya and Fyuren out of the way as a freefalling bulkhead hurtled down upon them. The interface table shattered in a spray of sparks and arcing. Fyuren found his tablet, beneath a few shards of broken table, glass, and shorted cable. Its screen was cracked, to his chagrin, but it appeared functional.

"Can you still make it work?" asked Gast.

"Not without the interface, right?" asked Fenk.

"Luckily, he didn't wipe the tablet's disk, so I still have all the code," replied Fyuren.

More sounds of groaning came from above. Expecting another trap, the party looked up to see the trusses and chains supporting the drive buckling. The chassis began to whine under the weight of the machine.

"Swine!" shouted Neliya.

The Nightshift charged toward the device and put themselves between it and the floor. With all their combined might, they pushed it upwards.

Kajil's voice blared through the intercomm, "What's taking so long? Gelfri's gaining on us."

The ship shuddered violently as fire struck from both the forward and the rear. Bullets burst from the rear mass-drivers to block incoming missiles, but many hostile volleys found their mark on the hull of the ancient ship.

Allo's voice came over the intercom in worried shouts, "Fyuren! I've charged all the tunneller's capacitors. That's all I can give you. If you're going to do something, do it now!"

The group looked to each other decisively and nodded. Then the focus turned to Fyuren, who cleared his head with a deep breath. "Neliya, I need that drive back up to level height. Mister Indra and Borig, find any more traps. Dad, give me a hand with the interface!"

Gast leaped agilely up the levels of bulkhead as he scanned the machine. He caught sight of a shorted wire connected to a bottle of flammable liquid. He summoned the bottle into his hand, and threw it down the corridor. Borig swung across the room on the hanging cables, gathering any booby-traps he could see.

Neliya moved over to the Nightshift, already blowing their bellows under the weight of the contraption. She and a few of the shorter creatures fetched unused beams and propped up the machine.

Fenk and Fyuren upturned the remains of the interface, sifting through the twisted cables and frayed wiring. More than once, a live wire gave them a jolt, but they ignored it. Fyuren found the plug for his tablet, just as his father handed him the connection module. He twisted the matching wires around each other and taped them up.

"Ready!" he yelled.

At the worst time, another blast rocked the ship horribly. The Nightshift's makeshift support almost collapsed. Neliya, Swine, and his crew backed away as the device rattled.

"Shorts! We've lost the tokamak," cried Allo over the intercom. "We ain't got power 'cept what's in those caps! Do it already!"

"Gast! Get me on the device!" Fyuren ordered

Gast leapt from his perch and sprinted to Fyuren's side. The boy suddenly became weightless, as Gast's pulsating arm threw him into the air. He landed near the input port, shoved the module into the socket, and hit 'go' on the tablet screen.

Beneath him, the device whirred to life. All went dark but for the fires and embers from the battle ongoing. The device's humming grew louder, into a scream worse than Fyuren had ever heard. A stream of overpowering white energy blasted through the cables and tethers, imbuing the chassis of the *Ranegr* with an ethereal hue.

Then there was timelessness.

14 | I had fun, Neliya

Fyuren coursed through a vast ocean. The water – if it was water – allowed him to pass through it effortlessly. Dots of light passed by him fleetingly, their colours mixing with the fluid's shimmering blue haze. Like a curious toddler, he reached out to grab them. But they slipped through his fingers like blobs of dye in the currents. He saw a boy floating before him, a hand outstretched in friendship.

"We will teach you," said the boy.

Though he hesitated, Fyuren felt calm, welcomed, and accepted. He reached out cautiously, but optimistically.

The hand grabbed him, the water vanished, and his eyes opened. He looked through the smoke, illuminated by dim, flickering lights, and saw Neliya's face.

"Fyuren! Are you alright?" she asked.

"What happened?" he exclaimed.

"Everything's trashed," replied Neliya. "Did the jump work?"

"Yeah, we should be near the *Othala*," said Fyuren breathlessly. The room was a complete wreck, utterly unrecognisable from before. Fyuren knew, just by looking, that his modified TIM device was beyond repair. "Where're Dad and Mister Indra?"

"Mister Indra's over there somewhere, looking for your dad," said Neliya, pointing in the direction of a source of some noise that her friend hadn't yet noticed.

Suddenly, a crashing sound and clanging reverberated from behind them. Several Nightshift survivors came into the light. One of them nursed a bruised Swine.

"Swine!" exclaimed Neliya, scrambling over to support him.

"M'lady," mumbled the exhausted, concussed creature. With the last of his energy, he said, "Glad t'have help'd a nice lass like ya."

Neliya gave an incredulous grieved smile, which he returned before falling unconscious. "Take him somewhere safe, and make sure you're all looked after!" she commanded the creatures. With tired nods, they headed down the hall.

"Over here," called out the voice of Gast.

Neliya and Fyuren navigated the wreckage toward Gast's calls. As they drew nearer they could see Gast and Borig's silhouettes, shovelling the derelict aside. Nearer still, they heard groaning beneath the rubble, and Fenk pushed through the mess. A red trail of blood dribbled down from a gash in his forehead.

Fyuren was careful, but fervent, when he threw his arms around his father. He looked up at the man and said, "We should be home now!"

"He doesn't know," retorted a sceptical Borig. "He hasn't even looked out a window yet."

"We'll find a window then," said Fyuren. "And I'll need my tablet."

"We'll buy you a new one," responded Fenk. Neliya and Gast were amazed that Fenk could still think of spoiling his son while sporting a broken arm. However, Fyuren insisted, "No, my tablet has the tunnelling solution and all the test data."

Borig darted around the sparking hardware and over the fallen bulkheads and cables, and scraped around the trash. He reached for a glint of light in the mess, and procured the tablet. When Fyuren tested it, the screen was unresponsive.

"I can still get the data off it," he said confidently as he shoved it into the carry bag that hung from his shoulders.

The group moved down the nearest corridor, illuminated by the flickering light from Gast's limb. Shadows came to life on their own, dredging up Neliya and Fyuren's earliest memories of the *Ranegr*. More than once, Neliya imagined the stranger who came to be known as Allo was herding her around. She caught a glimpse of Fyuren's perturbed face in the failing light, and knew he felt the same.

But we're almost home, she thought. *The crazy trip is almost over.*

The subtle sound of voices echoed through the dark, lonely corridor. The group paused to strain their ears.

Fyuren barked, "Kajil!"

"Fyuren?" came a soft reply.

"Kajil!" cried Neliya delightedly.

"Where're ya?" responded the voice.

Fyuren grabbed Gast's arm and pointed it to the wall. "Corridor seventeen, subjunction one. Keep yelling, and we'll follow your voice."

The group picked up the pace, blindly scrambling their way through the passageway toward the sounds of familiar voices growing louder. Another faint source of light filled the corridors up ahead. There was Kajil, almost as beaten-up as Fenk, with Dennie, Allo, and the remainder of the bridge and tokamak crews.

"Boy, am I glad to see ya!" exclaimed Kajil. "What happened with the jump?"

"Should've worked," said Fyuren.

"Ya dun't fudged ya math or somethin'?" asked Kajil, to which Fyuren gave a confused look. Kajil limped toward a nearby viewport, which gave a vista of stars that almost made Fyuren faint: a star close enough for the *Ranegr* to be in its solar system. Near it he saw a large planet with several moons.

"Looks like a comet catcher," Kajil said. "Dunno any stars with catcher planets near the Pebhasid station."

"The *Othala*'s not near any system either," said Fenk. "Won't be for another ten years."

"We're supposed to be at the *Othala*! What happened?" Neliya demanded.

Fyuren grew flustered. "I don't know! All the data's in my dead tablet! I don't know, okay?"

Neliya was shocked and taken aback. She'd never heard Fyuren say "I don't know" so many times in such a short period.

Fenk swatted away the medic tending to him, and walked toward his son. He gingerly dropped to his knees and wiped the tears from his son's face.

"Sorry, son," he said gently.

Fyuren growled, "No, I must've made a mistake. Now we're lost, *again!*"

Fenk embraced him with his free hand. "We'll find a way out of it. We'll find a way to get the ship back together and try it again." He turned to Kajil, whose lips were twisted into an irritated sneer.

Allo interjected, "We could try the backup PSU on the back deck. We could start it up, and work somethin' out there."

"See?" exclaimed Fenk enthusiastically, meeting Fyuren's dejected face with a smile. "We still have a shot. We can still do this."

"I'm in," said Neliya.

"So am I," said Gast. "We still have to rescue Zeers."

"But I'll need a smart kid to help," Allo added.

Kajil gave a tired sigh and nodded in agreement. All eyes fell on Fyuren, who silently acquiesced.

The group slowly made their way toward the aft tactical deck. They ran into a few miners on the way.

"The Quartermaster still brig'd?" Kajil asked one of them.

"Nup," replied one of the miners. "Most brig cells go' damaged in the fight. Lots 'o bodies. But ol' Q wasn't one of 'em."

A few breathed distressed sighs, but Gast interjected, "We don't have time to search. If the only PSU is on the tactical deck, then he'll obviously head there anyway. We might catch him on the way."

"Wouldn't be so sure," said Dennie. "Earlier, I spot'd a missin' escape pod on the lower deck."

"So he jumped ship?" asked Neliya.

"He's stuffed now," intoned Allo with a grin. "We in the middle of nowhere. He's gone now."

Kajil chuckled at the Quartermaster's predicament as the group pressed on.

Fyuren trudged alongside his father. His head was turned down to his feet as his run-down mind sifted through what calculations he could recall. But he always wound up dawdling on thoughts of his mother's cooking and the cake she made for his last birthday before the start of a trip he scornfully begged to be over.

He let his eyes drift to a nearby viewport. Neliya nodded for Fenk to walk ahead. The group moved past them, except for Borig, who remained a bit further behind in watch.

Fyuren pointed to a patch of space and mumbled, "That's where the *Othala* is." A tear trickled down his cheek.

Neliya pursed her trembling lips to keep herself from crying as well. She took him by the shoulders and looked at him with as much resolve as possible.

"Somewhere in your head there's a way," she proclaimed. "You will see your mum again."

Fyuren threw his arms around her, and she held him tight. She clenched her face to hold back her grief, while Fyuren's chest let his own out in small shovelfuls of heaves and sobs. Then, as Fyuren gazed out the viewport while still gripping his friend tightly, he said something Neliya would never have expected.

"I wish Zeers were here. When I had my big brother and big sister, I knew I could do it."

Now Neliya couldn't control herself, and she wept. At the end of the hall, the group waited. They all gazed at the sight of two friends comforting each other. Kajil, Allo, Dennie, Borig, and Swine each felt a lump in their throat. Fenk and Gast shuffled, if only to vent their own disappointment.

"We have to keep going," Kajil said gently.

Just as they began moving, Fyuren noticed something in the viewport. Too late did he recognise it.

"Meteor!" he cried in a panic.

Borig swiftly grabbed the pair and yanked them out of the way. There was a deafening crash and explosion, and the friends lost their senses in the confusion. Neliya caught herself on a bulkhead and steadied herself.

"Big Brother's old ship is holey," said Borig as he manually sealed the hatch.

"Holy?" shouted Neliya.

"Space rock wanted to say hello and glomped too hard," said Borig.

Fyuren pressed his face to the window. A dent, like an open wound, marred the hull and bled gas and electrical sparks.

"Dad!" he screamed, his palms pressed against the frosting glass.

"Air's escaping," said Borig with a cough. "Need to get off ship."

"Where to?" asked Neliya.

"*Anywhere!*"

Borig grabbed Neliya and Fyuren, and threw them down the passage. He shoved them toward a set of escape-pods, and opened one hatch and threw Fyuren into it. Wasting no time, he bashed the eject button, and Neliya watched Fyuren's face disappear with the pod. Then Borig dragged Neliya to the next pod. It was the only other pod that appeared to be working.

"Borig, what about you?" asked Neliya.

"Only one pod," said the little man.

"No! Come with me!" cried Neliya.

"No room! Go now!" said Borig.

Neliya struggled as Borig tried to push her into the pod. He swiftly bit her on the arm and she released his hands with a shriek. The hatch slammed shut on her. She pressed her face and palms to the glass.

Borig hovered his hand over the eject button, and smiled at his friend. "I had fun, Neliya."

Then he was gone.

15 | Chigua!

Neliya could always tell between natural and artificial light. The latter was always so uniform and consistent, as if photons came off a factory floor after being scrutinised by a machine for purity and coherence.

She hated it.

Natural light was unstable, erratic, and the only thing constant about it was the change in its mix of colours. Most beautiful, she believed, was the light from a sun. On the *Othala*, when she wanted that kind of light, a candle would serve as a substitute. It would flicker erratically in response to her breath and trembling hands. Though it gave her a fix, it often left her with wax burns that grew harder to hide the longer she went without real sunlight. But she hadn't seen candlelight, much less sunlight, for a very long time. Now, it hit her face squarely and pulled her from a deep sleep.

When she opened her eyes, she expected to see rusted bulkheads and drab light-globes, and hear the hum of beyond-ancient systems limping well beyond their design life. Instead, she saw a white-painted ceiling, pleasantly illuminated by early morning sunlight.

A frightened gasp split the silence. She tilted her head and saw a wide-eyed little girl kneeling next to her, nervously squeezing the water out of a cool cloth. Neliya wasn't sure if the girl was sick, or just terrified, by the pale tint of her skin. Then, Neliya saw the twitching, upswept ears, and knew she wasn't home.

She opened her mouth to speak. The girl suddenly turned and scrambled down a ladder.

Neliya heard the child cry, "*Abu-ken, Rii-tuan omyottune!*"

She sighed with frustration. Her head began to ache as she let it fall back on her pillow.

Still not home, and the Ranegr is …

Then she remembered Borig's smile in those last moments. She clamped her eyes shut to hold back her grief.

Don't cry, Neliya! Why not? Borig died, I don't know if the Ranegr survived the meteor! Zeers is gone, and Fyuren … Fyuren!

She sat up, overcoming her fatigue. She found herself on a small futon. Someone had dressed her in white bedclothes, and bandaged the bruises and cuts along her arms. Fyuren lay unconscious next to her, his flushed face sporting its own collection of wounds. When Neliya reached out to him, a powerful burning sensation coursed through her back. She jerked back, gritting her teeth.

What the hell is going on?

The little girl returned with an older woman, who approached cautiously. Neliya looked up, her eyes darting between the woman and the child behind her. A haze of frustration, pain, and panic fuelled her agitation. She knew these people were trying to help, but her body would not stop shaking, and the pain along her back would not go away.

"Where am I?" she muttered. The alien woman returned a look of concern and confusion as the little girl clung to her tighter. She finally gathered the resolve and placed a hand on her chest.

"Sukete," she muttered.

Neliya lifted a shaky hand, pointing to the woman. "Sukete?" The woman responded with a relieved smile and nodded. Neliya's outstretched finger drifted to the little girl, whose ears ruffled like an insect's wings.

"Uenda," said the mother.

Neliya's hand fell to her chest, and she said her name. Her nerves began to quiet, but the pain in her back continued to bother her. Sukete turned her over and replaced the bandage over a deep gash on her back. Though the alien mother's treatment felt gentle, Neliya still growled through tightly gritted teeth. When the wound was re-dressed, Uenda handed Neliya a dull-coloured ceramic bowl. She mimed eating, and then made a gesture either explaining that it was hot, or some weird fish dance. Neliya eyed the steaming white goo hesitantly.

"*Chigua! Ueo chigua!*" exclaimed Uenda. "*Te, Rii-tuan.*"

Sukete grimaced at Uenda as if she'd said something silly or rude. Neliya grinned weakly, before trying her luck with the food. It felt very similar to porridge, although the milky part tasted a bit strange. She ate some more, growing more accustomed to it.

"Ueo?" asked Sukete.

Is it good?

"Yes … umm … ueo," Neliya stammered hoarsely. Sukete bowed with a smile.

Neliya looked to Fyuren, still unconscious. His lips moved erratically as if whispering in tongues.

"Fyuren?" she said, pointing a finger at her friend.

"*Ae*," said Sukete with a reassuring smile. At that moment, a third face appeared at the top of the ladder. This one was a boy, as far as Neliya could tell. He carried with him a smaller bowl, filled with a clear broth. His eyes met with her.

"Edo," he said, pointing to himself. Neliya responded in kind, and received a smile that drew out her own.

Sukete said something to the boy, pointing curtly to Fyuren before descending the ladder. Edo moved over to Fyuren's bedside and began carefully spooning the broth into the near-comatose Mydian's mouth. When he was finished, he glanced at Neliya again with a smile that said, *Glad you're alright*. Then he left.

Uenda stayed silent, her eyes diverted down as she rocked nervously. The silence started to irritate Neliya. She handed the empty bowl to the girl, grabbing her hand before she left.

"What planet is this?" she stammered.

Uenda's ears pricked, and she scrambled down the ladder.

Good one, Neliya! That's probably the worst insult imaginable in their language.

Not long after, Uenda hurried back up the ladder with scrunched up paper in one hand and a few pencils in the other. She abruptly shoved the papers in Neliya's face. "*Meyo!*"

The stack resembled a picture book, albeit in an art form reminiscent of her pre-school days.

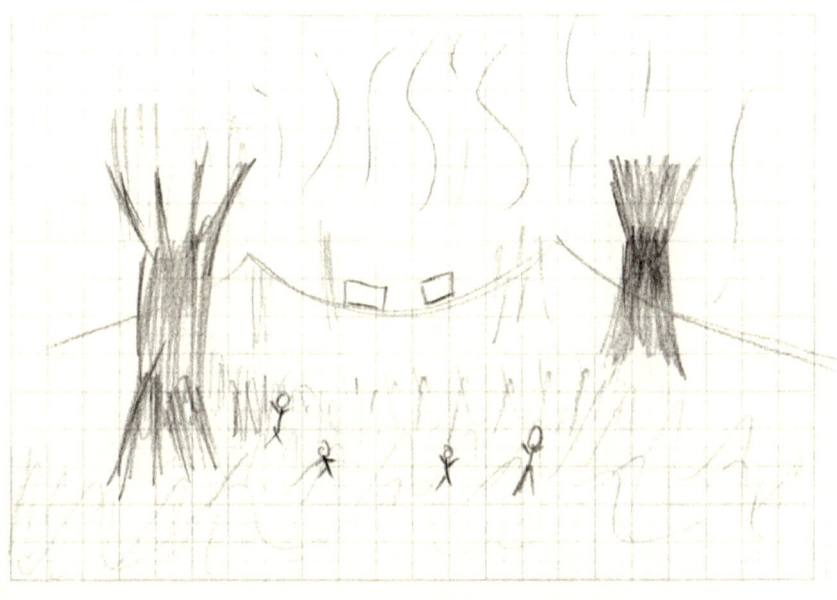

Neliya grinned as she flipped through the story. Uenda began to smile as well, and offered Neliya a pencil. She took the hint, and set about scribbling her story.

Sukete came back to find paper and pencil shavings littered over Neliya's futon. Uenda finished a drawing and showed it to her: four people, walking hand in hand and smiling. Sukete's saw the picture stab Neliya through the heart. Before the girl could break down, Sukete beckoned her to stand and led her down the ladder.

The landing where Neliya had been sleeping sat atop a wardrobe. The adjoining room had similarly polished wooden flooring and white painted walls adorned with photos and paintings. One of the walls was lined with a quartet of hanging scrolls. Each of them bore a different glyph.

Sukete pointed to the scrolls, from left to right, and said, "Odentii, Sukete, Edo, Uenda."

Family name plates, Neliya concluded.

Her eyes scanned the rest of the house. The roof curved upward, meeting at a hole directly above an open hearth in the centre of the room. She could see green fields outside, with a few tractors and other farming equipment also visible near the house.

Then she noticed Uenda with a man who appeared as old as Sukete. He nodded politely, and returned his attention to Neliya's drawings in his hand. Sukete then led Neliya into a room that smelled of soap and water.

"*Myuran,*" she said.

Neliya looked around. The floor was tiled, the walls were made of treated wood with a large gap at the top to let sunlight in. There were a few bath stools, water buckets and faucets.

Sukete locked the door and motioned her to remove her bedclothes. Neliya kept quiet as Sukete gingerly cleaned the wound on her back, the alien ointment stinging not nearly as much as before.

Sukete's care reminded Neliya of Kagoolie, comforting her in her distress all that time ago. Not just her; all her friends on the *Ranegr* had given her the strength to survive. Now they were floating in space, in all likelihood dead,

Fyuren and Zeers' fathers with them.

And Zeers, once her strongest pillar, had been snatched from her arms and made a monster.

Sukete watched the alien child break down in front of her. The woman gently pulled Neliya's hands away, and wiped the dirt from her flushed mess of a face, soaking the tears away as more came. Then she began to sing softly. The words were completely unintelligible, but the pleasant melody and Sukete's soothing voice made Neliya feel as if she were looking into a mother's eyes. Though the feeling was wistful, it calmed the tumult in her mind long enough to remember.

Fyuren's with me. He's sick now, but he'll get better. And those escape pods are probably still where we crashed. He can probably use them to call for help. Plus, I've fallen in with kind people. I'll be alright.

Neliya gave Sukete the first genuine smile she'd given in a long while.

16 | We're stuck here

The hum of sunlight on her eyes threw Neliya into the waking world, where her re-embodied senses struck her fatigued body. Her dreams receded into her bubbling thoughts like a shy creature retreating into its hovel. The morning sun notwithstanding, the comfortable futon, coupled with a snoozing Uenda snuggled up to her like a teddy bear, made sleeping in more enticing than anything else.

Another force, in the form of a hand shaking her shoulder, woke her again. She turned over and smiled in delight to see Fyuren, awake and speaking.

"Neliya, where are we?" he droned.

She almost screamed with joy, but let it come out in a low whisper, "Fyuren!" The boy repeated his question, which she dodged as she sat up to embrace him. "Are you alright? You were sick for days."

"I'm fine, Neliya. Where are we?" Fyuren urged.

"If I'm pronouncing this right, we're on a planet the inhabitants call Ondyarii," replied Neliya.

Fyuren's eyes widened, first in confusion, then in concern. His brow furrowed as he tried to collect his memories. "We must be on a planet in the system the *Ranegr* came into." He scrambled to his feet, and fell flat on his face.

Neliya helped him up. "Careful, you haven't walked for a while."

Fyuren grew more flummoxed at his surroundings. "What is this place?"

"The house of Odentii and Sukete Andou, on the outskirts of Medan village." Neliya indicated the sleeping girl nearby. "That's their daughter, Uenda."

"They're not Mydian," said Fyuren.

"They call themselves Neiren," said Neliya. "They found our escape pods and brought us here. Sukete's been looking after us. The whole family has, really."

Fyuren's eyes took in the room. He noticed the window, and with Neliya's help, hobbled to it. The sun was not yet above the horizon, but near enough to cast a cyan haze into the atmosphere and a shadow over a gas giant looming over the mountains. Its gibbous phase revealed currents and storms, swirling in varying shades of purple and red, distorted by the atmosphere.

"Beautiful, isn't it?" mused Neliya. "I remember seeing the Comet-Catcher in the Lethanis System on an excursion once, but I've never seen one from one of its moons."

Fyuren went into a panic. "We can't be on this planet, it's not real. There's no way a gas giant's moon can support life. Something's wrong."

Neliya lowered the hyperventilating boy to the floor, placing his back up against the wall. "Please, calm down. This planet seems to be just fine. It's got air, life, and people are farming."

Fyuren grew more frantic as his mind conceived of every negative outcome. Neliya held his shoulder to steady him and placed her hand over his mouth, silencing him.

"Listen," she said firmly. "All I know is that we've fallen into the care of some really nice people. But we've also crashed right into their backyard. I'm trying to learn their language so I can explain what's going on. I need you to keep calm while I do that, and so that *you* can figure out how we can get back to the *Ranegr*." She released his mouth.

With a teary huff, he rasped, "How?"

"Can't we use the escape pods?" asked Neliya.

"Oh, yeah, escape pods," said Fyuren sardonically. "While I'm at it, why don't I just whip together some chewing gum and paper clips and make a fusion reactor out of it?"

Neliya ignored his belligerent sarcasm. "Fyuren, there has to be something you can use in those pods."

Fyuren pursed his lip, glaring aimlessly as he wrestled with his distress. "Fine," he quietly barked.

Sunlight cascaded through the window and woke Uenda. She completely ignored Fyuren's awakening and leapt down the ladder, calling for Neliya to follow. Neliya helped her friend down the ladder and into the living space. Fyuren limped gingerly on his sore legs. He scowled at Sukete, who knelt on the floor near the open hearth, a gentle flame rising within.

"Why is she lighting a fire inside?" exclaimed Fyuren under his breath.

Neliya pointed out the hole in the roof. "Please stop fretting and just say thanks."

"Oh, and how might I say that?" retorted the boy.

Neliya ignored him and sat at the hearth opposite Sukete. "Gokidai,

Sukete-ken." She clumsily mimicked the woman's posture, sitting on her heels. Fyuren sat cross-legged on the cushion.

"How long have you been learning this language?" he asked.

"A few days," she replied. Fyuren's brow ascended higher.

"Tell 'em we want off this moon before it's torn apart by a gas giant," snapped Fyuren. His tone caught a concerned look from Sukete. Neliya could only apologise, and hoped Sukete would understand her friend's frustration.

"Once we've eaten, *then* we'll talk about finding the pods," she whispered irately. "Until then, try to be polite."

Fyuren slumped and once again allowed his eyes to wander about the place. A bellow of "Gokidai, Rii-tuan!" alerted him to the arrival of Uenda, holding plates of raw meat and what looked like eggs. Neliya responded with a smile.

"What did she call you?" asked Fyuren.

"Rii-tuan," said Neliya. "I think it means *Little Star*."

"You sure it's not a derogatory comment?" scoffed Fyuren. Neliya ignored him.

The Mydians watched silently as Sukete placed a metal pan over a grating on the hearth, applied some oil, and placed the meat rashers and eggs into it. A handful of spices followed, and a pleasant aroma wafted from the pan.

Fyuren, less interested in the culture, noticed something about Sukete and Uenda apart from the ears. "They've got five fingers."

"So what?" asked Neliya.

"We've got four," said the boy, wiggling his hands in the air.

"So? Earthens have five and Ranians have six. They're aliens!" said Neliya.

"Aliens who somehow evolved on a *moon of a gas giant*," he enunciated the last part as if it were something to inspire awe and shock.

Neliya was not impressed and she droned, "Yes, it's fascinating. You can write a book about it when we get back home, but for now, be quiet."

At that moment, Edo emerged from the bathroom. He took a place next to Neliya, sending her a polite smile that made Fyuren even more nervous and agitated than before. Then Odentii appeared at the door, with another man in tow. In contrast to Odentii's fixed, serious appearance and slender physique, his companion was shorter and stouter. His light grey robes reached snugly around his form, tied together with a sash. Both men uttered an unfamiliar greeting and sat at the hearth.

Sukete handed plates of food around. Neliya held a plate to Fyuren, leaning down to whisper, "Wait until I say." When all were served, Sukete motioned them to eat, and the family replied with a resounding chorus of "Okkarai Atesu!" and the meal began.

Neliya imitated the aliens' manners, putting her days of practice to the test. She smiled tentatively at her handling of the two slender stick-shaped eating implements. Fyuren had a much more apprehensive look at the food, especially the bowl of what, to him, looked like snot.

"It's porridge, Fyuren," whispered Neliya.

"I never liked porridge," protested Fyuren.

Neliya just glared at him, and he obeyed. The brief lapse in his sour mood told Neliya he didn't dislike the stuff, and she returned to her own food.

Edo, Uenda, and Sukete spoke with Neliya, teaching her new words: *tenu* for egg, *hakuzo* for wood, *shakona* for hearth, *wacha* for eating sticks. Meanwhile, Odentii spoke in a hush with their stout guest, both stealing glances at the Mydians. Eventually, Odentii called out to Neliya. When he had her attention, he procured her drawings from his robes, and pointed to a rendition of the escape pods.

"I think they're asking if we want to see the pods," Neliya translated.

"Yes, we would like to see the pods, please!" shouted Fyuren, nodding vehemently with a very forced smile.

Neliya didn't have time to react before Odentii and his partner stood and entered a fast-paced yet short-lived conversation. The man promptly exited the house, and shouted at other people Neliya couldn't see. Odentii and Edo went into the shed outside.

Sukete gave the Mydians some clothes that were slightly too big for them, but were comfortable enough. Then Uenda half-dragged them, with an excited grin, to the shed where Odentii stood with a carriage. The six-legged beast reined to the carriage twitched irritably when the aliens approached. Odentii explained that the animal was called *mashi*, and tried to assure them it was safe. Fyuren kept scanning the area, eyeing a nearby gathering of curious villagers herded by the man from breakfast.

Neliya, Fyuren, and Uenda rode in the back of the carriage. Odentii drove the carriage along the road. The rabble of inquisitive villagers followed behind, eyeing the aliens with innumerable questions. Whenever one made eye contact with Fyuren, the irked prodigy glared at them. Prompted by suspicion of alien superpowers, many of the villagers withdrew from him. They had a much nicer opinion of Neliya, however. When they looked at her, she simply smiled politely back.

Uenda continued teaching Neliya words, faster than the Mydian could accord them to memory. Questions were a tough endeavour for both parties, but with each word it grew easier. Eventually, Uenda asked a question that nearly sent Neliya off the carriage with laughter.

"What's the matter?" asked Fyuren.

"Uenda asked why your ears are so big and round," said Neliya as she wiped a tear from her eye. She sobered to see Fyuren scrambling to the front of the carriage, wearing an expression similar to when he and Zeers argued about going home. She turned to the curious group and motioned them away. She then turned to Fyuren, who sat hugging his knees, his eyes gazing fixedly forward. He looked like a psychiatric patient by the way he rocked back and forth, and she let him be.

Uenda took up a seat next to her on the edge of the carriage.

"*Rugu-tuan's* angry?" she asked, the words making more sense to Neliya. "At me?"

Neliya shook her head. "Everything."

Uenda simply nodded, her eyebrows raised obliviously, and gazed back down the path they had travelled.

They approached the boundaries of the forest, and the mashi grew restless in the thickening brush. Odentii pulled back on the reins, secured the carriage to a nearby tree for the beast to graze, and announced that they would need to go on foot.

Neliya held the slouching Fyuren close, an arm around his shoulder, and motioned for Odentii to lead the way. Uenda caught up to her father and walked hand-in-hand with him. The forest passage was long and strewn with fresh tracks. Grasses had grown unchecked in the forest, only to be trampled under the feet of bewildered residents on their journey to the crash site. Neliya still drew a blank on her memories of the landing, even when the group entered a clearing and the crash site came into view in the distance.

"There's where we landed," she said to a barely listening Fyuren. "I don't suppose they'd be space-worthy?"

"The only engines they have are descent thrusters," muttered Fyuren. "They wouldn't get us anywhere."

Neliya pressed, "They'd have a communications system, wouldn't they?"

"Shut up!" Fyuren barked, pushing away from her. He glared up at the girl, frustrated, defeated, and angry. "Stop pretending that there's still hope we can get home. We're stuck here!"

Neliya huffed, "How can you say that? You don't even know what happened during the jump."

"What does it matter?" screamed Fyuren. "Sure, my tablet would have the data from the jump. All it'd tell me is that I forgot to carry the one somewhere. I'd still be stuck here. We should be home! Not here! I shouldn't have had to develop a tunnelling solution for a crazy Drifter captain! And I shouldn't be stuck here on a backwater planet in the middle of nowhere, who knows how far from my Mum and Dad!" At the mention of his father, Fyuren's histrionics stopped, his breathing shallowed, and he began to sob. His shoulders heaved, slumping under the burden of his predicament. "What if Dad is dead? That meteor crashed right into the *Ranegr*. What if Dad and Mister Indra weren't lucky, and they died?" He fell into Neliya's arms, and trembled in her embrace. Every sound he made was a thorn in her side as she tried to hold back her own grief for his sake.

"This isn't fair!" Fyuren moaned. "Why did that stupid Sidha let the bioplants fail? Why did our tunneller stuff up? Why did Zeers go crazy? Why couldn't that TIM device just bloody-well work!? Why am I not with my

Mum and Dad right now!?"

And he cried deep, heaving wails of grief, frustration, and rage. None of the villagers needed to understand Myddish to know exactly what was going on, and even they could not prevent their eyes stinging with sympathy. And Neliya, being so close to the epicentre of this fountain of anguish, felt the brunt of it.

No longer able to stand it, she pushed Fyuren to arms length, bellowed, "Snap out of it!" and slapped him across the face. The blow knocked him off balance, the surprise jumbling the state of angst that had claimed his mind. Thoughts and feelings collided and shattered in his brain until it went blank. He stood, doubled over and panting, his cheeks wet with salty tears, his eyes blankly staring at the ground beneath his feet.

"Get a grip, you stupid little child!" barked Neliya. "It's time for you to get it: you're smart! Smarter than me. And I'll be dead if I let you give up just because of another setback. Even if I have to drag you by your big round ears, you're going to find a way out of this! You got that, Shorts?"

Fyuren's eyes did not leave hers, and he did not make a sound. He cringed when she used his Pebhorda nickname, and at that her temper broke. Her shoulders slumped with fatigue, recalling her own breakdown upon seeing Uenda's drawings of her family.

"I can barely remember what they look like," she mumbled. "My Mum and Dad, I mean. We've been gone so long. Last time I saw them, I was still a little girl. Now," she looked down her body, "I look like I could have kids of my own."

Fyuren gave a smirk, which turned into a grin.

"What?" asked Neliya, her own lips cracking.

Fyuren's grin overpowered his self-control. "I'll have to resize your spacesuit again."

Neliya didn't get the chance to retaliate before Fyuren was tackled by a small creature in a broad-brimmed hat. Uenda perched on all fours above the boy, pinning him down with surprising strength. She giggled, exclaiming something in her language.

"What's she saying?" asked the bewildered boy. Neliya said nothing.

Uenda gazed at Fyuren with a mischievous look in her eye, and proceeded to tickle him unrelentingly. The boy writhed in agony, begging Neliya for help. She could only fall to her knees and giggle at the scene.

Odentii beheld the sight from a distance, his lips upturned. He turned to his stout companion from breakfast and mumbled, "As I thought, Idoru. They are just children."

Idoru nodded knowingly. Those swirling images of attacks from the sky that had plagued his mind and those of the villagers disappeared at the sight of Uenda playing with the alien children. In that moment, the apprehension that had gripped entire group of onlookers wafted away like dry leaves in the wind, and all that remained was a single realisation.

"They're just lost children trying to get home," intoned Idoru. With a relieved smile, he added, "Madokai will be pleased."

17 | We just want to go home

The group returned in late afternoon, the carriage loaded with parts from the crashed pods. Fyuren hadn't a clue what he might do with them, since his first goal was to fix his tablet's screen and get the data from the CTN jump. Odentii let him use the workshop next to the shed, which was dusty and full of tools. Some tools looked like they were regularly used and maintained, while others, evidently heirlooms, were rusted from years of disuse. Fyuren cleared a workbench and set up his equipment there. Neliya and Odentii stood to the side, watching the boy work.

"This'll take a while," he said.

"It can't be as hard as that crazy radius thing, can it?" retorted Neliya.

"*Krah-tzee!*" corrected Fyuren. "And seriously, it'll be a while because I have to find a way to connect my tablet to this ancient display, using whatever I can find in this primitive barn." Normally, he would have gone on like that until someone interrupted him. But upon noticing Neliya's stifled grin, he glared at her. "You think making fun of me is going to motivate me?"

"Just a little," jibed Neliya.

Fyuren quietly pointed to the door, and then set to work.

Days passed.

At first, Sukete worried when Fyuren ignored calls for dinner. As Neliya learned more of the language, she could explain that this was how he worked, and it was best he not be disturbed. That, however, left her with little else to do. So she settled into a routine of helping Sukete make food, leaving a tray on a table in the workshop for her friend, and bussing the used tray from the previous meal. At the same time, she helped Odentii and Edo with farm work to become more proficient at their language, which she learned was called Aimorein. Odentii welcomed the help as well, so that he could learn Myddish.

At one point, Neliya commented that Odentii seemed to learn Myddish faster than she could learn Aimorein. Odentii laughed and welcomed the complement. He explained that he was fluent in languages spoken elsewhere on Ondyarii.

"It helps that I have relatives across the western seas in Kehandou," he explained.

Neliya enjoyed the farm work and linguistics lessons. The routine also helped her adapt to the length of Ondyarii's day and night, about a third shorter than the *Ranegr* day. She also learned that months were measured by the position of the gas giant that the moon orbited, which was called Sikai.

Uenda had taken an exceptional liking to Neliya, wishing to be near her all the time. The little girl helped the most with new words. She was the most hyperactive girl Neliya had ever met, and had the greatest fascination with new discoveries. When there was little to do, Neliya would opt to sit with Uenda and ask about the various flowers.

One day, she went outside to see the little girl marching around the garden, a long-stalked flower with white petals held in her hand like a baton. She scanned the garden purposefully. Suddenly, she charged toward one of the flowers. She gingerly pulled a tiny green grub off the stalk and chided it about eating the plants, before flicking it onto the lawn. Neliya couldn't help but chuckle at the little captain of the guard.

It was helpful having Uenda as a companion while Fyuren was isolated in his work. When he was designing the *Ranegr*'s TIM device, Neliya had Zeers and the others to talk to. Here, she was glad for the replacement.

The only downside was when Uenda insisted on dragging Neliya into the village proper on errands for Sukete. For the first few weeks, her yellow skin earned quite a few disconcerted stares from the townspeople, and the language barrier didn't help at all. However, as her fluency developed, so did the invisible wall between her and the people. Soon, she learned their names, and they remembered her name, until she found herself looking forward to speaking to the neighbours in Medan.

By the end of the first month, Neliya started to worry that Fyuren wasn't sleeping properly. She sometimes found him curled up in a makeshift bed in the shed. It became a common topic of conversation between her and Sukete, usually while they made dinner.

"Maybe I over encouraged him," she said to Sukete, handing her a bowl of whisked egg.

"Does he usually work like this?" asked Sukete as she sampled some soup for taste.

"When he's really motivated," said Neliya.

Half way through the third month, Neliya had had enough. She entered the workshop, finding Fyuren in the same clothes he'd worn to the crash site, his face sunken and tired, and his eyes maniacally focused on the contraption he was assembling.

"Have you managed to get the tablet working?" she stammered, having not spoken Myddish for a while.

"Ages ago," returned the boy.

"Why didn't you tell me?" exclaimed Neliya.

Fyuren groaned, "Oh gee, I dunno, maybe I was busy trying to find a way out of here. Now can you just let me work?" He paused to finish soldering a connection, and then pointed the smoking hot iron to the wall behind him. "And take her with you."

Neliya looked over, and saw movement behind a stack of old tractor parts. Her hands on her hips, she commanded, "Uenda, out here now."

Uenda sheepishly revealed herself. By the dirt on her clothes and face, Neliya guessed she'd been hiding in the workshop for a while.

"It's not fair, Rii-tuan," she pouted. "Why do only you and Daddy get to see? I want to know what Rugu-tuan is doing. It looks interesting."

"He needs to be alone," chided Neliya. "Go inside and get cleaned up for dinner." Uenda moaned longingly. "Go," said the Mydian firmly.

"Yes, Ma'am," said the girl, before exiting the workshop.

"Sounds like you're getting better," mumbled Fyuren as he blew away smoke from the device. "Now leave."

"I'm not going," said Neliya in Aimorein, the gears in her brain grinding as she switched back to Myddish.

"I don't speak the language, and I'm busy," he said. "Go away."

"No," returned the girl. Fyuren shoved the soldering iron into its cradle and blasted a frustrated glare at her. Before he could say anything, his expression morphed into one of surprise.

"Wow, you look really different," he mumbled.

"What do you mean?" Neliya asked as she looked down at herself. She had different clothes, courtesy of Sukete's wardrobe, but she couldn't see anything else beyond superficial changes.

"Your eyes look a little different, and you're growing in brown roots," said Fyuren as he indicated her face and hair.

"Maybe the food I've been eating," muttered the girl. "Also, I've been running in the morning, so I might have lost a little weight."

"And hanging out with that whiny girl," Fyuren jibed as his interest subsided and he turned back to his work.

"Don't say that about Uenda, she's nice," chided Neliya.

Fyuren tapped the soldering iron to the circuit, and blew away the puffs of smoke. "Whatever, just don't get too close to her, or that older lady," he said between taps and checks. "The last thing I want is you getting attached and having to drag you away."

"You don't need to worry about that," interjected the girl. "I'm plenty sensible."

"We'll see," droned the boy.

Neliya studied him a moment longer, and waited until he stowed the soldering iron and started inspecting the circuit.

"You look like you've just finished something," she intoned. "Sounds like you could use a break before moving on!"

"No chance," growled Fyuren.

"No choice," replied the girl. She wrapped her arm around his waist and lifted him off his seat. By the time Fyuren realised what had happened, she'd already carried him out of the workshop.

"Let go, Neliya," barked the boy, struggling to free himself. But while his mind was fully awake, his body was too tired to put up a solid fight. Sukete was taken aback by the ruckus, as were Odentii and his stout partner, who had walked into the house just after them.

"Don't mind, everyone," said Neliya in Aimorein. "Fyuren needs a bath, so I'm giving him one."

"Wait, Neliya," cried Sukete over Fyuren's protests. "Uenda is washing now."

"That's ok, I'm sure she won't mind washing Fyuren's back," replied the girl. She approached the bathroom door and knocked. "Uenda? Rugu-tuan's decided he wants to have a bath too. Is that alright?" Neliya relished the fact that Fyuren hadn't a clue what she was saying. She plopped him on the floor in front of the bathroom door and opened it. Uenda sat there, completely covered in soap bubbles, with an adorable grin on her face.

"She's going to wash your back," said Neliya.

Fyuren's face went pale.

The sky had darkened, and the warming light of the fire in the hearth flooded the room. The family and their two alien guests ate around the hearth. Odentii's stout friend, Idoru, had also joined them for dinner, and eyed the pair thoughtfully. Fyuren was hardly concerned with the man, however. His face was still warm from the embarrassment of being bathed against his will by the hyperactive child next to him.

"I should have worked harder at sports," he grumbled.

"Look on the positive side," said Neliya. "You smell a lot better than you did before." Fyuren shot her a glare she ignored as she patted Uenda and said in Aimorein, "Isn't that right? Rugu-tuan was smelly."

"Smelly!" exclaimed Uenda through a mouthful of salad and rice. Sukete and Edo chuckled at the joke. Even Fyuren's mood was not so sour as to keep him from smirking slightly.

"Ha, so you can't keep a bad mood up," said Neliya. "If you're lucky, Rugu-tuan won't be your nickname much longer."

"What does that mean?" asked Fyuren half-interested.

"*Grumbleguts*," replied Neliya, before continuing her banter with Uenda.

Fyuren watched her babble with the little girl, and added sarcastically, "Since you're fluent now, how about you tell her to stop bugging me while I work?"

"Certainly I will tell her," said Odentii.

Fyuren almost dropped his bowl. "You understand me?"

"Little," replied Odentii, his pronunciation slightly off.

"I too," interjected Edo.

Sukete raised her hand with a smile. Fyuren turned to Neliya, astonished.

"If you hadn't locked yourself away, you might have learned a bit yourself," said the girl as she expertly twirled the eating sticks in her hand and shovelled slices of meat into her mouth with them.

At that point, the stout stranger spoke, but he still used Aimorein words.

"This leader of village, Idoru," said Odentii, translating for the man. The man bowed reverently.

Neliya bowed in reply, "It is an honour to learn your name."

Idoru continued to speak, with Odentii translating, "Our village of Medan waited for you to learn our speech. Now we'll know your plan. We meet the town. You tell everyone."

Neliya exchanged glances with Fyuren, and both gulped nervously for different reasons. But neither voiced concerns, and they agreed to meet the village elders.

When dinner was finished, Sukete brought Neliya into the master bedroom and procured an off-white dress robe with red lining. The Mydian looked in the mirror, studying her appearance in the alien garb that was slightly too big for her. As she twirled for Sukete and Uenda, she caught a sudden glimpse of Kagoolie and Deloorie. She blinked and the vision was gone.

"Rii-tuan is beautiful in Mummy's *mekato*!" shouted Uenda. Neliya accorded the new word to memory with reddened cheeks. She noticed the messy state of her locks and grumbled, "What about my hair? It looks bad."

Sukete's lips pursed with disappointment, "We don't have time now."

On Odentii's call, Sukete wrapped Neliya in a shawl before fetching one for herself and her daughter. They climbed onto the carriage. Fyuren had been lent one of Edo's old formal robes, and had found himself a comfortable spot at the back of the carriage.

The farm was a fair distance from the village proper. The path took them past other farms and livestock grazing grounds. The owners of those grounds were rounding herds of bizarre bird-like creatures into the pens as the sun slipped below.

"They called kanbi. That is meat we eat," said Odentii in Myddish.

"Hmm, they look like kerec with a mouth and no feathers, and taste like kogruk," muttered Fyuren, stealing a barely interested glance before returning to his musing.

The lights of the town slowly came into view. As at the house of Andou, oil lamps and open fires illuminated these houses. Most rooves were thatched with sturdy tree-bark, others with ceramic tiles, and their edges curved elegantly. Each structure's foundation pillars were visible beneath them, serving as shelter for pets and small stray animals.

Commotion brewed at the Mydians' arrival, as lamp-bearing villagers turned, following their twitching ears, to gawk for a moment. Then they followed the Andou entourage toward the temple in the middle of town.

Fyuren hopped off the carriage and joined hands with Neliya. He pretended he was less fazed than he actually was, while Neliya wore her nervousness on her sleeve. She let her eyes wander, unable to control them even if she wanted to. Wooden pylons of a slight vase shape held up an inner structure spacious enough to house only a subset of the village, that being the governing body or small groups of worshipers. That didn't stop the rest of the village from piling at windows and doors to hear the story of the children from the sky.

Idols sat along the walls of the hall. Their tiered elevations tended toward more illustrious designs and denser decorations, up to the highest level, where statues of a man and woman sat surrounded by effigies of servants and luxury.

Right in front of these idols sat the Medan elder council. Idoru shared the middle with an old lady with a fixed gaze, directed at the Mydians from the moment they entered the hall. The one furthest to the left struck a plate with a reverent flourish, and with a squeaky voice proclaimed a strange word Neliya couldn't understand. He had to do it several times, each time as calm and reserved as the first, until the crowded hall quieted down.

Without realising it, Neliya and Fyuren wound up at the front of the crowd. The amazing idols and effigies felt very foreboding to them. Their downward gaze struck Neliya and Fyuren's heads, demeaning and shrinking them.

Fizzle and drizzle …

A burning chill vibrated up Neliya's spine. She quickly realised the crowd had bowed and murmured a prayer of respect to the idols and the council. She immediately did the same, ignoring Fyuren's scoff. She fought to control her own trembling and begged the statues not to remind her of Littles or Gelfri. She felt a hand on her shoulder, and saw Odentii next to her. The people had finished their prayer, and beset her with expectant gazes.

Idoru addressed the village, "These two have fallen from the sky. They are named Neliya and Fyuren." Neliya bowed to the council reflexively, before giving in to the compulsion to do the same to the crowd. The hall simmered with disapproving murmurs as she coaxed a modicum of politeness out of her recalcitrant friend. A soft clang from the bellman silenced the hall, and signalled Idoru to continue. "They have learned our tongue, and will now explain themselves." The gaze of the council fell to the Mydians.

Neliya looked to Fyuren, and nodded to indicate that he should do the talking and she would translate.

It's worse than a science conference presentation, he thought. He tried to make his explanation as simple as possible for her.

"We lived on a ship, travelling from one star to another. Our people can't travel very fast between stars. Well, we can, but it's dangerous. So we travel on ships with machines to help us live for many years. Neliya and I grew up on a colony ship called the *Othala*.

"The machines that kept us alive broke down, and we had to escape while the crew tried to fix them. We used the dangerous method. An accident happened, and we were lost. We were picked up by another ship, outside the law, called the *Ranegr*. When the captain learned of my intelligence, he made me develop a machine that would transport the *Ranegr* using the dangerous method. I did, and he imprisoned us. We escaped, stole the *Ranegr* from him and tried to return home."

He paused, and Neliya wondered if he was going to actually explain what happened in the jump. She winced at the idea of having to translate a complex exposition.

"Just as we used the machine, it malfunctioned. And it sent us to this unknown planet. The *Ranegr* was damaged, and we had to escape in those pods."

When Neliya finished translating, Idoru went into a moment of thought, conversing under his breath with his neighbours. All Neliya could do was hope her grasp of the language was enough. Odentii's considerable linguistic skills notwithstanding, she wondered whether the meaning was properly conveyed.

Finally, the village leader spoke.

"He asked to know how we plan to get home," Neliya translated.

"The device you dragged me away from was a communicator," Fyuren began, his words initially directed at Neliya. The girl snapped her fingers to stop him and pointed briefly to the council. Then she paused, wetting her lips thoughtfully, before bowing and stating reverently, "Forgive our rudeness."

"Please continue, young lady," said the old lady, in an unexpectedly casual tone. Neliya nodded, spoke a few more phrases, and then looked to Fyuren.

"You told them I'm making a communicator?" he said.

"Yes, talk to *them*," urged Neliya.

Fyuren sighed, his irritation growing.

"What are we doing here?" he said. "They won't be able to help us."

"Are you really doing this now?" Neliya growled softly. "We crashed into their backyard. The least we can do is explain ourselves. Now, *talk – to – them*."

"Fine," Fyuren growled silently. To the council, he blurted, "I will call the *Ranegr* for help."

Idoru spoke again, "You want to bring others here?" A concerned murmur spread through the hall.

"Only so they can rescue us," Neliya explained in Aimorein. She directed her gaze over her shoulder. "We just want to go home."

Idoru paused, allowing the lady next to him to ask a question of her own.

"She asked where the *Ranegr* is right now," Neliya uttered.

"I don't know," said Fyuren. "Without a telescope or a map of the solar system, I can't work out where it is."

The council was taken aback by Neliya's translation, because she left out the parts she couldn't translate. But Odentii knew better.

"Neliya, what means 'telescope?'" asked the man.

Neliya panted, tired from overuse of her brain. Rubbing her sore head, she turned to him and described the device. The moment he heard the words "star" and "looking," Odentii knew straight away what she meant. He quickly engaged in a back and forth with the council that Neliya could hardly keep up with. Finally, he turned to the children and said, "Our governor, the Saajya, has map of stars. We can give."

Fyuren's heart raced with excitement. Chewing his lip, he thought quickly, trying not to assume that these people had accurate understanding of celestial mechanics. He ultimately decided to give them the benefit of the doubt.

"Odentii, can I have them, please?" he said.

18 | Let's get to work

The Saajya, bedizened with the colourful garb of an Aimoren government official, sat in pensive thought. His eyes scanned the scroll before him, his lips tightening imperceptibly at the end of each sentence. Beneath that demeanour, he was quite unsettled, and the handmaid gently wafting him with a fan did little to help him.

Idoru sat before the Saajya, looking up at the ruler sitting on the wooden dais, the heat from a small ceremonial flame rippling the air between them. The mood of their private meetings was always disturbing, due to the Saajya's control over the lands in the prefecture, and thus Idoru's livelihood. And recent events, having caught the inquisitive eyes of neighbouring rulers, made the mood even tenser. Idoru did everything in his power to avoid gulping nervously. As if sensing the dryness in his throat, the Saajya's finger twitched at the handmaid, who poured tea into a small cup and handed it to Idoru.

"Gratitude," said Idoru in a hoarse whisper. He took a placid sip, swallowed, and then made a soft hissing sound through his teeth to the handmaid, who bowed in acceptance of his non-verbal complement, and returned to her lord's side.

The tea calmed Idoru's nerves, but not by much.

The Saajya finished his fifth reread, and then set the scroll into the flame.

"I am sure you can understand the need for absolute discretion," said the Saajya. Idoru bowed, but said nothing. "I must hear it from your mouth. Are you certain there will be no others?"

"*They* are certain, Madokai," said Idoru, uttering the salutation with as much conviction as he could muster.

"And you trust them?" replied the Saajya.

Idoru straightened his back. "They are children, and there was not a shred of falsehood in their eyes when they said they wanted only to go home."

"Assuming you would know falsehood were it in the eyes of children such as these," said the Saajya, withdrawing his hand into the baggy sleeve of his long coat. "There is precedent for children as infiltrators."

Idoru's lips tightened, and his gaze left the floor to look for once at the Saajya. "If you so believed, Madokai, you would have insisted the children be brought here under guard and in secret. You would interrogate them until you were certain of their intentions." He paused while he attempted to gauge the Saajya's reaction, which was difficult in the light of the man's unchanging expression. "I do not think you really believe that these children would harbour ill intentions for us. Even so, was it not one of your ancestors who was faced with a decision much like this?"

"You refer to the Great War of the West?" muttered the Saajya.

"A supplicant pleading for asylum," Idoru continued. "A banished prince, thought dead by his kingdom, an enemy of Aimore no less!"

"That prince then went on to engage our country in war," the Saajya interjected, his tone stern. "This may perhaps lead to something such as that, but on a far greater scale."

"Did we not win the conflict?" asked Idoru, holding his gaze.

"We did. Yet, I fear a war such as the one I imagine now, if the present situation were to take a similar course. And what price would our people have to pay for victory with respect to the magnitude of the conflict?"

"Imagine the conflict if we don't help them," said Idoru.

The Saajya's eyes narrowed. "If these children speak truth, then they are two, compared to an incomprehensibly large society. Think you that they are worth a war to retrieve?"

"No, and you know a war will not happen for them," retorted Idoru. "Only one vessel is out there looking for them, and its only concern for us is the children in our care. As far as I am concerned, it is irrelevant. I want to help these children." Idoru's tone was resolved, and his gaze remained fixed on the Saajya.

The Saajya summoned into his mind a dear image of two children and a mother. Then he turned to Idoru and said, "As do I."

The tension in Idoru's back slowly ebbed away.

I should really retire and hand this position to my son.

The Saajya continued, "However, I must consider other matters that play a part."

Idoru nodded, relieved to know where the Saajya's true concerns lay.

"Does Eranon know of the children?" he asked.

The Saajya sneered. "Think you I would allow my arch rival or any of his vassals to know of such a presence? He knows not even of the impact. As far as his agents are aware, naught but shooting stars and dust made landfall near Medan. Pago and Fahai think that fairies came from the sky to grant our prefecture a bountiful crop."

Idoru scoffed, and didn't regain his composure before the Saajya noticed and responded with a brief crack of his lips.

"It's what happens when you allow paranoia or cults to dominate your populace," said Idoru. "I assume you will be doing your part to confuse them?"

"I have already asked my spies to spread false stories and myths about the falling star," said the Saajya, a twinge of pride to his monotone. "I have also petitioned the High Saajya to feign ignorance to the Kehan. While we are now in an alliance with the west, the tensions between them and the Far East have disquieted the High Saajya about happenings in Medan. If these children may hold some advantage they may press …"

The men sat in silence for a moment, pondering and digesting the information they had exchanged. After several cups of tea, Idoru spoke first.

"I will keep the children in Medan, and establish a false shrine of pebbles, effigies of a fallen star. Should a pilgrimage be made, we will have the necessary theatrics to dispel rumours."

The Saajya replied with a nod. "Know that the High Saajya is with us. I will continue to shroud their existence in rumour. Let us ensure the children leave safely and our world remains without knowledge of them."

Idoru bowed reverently, stood, and left the room.

The forest was quiet, save for the buzz of insects and the occasional ruffle of foliage by a forager eking out its next meal. All of it was typical of a summer on any planet, even if that planet was a moon of a gas giant.

A creature dashed and bounded over brush and log, giggling excitedly, her ears beating the air around her head, over which she held a well-used canvas bag. An assailant pursued her speedily. The nimble leader slid easily down a dirt slope toward her quarry, while her follower took her time with the descent. At the bottom, she stumbled as she caught her breath.

"Uenda!" Neliya called out between strangled pants.

"Hurry up, Rii-tuan! We're so close to the *nageyo* nest!" exclaimed the impatient girl, her ears twitching with irritation. In the next instant she soared over the bushes and out of sight. Neliya resumed her chase with an incredulous chuckle.

Aren't you supposed to be really athletic? She asked herself, thinking partly in Aimorein. *I guess running on a planet isn't quite the same as on a ship.*

Lost in her musings, Neliya almost ran over Uenda, who had stopped in front of a tall tree with a sloped trunk. She slumped onto her knees to catch her breath, while the little Neiren tomboy glared upwards with intent.

"They've built their nest higher," whispered Uenda. "Dunchi-ken is getting smarter."

"Who's Dunchi-ken?" asked Neliya, her throat stinging from the panting.

"See?" blurted Uenda in a whisper, her finger outstretched toward a fuzzy bulb hanging from a branch high in the tree. Neliya strained her eyes, her hand held up to block the afternoon sunlight. It wasn't fuzz around the bulb, but a cloud of flying insects.

"Are those nageyo?" she asked.

"Uh-huh! Time to steal some *nagejenshi!*" exclaimed the girl, her brow furrowed with determination. She fastened her sack over her shoulder and strode over to the tree, kicking off her wooden sandals. Uenda suddenly shot a quarter of the way up the tree, pulling herself up on the notches of old branches.

The girl scaled the tree with practiced grace, making very little sound so as not to distract the strange insects going about their business high above. Homing in on her target, Uenda slowed her pace, until she reached the branch just under the nest. She took a seat, and calmly unfastened her bag.

Uenda procured a small knife from the bag and held it in between her teeth. Then out came a spiny seed the size of her fist, and a box of matches. The little girl grinned victoriously through her clenched teeth as she eyed the nest. She looked over the treetops for any incoming wind gusts, before striking a match. Soon, the seed was smoking nicely. With malevolent glee, Uenda held the seed up toward the nest, letting its smoke invade the tunnels within the waxy bulb. The insects moved for the hive, climbing their way in, as if to save the treasure held therein. A few brave souls, however, saw their arch-enemy and defended.

Then Uenda rose, balancing on the branch. Drawing the knife from her mouth, she plunged it into the nest, expertly cutting out a chunk of it. Ignoring the sharp stings on her exposed arms, Uenda licked the knife clean, and held out her canvas bag to catch the oozing slimy mass of wax.

"*Rachi!*" she exclaimed, leaping from the branch and sliding down the slope of the tree like a slippery-dip. "Let's go, Rii-tuan!"

"What?" replied a bewildered Neliya. The buzzing grew very loud, and she saw a cloud of angry bugs flying towards her. With a squeal she chased the little girl into the woods.

The sound of angry nageyo mobs eventually subsided as the girls outran them. They kept running though, mostly due to Neliya being overwhelmed with the desire to not be swarmed by alien bugs. When they came to a clearing, she stopped, and allowed herself a break.

"Next time," she barked. "You tell me exactly what we're doing! You realise what alien bugs could do to me!"

Uenda's face cracked at the scolding, and through watering and shocked eyes, she said, "But you told me to show you! You said you wanted to see Ondyarii, so I showed you." Neliya saw the heartbroken look in the girl's face. Uenda's cheeks began to redden, and her lips folded outwards. "Rii-tuan is so mean!"

Oh no, this is just like when Fyuren kicked her out of the workshop, thought Neliya.

"Okay, okay, stop it, Uenda," she pleaded, wrapping her arms around the girl. "I didn't mean to yell at you. I was just scared."

"Why? They're just nageyo," mumbled Uenda through tears she tried to stop. "The *sasu* don't hurt that bad."

"Sasu?" asked Neliya, another word she didn't understand. Uenda brandished the reddish purple blotches on her forearms. "Stings!"

"They're not that bad, and they'll heal in a while," Uenda insisted.

"But look at all of them!" shouted Neliya. "Your mother's going to be mad at me for not looking after you!"

Uenda fumed. "But I do this all the time, Rii-tuan!" She held up the canvas bag, adding, "And I got some nagejenshi. We can eat it."

"What is that stuff, anyway?" asked Neliya.

Uenda sniffed back the last of her tears and, with a grin, opened the bag to show the contents: a sickly mess of hexagon-shaped cells, most of which were broken, and covered in a sticky orange goo. Throw in twitching, fidgeting nageyo caught up in the mass and white grubs visible in some of the cells. It made for an icky sight. Neliya gagged when Uenda broke off a small piece of the mass. Tendrils of goo connected the piece to the whole, growing thinner as Uenda brought it up to her mouth. Her eyes lit up with glee.

"Have some, Rii-tuan!" she chirped.

Neliya's courage almost left her when Uenda ate a piece that had a grub in it. Uenda shot her another expectant look. She took a deep breath, and then touched her finger to the sticky ooze. Pushing her nerve, she grabbed a piece, and without looking at it, put it straight into her mouth.

With the goo dripping down her chin, she exclaimed, "Ueo!"

"Isn't it?" said Uenda. "We'll take this home and Mummy can make some *motosu* with it."

Hand in hand, the girls headed back through the woods to the village. As they passed through the town, some of the people bowed politely and chuckled at their closeness. Were it not for that their heritage was light years apart, a passer-by would think the two girls were sisters by how they walked through the crowd.

At home, an elderly couple greeted them at the hearth. Neliya quickly recognised one of them as the matriarch of the village council.

"Grandma! Grandpa!" Uenda shouted upon recognising them. Seeming to ignore Neliya for the moment, she held up the canvas bag. "Mummy's going to make motosu!" Sukete took the bag, and chided Uenda for pestering the bugs, though it was more ritualistic than serious. Meanwhile, the grandparents bowed politely to Neliya, the lady still wearing that smile uncharacteristic of an official.

"Gokidai, Neliya-eru," said the lady. "You don't remember me, do you?"

"I remember you, but I don't think I know your names, sorry," replied Neliya, mirroring their reverence.

"I am Arika, and this is my husband Jikyo," said the lady. "We are Sukete's parents."

"I'm glad to finally meet you," Neliya bowed.

"Thank you for being a wonderful elder sister for our granddaughter," said Jikyo before offering her a cup of tea. Sukete set out a plate of the delicious goo for the girls to share, which Neliya enjoyed despite the writhing presence of those strange bugs.

"You wait, Rii-tuan, Mummy's motosu is the best!" Then Uenda shouted over her shoulder to the kitchen, "Hey, Mummy! Rii-tuan doesn't know nageyo!"

"Of course she wouldn't, Uenda dear," said Arika. "They'd have some other kind of insect."

"But nothing that makes sweets," said Neliya. Eyeing Uenda's arms, she added, "We have plenty that sting though."

"I think you were stung too," said Jikyo.

Neliya checked her arm, and it was as if her nerves shot to attention like lazy cadets upon the arrival of their drill sergeant. A powerful itch crackled along her skin from a purple welt with red edges, the size of her palm.

Uenda panicked, "Uah! Rii-tuan got stung!"

Jikyo quickly restrained Neliya's arm that reached to scratch the blemish. He called for Sukete, who appeared with the medicine box. Though the salve she applied soothed the itch, the bandage that followed only shielded the agonising welt from Neliya's scratch-happy fingernails. She was able to pull her mind away from it by helping Arika calm a very distressed Uenda.

"I got Rii-tuan stung!" Uenda's eyes bubbled with tears.

"I'm alright now! It's just itchy," said Neliya, stroking the girl's hair soothingly.

Uenda cried, "Big Brother said I shouldn't take you to see the nageyo or the sting would make your arm fall off!"

Neliya glanced at Sukete with an incredulous look. The mother only shook her head in dismay. "I hate it when Edo tells her scary stories."

The sound of Myddish words, spoken through a croaky, tired voice, announced Fyuren's presence at the door. "What's Hyper Beanbag's problem?"

Neliya scoffed, "Hyper Beanbag? You looking to give her a nickname, Grumbleguts?"

"It's only fair," replied the boy, who once again looked in desperate need of a bath and good night's sleep. "What's wrong with her?"

Sheepishly, Neliya rolled back her sleeve to reveal the bandage. Fyuren froze, his entire face a petrified expression of horror.

"You idiot! A sting?" he roared. "You have any idea what alien bugs can do to us? You want to die here?"

Neliya tried to find a window to calm her friend amid the onslaught. But be it the lack of sleep or the stress of repeated failure to return home, Fyuren's savagery hit a new high. The berating stopped unexpectedly and Neliya looked up to see Fyuren, his arms held firmly against his chest by Edo.

"Calm self," he said quietly.

The Mydian's aggression grew, before his breathing slowed. When Fyuren was calm, Edo released him. Traces of confusion flashed in and out of his vacant eyes. Neliya approached him, "Are you alright?"

"Sorry, it was another outburst," he said.

"A bad one," replied Neliya.

"The sting alright?" asked Fyuren.

"Yes, it's fine. Sukete put something on it. You should thank Edo for getting you out of it without bashing you up."

Embarrassed, Fyuren turned to regard Edo. Then he asked over his shoulder, "How do you say sorry?" Neliya whispered the word in his ear, and he timidly uttered, "*Ubomatasu.*"

The room simmered with an embarrassing silence, which Odentii's appearance at the door broke.

"What's going on here?" asked Odentii jovially.

"Nothing, father," said Edo with a smile. "Welcome back."

Odentii turned to Fyuren and in Myddish he said, "I have something for you."

He took Fyuren and Neliya to the workshop. By the door sat a thick canvas bag full of scrolls and books. He took the largest scroll and rolled it out on top of Fyuren's mountain of hardware. The writing was completely different from any Aimorein text Neliya had seen, but both she and Fyuren recognised the concentric and criss-crossing ellipses drawn onto the paper.

"This is map of solar system," said Odentii. "Obviously, you won't be able to read Kehain Tao-Hua but I can help."

Fyuren exchanged excited glances with Neliya. "Well, let's get to work."

19 | Rii-tuan's hair's been eaten!

Neliya pulled back her waist-length locks, clutching her nose while grinning triumphantly.

"Found another one!" she yelled. Edo stood up from behind the brush of sliver-garlic and brought his scythe. He looked at the mass of furry mould smeared across the stalks of several plants, and sliced them away at the roots. Tendrils of green-white ooze tethered the stalk to the ground.

"This one's gone all the way into the roots," said Edo, half annoyed, half dismayed. "At least we'll have plenty of feed for the mashi."

Neliya bent down with a hand spade and hacked the root out of the earth, tossing the herbaceous tangle into a nearby basket. They pulled apart the neighbouring stalks, looking for more infected plants.

"Can't smell any more?" asked Edo.

Neliya's nose scrunched, "It's probably overpowered by what's in the basket already."

"Any chance Fyuren would come up with a nice *kusin* killer? Something we could just spray on the whole crop?"

"And give him an even bigger sleep debt?" jibed Neliya. "Besides, it's good enough that I can smell it better than you."

"I can't smell it at all," chuckled Edo.

"Makes me want to vomit," rasped Neliya through strained breaths.

"Let's take a break then," said Edo. "And I think father wants a hand with loading the last quarter crop."

Neliya followed Edo toward where Odentii stood waving for help. She quickly passed him to avoid the nose-piercing smell from the basket Edo carried. Not that it was as bad as the *Ranegr*'s tokamak cooling pipes, but it was close. She started helping Odentii load the tractor with crates of sliver-garlic, while Edo tossed the infected stalks in the animal feed.

"I'll sow barley next season, so don't worry about kusin fungus," said Odentii upon noticing Neliya's stifled gags. He turned to Edo. "Set up for *haisou* and we'll practice when I get back."

Neliya and Edo heaved the last of the crates onto the tractor, and waved to Odentii as he left for the village's loading silo. Then they looked to each other.

"I'm in the mood for some tea," said Edo.

Sukete's calling interrupted them. "Neliya? Could you go collect some kindling?"

"Ugh, and I was hoping for a break and some tea," Neliya murmured.

"How about I help you," said Edo, his gaze concealing a certain boldness that made Neliya giddy. She was about to refuse, but Edo cut her off. "Come on, it'll get done faster that way. Grab the *youkuro* and let's go."

Neliya acquiesced with a smile. Picking up the kindling basket on the front porch, she slung its straps over her shoulder and headed for the woods.

"It's not too heavy?" Edo asked when the youkuro reached half capacity.

"Nope," Neliya grunted, shifting the weight slightly.

Edo shrugged, and kept on walking down the path. His eyes drifted toward the sky. "Are you looking forward to finding your ship?"

"Yeah," Neliya droned.

"That doesn't sound very excited," intoned Edo. "Perhaps you like it here?"

"Perhaps the youkuro is just dampening my spirits," replied Neliya curtly.

"Then let me take it," chided Edo.

Neliya protested, but silently was glad for the respite. Edo's face strained a little as he took on the sudden load, but he quickly adjusted his balance and began moving forward.

"Now are you excited about finding the ship?" Edo pressed.

"Yes," said Neliya irately, shoving a few more sticks in the basket.

"You still don't sound excited," returned Edo with a grin.

Neliya wanted to argue more, looking for other explanations for her lack of enthusiasm, but found nothing convincing. Finally, with a fume of frustration, she said, "When Fyuren actually finds the ship, then I'll be excited."

"Understood, Rii-tuan," chuckled Edo. Neliya shot him a menacing look, which she couldn't hold when her glance met his. Both faces cracked into laughter. As they sobered, Edo looked to the sky and mumbled, "I should get back soon and set up the haisou targets."

Neliya frowned, "What's haisou?"

"Oh, it's a sport Father and I play," Edo explained. "You use a *nauya* – a wooden stick with a string hooked to both ends – and shoot smaller sticks at a target. Grandfather Jikyo, Father, and I participate in a tournament every year. But we haven't had a chance to practice because certain people fell out of the sky."

Neliya pursed her lips. "Sorry for bothering you." She pondered the game Edo described, and it elicited in her mind a recollection of a corkboard full of holes, barely able to hold the darts Allo had tried to throw into its centre.

"Maybe I could help you practice," she said. "On the *Ranegr*, we had a game called darts. You throw sharp things at a target in that game. I was *really* good at that game."

"Really?" asked Edo.

"The first time I played, I hit the centre first try," said Neliya with a grin. "And my friend Jugga said it was just luck and told me to go again. I went again, and still got it. Jugga was looking really silly, so he bet that I couldn't do it a third time. And I did. But he was a bit of a sore loser and poured a drink all over me."

"What?" exclaimed Edo, a disgusted look on his face.

Neliya giggled, "It's alright, I got him back." She laughed as she replayed their tickle war in her head. More memories resurfaced: of Zeers and Fyuren dancing and singing along with the crew; of meals on the *Ranegr* shuttle, during their mining excursion; and of a landslide on a rogue planet.

Neliya stopped dead in her tracks, and her knees shook. Her leg, marred with an ugly scar, tingled as scraps of memories, without her permission, assembled themselves into a horrific image of beloved friends, crushed to death under a thousand tonnes of temellut ore. Her face twisted into a flushed mess and she cupped her lips. When Edo nervously asked her what was wrong, she cringed to hold back her grief and push away her bad memories.

But they came out anyway.

She felt two hands on her shoulders. She looked up into Edo's face. The youkuro sat beside them, and without it he had risen to his full height.

"Whenever my mother is upset, my father does this to calm her," he said, before gently pulling her into his embrace. Neliya's mind flooded with thoughts, triggered by the texture of his jacket against her face. At first she was filled with visions of being in Zeers' arms. Then, slowly, the sensations changed to something different, not unlike the alien air of Ondyarii filling her lungs after so long on the *Ranegr*. Her arms moved on their own, dragging her recalcitrant mind with them, reciprocating Edo's embrace.

This will make you feel better, her limbs roared at her grieving mind. And it did.

"Uah! Rii-tuan and Brother Edo are hugging!" screeched Uenda from above. Before the pair could look up, Uenda was already halfway down a tall tree, a canvas bag in her hand. "Rii-tuan! Did Brother Edo tell you he likes you?" Before the Mydian could get a sentence out, Uenda let out an overjoyed, "Wahoo! Big Brother Edo! Rii-tuan! *Sayei! Sayei! Sayei!*"

"*Sayen*, you idiot," corrected Edo.

"Oh! Sayen, you say," exclaimed Uenda, her grin even bigger. She proceeded to dance around the pair, repeating the word Neliya assumed meant *love*, until Edo tripped her, and held her upside down.

"Look at this, Neliya," he bellowed like Jugga. "We got us some nice wild game for dinner, eh?" He carried the shrieking, giggling creature down the path, bickering with his little sister in a way that drew out Neliya's bliss like a narcotic salve. Edo looked over his shoulder at her, a brief genuine smile cracking through his jesting, and the idea of him confessing his love to her very quickly appealed to her. She shook it off, hoisted the youkuro onto her shoulders, and followed them.

A bit further up the path Edo released his sister and she galloped out in front of him toward the house. Edo lagged a little to match Neliya's pace, and by the time they reached the front porch, Uenda had already spilled the gossip about their hugging in the woods. Sukete was beaming between her chuckles as Edo tried to explain what really happened, only to receive a chiding about gentlemanly behaviour from Odentii. Neliya would have joined in the commotion, but she was much too busy trying to untangle her hair from the weaving of the youkuro. When she finally made it to the door, her blonde-tipped brown hair was a complete frazzle.

"Uah! Rii-tuan's hair's been eaten," exclaimed Uenda.

Sukete grimaced. "Neliya, maybe we should cut your hair so you don't have this problem again."

"That would be nice," said Neliya. Then, the topic of hair reminded her of things she'd noticed when she ran errands in the village. "Actually … I was just hoping," Neliya stammered as she rubbed her frazzled hair between her fingers, "I've noticed girls going around the village with their hair in a certain way. Short hair and a really long braid out the back."

Sukete smiled. "Would you like that?"

Neliya nodded excitedly. Sukete led her to the front porch and knelt behind her. She unfolded a bag full of scissors, brushes, and combs, along with a bag of coloured beads and a length of bright orange cloth. Sukete huffed a moment as she studied the mass of hair before her, even taking a moment to gently stroke it, before she started brushing it out.

Neliya sat quietly, though her insides writhed giddily at the pull of the brush and Sukete's hands through her hair. The only person to touch her hair was Kagoolie, when the elderly Earthen had washed it long ago, and it was comforting and nice. This felt quite different.

"Do Mydians style their own hair?" asked Sukete.

"No, we usually pay someone to do it," replied Neliya. "But they were always so scratchy and did everything as fast as they could so they get more customers. But now, someone's taking their time."

"Mummy does my hair a lot," said Uenda, who sat against the porch railing with her knees to her chest, smiling at the scene.

"Like a mother should," said Neliya.

"Your mother never did this?" asked Sukete.

"Never," said Neliya. "She worked all the time, and I guess I never thought I needed it. But now, I really think I've been missing something."

Sukete smiled warmly. She set the brush down and picked up some scissors.

"I'm going to start cutting now," she said.

Neliya remained absolutely still. Her ears filled with the sounds of keratin strands giving way to the blades, like the tearing of old paper. The remains of her blonde hair wafted unceremoniously to the floor, having lost any meaning to her. The sounds and smells of the world around her, the fading late afternoon sun, and the hands of the woman brushing away dust-like hair fragments occupied her every ounce of attention.

Kagoolie was comforting; Zeers' arm around her felt romantic; being with her friends was fun and calming. But never before had she felt this. Part of her wondered, very silently amidst her smiling, whether this what she always wanted whenever she got the rare hug from the mother she could barely remember.

Not comfort or romance ... Just motherly ...

Unfortunately, Neliya had little chance to enjoy the moment before Uenda bellowed, "Hey, Mummy, can you do my hair in that style too?"

"No, Uenda," said Sukete firmly. "You're too young."

Uenda pouted, "No fair. I want pretty hair like Rii-tuan."

"No, you need to wait," said Sukete. Uenda frowned, before stomping off the porch and toward Odentii and Edo, who had set up targets on the field and were preparing for their practice.

Neliya chuckled, "What do you mean by too young?"

"This style is for *Yupete*, the women who aren't married yet," said Sukete. "Uenda's too young for that. She's only three years old. When she turns eight, her body will become ready to bear children, and I will style her hair in this way. That's when I'll tell her about the ways between men and women."

Neliya's head suddenly felt like it was a pressure cooker, as her mind recalled certain school classes from another lifetime. Images popped into her head that she really wished she could keep out as her cheeks went crimson.

"Oh, I see," she coughed nervously. Another thought suddenly occurred to her. "Maybe you shouldn't be styling my hair then."

"I'm sure you'll be alright," said Sukete. "It'll be practice for me ... The styling at least." She too cleared her throat as she threaded her fingers through Neliya's untangled hair.

Be it curiosity or just idiocy, something possessed Neliya to say, "You can also tell me, if you like."

Sukete's cheeks reddened and she swallowed nervously. She slowly began describing to Neliya how Neiren marry and conceive their children, all the while styling the girl's long hair.

Neliya's heart thumped in her chest and her skin tingled with embarrassment and gaucheness. Soon, that gaucheness gave way to calmness, and a warm feeling of honesty.

"That sounds a lot like how Mydians work, too," she mumbled when Sukete finished. She looked over her shoulder at Sukete, whose cheeks were shaded pink. "But Mydian girls don't have that kind of monthly … *event*. It sounds really uncomfortable."

Sukete shrugged, "We get used to it." She eyed Uenda, cheering on Edo as he fired a long arrow from strung bow toward a target. She whispered to Neliya, "I think Uenda will complain a lot."

Neliya cringed at the thought of Uenda being in pain, but put it aside as Sukete returned to styling her hair. Her eyes fell on Edo, his brow knitted with concentration as he aimed another arrow at the target. The feeling of his arms around her warmed her entire body.

"You and Edo were hugging?" said Sukete, as if reading her mind.

Neliya choked on her breath. "Is that bad?"

"Of course not," said Sukete. "Edo is a good man, and that is how Odentii and I raised him. I'm glad he's trying to make you feel happy."

Neliya pursed her lips as she thought about what Sukete had explained to her about the Neiren. Her eyes couldn't help but fixate upon the boy on the field, and a wish started to materialise in her heart.

"Done!" announced Sukete. She held a mirror up in front of Neliya. Her auburn bangs, riddled with coloured beads, were still long, while much of her hair was cut quite short, though still longer than a boy's style. She ran her hands over her head, until she reached what felt like a tail protruding from the base of her skull. It was a long braid that reached midway down her back, interwoven with an orange cloth.

"It's beautiful!" Neliya murmured.

Later that night, as Fyuren worked in the workshop, a tray fell on the bench-top, perfectly on time. But the delivery girl didn't depart as quickly as he'd hoped.

"Are you gonna drag me to the bath again?" he mumbled after finishing another line of code.

"You don't stink, so I don't need to," returned the girl.

"Well, thanks for the food, but I'm busy," said Fyuren.

Neliya fumed, "Hey, take a break and have a look!"

Fyuren saved his work, turned to the girl, and his jaw dropped.

"Who are you?" he exclaimed.

"Very funny," said Neliya. She then twirled to show him her new look. "It's the style for unmarried women."

"With that look, you're not likely to be unmarried for long," said the bewildered boy, who flushed for the first time since Neliya had met him.

Neliya fawned with a grin, "Aren't you sweet, Fyuren?"

"I'm sure your boyfriend loves it too," retorted Fyuren. When Neliya shot him surprised look, he added, "I heard the commotion about you and that Edo guy hugging. I can pick up a few things, though I'm not as good as you."

"Edo was just trying to cheer me up," Neliya explained.

Fyuren just shrugged and went back to his work. Neliya sat next to him, looking over his shoulder at the disorganized jumble of circuits and parts strewn around the table in front of him.

"Sorry I didn't get a chance to ask, since it's harvest time, but have you found the *Ranegr*?" she asked.

"I think so." He brought up the results of his telemetry calculations. The screen presented a simple three-dimensional view of the solar system. Fyuren tapped a flickering widget. A blip blinked near the fourth planet, labelled *Sky*.

"You spelled Sikai wrong," said Neliya.

"Whatever," said Fyuren hastily. "The *Ranegr* was thrown out of the CTN here. Its trajectory at the time was going to take it almost directly into the sun. Then," – the blip collided with another blip – "the meteorite hits. There's really something to be said about whoever built that ship. Even though it got all smashed up, it still had enough sensors to record all the telemetry.

"From that, I was able to work out a number of possible courses the *Ranegr* could have taken." He tapped a few more widgets, and six curves erupted from the blip representing the *Ranegr*. Most of them went around the sun, in a long arc that, as Fyuren animated the view, brought them close to Sikai. "Assuming they stay on a free-fall path, in about four months, the *Ranegr* should pass close to Undarli."

"Ondyarii," corrected Neliya.

"I get it, Neliya, you're smart," jibed Fyuren. Neliya shot him a wide-eyed look. He continued his presentation. "If I can get the communicator working, we should be able to get them to send the shuttle to come and pick us up."

Neliya nodded slowly, a hesitantly positive look on her face. "We'll be able to get back."

"Well, there's still a problem," Fyuren added, his burdened brow furrowing with irritated concern. Neliya raised her eyebrows. "*Si-kai* is going to eclipse the sun in about a week, which'll block our line-of-sight."

"That's on *Chisafenu*, Winter's End," said Neliya. "Then we have a clear view?"

"Nope, the *Ranegr* will pass behind the sun around then. We'll only have a short time to communicate."

Neliya gave him a pat on the back, "I'm sure you can do it."

"Hopefully the TIM device is fine and we can try the jump again," said Fyuren, his weary eyes showing signs of excitement. "We could actually go home."

"Yeah," said Neliya, though her voice betrayed little enthusiasm.

Fyuren's jaw dropped. "What's the matter? You get me pumped, and then you're just, 'Yeah!'"

"Nah, I'm just a little tired," she murmured.

Her eyes wandered to the small pile of scrolled-up star maps underneath Fyuren's carry bag. Longing to see the unique writing on those maps, she reached for one of the scrolls. The pile collapsed gently, taking Fyuren's bag with it. An odd clattering sound caught her ears. Suddenly Fyuren snatched the bag away.

"What's in the bag?" she asked with an inquisitive chuckle. He gave no response. "Seriously, what's in it?"

"Nothing!" barked the boy.

Neliya heard the same clattering sound, this time from behind Fyuren. She caught a glimpse of the blue, glittering jewel as Fyuren snatched up the secret treasure and clasped it desperately. Her expression turned to bewilderment, and she prised Fyuren's hand open to see the large sapphire in his hand.

"Where did you get that?" she uttered.

"It was on the rogue planet, in that cave," he explained.

"You stole it?" exclaimed Neliya.

"Some ancient relic on an abandoned planet! Who's gonna miss it?" retorted Fyuren. He added with a stammer, "Also …"

Neliya cocked her head. "Also, what?" She leaned forward expectantly, but Fyuren shut his mouth and ended the conversation. She pressed a moment longer, but he shut her off, the sapphire still held preciously to his chest.

Don't press it, she ordered herself. *We don't need another outburst at this time. He'll tell me when he wants … he always does.*

She stood up and uttered, "If nothing else, it'll make a good souvenir."

20 | If you wanna save that kid …

A bleary-eyed Kajil rubbed his face. The dented metal cup of water before him looked tastier than a nice pint. The dryness of his throat goaded him to down the lot. His shaking hand brought the rim of the cup to his mouth and he took enough to wet his lips.

Hang on, Kajil! If Allo gets this drivin' on, you'll up 'n' endin' a whole tank.

"I'm almost there," rasped the voice of Allo through the console. Kajil focused on the screen in front of him. The static-ridden video feed was at least enough for Kajil to see Allo squeezing through a labyrinth of large gearing, barely a few metres from the vacuum of space. A single misstep and they'd be sucked out into the void, or crushed under the gears of the solar panel alignment mechanism.

"We ought to be wearing space suits," said Fenk, a few metres behind Allo. "How's our exposure looking, Kajil?"

"'Nother ten mins, then you'll ge' radio-burn'd," replied Kajil, eyeing the gauges and hoping he read them properly. He put his hand over the microphone and leaned toward the creature seated at the console nearby. "Oi, Swine! What's the bioplant's cap's charge lookin'?"

"We're at two-fifs," replied Swine, his face as sickly as Kajil's from hours of stress and staring at monitors. "If they can fix the broken stuff, caps should fill."

Considerin' our luck, that's a pretty massive 'if', thought Kajil. He eyed Swine's complexion, and cringed at the cracked lips and parched skin. He said, "Let me know if you need a break."

Kajil almost shrieked with panic when Allo let out a grunt that sounded like a cry of pain.

"There we go!" growled Allo with exhausted triumph. "We're as ready as we'll ever be."

"Then get in here, and we'll fire it up," said Kajil.

Allo and Fenk took a controller from their pockets and held the trigger. Their harnesses let out a hiss and the massive transmission structure accelerated away from them. They reached the aerie and purposefully marched into the solar control room. The repair teams had gathered there, and some checked their radiation exposure while others took seats at consoles.

"Bring the actuators online," said the engineer.

"Actuators online," said Swine, straightening in anticipation of success.

A high-pitched hum reverberated through the room, originating deep within the hull of the ship. Allo watched a feed of the actuator chamber, and saw the huge coiled motors revolving at an ever-increasing rate.

"Connect stage one, first gear," Allo proclaimed.

"Aye," bellowed Kajil, punching the command into the console.

There was a sudden shudder as the motor made contact, and it struggled a moment before speeding up again. All in the room held their breath, unwilling to release it until the job was done. Allo ordered the next stage, and the next, each new stage accompanied by an abrupt shake of the ship and a sharp intake of breath.

"We're almost out of power!" cried Swine, his voice barely audible over the intense screech.

Allo breathed in his resolve, and bellowed, "Final stage, third gear!"

As the gears changed, the drive shaft's speed faltered. The lights flickered and the actuators groaned under the sudden stress. Allo eyed the video feed, and saw sparks and explosions around the main coil assembly. The crew's optimism rose cautiously as the actuators screeched louder.

"Engage the final clutch," commanded Allo.

Kajil slammed his fist on the clutch control button, and the tremors ended in an unexpected jolt, followed by the spectacular sound of moving solar panels.

"Panels are coming into alignment," Kajil announced. "In three, two, one!"

The chassis endured one last jolt before the actuators were released. The massive gear structure spun freely for a moment before coming to a stop, and the room fell silent. Everyone stared expectantly at the screen, wringing their hands as if they held cloths soaked with their own anxiety. Their mood broke as gauges appeared on the screens before them, glowing with the humming influx of energy.

"We go' power," mumbled Kajil. Tapping a radio widget on the screen, he uttered, "Deloorie, how are the caps lookin'?"

There was a tense pause, followed by a static-filled response.

"Charging," came an abrasive female voice. "At forty-two per cent ...

forty-five per cent … And still risin'!"

With that, the room burst into applause and victorious roars. The crew embraced each other, giving pats on backs, and allowing themselves a jovial moment. Kajil leaned back in his chair, grabbed the cup in front of him, and downed it.

Cheers emanated from a bowl around which the *Ranegr*'s crew had gathered. A small but steady trickle of water flowed out of a faucet connected to the bioplant. A smaller group of men and women stood on a platform above the limping machine, emptying buckets of waste into the intake. The stench that had filled the habitable areas of the derelict ship would soon lift, along with the morale of the daunted crew.

Moments later, a few of the farming crew appeared to announce fertiliser coming out of the plant as well, and the promise of more food. Fenk joined the Drifter crew in celebration. They all laughed, chatted, and drank as if the water were fine liquor.

An angry bellow echoed through the hallway, drawing the attention of the farming crew in the next chamber over. Gast stood at the door to the bioplant chamber, staring down the crew with an expression of rage.

"What in the name of all things sacred and holy are you doing?" he screamed. "Most of your crew is dead, my son is goddess-knows-where, and those two children are stranded on some planet in the middle of nowhere. But you have water! Yahoo!"

Kajil spoke up, "Indra, we're jitters about Zeers, and Neliya and Fyuren. But we've been in the wars, too. We need some morale." He pushed through to the dripping pipe. "C'mon, lemme fill your bottle," he offered politely.

"I'll be for morale when I have the children I came for," spat Gast, his mechanical limb quaking with fury. "If you'd cared for them, you'd have let them go!" And then he strutted down the corridor.

A buzz of conversation flooded from the bioplant chamber, and much of it was from infuriated Nightshift workers.

"I oughta bash his head in with his own arm," barked one of them.

"That's enough," warned Swine.

"No, Swine, it's total pish, it is," protested the worker. "Didn't we work out them kiddies were on an 'abitable rock anyway? What's he wingin' about, poopin' on our happy time?"

"Yeah," interjected an equally indignant lizard creature, thrusting his cup forward in accord. "We took it from his little girl, and now we have to deal with him?"

"Nel ain't his daughter," said Kajil quietly before Swine could bellow a retort.

"And Fyuren's my son," droned Fenk, leaning against the frame of the doorway.

The crew exchanged glances with others in the room, seeing the solemn expressions on most faces, especially Kajil and Allo. A sudden shudder of understanding overfell them, and they withdrew.

Kajil took the chance, and turned to Allo. "Go sleep, then get life support goin'. If you can get us to the main hangar, great."

Allo nodded, but said nothing. He filled his cup with water and left. Then Kajil turned to Swine.

"Keep glimpses on your men," he said. Swine nodded, before herding the Nightshift workers away. Kajil then turned and went after Gast, pulling the despondent Fenk along with him. When they were out of ear-reach, he asked, "You feel the same?"

Fenk loosened the dirty worn-out collar of his Mydian military uniform. "Somewhat. I feel a little guilty for getting caught up in the party. Like I almost forgot my son was out there."

"You didn't forget, shut up!" chided Kajil. "You saw they'd landed safely before the scanners konked it. I saw in ya face, how chill'd you were. So don't act all guilty like that, or you won't be helpful anymore." Kajil started marching down the hall. "Now c'mon and help me knock some sense into that Military Alchemist."

These guys'd make great soldiers, thought Fenk with an incredulous smile.

They passed a group of Pebhasid soldiers, their blue uniforms, like Fenk's, sullied by weeks of ongoing hardship. Kajil asked them whether they'd seen Gast, and the leader pointed them in the right direction. The man's tone was genuine enough, but Fenk could sense tension simmering beneath.

"I once did joint manoeuvres with Ranians and Aquilans," he intoned when they were out of ear-reach. "You could feel it, even when they were being honest with each other, that they'd love the chance to bite each other's heads off."

"Can't really blame 'em, though," said Kajil. "Most of 'em were loyal to the last Pebhasid. And Gelfri off'ed him."

"But you've managed to make peace," said Fenk, checking around a corner before proceeding.

"Yeah, only 'cause we hated Gelfri too," snorted Kajil.

Fenk patted him on the shoulder. "Fyuren mentioned you'd be the new captain, didn't he? You do the job pretty well. You got enemy soldiers and those Nightshift workers to work together. You're a real leader, Mister Kajil."

"Whoa, just Kajil, mate," replied Kajil, shaking off the onslaught of compliments. "Plus, I dun't made this happen on me own. It was the kiddies. All of 'em. We all got together to help them, 'cause they helped us, and they didn't even wanna be here." Fenk smiled as he thought proudly of the person his son had become. "C'mon, man, we need to find that grumpy idiot," said Kajil, giving the pilot a slap on the shoulder that was more painful than playful. "Seriously, I pat Fyuren harder than that and he don't flinch!"

"He's a strong kid," said Fenk.

"Gets it from his Mum, eh?" asked Kajil.

Fenk gripped his head with worry. "Oh, by the goddess, Janice! I don't want to imagine how she's feeling right now."

From around the corner, Gast bellowed with an accusatory tone, "You can't even remember your wife now, Orthos?"

The ethereal orange glow of Gast's mechanical limb faintly illuminated the dark passageway, pulsating as it passed over a slight hull weakness. Metallic striae bled across the weakness like a suture, healing itself in response to his presence. Intimidated by the power of the Megin technology, Kajil and Fenk kept their distance until the Military Alchemist was finished.

"Well?" barked Gast, flexing his mechanical fingers to relax them.

Fenk cleared his throat. "With respect, sir, I have not forgotten Janice at all. She let me leave, knowing I may be gone a long time without contact. And I know my son lives on that planet. I have merely put both of them at the back of my mind, because I cannot return my son home if I am dead."

Gast did not respond.

Frustrated, Kajil added, "And you can't help Zeers if ya mind's as sewer'd as him." No response. Kajil chewed his lip thoughtfully, and a moment later his face twisted into a cocky smirk. "I mean, you can run ya wacky mind-power stunts to repair the hull. But can ya fix a kid's brain?"

Finally Gast yelled over his shoulder, "The time has passed! Zeers is beyond help now."

That got him, thought Kajil.

"Oh really?" he taunted, his arms crossed pompously. "Seems an excuse to be negative to me. Eh, Fenk?" The pilot beside him grew very nervous, and tried to put a stop to the taunting. Kajil continued, raising his voice over Fenk's pleading. "Y'know, it took his head gotten jammed with a brainwasher for Zeers to act like this. Maybe *you're* a little screwy'd as well." Gast's limb began to hum, a faint orange hue brewing within its mechanisms. Kajil gulped, and steeled his resolve. "I'm wonderin' if Littles really did go bad. If I were him, *I'd* sell out *my* friends to keep away from you."

That was the last straw. Kajil suddenly found his weight jerked down the corridor. He flew through the air toward Gast's outstretched glowing limb.

"Commander Indra!" shouted Fenk desperately.

Kajil's grin widened, and he clenched his fist, landing a crushing blow directly on Gast's face. The Military Alchemist was slammed back-first against the wall, and crumpled to the floor in a daze. Kajil landed next to the man, shaken from the sudden stop. Gast regained his sense quickly and lunged at his attacker. Kajil beat him to the blow, head-butting him, and wrestling with him. Gast's glare was rank with utter rage, which made the fight all-too-easy for his opponent. Kajil allowed him the upper-hand for a moment, letting himself be pushed back against the bulkhead. Gast raised his limb, and with his mind activated it.

"Wrong move, Littles Senior," spat Kajil cockily. He clamped his broad hand around the wrist of the weaponed appendage and deflected it. Gast yelped at the sudden stress on his joints, and weakened his grip. Kajil drove him, face first, into the floor, holding the limb behind his back.

He overcame a Military Alchemist, Fenk marvelled. *Who is this man?*

Gast struggled, but Kajil forced him down.

"Shut up or I tear it off!" barked Kajil. Gast continued to protest, but he found his assailant too strong and heavy to overcome in his position. Kajil leaned down, lowering his voice. "Not that crash hot, are ya?" his voice bubbled rebukingly, without taunt. "Ya woman karks it, you can't hack it, could ya?"

"What would you know?" growled Gast.

Kajil sneered. "What Zeers told me: Dumped him with a friend, and hardly ever see him. Absorbed in your work, too."

"I work to provide for him! What more can he ask for?" retorted Gast.

Kajil leaned down to grumble into his ear, "How about not feelin' like you blame him for what happened to her?" Gast's heart skipped a beat, his eyes shaking visibly with stunned realisation. Kajil tried not to grin triumphantly, and forced a stern expression upon his face. "If you wanna save that kid, I'd start with tellin' him that."

With that, Kajil released the man, and pulled him to his feet.

"And one more thing," he said, his hand still firmly gripping Gast's. "If we wanna knees-up, we're bloody-well gonna. Got it?"

Gast huffed, and nodded.

Kajil walked away, past a flabbergasted Fenk and around the corner. Fenk apologised to the superior officer for not intervening, but Gast wasn't listening. The pilot followed Kajil down the hall, and turned a corner to find the man with his back against the wall. His face was pale with pent-up terror.

"Thought I was gonna die back there," he rasped.

Fenk could only wonder, *Who **is** this man?*

Before Fenk could speak, Deloorie appeared around the corner, showing cracks of a smile for the first time in weeks.

"Fyuren's made contact," she cried.

21 | What's on the to-do list?

Kajil burst onto the auxiliary bridge, Fenk and Gast in tow. Dennie sat at the communications terminal, nervously twisting dials and punching commands into the interface to clear up the signal. Allo and Kagoolie stood behind her, wearing smiles like children about to meet a long lost and much loved relative.

Dennie delicately twisted a dial, listening carefully to the feed in the headphones. "That's the best I can do," she said, pulling the headphones out of the jack. A static-filled channel burst from the speakers, and interlaced within was a voice they had longed to hear.

"Can you hear me now?" asked Fyuren's disembodied voice.

"Yes!" roared the group in unison.

"Agh! Too loud," came a second voice.

"Neliya, dat you?" asked Kagoolie.

"Kagoolie!" exclaimed Neliya. "You're alright!"

"You too, eh!" replied the old lady. "Deloorie is here too, and Kajil, *and* Gast and Fenk too."

"Dad!" cried Fyuren's voice.

Fenk sniffed away the reddening of his eyes. "Fyuren, I'll never get over how smart you are. But the question is, are *you* and Neliya alright?"

"We're fine," said Fyuren. "I'd have called sooner, but I had to fix my tablet, and we had a bit of a language barrier to get around."

"Language barrier?" asked Kajil. "That planet got people on it?"

"Lovely people," said Neliya. "They're called Neiren—"

Fyuren's voice quickly cut in. "Before she starts telling stories, I need Allo to get together all the data on the status of the ship and the TIM device."

Allo sprinted to a console nearby and compiled Fyuren's request.

Meanwhile, the others listened intently as the children told their story. By the end of it, most wore relieved smiles on their faces, including Gast.

Having arrived halfway through the telling, Swine was the first to speak up. "We thought you two'd be stuck on a wilderness! Huntin' for food and stuff."

"Ugh! You think we'd have called so soon if that'd happened?" returned Fyuren. "Hey, Allo, how's the download coming?"

"Going," Allo drew out the word, "now! It should be transmitting now."

"Yep, it's coming now," replied Fyuren. "Now listen up. At night we can still communicate, but the signal will be a bit degraded. But in about five days, you'll be on the other side of the sun and won't be in range for another three months or so."

Fenk's mouth was agape, and he felt like he was hanging from a frayed thread over a chasm.

Gast, having recovered from his thrashing at Kajil's hand, spoke up shrewdly, "You didn't hack together a comm-link just to say 'hello.'"

"Nope," said Fyuren. "You guys have got five days of me helping to get the *Ranegr* working again. After that, you'll have three months to finish it. In four months, the *Ranegr* will pass close to this planet, and you can come pick us up. And then, we go after Zeers."

Members of the group exchanged glances, and grew confident at the sound of the prodigy's voice. Then they turned to Fenk.

He leaned toward the console and said, "Okay, Fyuren, what's on the to-do list?"

Fenk floated down the corridor, holding to the toolbox tightly. His zero-gravity training notwithstanding, the ancient ship and the equally aged space-suit that clung to his skin made for a disquieting experience.

"Alright, Dad," said Fyuren's crackly voice. "Things should start looking familiar now."

"Yeah, even though I've only seen this place once," replied Fenk. The rays cast by his helmet-mounted torches diffused in the space around him, casting shadows about that reminded him of tense scenes in horror films. He distracted himself by conversing with his son.

"Haven't had a chance to ask," he said. "The Andor's a nice family?"

"Nice enough, if a little nosy," replied Fyuren.

"Nosy?" asked Fenk.

"They won't just let me work," whined Fyuren. "Especially hyper beanbag, Wenda."

Fenk grimaced. "But they're feeding you, right? And they let you use their workshop too. You can't blame them for being curious. You're the one in their space, after all."

Fyuren fumed, "Yeah, but it's so bothersome to explain things to people who wouldn't understand me even if I spoke the language!"

"Why don't you try to learn the language?" Fenk suggested, grunting slightly as he pushed aside some floating junk. "Maybe Odentir can be an assistant."

"Dad, I don't need an assistant," Fyuren retorted curtly. "I shouldn't even be here. I should be there with you, doing the job I'm making you do."

"Ha, didn't you learn your lesson?" scoffed Fenk, allowing himself a snide grin amidst his deep breathing. "Didn't Kagoolie say it? Thing's aren't always how you suppose them. You're there; I'm here. And if I were you, I'd spend some time learning about the planet you're on. It's people and culture."

The sound of his son's sighs bubbled through the speaker. "I'll try," mumbled Fyuren. "You should be near the chamber now."

Fenk looked up from the fallen truss over which he stepped, and saw the chamber. Streaks of blue light flooded the room, speckled with dust particles suspended in the space within. "It's like moonlight," he mused.

"Oh, crap, I didn't think of this," grumbled Fyuren. "That's not moonlight. The meteor must've busted a few holes in the hull around there. No wonder we couldn't get the life-support up. The *Ranegr* is near a comet catcher near the sun ... I think Odentir called it Komoroi."

Fenk peered out into the chamber, and his gaze wandered about the room. The hull sported several tears, with visible melting and blistering around the edges. The areas illuminated were equally damaged by radiation.

"A gas giant reflecting light from the sun, and I'm right in the middle of it. What could go wrong?"

"Dad, don't worry about it. We'll look for another way."

"It's taken us hours to get here," replied Fenk. "I'll just get the thing now."

"The radiation will set you on fire," snapped Fyuren.

"Everyone else is doing their job, so I gotta do mine," said Fenk, breathing deeply and exhaling his resolve. He climbed down the support trusses toward the floor. He looked over and saw the TIM device, safely in the shadows of the radiation. Like a nimble lizard, he moved along the litter. His heart started to race as he neared the radiation spots, and the frayed wires and broken support structures melting under the relentless onslaught. Then he saw a gnarled hand, protruding from beneath the rubble. He gave it a pull, finding it connected to nothing. He inhaled sharply.

"Dad, everything alright?" came Fyuren's voice. "Your heart beat just–"

"Yeah, just found one of the missing crew – or part thereof," the pilot interjected. He gingerly held the hand in the light, and watched the skin bubble and melt like a roast in an oven. He dropped it in shock, watching the limb rapidly liquefy and disintegrate. "Ah, yep. Now I know what we're dealing with."

"Dad, turn back and find another way," said Fyuren.

Fenk ignored him, and scanned the area, licking his dry lips. "Fyuren, radio silence until I say. If I start screaming in agony, well … panic."

"Dad," Fyuren protested worriedly.

"Radio silence," snapped the pilot. In a determined business-like manner, he grabbed a handy stray cable, and used it to tie his toolbox to his back. Then he clambered toward an opening in the curtain of light. He curved his body to fit through the shadowy canals in his path, keeping his quarry in sight. His hand slipped and he rolled forward, coming very near a light streak. He stopped himself, but not before his helmet caught a small dose, and the glass deformed on the right side. Fenk pushed onward, his vision slightly hampered by the defect in his helmet's view. He cleared the radioactive minefield and leapt through the zero-gravity space toward the derelict device.

"I'm through," he blurted with strangled relief. "I slipped slightly and my helmet got zapped. Sight's a little blurry, but everything else is fine."

"Seriously, you shouldn't have done that," Fyuren urged.

"I'm here now. Let's get to work," Fenk commanded.

Fyuren obediently walked his father through the task of removing the amplifier housing around the TIM device. Metal plates and components were thrown away piece by piece. At first they were gigantic, almost as large as Fenk was tall, but they steadily grew smaller. The last components were hewn away, revealing the tiny TIM device held within.

"How does it look, Dad?" asked Fyuren, and the seriousness of the situation overcame them both.

"Umm," droned Fenk, looking over the unfamiliar device. "Can you get my helmet cameras working, so you can see for yourself?"

"Tried that tons of times when I was on-board." Another sigh reverberated through Fenk's helmet. "Let's just get it back to the aft bridge. Allo can take some pictures and send them over."

"Roger that," replied Fenk, grabbing a wrench and working at the device's scaffolding. He removed all the bolts and securing frames, and the device lifted out of the housing. "I can't believe how small this thing is. Have I missed something?"

"Nope, that's it," said Fyuren curtly. "Get it back to the bridge."

"Yes, sir," Fenk proclaimed, slinging the toolbox and retrieved device onto his back.

An unsettling pitter-patter, like the noise just before rain, emanated from the hull, along the chassis, and through Fenk's feet. It wasn't rain that followed, but hail. Bullet-like particles screamed through the chamber, widening the holes above and making new holes along the corridors Fenk had come through. Fenk dived for cover just in time to see radiation flood through the chamber and adjacent passageways. He was trapped.

"Fyuren, can you find me another way around?" he asked.

"You could head down the corridors on the upper level toward the resomators, and then meet up with Allo at the tokamak," replied Fyuren.

Fenk looked around, but couldn't see to the upper levels without stepping into the light, and that was out of the question. He eyed the discarded TIM casing, its metal surface taking the full brunt of the radiation. The metal cast a decent shadow, enough for him to hide within.

"Got myself a little shield here," he announced. "I'm going to use it to get a look at the upper levels."

"Careful, Dad," said Fyuren. "You're in the comet catcher's rings, so you're getting hammered with dust and small rocks."

"I'll keep that in mind," said the pilot, lifting the plate over his head like an umbrella. He breathed in, then pushed off the wall and into the light. Straining his stomach muscles he forced his body under the haven of the plate's shadow. He then peeked out slightly, to see the upper levels.

Every passageway he saw was flooded with the blue light, illuminating it gently as if it were as harmless as lamplight. Fenk quickly abandoned the plan of meeting with Allo, and looked toward the passageway from which he had entered. The debris had cut through several bulkheads before reaching the floor before him, glowing like embers in a fireplace. The radiation dribbled through the holes in small streams, but there were enough of them to be of concern.

"All the corridors are flooded with radiation and my shield won't fit in them," Fenk explained, looking around for another exit.

"Stay put, and Allo'll come with a plasma cutter," said Fyuren.

"I only have about twenty minutes of oh-two left," replied Fenk, his gaze falling upon the blanket of innocent blue light. He paused for a moment, and then looked up to the now gaping hole in the hull. He licked his lips almost mischievously. "I got a better idea," he murmured through grinning teeth. "I'll be a turtle-bug on the hull." He set down his shield and procured the grapple gun from the toolbox. He attached one end of its line to the harness around his waist. Then, with another length of cable, he fastened the shield to his back and the TIM device to his chest.

"Dad, forget it," said Fyuren.

"My air won't last long enough," protested Fenk, securing the shield in place.

"It's not just radiation out there, Dad," cried Fyuren. "Dust and space rocks too!"

"Fyuren, you're too much like your mother," said the pilot, shaking his head clear. "If there's one thing this trip should teach you, it's that if you always play it safe, you'll never learn anything new."

With no further thought, he pushed away from the platform. His heart thumped with excitement as his momentum carried him upwards through the layers of solar wind-beaten hull. Out the corner of his eye he saw the darkness of space, and hazy blue glimmers of the comet catcher's atmosphere. He looked down and saw the browning ceramic hull of the *Ranegr*.

"Now," he muttered, targeting the hull just above the breach and firing. The hook connected, and yanked him by the waist back to the ship. His landing accompanied a victorious grunt. "I'm on the hull," he announced. "And still in one piece."

"Dad, you're an idiot," chided Fyuren. "I'm telling Mum when we get back."

Fenk couldn't hold back chuckles, though it pained him with his doubled over posture. "Okay, Fyuren, tell me where to go."

Fyuren directed him to an airlock on a side of the ship facing neither the sun nor the comet catcher. He moved with the grapple gun, firing at visible targets and climbing along the rope, the shield protecting him like a turtle shell. When he passed into the ship's shadow he was glad to be rid of the bulky shield. The airlock, luckily, still had some power in its circuits, and granted him access.

When the gravity generators kicked in, Fenk fell to the floor, overcome by dizziness and the unexpected weight of the TIM device strapped to his chest. He crawled out of the airlock and leaned against the wall of the corridor. He sat quietly for a moment, then pulled himself to his feet, lifted the TIM device over his shoulder, and headed down the corridor.

As he rounded a corner, Fenk heard whispering from a room nearby. At first he paid it no mind, until his ears burned with the mention of tunnellers. Curious, he peeked into the room, and saw a trio in Pebhasid uniforms hovering around screen and keyboard, connected to a device emitting a soft green hue.

That's an IMS console, he thought.

He squinted to read the chat screen, and gasped upon recognising with whom they were communicating. The soldiers swivelled in alarm. One of them suddenly grabbed a heavy piece of broken bulkhead and smashed the console, while the other two lunged at Fenk. He dodged one and brought his elbow down upon his unguarded head. He leapt out of the way of the second soldier, and slammed the communicator button on his wrist.

"Alarm! Alarm! Pebhasid soldiers have an interstellar communicator and have alerted hostiles to our location. Assistance to Level Nine Subjunction Twenty-Three!"

The enemies, determined to silence him, threw spirited punches and blows. But they were no match for the trained Mydian soldier. Then the third entered the fray with a knife drawn, and Fenk found himself overcome. But the knife suddenly flew out of the foe's hand as if moving on its own, and plunged into the man's own neck. His comrades stopped, horrified, as he slumped, gurgling for his final breaths. They turned to see Gast, his Megin limb outstretched. With a wave of the mechanical arm, the knife launched itself into the next soldier, and he fell. The knife stopped short of bisecting the third man's neck, and he backed against the wall, trembling in awe and panic.

Fenk gave a nod of gratitude in Gast's direction, before both men turned to their prisoner.

"He was using an IMS," Fenk explained. "I saw what they were writing and to whom."

"You won't find out how much they know," barked the soldier, a grin on his face though his voice was riddled with fear. "I destroyed the console, and I'll die before I tell you."

"No, you'll tell first," rasped the Military Alchemist.

22 | Tragedies happen all the time

Deloorie's shaking hand reached for the wrong wrench, yet again. She threw it back with a growl.

Damn irrigation pump, she cursed. *Why won't you work for more than a minute?!*

She finally found the right wrench, and despite her trembling, she managed to get it fitted to the bolt. She panted dryly and began to push on the valve.

I just have to get this valve open. This damn, bloody, stupid rusted valve!

The wrench slipped, and she let out a screech of pain. The farming crew stood erect with alarm, some coming to her aid. She stood there, grimacing with frustration, cradling a deep gash that started from her hand and ran down her wrist. Blood dribbled in a steady flow along her fingers and puddled on the floor.

"Get away! I don't need help!" roared Deloorie, pushing the others away with her free hand while the other dangled by her side.

Kagoolie put herself between Deloorie and the crew, and stared intently at her. Deloorie's exhausted gaze met the old lady's determined eyes.

"Ya'll drain out," said the old lady curtly. "Ya won't live 'til the crops flower."

"Just give me a bandage," barked Deloorie, who saw nothing but red.

Kagoolie slapped her forcefully. Deloorie returned an indignant gaze, but was struck again before she could protest. Kagoolie, frail though she seemed, continued to assail her with painful-looking strikes. Finally, Deloorie was silent.

"Get into da next room and clean dat cut," barked the old lady.

Deloorie pulled herself to her feet, dazed from the onslaught no one would have expected from the kindly old lady. She trudged out of the room, her eyes glued to the floor so as avoid the gazes of her kin. She squeezed her wounded hand tightly while running it under the flowing water in the bioplant chamber. Kagoolie appeared and forced her to sit on a stool. Despite her own fury at the younger woman's behaviour, Kagoolie was gentle as she applied some disinfectant, the bite of which made Deloorie twitch.

"It was horrible," said Kagoolie. "Dat's clear. But you ain't gunna pretend only you lost someone."

As if her words were a herald, Gast entered the room, moving toward the water faucet for a much-needed drink. Her point made, Kagoolie stood, glaring down at the woman. Deloorie's lips pursed to stifle her protests, her brow furrowed in an ugly hybrid of anger and sorrow.

Kagoolie said, "Think about da kiddies, Neliya 'n' Fyuren. And Zeers too. Dey need our help now." Walking toward the door, she added, "Eat something. You ain't had your ration fa days." And then she left Deloorie alone with the Military Alchemist. At first she paid him no mind, her own pensive mind swimming with angst and fatigue, the nerves along her arm burning.

Massaging the interface between his muscles and his mechanical limb, Gast strolled toward the ration cabinet and took two small biscuits from it. One he bit down on, offering the other to Deloorie. She took the food and nibbled at it, but said nothing. Gast leaned against the bioplant, which silently chugged away processing effluent into its vital elements.

After a few minutes of silence, he finally said, "Tragedies happen all the time. Children lose parents, men lose wives, women lose husbands, and people lose friends. Sometimes they're taken away from us, other times they just go. And we never find out where they went or what happened to them. Some people can't deal with that, no matter what training they've undergone, no matter how strong or smart they think they are."

Deloorie began to fidget.

Gast went on, "Eventually, we find ourselves shunning anything that reminds us of them, seeking out a place where the ones we love don't exist. But they aren't havens; they're prisons. We never truly realise it until we lose more things precious to us."

Deloorie opened her mouth to speak, but it was thick with grief and she gave a harsh cough. Then she said, "There's gotta be a way to save Zeers." Her tone was flat and half-hearted, and to Gast it sounded like a recording of his own thoughts played aloud.

"That's what I'm working towards," he said. "What are you working towards?"

Deloorie gave no answer, and Gast didn't expect one. He instead left her to her thoughts.

The auxiliary bridge was littered with people, but few were actually doing much. Groups of Nightshift, farm, and hangar crew played games with salvaged playing cards or sat quietly around small heater lamps. Others managed the systems that still functioned. The rest of the crew had turned to looking for more potential traitors among the Pebhasid soldiers.

Allo studied the sabotaged IMS the Pebhasid soldiers had brought on-board. Dennie sat at the communications terminal, transferring photos of the TIM device to the planet.

"Kajil and everyone still with the soldier," came Fyuren's voice through the radio.

"Yep," replied Dennie.

"They'd better hurry up," said Fyuren, his voice growing impatient. "We're about an hour and a half to blackout."

"Shouldn't you be getting ready for that party? Cheese-a-feeno?" asked Dennie.

"Yeah, Edo lent me some of his old clothes," said Fyuren. Dennie could hear an excited little girl, speaking unintelligible gibberish. Neliya's voice followed, speaking the same alien tongue.

"Neliya sounds like she's settling in just fine," chuckled Dennie. "She mightn't want to leave."

Fyuren moaned, "Don't say that. I don't want another Littles."

Dennie chuckled, recalling fondly the first time she'd actually spoken to her two favourite crew members. It had been so long since then.

Before this crazy fiasco, I was just a kitchen hand. Now I'm a comms officer.

She was snapped out of her reverie by a blinking alert on the screen. "The images should have finished transferring."

"Yep, got 'em," said Fyuren. An incoherent mumble of verbalised thought crackled through the channel before he said, "TIM device looks just like I left it. I can't see anything wrong with it, really. But I'll need to look at it in better detail once we get back on board."

Allo stood up from the broken IMS with a sigh.

"Fyuren," he said into the microphone. "That little bugger done a real number on the IMS. Whole thing's croaked."

"Damn! We could have used that to contact the *Othala*," Fyuren growled. "What about the secondary storage? If that's fine, we can find out what they were talking about."

Allo smacked his head. "Duh. I shoulda thought of that."

"Maybe 'cause you ain't snooz'd for a week," mumbled Dennie. Allo paid her jibe no attention and fumbled around with the IMS circuitry, looking under and around the chassis of the device, until he found a small module slotted to the motherboard.

"Got it!" he exclaimed, prising the palm-sized device from its mooring. He scurried to a nearby terminal. Blinking fiercely and sighing as if it would shoo away his fatigue, Allo slotted the drive into the terminal and began scanning the contents. He finally managed to locate the logs despite his hazy mind, but was met with defeat when he saw the contents. "Dammit, they're all encoded," he groaned, rubbing his drained face.

"Allo, transfer the files to me, and go to sleep. You're no use to us the way you are," said Fyuren.

Allo breathed deeply, rubbing his hands over his face and through his hair, before letting them drop to his sides. The boy's words overwhelmed his desire to work any further.

"Ain't you come a long way, Shorts," he chuckled.

"You and Malse were good teachers," replied the boy.

Allo walked back to the console, and haphazardly typed the commands to initiate the data transfer. Then he trudged toward the barracks down the hall, ignoring four individuals who passed him with purpose.

"Fyuren's on the channel?" Gast asked. Dennie nodded.

"Mute it," snapped Kajil. "He dun't need to know this just yet."

Dennie tapped the blue silencer widget on her terminal, and turned to listen. The crew directed their attention at the three men and Swine who appeared behind them, rubbing his hands clean as if retiring from a strenuous workout.

"So, what'd Pebha-scum say?" asked a Nightshift worker.

"It's Gelfri," announced Kajil. "He go' our pos, and he's comin' for the *Ranegr.*"

A frustrated cry radiated through the group. Panic settled in next, and some were quick to throw accusations at Kajil.

"You said we hadda work with them Pebhasid mutts," barked one disgruntled miner.

"We shoulda blown 'em out the airlock like we did with all stowaways!" roared a slime-covered Nightshift worker.

A repetitive banging began to overshadow all other argumentative noise in the room, and all eyes turned to Dennie. In her hand was a metal cup, which she whacked against the bulkhead. Her eyes glimmered with determination, and she bellowed, "Everybody calm down!" The room fell silent. The animosity withdrew into everyone's mind but did not disappear. When Dennie was satisfied she had everyone's attention, she turned to Kajil and asked, "He needs a TIM device to get here, otherwise it'd take yonks, right?"

"Yep. And Gelfri ain't go' one. Even if he did, chances are his mob won't get Fyuren's designs anyway," said Kajil.

"How do you know that Pebhasid scum wasn't pullin' a leg, eh?" asked a sceptical farmer. A murmur of unsteady concordance simmered through the room.

"Oh, he wasn't lyin'," said Swine with a grin. "Threaten a certain body part, and any man'll squeal like a stuck boar."

At that, the mood shifted into one of cautious laughter.

"So he won't bug us a while still," said Kajil, a smile riding on his face. "We've go' the shuttle, and the TIM device. We wait out the rest of this orbit, pick up the kids, Fyuren sets up the tunneller, 'n' we're outta here."

A miner laughed sarcastically, "Yeah, but Gelfri ain't stupid, he'll figure it out."

"And there's Zeers to worry about as well," said Deloorie, appearing behind Kajil with Kagoolie and a few other farmers in tow. She eyed Gast expectantly.

"Zeers is on my mind, yes," Gast admitted. "But I won't be able to save him if I'm dead or caught. So he must go to the back of my mind for now."

Fenk suppressed a smile as he added, "As for Gelfri, the traitor said his scientists were having trouble just working out where to begin on Fyuren's work. I think we'll have plenty of time."

The crew fell into thought, much of their concern dissipating but enough remaining to be noticeable on their faces.

"We gonna tell Fyuren?" asked Dennie.

"No," said Fenk curtly. "He's trying to work the ship's problems. He doesn't need anymore pressure."

Kajil and Gast nodded in agreement.

"Unmute it, and we'll talk the plan," said Kajil. "We got less than an hour to blackout."

Dennie pressed the silencer widget, and Fyuren's voice came through the speaker.

"Fyuren, you still there?" asked Fenk.

"Yep," replied Fyuren's voice, though it was slightly deepened and static accompanied it.

"Whoa, did your voice break?" jibed the pilot.

Fyuren curtly replied, "No, it's the time-dilation effect of the sun's gravity—"

"You're smart, we get it!" bellowed the crew.

"You've spent way too much time around Neliya and Zeers," stammered the prodigy. The channel crackled with the laughter of the crew, as well as a brief chuckle from Fyuren. Eventually there was quiet, and Kajil brought Fyuren back to point.

"The flight'll be tricky, since we don't want to alert the natives," said Fyuren. "Most neighbouring villages just think our pods were meteorites, and our hosts are trying to keep it that way. Based on the geography of the area, I think you should bring the shuttle along this descent vector."

A map popped up on Dennie's screen. A red line streaked upwards from an ocean at the equator, toward an island off the coast of a great continent. It came to rest at a small valley near the island coast.

"That'll be a tough landing," said Fenk nervously.

"I've tried it as many ways as I can think," replied Fyuren. "With this, you have the lowest chance of being seen."

Kajil shook his head. "Send ya calc's 'n' I'll get Allo to double check 'em."

"Will do." An electronic beep reverberated through the channel. "Ah, the logs have finished decrypting," said Fyuren.

"What logs?" asked Fenk.

"Logs from the Pebhasid soldier's IMS," replied the boy. Kajil glared at Dennie with wide-eyes.

"We sent it before you came," she said sheepishly.

"Fyuren, just send it back to us," said Fenk.

"But I wanna know how close Gelfri is to a working tunneller," said Fyuren. Kajil's eyes widened even more. Fenk inhaled sharply. Fyuren went on, "I figured Gelfri'd be coming. By the looks of the logs, he's nowhere near a working TIM device. So we'll have plenty of time." Fyuren's tone turned cautious. "Wait a minute. What does *jadhu sgan* mean?"

Brows furrowed in confusion. The word seemed familiar, but Kajil couldn't place it. Dennie, however, could. "It's old Pebhorda speak. Means 'Platter village.'"

Gast and Fenk's faces darkened, and they exchanged panicked glances.

"Platter village," said Fyuren. "It's a common name for a *Velhig*-class MCV. They're planning to commandeer a Mydian vessel."

"They can't have," exclaimed Fenk. "Velhig are short-range only … unless it's a–"

"Science vessel," interjected Fyuren. "It says here they're going after the *Kulanki*."

Kajil irately looked back and forth between the console and the two Mydian soldiers. "So what?"

"The *Kulanki* is researching tunnelling," said Fyuren. "I based my work on their research."

"So they *can* come and get us!" cried one of the farmers.

"Wait!" shouted Kajil, silencing the panic temporarily. To the console he said, "Fyuren, he still needs your work to take a big ship, right?"

"Of course, but he's got scientists whose work I based mine on," said Fyuren. "If he's got their help, we mightn't have much time."

Kajil cut off everyone else, and spoke – almost shouting – into the microphone, "But he ain't go' one yet?"

"No," snapped Fyuren. "We're still alright, nothing has changed."

Kajil stepped back from the console, his back wet with a cold sweat. Fenk's heart thumped like he was back in space again, trying to dodge meteorites and solar winds. Gast's limb trembled, and it strained his joints. The room was very tense for a long while.

"Nothing's changed, alright?" exclaimed Deloorie, shaking herself free of her trepidation. "We can still get out of here, before Gelfri even has a working tunneller." She gripped Kajil's shoulder, and looked him in the eye. "What do we need?"

Kajil sighed again, palming his face.

"We need power to the device," said Gast.

"Tokamak can't be restarted," added Fenk.

"Let me see if I can do something about it," said Fyuren. "We get the power working and we're out of here."

The channel began to decay with static. Fenk moved to the console in alarm. "Fyuren?"

"Channel's be ... off ... ooner than ... thought," said the disembodied voice of his son. "I'll g ... power sou ... orking, and we ... out of here. See you ... ew months."

The channel died.

23 | A cold, icy flame

Space rippled silently with the movement of a dome-shaped spacecraft, cutting a swath through the interstellar medium to be felt centuries from now on some distant planet's atmosphere. An MCV of the lower-end designs tenaciously carried within its dome a small village of scientists and their families. Swivelling antennae, sensitive to all manner of radiation, scanned the surroundings.

A pulse surged through space and struck the port antenna, sending electrical signals vibrating along the ceramic nerves of the vessel to a terminal, in front of which a bored navigator sat playing video games. Interstellar science missions were rarely eventful, hence the officer's twitch of fright at the pinging widget on his screen.

"Uh, Captain," he said, rousing the daydreaming commander.

"Report," yawned the captain, walking over with bleary eyes. His eyes grew more attentive as he studied the report. "Communications? Can the cruiser on the port flank confirm our readings?"

Following a brief back-and-forth, the communications officer replied, "Port flank confirms readings. One heavy cruiser class vessel and five … correction! *Six* frigates on intercept course. Drifter markings sighted."

The captain straightened up, elation in his face as obvious as a pimple on his nose.

Skirmish with Drifters! What a wonderful way to finish this dull trip, he thought.

"Inform the residents, sound general quarters," proclaimed the captain. "Helm, hard to port. The escort will assume defensive pattern three."

"Think we can beat 'em?" asked the cocky first officer.

"We're Mydians," replied the captain, as if it were an obvious victory.

The fleet came about, the inertial forces throwing off some of the residents as they reluctantly abandoned their work. Shelters filled with parents and children, while security staff prepared to defend the populace. Ions around the ships bubbled with the sound of weapons taking aim. The moment the ships came within range, the captain sent out a hailing beacon.

"This is the science MCV *Kulanki*. Please identify yourselves."

A man no older than seventeen appeared on the screen. Saggy manic eyes crowned an insidiously joyful grin so wide it twisted the tattoo above his eye. He responded with a snide tone. "This is Littles, Representative of the Pebhasid Gelfri the Great! This is his territory. Now if you cooperative clouts would be so kind as to walk out the airlock, that'd be groovy."

The captain scoffed with bewilderment at the boy's brazenness. "This is a science vessel belonging to the Mydian Republic. We mean no conflict, and will gladly set course out of this region of space."

"Oh, oh, I'm sorry," replied the Pebhasid captain sardonically. "I guess you didn't understand me. I meant to say, 'Your shiny ship is ours, so die please.'"

The captain's face grew stern, his jaw tightening.

"Clearly your intentions are hostile," he muttered. "Withdraw or we shall defend ourselves."

Littles chirped, "Ah, you're such a complacent captain. And so eager to please!"

The channel was suddenly severed.

Aboard the Pebhorda cruiser, Littles rose, twirling his long braid through his fingers. "Frigates one through four, locomote upon their lateral lines. Five to seven, assemble affront our anterior. The *Shar-Ranegr* will now advance!"

Fusion drives roared to life as two frigates approached the MCV from either side. Space lit up with the flashes of mass-driver cannons opening fire from both sides, pounding into the ceramic armour of the warring vessels. Littles fumbled with the gold buttons on his shirt as he eyed the approaching MCV and listened to the damage reports from the advancing frigates.

"Frigate three is suffering heavy fire, and the enemy fleet is pushing past them," reported the tactics officer.

"Frigate four sunk," announced the first officer.

Littles pursed his lips, bored with the lack of progress and the losses. "You know what? Stuff it. I don't care if those testy tunnellers don't like the EMP. Mine survived just fine."

"My lord, I would advise against it," said the first officer. He was silenced when a knife, drawn from Littles' belt, veered dangerously close to his jugular vein.

"Engineering," he muttered into his headset. "Are the capacitors charged?"

"Yes, my lord," came the reply.

"Frigates five through seven, get the flib out of my way!" roared Littles.

The frigates scrambled out of the line of fire, but not fast enough for their commander's taste. Littles' hand neared a blue flashing icon on the screen before him.

"My lord, they have not moved," warned the first officer.

"Who gives a toss?" rasped Littles, pressing his finger to the icon.

A white-hot discharge burst from the wings of the *Shar-Ranegr*, crackling the invisible gas in front of them. The *Kulanki* was engulfed in a cloud of sparks and shimmers, and gas burst from ruptures and tears in the hull. It began to pitch, as did most of the escort fleet. The ones that were not caught in the EMP now stood out-numbered. The battle devolved into a slaughter, playing out before Littles as he malevolently chortled:

> Here we are at the platter village,
> Lovely target to plunder and pillage.
> Oppose the Pebhasid, although you try,
> You'll meet me, and in the vacuum die.

Small dots flew from the *Kulanki* and vanished in puffs of purple light, sending a nostalgic tremor down Littles' spine. His eyes widened.

"Ha! Did I not say those tenacious tunnellers would be fine?" he exclaimed to his first officer.

"My lord," warned the helm, drawing Littles' attention to the viewport. A few of the escort's smaller ships began to accelerate, their course bringing them right at the *Shar-Ranegr*. Littles jumped up and down, clapping his hands together.

The first officer cried, "Shoot them down!"

With a horrendous snarl, Littles pulled the officer into a suffocating head-lock, and directed his eyes at the ships. They drew nearer, and accelerated. Upon Littles' order, the Pebhorda ships directed every cannon at the ramming ships, dissolving them in a barrage of fire. When there were no more ships, Littles giggled, and leaned toward the first officer's ear.

"I give the orders here!" He gave the first officer a peck on the cheek before releasing him, and delivered a punch between the man's eyes, knocking him to the ground. Then Littles straightened out his clothes and hair, and addressed the crew.

"Open a channel on the emergency band!" he snapped. The radio crackled with sounds of battle damage, explosions, and crewmen moaning in pain and dismay. "This is Littles of the Pebhasid Gelfri. Your escort fleet has been neutralised. Lay down all weapons and surrender, and you won't be treated *too* harshly. Any turgid tunnellers tryin' to take-off will be totalled by my terrific turrets." The channel closed without response. Then Littles crouched down to look at his semi-conscious first officer. "I want boarding parties and skeleton crews ready yesterday. Bring me every tunneller they have left."

Littles stretched out on the deep and comfortable chair he'd reappropriated from the Pebhasid headquarters before departure. A satisfied chuckle burst from his lips before he leaned back with a sigh. His hand absentmindedly slipped behind his neck to gingerly touch the base of his skull. The lesion had shrunk further. One would have thought it a tiny cyst, unworthy of concern.

It's slowly shrunk away since that beastly bitch disappeared.

The lesion pulsed at the thought.

No! Keep the wedge out, Littles. Keep the grin on your face, the bad stuff erase …

The captain's thoughts calmed, and he snuggled into the chair, giving himself a break from all the hassles of late. He sighed at the work on his desk. Inventories needed to be counted, prisoners needed evaluation, and the ships needed repairs. When Littles saw the work in front of him, he threw his hands up in dismay.

Who'd've thought the Pebhorda had so much boring bureaucracy? The only interesting item here is the report of a Military Alchemist. Too bad the clown'd been crushed by a bulkhead. Helped me get my hands on four of their tunnellers though. I should thank the god of bulkheads. Now we can go get that ghastly girl and my ship!

"Ghastly girl, am I?" muttered a female voice Littles had come to dread. He sat up, and saw Neliya before him. She wore a thin-fabric white dress that clung suggestively to her body, her sly voice filling Littles with passion and fury at the same time.

"How did you get here?" he snapped.

Neliya cocked her head, her expression pained, and she seductively murmured, "Is that how you greet an old flame?"

"A cold, icy flame," spat Littles, the flesh around his lesion numb. "You changed your hair colour, I see."

The girl stroked her auburn mane. "He liked this colour." Littles' breath hitched for the tone of her voice had changed. Her eyes locked onto him. Her hands drifted up her sides, the fingertips gently grazing along the fabric of her flimsy garment, ascending her slender neck. "He'd dream about it … long for it …" Littles' breath faltered, his heart skipped beats, and his lips dried up. Neliya drew near, and cupped his cheeks, and she gazed into his eyes. Her grip then tightened. "When he had it, you took it from him."

Littles jumped at the accusation. His lesion caught fire but he was too paralysed with fear to grip it.

"Why did you take me from him?" asked the being who was no longer Neliya. "He was happy with me. You took me away from him"

"I don't care about him," snapped Littles, finding the strength to slap his hands over his ears. "I am now a Pebhorda, a captain of the stars. He's nothing, meaningless!"

Two hands tore his arms away and pinned him to the chair. The nightmare straddled him, her hair flaring away as if blown back by a great windstorm. Her jaw detached from her skull, and her mouth bore sharp incisors. Littles struggled, his horrified gasps stifled by a bizarre tentacle that burst from his lesion and strangled him. His bulging eyes flew open as he wheezed for breath. The thing violently hissed, and poisonous lips mashed against the bluing rim of Littles' mouth, and sharp canines tore at his lips.

His face suddenly met with a metal floor. He lay there, trembling with fear, hoping that if he remained still, the creature would leave him in peace.

Leave me be. Take the wedge and get gone, do not make me forlorn.

Repeating this over and over again, he regained the desire to move only with great pain and time, pulling his knees to his chest and clutching them tightly. He gave a sudden strangled gasp, and then sat up, bewildered at the vision. Frustrated, he hit his head against the steel floor.

The same damn dream.

A beeping sound emanated from the desktop console. It was a sound he recognised well. He pulled himself to his feet, though from the waist down ached as if every tendon were filled with glass shards. He hobbled to the console and accepted the communiqué.

"Gelfri!" he said with lazy sincerity. "You look horrendously horrible."

The Pebhasid wiped a soaking handkerchief across his deep-red face, and widened his eyes to relieve the searing pain reverberating through him.

"Says the insufferable insomniac," he retorted. "Femie still bothering you?"

Littles' neck jerked at the mention. "I'll manage."

"Ah, 'course you will," sighed Gelfri. "Mum used to bug me a bit after I got the *Ranegr*. Never fear, my fatigued friend. We Pebhorda persist and pulverise the pests that plague us."

Littles pursed his lips determinedly, and nodded with a concordant grunt.

"How goes your trial?" he asked.

"Difficult, I must say. But I will make better use of it than its former owner. Now that pleasantries are aside ..." Gelfri grabbed the camera violently. "Why did you use the EMP on those ships!? Did I not *specifically* order you to be careful with them, you imbecilic insufferable ignoramus!?"

"Oh, get over it, Gelfri!" retorted Littles. "A few got damaged, the rest are fine."

"How many?" rasped the Pebhasid.

"Four," said Littles.

The Pebhasid almost burst a blood vessel. "Four! Did I just hear the word *four* escape your lips?"

"Yep," replied Littles, his eyes focused on cleaning his fingernails.

"Oh, well, we might be able to get, say, *ten troops* through the CTN," barked Gelfri.

"Shorts got the *Ranegr* to run with just one," returned Littles. "I've got four, so we can get four entire troop transports through."

Gelfri buried his face in his hands, desperate to manage both the pain coursing through his body and the frustration his protégé was inflicting upon him. "Littles, I've got the best scientists working on Shorts' stuff. They've been working for *months* and they say they haven't even scratched the surface!"

Littles scoffed, a grin riding on his lips. "Well, I just hijacked an entire MCV worth of scientists that can help. Plus their families as, shall we say, incentive? *I'll* get the TIM device working. You just focus on finding those rambunctious *Ranegr*-stealing rascals."

"I got a data burst through the communications network," said Gelfri.

"You found them!" shouted Littles, his lesion quivering with sickening excitement.

"In a star system about seven light years away," said Gelfri. "*Ranegr* is intact, and they're tryin' to repair the TIM device for another jump."

"How much time do we have?" asked Littles.

"Last data burst said they wouldn't be able to leave for another three months or so," said the Pebhasid.

Littles gritted his teeth, and straightened to his full height. Determination ignited a fire in his bleary eyes. "We've set a return course at full speed. E.T.A. two weeks."

"Do better," returned Gelfri, before shutting off the link.

A rabble of very nervous and outraged Mydians filled the hangar of the *Shar-Ranegr*. Hardly half the size of the real *Ranegr*'s great maw, it was less than a speckle of the legendary vessel. Instead Littles had to settle for this cheep imitation.

Not much longer.

The people below looked up, expecting answers regarding the whereabouts of their families and loved ones. At first Littles gave no response, instead studying them a moment. "I am Littles, representative of Pebhasid Gelfri the Great. You are now subservient to me."

"We are subservient to the Mydian republic," retorted one person, nearest to Littles and gazing up at him defiantly.

"State your name, rebellious renegade," said Littles. The scientist gave it, and Littles uttered a summons into his radio. A screen appeared on the wall of the hangar, within view of everyone. Jaws dropped in horror at the screen's contents. "This is your family, is it not?" Littles asked the man below. The man gasped at the image of his loved ones, shivering with the same terror that froze his blood.

"What is this?" the man snapped.

"There's a petulant prodigy, who figured out how to attach a TIM device to a ship larger than a small desk," Littles explained. "We need your help to implement his revolutionary research. Make it work, and you and your families will be freed."

"And if we refuse?" asked the first man.

Littles uttered a command into his radio. Suddenly, the trembling people on the screen let out silent screams, their expressions of anguish chilling all who viewed it. The children crumpled first, gasping for breath, while their mother reached desperately for them. Finally, she succumbed. The man dropped to his knees in the middle of the crowd, unable to breathe from the grief that gripped his heart.

"In case you were wondering what'll happen if you don't help us ... that's it," said Littles with a chilling tone.

The man wailed on the ground. His colleagues glared upwards, their teeth clenched and their eyes watering. Yet none dared speak up in disapproval, their own families in mind.

"Now that's settled, I'll have the data delivered to you so you can get started," said Littles, straightening out his clothes and walking down the boardwalk. His first officer waited for him at the end.

"Report," he grunted.

"Their vitals are stable," replied the first officer. "The gas should wear off in an hour."

Littles grunted with satisfaction. Eyeing the distraught scientist on the floor, he said, "Have the guards take him to their cell. Keep them separate from the rest." As if sensing the officer's perplexity, he added, "Theatrics work better when convincing someone."

Littles marched down the hallway. "Tell the engineers to squeeze as much delta-vee out of the drives as they can. I want to be back at the Pebhasid before two weeks."

24 | I'm just happy

Uenda leapt off the front porch, her pretty blue mekato dress waving as she sailed through the air. Upon landing, she almost tripped on her wooden sandals, but steadied herself. She stood next to Fyuren, who wore trousers and a shirt Edo lent him.

"Hurry up! We'll be late," she bellowed in a high-pitched voice riddled with excitement.

"Uenda, it's not even sundown yet," chided Sukete as she tied a cyan shawl over the shoulders of her green mekato. "And be careful! Grandma went to a lot of effort to make those floral patterns."

Uenda stood up from the ground.

"But we should make sure bugs don't get stomped on," she said, holding up a many-legged insect, at which Fyuren balked.

Sukete smiled at her daughter's thoughtful nature. She strode over to Neliya, and fastened the white shawl around her indigo mekato. She stepped back to look at the girl. The star-speckled pattern, glimmering as she moved, befitted the Mydian like nothing Sukete had seen her wear.

"You wear it perfectly," Sukete proclaimed.

"It's a good thing I measured you before making it," said Arika, approaching from behind to straighten out the fabric.

Neliya felt queasy with embarrassment, "I feel so spoiled." At that, Arika and Sukete burst into laughter.

"Don't be silly," exclaimed Arika. "You're part of the family!"

Neliya's heart bubbled warmly at the sentiment, and she gave the ladies a grateful hug. She looked over her shoulder to see the blue symbol embroidered into the shawl's fabric. It fascinated her, though she couldn't figure out why.

"That's the *Sheso Muzai*, symbolising joy and prosperity," said Sukete.

Uenda appeared at the door. "Come on! Grumble-guts is saying things." Then she saw Neliya's attire. "Oooh! Rii-tuan's beautiful!"

"Thank you very much, Uenda," replied Neliya. "And to you as well, Arika."

"Shall we go?" said Sukete, picking up her small purse. The four women strode out the door, Sukete locking it behind her. Fyuren stood entranced by Neliya's appearance.

"Whoever made that dress is a genius," he commented with red-hued cheeks. Arika beamed when Neliya translated his words. As they climbed onto the carriage, he was struck by the shawl and the symbol it bore.

"That symbol's the old Alchemic symbol for silver," he intoned.

"Really?" asked Neliya, her interest piqued. She nonchalantly looked over her shoulder, trying in vain to look at the marking. "I thought it looked familiar. Here it means prosperity."

Fyuren just shrugged and slumped back in his seat, shifting unsteadily as the carriage cleared a bump in the road. He wanted to ponder the symbol further, but another voice in his head roared, "Take a break!" He let Neliya jabber on with Arika and Sukete in the alien language he couldn't be bothered to learn. His gaze turned to the front of the carriage, where Uenda chatted with her father. The village came into view, a stack of wooden logs visible through the lingering mist of winter's final eclipse. He wanted to ask Neliya about it, but she was much too wrapped up in the conversation with the two other women. Instead of roping her into another translation job, he moved to the front of the carriage and sat next to Odentii.

"What's the pile of logs for?" he asked.

"To say farewell to winter," replied Odentii. "Neliya-eru explained it not?"

"She might've but I was too busy," said Fyuren.

Odentii chuckled incredulously. "You have a good head, but you seem … itee, how to say? Not interested in new things?"

Fyuren sighed, "I've never taken much to festivals. Even on the *Othala*."

Odentii smiled, adding, "Also, not going home."

"That's not so bad now that I know Dad's alright." He yawned, and absentmindedly gazed at the tents going up. "Dad told me to take a few days off before starting my work again, and that I should learn about Imarin culture."

"Aimoren," corrected Odentii.

"Sorry, *Aimoren*," said Fyuren, though his pronunciation was still lazy. "So, what is the pile of logs for?"

"This is *Chisafenu*, Winter's End," said Odentii. "I think Neliya-eru called pile a *bonfire*. We call it *shikana*. When the eclipse begins, we burn it to send away the last of winter. Then we have party for the next year."

Fyuren nodded, his eyebrows raised at the images the word 'party' recalled: memories of Kajil and Jugga's gang of hangar workers supplicating at the altar that was a beer keg; the tokamak crew tussling his hair roughly but familiarly; and the few of the bridge crew who saw it fit to join their celebrations. Then he recalled thoughts of Zeers, wearing a merry face the likes of which he'd never expressed before. Fyuren looked over his shoulder at Neliya, whose expression was of a hauntingly similar nature.

When they reached the village proper, Odentii reined the mashi to a stable set aside for travelling guests, and the group made their way to the centre of town on foot. Tents of many different colours had gone up, along with signs advertising food stalls and games. The town square had been given a wide berth except for the men who were hurriedly lifting the last logs on to the pile. Neliya easily picked out Edo in the rabble.

Like all the other workers, Edo was wearing little more than a pair of shorts and a white sweatband. Fyuren glanced over at Neliya, and scoffed when he saw her blush. When Edo saw Neliya, steam seemed to erupt from his ears – although the heavy wood might have had something to do with it. Fyuren turned away and hid his grin behind his hand. As he sobered himself, he felt the hairs behind his ears ruffle subtly at the confused stares from people around him.

"Odentir?" he said.

"*Rusuo*," whispered Odentii. Of the few words Fyuren understood, it echoed in his mind and he was quiet. Odentii leaned down to whisper in his ear, "People from other towns came. If someone asks, we caring for disfigured relatives from other country. Understand?"

"You couldn't have mentioned that earlier?" Fyuren asked, concern exacerbating the nervous tingle running down his back.

"Thought you would not notice," replied Odentii with a grin. "And it is *Odentii*." He put his arm around Fyuren, pulling the boy to his front and placing his hands on his shoulders. "Now," he looked up at the sky, where the silhouette of Sikai grew nearer to the sun.

The gas giant's rings lit up like a translucent sash about the planet's girth. The rabble of near-naked men retreated from the log pile, out of breath and wiping the sweat dribbling from their brows. Despite their fatigue, they wore grins of camaraderie. Then Idoru appeared, his purple and red robes clean and pressed just for the occasion. He carried a torch in one hand. With the other, he pointed to the sun vanishing behind Sikai's disk.

Idoru began to sing, and the jovial posse of men locked hands and joined in the chorus.

> *Arii ze enomai sikai ma shipe*
> *Chinne ma kyauna mi pottahya uni.*
> *Itezasho nape, aimore riise*
> *Wara ma umaga mi meze u yani.*
>
> *Amuppe! Atuppe! Rawappai atesu.*
> *Mode ze yuyunai nettopai ape.*
> *Chinne ma kyaunadyo suke mi konu*
> *Yao taku mona atupposu ze.*

Neliya knew the song backwards, and her mind crackled with the meaning therein: "The sun is sleeping behind Sikai, so let us say goodbye to the worries of yesteryear. It is a new time, our silver isle glimmers like the river of stars in the sky. Wash your bodies! Wash your clothes! It's time to laugh and cheer. Now you can relax, enjoy it while you can. Take the worries of yesterday, drown them in water. Wash them clean, the bad away, like dirty laundry."

The song repeated, and the whole crowd sang along. The song was like a celestial lullaby, and sent the sun to sleep behind Sikai. The crowd chanted the final lines with gusto, as Idoru hurled the torch into the log pile. A roar of applause from the townspeople heralded the growl of the fire's birth, and Idoru bade the people to enjoy the festival, and look forward to the New Year.

The crowd dispersed, drawn to the stalls and food stands waiting to cash in on the celebrations. Fyuren approached Neliya, who stood mesmerised by the festivities. She was whisked away by Uenda, and he resigned himself to watching her try some bizarre foodstuffs, like fried creatures with tentacles and something called *yagupae*. The sight of her popping the marinated squishy things into her mouth convinced him she didn't really understand the language, because he was certain she was eating some animal's eyes.

"Ueo!" she exclaimed in a very Uenda-esque manner.

Other stalls sold sweets, and soon Neliya and Uenda were walking hand-in-hand down the aisle of shops with technicolour toffees in their free hands. A mask clung to the side of Neliya's head, adorned with splashes of blue and orange, complementing each other in a unique artistic pattern of a face. Soon Neliya was the one pulling Uenda toward a stall that had caught her eye.

Neliya leaned over the metal tub at the stall, eyes radiating amazement, then traded some coins for a wooden stick with a string lasso, with which she laboured futilely to catch whatever was swimming in that tub.

"Sounds like a tough game, eh?" asked Fyuren.

"It's too hard," moaned a disappointed Neliya.

"Itee ..." Arika intoned, noting the confused looks their Myddish conversation was eliciting. Neliya and Fyuren quickly got the message and they moved along. She put her arm around his shoulders, and whispered in his ear. "I think you should have learned a bit more Aimorein."

"Wouldn't have had the time to contact the *Ranegr*," droned Fyuren. "Plus, you seem to be doing just fine. Better than fine."

Neliya looked down at the ground, her hand clenched slightly.

"Will you be able to say goodbye, Neliya?" Fyuren anticipated she'd either say 'no' or lie.

The girl walked silently a moment, her eyes drifting up to the sky and lamenting she could see no stars against the inky blackness of the eclipsed sky. She finally said, "You've gotten a lot taller, Fyuren-ken." She then ran back to Sukete, Arika, and Uenda. He watched her back, having seen the same scene whenever Zeers ran off to meet Jugga and Kajil's gang.

At least no one's going to put something in her brain and make her crazy, he thought hopefully.

Edo, Odentii, and Jikyo met with the ladies after their Haisou tournament. Jikyo seemed a bit disappointed that he'd lost for the team, but his son-in-law and grandson were in much higher spirits. Uenda took it upon herself to ramble to Odentii about Neliya trying every different kind of food, and their attempts to catch animals out of the tubs. Arika took to comforting her husband after his loss, while Neliya apologised to Edo for missing his game.

"It's alright. I'd've been embarrassed if you saw me play like that," said Edo. He awkwardly scratched the back of his head and chuckled. "I was worried I wouldn't make it to the end of the game, since I haven't had much practice lately."

Neliya grimaced, and said, "Because of us dropping in ... literally."

Edo grinned confidently, "Next year, we'll definitely win."

The men partook of a long-awaited meal on a bench near the bonfire. It still burned with a gentler flame, the tendrils of which flittered, like bright-red ghosts dancing to the music played by a small band of musicians nearby. The voice of the music came from a stringed instrument Neliya had never seen before. The woman, whose nationality was clearly not Aimoren, drew a stick along the strings, producing a sound hauntingly similar to a child's singing.

"That's called a *koeri*," said Sukete when Neliya asked. The Mydian said nothing further, and walked into the square. The music took control of her body, and she began to dance.

Her rational mind gone to oblivion, Neliya felt like she were once again flying over those clouds of manifold colours. With a smile the likes of which neither had ever seen, she grabbed Sukete and Fyuren and roped them into her dance. A loud belch of laughter burst from Uenda, and she followed. Neliya pulled others in, and soon a whole crowd girdled the bonfire, dancing to the koeri's music.

Neliya saw Edo, transfixed by her grace, and beckoned him to come. Edo leaned away with an amused smile. Odentii gave him a push, launching him within Neliya's reach and she took his hand. Drunk on the music and the fun, they danced through every tune the musician sang through the strings of her koeri.

Neliya lay wide awake that night. Uenda nestled against her shoulder and slept so peacefully not even Neliya's restless fidgeting woke her. Not wanting to disturb the girl, Neliya edged out of the futon and left the room. The house was dark save for the slivers of light that trickled under the front door.

Outside, a sparkling river bisected the sky, interspersed with mottles of bulbous wisps. The light of a trillion far-away suns and planets pitter-pattered across the landscape, imbuing it with a light cyan, unlike the purple luminance it enjoyed when Sikai dominated the sky. Compared to this, Neliya's lookout on the *Othala* was like a child's finger-painting. The sight of Edo, lying on a mat in the middle of the bare field, only made it better.

She walked across the field, the loamy earth squishing under her weight, and put her head between his gaze and the sky above.

"Can't sleep?" asked Edo.

"I should say the same thing," replied Neliya.

Edo shrugged. "On Chisafenu, I always come out to look at the night sky. I was going to invite you, but father would've disapproved."

Neliya popped down on the mat next to him, and looked upward.

"It's amazing," she said breathlessly. "It's really familiar, but still beautiful."

"Don't the stars change from the *Othala* to here?" asked Edo.

"Fyuren said that we're not far away enough for much change. It's amazing how close we really are." Edo smiled silently, allowing Neliya to continue chattering. "Fyuren, Zeers, and I, we had a place on the *Othala*, where we could see the stars. We'd go there often when we got sick of the city. We'd sit really close to the window, and block out everything so all we saw were stars." She raised an outstretched finger. "You see there? That's where Lethanis is."

Edo chuckled with amazement. "That's Shanibona, the home of the river queen, Muneuo. You remember the big statue in the shrine? Muneuo is the small one next to the big woman statue.

"The legend says the demon Aeguro battled Sikai for dominion of the sky. Their fight caused a great flood that destroyed a village, and Muneuo was washed down the river. Sikai, victorious over Aeguro, took pity upon Muneuo, for it was his conduct that led to her loss. So he sent the dragon Tashua to fetch her from the river. While Sikai petitioned the great gods for a home for Muneuo, Tashua took the form of a boy named Kouhi and stayed with the girl. Together they grew, though Muneuo did not know Kouhi was a dragon, and they fell in love. But, you see, the great gods would never permit an immortal dragon to be with a mortal, for they could not be in two worlds at once forever. When Muneuo saw him as a dragon, her feelings remained. So she said to the great gods, 'Make me a dragon, so that I can be with Tashua.' Though they couldn't grant such a wish, they were moved by her purity and spirit, and brought her to the palace of Shanibona, at the mouth of the celestial river, and gave her a room within its walls. They commanded Tashua to be her guardian, and would allow him, once every five years, to become Kouhi and be with Muneuo."

Edo relished the wonder in Neliya's eyes. He smiled, and then directed her gaze to a faint speck closer to the horizon. "It's hard to see, but Tashua is right there. In a year and a bit, it will be near to Shanibona, and the lovers can meet again."

Neliya bit her lip, and she turned to Edo. She saw a flash of Zeers' face, though he had a smile she forgot her friend could wear. She lost hold of the reins on her mind and it dragged her into visions of Zeers: the sound of his laughter, the feel of his shoulder as she laid her head on it, and of his hand in hers.

That feeling seemed a little too real, and she quickly realised Edo had gripped her hand gently. Zeers slowly faded, and Edo remained. His face solidified in her mind, and drowned out any other thoughts.

Edo sat up and pulled out a paper envelope. "I wanted to give this to you earlier, so you could wear it at the festival, but I couldn't find the right time."

Neliya took it and opened it. Out came a long leather filament, from which hung a stone. It was as if someone had moulded a fragment of the sky above her head. In the pale light it diffracted more colours than she knew existed.

"The stone is called *fueshen*," Edo explained. "When you contacted your ship, it looked like you might get to go home. I just wanted to give you something to remember me by."

Neliya was too transfixed by the pendant to notice Edo's nervous fidgeting.

"Thank you, Edo," she said, and then leaned over to kiss him. The motion was over in less than a second, but the moment after, where they were still very close, drew out like the tail of a shooting star. Neliya was the first to come to her senses. The first thing she did was stifle herself.

"I'm sorry, I don't know why," she babbled.

Edo responded very quickly. "It's alright, that felt nice!"

Neliya couldn't stop stammering, and her face burned enough to start a wildfire. "Do Neiren do that?"

"Sometimes, but not so suddenly," chuckled Edo.

Neliya fell silent, save for the steam hissing out her ears. Her frantic thoughts were evident in the twitching and darting of her eyes, and Edo decided he had to make a move. He took the pendant from her and hung it over her neck.

"I'm glad you like it," he said with a shaky smile.

Neliya nodded like a girl half her age, but was still silent. She saw movement out the corner of her eye, and looked up in time to see Edo's glimmering eyes. She felt his hands on her shoulders, and his lips brush against hers. She inhaled sharply at his action, but her body stayed right where it sat, unwilling to move away from him. Her chest burned with warmth enough to shoo away a blizzard as she pressed against his lips with her own.

Edo pulled away slowly and panted softly, "I wanted to do that for a long time."

Neliya's brain was too frazzled for anything other than the widest smile she'd ever given. Her hands crept up and threaded her fingers through his. She kissed him again, and her body trembled with joy.

Edo broke this kiss and said, "Are you cold? Would you like to go inside?"

"No," Neliya whispered. "I'd like to stay and keep looking at the stars."

Edo grinned, and lay back down on the mat. Neliya followed, and shuffled into his embrace. Neliya stroked the pendant around her neck, and gave him a smile more grateful than happy.

"You're not cold?" he asked nervously.

"No," she said bluntly. "I'm just happy."

She snuggled up to him and gripped the pendant around her neck. They both knew they'd have to go back indoors or risk catching a cold or a lecture from Edo's parents. Sharing a common mind, they prayed to the sky to slow time. And for that moment, Neliya forgot about anything else.

25 | This will get us home

Barely three days after Chisafenu – most of it spent sleeping – Fyuren was back to work. Initially, he wasn't as reclusive as before, and could be seen pacing around the field in thought. He even took to offering his nose to look for kusin in the last of the sliver-garlic crop, though he was only looking to use Neliya as a soundboard. After a few days of that, he was back in the workshop, the hours punctuated by the occasional frustrated growl.

One day he sat in the workshop, running his thumbnail back and forth over his lips as he stared at the tokamak readings Allo had sent him. But his mind was hardly focused on the data. He kept recalling an image of Neliya and Edo, hand in hand as they walked toward the northern fields. The sight, which he'd beheld for the last few mornings, drove him to distraction.

So help me, if she doesn't come home with me, he thought, his blood pressure rising. With a growl, he internally chanted his mantra: *Just get Mister Indra to convince her to leave when he gets here.*

It helped him whenever he became stuck in a thought loop. With a sigh, he rubbed his reddened eyes and returned his focus to the calculations before him. A few hundred lines of code whizzed past the screen, his gaze carefully scrutinising them for mistakes. Then he set the program running, and awaited the output. Luckily, the mathematics of fusion weren't nearly as complex or strenuous as tunnelling. And yet his simulation of the *Ranegr's* tokamak still resulted in failure.

Calm!

He gripped the sides of his head upon feeling the familiar tingle of an oncoming outburst. Chewing his lip, he pushed the frustration-induced tantrum down into his gut and left it there before studying the output of the program.

Always the same thing. Not even at the Ranegr's current position, and using reflected light from the comet catcher. There just isn't enough power to achieve ignition.

Fyuren rubbed his temples. For the fifth time that day, his mind scanned for alternatives to the dozen solutions he'd already tried.

What about a solar prominence? That'd have enough power for ten tokamaks!

The idea grew increasingly appealing as he considered it with the assets at hand, until another part of his mind ran an abysmal reality check.

They're too unpredictable! It'd be like trying to channel a bolt of lightning into a speeding car with no steering wheel.

His optimism lobe fought back reflexively, trying to keep the idea alive, but it was a losing battle against the sheer power of logic and knowledge. Finally he raised the white flag and slumped back onto his chair.

Frustrated by his code, displayed mockingly on the screen, he stood and paced the workshop. When that did little to help, he left with a growl. Odentii and Sukete looked up from their perch on the front porch, and stood with concerned expressions as he exited the shed, a defeated scowl on his face.

"Fyuren-eru," Odentii called out to him.

"I'm going for a walk," Fyuren replied over his shoulder. He tried to remain as calm as possible, but the words still left him in a shout.

He wandered out of the gate and down the track toward the village. Usually a walk helped his thought processes, even when on the *Ranegr*. But he was still unaccustomed to the air on this planet. The unfamiliar scents drove him to greater distraction.

Remember though, you felt the same about the Ranegr at first. Then again, you had Neliya and Zeers with you. Now she's gone off with hyper beanbag, and he's gone coo-coo pants.

He stopped, his arm hairs standing on end as his stomach filled with bile.

Ugh! That sounds like Gelfri!

He slumped down against a tree next to the path, his eyes wandering out over the land. The view, though pretty, failed to please him. He felt that, as a Mydian born in space, only a sight of the vast expanse could sate his desire for a moment's wonder.

If only being in space weren't so damn hard. Neliya on the other hand ... No wonder she loves it here, she never liked the Othala. Neither did Zeers. Maybe that's why Gelfri could brainwash him.

Feeling the murkiness of grief creeping up on him, he let out a sigh to shoo it away.

If Neliya were here, I could use her as a soundboard. Too bad she's off with her new boyfriend.

Absentmindedly, he touched the pouch hanging from his neck. The weight of the sapphire was odd, as if the matter within was denser than an ordinary sapphire. He took it out of the pouch and studied it. The sunlight bled through the matrix of the crystal, perfectly cut like the undisturbed surface of a still lake. It enchanted him, so much that, without realising, he pressed it to his lips.

A nostalgic feeling fell over him as if a dam had broken and poured torrents of water over his head. Fyuren began to fly through the currents, though he had no destination. Those familiar blobs of light passed near him, and with a lucid mind he reached out to them. Upon his touch they dissolved through his fingers, leaving a tingle in his palms. In his mind, he heard Neliya's humming voice, sighing with his every failed attempt to grasp the droplets. Then, at last, he caught one between both hands, and by incomprehensible compulsion he held it tight.

We will teach you, said a far away voice.

Fyuren's hands simmered with pleasant warmth, bright yellow light escaping through the skin of his fingers. He opened his hands to see a vibrantly glowing seed, growing outward into a sphere of radiant flame.

A star.

His eyes fluttered open. It was twilight. The grass around his heavy hands ruffled in the accelerating breeze. The sapphire lay in his lap, his vision of it blurred by the sleep dust that had gathered in his eyes. A sequence of equations and designs struck his mind like a scientific eureka. He quickly scooped the sapphire into the pouch and sprinted back to the Andou house.

Odentii and Neliya saw him return, and cautiously approached the boy, whose hands worked frantically with screwdrivers to dismantle a device from his crashed pod. The Mydian's brow was furrowed with concentration, though his eyes appeared blank. Finally the boy finished what he was doing, almost tearing apart the device and rending a reel of cyan wire from it. He held it up to Neliya.

"What's that?" she asked

"That is a superconducting ceramic wire," he said. "That's about four and a half metres. I need twenty-two." He indicated seven similar devices on the floor nearby. "Help me dismantle the others."

The night was a busy one, as Odentii, Edo, and Neliya became Fyuren's workhorses. Sukete decided to serve them dinner in the workshop, and she and Uenda watched them work on some contraption Fyuren refused to explain in any satisfying detail.

"It's a power source," was all he ever said.

Slowly the escape pod components were dissected, dismantled, and cannibalised into a small but intricate apparatus that took shape in front of Fyuren. It began with thick, tightly wound coils of the cyan wire, which were then assembled into a sphere, which was then quickly concealed in a metal containment vessel. Then came the glass breaking and melting into cylinders, slowly worked into structures of which neither Neliya nor their hosts could make sense. Eventually they stopped trying to discern the end goal of the exercise, and bid Fyuren good night. He waved silently and continued working.

The following morning, Odentii and Edo rose for Haisou practice, only to meet Fyuren seated on the front porch. The boy chewed his fingernails manically as he stared at a set of schematics. Odentii called out to him, and the boy shot up and faced him.

"I need your tractor!"

Moments later, Odentii moved his bulky tractor into the workshop. The engine's fumes flooded the shed with a dry, stuffy smell, prompting Fyuren to open all the windows he could find. He then clamped two thick cables onto what Odentii assured him was the engine battery, tethering the machine to the interconnected mess of wires, pipes, tanks, and cylinders.

"When I say, step on the accelerator and hold it," he said over the chug of the tractor's engine. Odentii hopped into the driver seat and positioned his foot. Fyuren jumped over cables and tanks toward his tablet, and punched in a single command. "Now!"

The tractor engine began to roar under Odentii's foot. Fyuren gazed quietly at the display, waiting for the system to reach that desired target. He nodded with satisfaction, and slowly engaged a lever.

The seams of his device began to glimmer with purple-white light, before settling into a dimmer but regular pulsating hum. Fyuren signalled Odentii, who switched off the tractor. Neliya and Sukete entered the workshop, yawning despite the concern and confusion riddling their faces. They approached the bench, where Fyuren stood, his downward gaze illuminated eerily with purple light from the device.

"That's not like any power source I've seen," said Neliya.

"Of course, it's not," replied Fyuren, his pensive face concealing raucous cries of triumphant satisfaction. "It's a polywell fusion reactor. It's just as powerful as a tokamak, at a hundredth the size. The first of its kind."

With a glad expression, Fyuren regarded her amazed expression. "This will get us home."

26 | I won't just remember you

Despite his achievement, Fyuren insisted he still had work to do before the *Ranegr* picked them up. That meant, unfortunately, that Odentii didn't get his workshop back. But if the man minded, he didn't show it. He was still much too distracted with farming the fallowed fields to the north, where, true to his word, he started sowing barley.

The walk up to the northern fields served as some good early morning exercise for Neliya and Edo, and a warm-up for the work of ploughing the soil. It also gave them the time to be alone together, for which an opportunity was rare. Edo often had to help Odentii and Sukete needed Neliya's help. Neliya couldn't even sneak out of her room at night, thanks to Uenda, who still refused to sleep on a separate futon from her.

"Rii-tuan is a good hug pillow," the little girl mumbled over breakfast one day.

"You should be old enough to sleep on your own," said Edo.

"You just want her to be *your* hug pillow, don't you?" Uenda retorted, shooting a knowing glance at the pendant around Neliya's neck. Sukete and Odentii chided their daughter for such inappropriate words, while Edo and Neliya tried to hide their flustered faces.

Ultimately, Neliya didn't mind Uenda's sleeping habits, even though she would have preferred Edo. She woke one morning from a wonderful dream, and although the dream steadily slipped through her fingers like mud in the rain, she could clearly remember the delightful feeling it gave her.

Uenda still slept, her lips upturned in serenity. Neliya slowly edged out of Uenda's grip, slipped on a pair of shoes, and went outside. The morning air felt crisp and cool as it entered her lungs, and her eyes drooped as she inhaled. She gazed out onto the field, where targets were laid out for Odentii and Edo's Haisou practice.

Sukete beckoned her to sit with her on the porch and watch them. Though the tea was tempting, something else tugged her out onto the field. She stepped off the porch, and approached the man.

"Gokidai, Neliya," said Odentii, having noticed her before his son.

"Sorry to break into your practice," she said sheepishly. "I was hoping, maybe, I could have a try."

Edo shot his father a glance that was too hopeful for even a dimwit to miss. Odentii handed her a spare nauya from a bag on the ground.

"This is my wife's, so be careful with it," he said with a stern warning.

Neliya eyed it like a precious heirloom. With a gaze over at Sukete, she said, "Should I? What about her?"

"I bring it out every day in the hopes she'll practice, but she never does," said Odentii with resigned disappointment. "Come, have a try."

Edo stepped aside with a gallant bow, and Neliya stepped up to the line in the dirt. She grabbed an arrow and, with considerable hesitation, hooked the shaft to the string. She shifted her position several times before pulling back on the string, which was much harder than she'd expected. Neliya splayed her hands to release the string, and twitched in pain as the recoil scraped her arm and the arrow scratched her fingers as it flew, ungracefully, toward the target.

"At least I hit," she mumbled with a grimace. "It's a lot harder than darts."

Edo stepped up. "Your posture's wrong, and you're holding the nauya and arrow too tightly."

"She managed to hit the target, despite her poor form," Odentii noted. "Much better than you or your mother." Odentii showed her the correct posture and slowly walked her through the method of notching the arrow and releasing it. Then she tried again.

"Make sure you breathe as well," instructed Odentii. "Breathe in as you pull back on the string, hold it as you centre your target, then breathe out when your arrow hits."

Neliya did as she was told, finding it surprisingly easy to calm herself and relax her fingers. The string flew harmlessly out of her fingers, and the arrow landed just inside the innermost circle. Not a prefect bullseye, but enough to launch every onlooker's eyebrows skyward.

"I did it!" she shrieked.

"Well done," exclaimed Edo. When Neliya made another mark within the circle, he chuckled in amazement. "You're a natural."

"Thank you, Edo," said Neliya with a restrained smile. She declined the offer to continue practicing, as the smell of tea drew her to Sukete on the porch. She handed Edo the nauya, and walked toward the tea-bearing lady with a spring in her step.

"That's very good, Neliya," said Sukete. "Is good eyesight a Mydian trait?"

"Nope, that's just me," said Neliya. She plopped down next to Sukete, who poured her a cup of tea from the nearby pot. "Don't you play anymore?"

Sukete shrugged, "I got so I didn't like getting up so early. You should keep practicing. Edo practices alone when his father gets busy in early summer, and he'd be glad for the partner."

Neliya pursed her lips, unintentionally stifling her smile. She recalled Edo's kiss on Chisafenu, and her gaze grew pensive. Sukete sensed unease growing in the Mydian, and she inquired. Neliya remained silent a while longer as she tried to rehearse what she wanted to say. Although it had made her indescribably happy, her dream had left her with a need to talk to someone who wasn't Edo. And she wasn't entirely sure that someone should be Sukete either. Finally she decided to get the load off her chest.

"Sukete, do you like me?" she asked clumsily.

Sukete frowned. "What kind of question is that? Of course I like you."

"No, I mean ... do you approve of me?" Neliya stammered, her heart thumping. "Would you disapprove if I ... k-kissed Edo?"

Sukete stared at her, deathly silent. A chortle suddenly burst past her lips and she grinned ecstatically.

"It was on Chisafenu, wasn't it?" she exclaimed, beaming as if she'd been given the prize of a lifetime. She pointed to the sparkling pendant around Neliya's neck. "I saw him buy that with his own money, and I knew what he had in mind." Sukete stroked Neliya's flushed cheek. "Of course I approve," she said.

Neliya's chest shuddered with a cold blast as she inhaled. A sickening sense of relief filled her, and she mumbled, "Thank you."

Sukete smiled as she took a big sip from her cup. Then she said, "I think you two look adorable, holding hands on the way to the north fields."

Neliya almost choked on her tea. She spluttered, "You could see?"

"So can Odentii," replied Sukete. "Speaking of which, is that why you've been trying to get Uenda to sleep on her own futon? So you can sneak into Edo's room at night?"

Neliya almost dropped her teacup as she threw a hand up and blabbered, "I don't mean to do *that!* It's just that, well, it'd be nice to spend some time alone."

Sukete's smile didn't falter as she eyed the yammering girl. She sipped her tea and said, "It's fine. You just want to be together as much as possible before you go."

Neliya gulped nervously, and looked away. Her eyes drifted to Edo and smiled at the mirth that filled her. She finally said, "Your son is a wonderful person, and I really like him. And if I have to go back to the *Othala*, I just want to be able to remember as much of him as I can."

Sukete shuffled toward her and snaked her arm over the girl's shoulder. She held her close, stroking her hair gently. As she rested her cheek against Neliya's head, she intoned, "Neliya, if you want to stay with us ... you're more than welcome." Neliya pulled away and glared at Sukete, utter surprise on her face. Sukete returned a resolute look. "We all love you. You're a wonderful daughter, and you'd be an even more wonderful daughter-in-law. So, if you want to stay, we'll be honoured to have you."

The hair on Neliya's skin stood on end as she processed Sukete's statement. Her eyes darted to Edo, and then to the workshop where Fyuren had isolated himself. Her mind was blank with indecisiveness. Sensing her unease, Sukete took her hand and said, "It's your choice. Your life. If you want to go back to the *Othala*, go. But staying here will make you happy …"

Finding no other response, Neliya smiled graciously.

"Staying here would make me happy," she said. "Getting to be with you, Odentii, and Uenda, and to stay with Edo."

Suddenly, a giggling creature tackled Neliya from behind and bellowed, "It's Brother Edo! Isn't it? Rii-tuan wants to marry big brother, right?"

Uenda yelled it with such fervent volume, even a deaf person a hundred metres away could have heard it. It was enough to make Neliya's cheeks turn into red-hot coals. She knew Edo heard his sister's too-excited-for-morning blurts, and it threw him off so much his arrow hit his father's target. Sukete made a less than half-hearted effort to quiet her daughter, but her own giddiness at the idea overpowered her sense of propriety.

Uenda continued to rock with her arms around Neliya's neck as she yelled, "Rii-tuan and Edo should get married! Then she can stay!"

The little girl's mischievous paroxysm settled down. Yet she continued to hum and nuzzle to Neliya's hair. The Mydian finally murmured, "Uenda."

"What is it, Big Sister Rii-tuan?" replied the jovial child.

Neliya turned to look the girl in the eye. "You stink!"

Sukete interjected, "And it's *Choteginhu*, so go and get ready."

The words echoed in Neliya's mind, *Day of the Dead*. Sukete had once explained that it was the day when people went to visit the Ancestors' graves on the mountain nearby. Edo and Odentii finished their practice and retreated to their rooms to get ready for the trip to the mountain cemetery. Neliya quickly asked how she could help, but Sukete held up a hand.

"You have some things you need to think about, don't you?" she said as she herded Uenda into the bathroom.

"Thinking about what?" asked Edo quizzically.

"Oh … just … lady stuff," Neliya stammered. Edo wanted to press further, but Sukete dragged him away to dress for their visit to the cemetery.

Neliya bade them good day as they departed in dark robes for the mountain path, leaving her alone. She glanced into the house, and felt a chill at its emptiness. Looking to the shed, she considered Fyuren's company.

He'd probably just ramble on, she thought with a grimace.

Then her eyes drifted to the sunlit outdoors. The forests beyond the field glimmered with deep green, and the skies above were pockmarked with fluffy clouds. Neliya's loneliness subsided, and with a resolute nod she tied her shawl over her shoulders and set out. She passed through the woods, down the hill, and into the fields to the southwest of the village. She filled her nose with the scents carried on the wind, and enjoyed the air flowing through her hair.

I haven't really had a chance to wander on my own, have I?

She paced about the fields a while longer, and wet her feet in a stream further south. Its flow drew her attention, and she followed it toward a patch of trees to the east. The hard dirt below her feet pressed against her weight as she stepped over earth-breaking roots. Her hands ran along their abrasive bark, scratching at her fingertips. The strong aromas of the trees' sap and flowers girdled her, and she came to a stop in the middle of the forest.

Her hand crept up to stroke the pendant, and her mind went to Sukete's offer. Her heart fluttered at the thought. She imagined waking every morning to the smell of Ondyarii's atmosphere, and feeling the warmth of a real sun every day. The images of endless days with Edo and Uenda excited her beyond belief.

Then she imagined watching the *Ranegr*'s shuttle take off, leaving her behind. Her body shivered with the sense of loss, and she wondered, *If I stay, what if I changed my mind?*

She sifted through her memories, searching hard for the slightest recollection of the *Othala* beyond its name. All she could remember was the spinning metal cylinder, the stagnant simulated lights, and the recycled water.

But Fyuren and Zeers were also there, she reminded herself. She let out a dry cough at the thought of Zeers, and what he'd done last they spoke. The muscles of her forehead tightened at the recollection and she pushed it away. She searched for any pleasant memory she could find of that other life, yet she found only the visions of days spent on auto-pilot: school, homework, prepare to take over the family business, listen to Fyuren rant, and stop Zeers embarrassing himself.

Frustrated, Neliya growled and kicked a small rock across the dirt path. She started to walk, then run, in order to shoo away the bothersome thoughts cluttering her mind. She lost track of how far she'd run long before she realised she was lost. An earth-breaking root caught her foot and sent her to the ground. She pulled herself to her feet and spat out a mouthful of dirt. Brushing herself off, she discovered, to her horror, that her pendant was gone.

There it sat on the ground. A small critter scampered down a nearby tree and grabbed the shiny gem. It looked at Neliya, the spots on its light brown fur vibrating with shock. It then turned and scurried away. Mortified, Neliya raced after the jewel thief. She kept the pest in her sights, bounding over tree trunks and sliding down hills. She shrieked with dismay as it vanished down a hole at the base of a mangled, ancient tree.

The hole was small, but big enough that she could fit through. After all, the *Ranegr*'s tokamak coolant pipes were narrower than this tunnel. As Neliya knelt down and crawled into the tunnel, a realisation came to her: *Back where I started.*

She lost her vision as soon as she entered the passage, and the air was thick with dust. Yet she persevered with determination to reclaim her treasure. The floor beneath her suddenly gave way and she slid forward. She reached blindly for anything she could grab to stop her descent, but found nothing. She hit the bottom of the slope, face first.

Her eyes stung from the murky, dry air around her. She pulled herself to her feet, coughed away the rest of the grit in her mouth, and looked around. A faint green hue gave form to her surroundings. Moss covered the walls, obscuring their luminescence only barely. She could see that the tunnel was tall enough for her to stand in, but not by much. It had also buckled in various places, through which the hungry trees above had plunged their roots.

Neliya was so surprised by what she found, she almost forgot why she'd crawled into the cavern. Her eyes, still sore from the dust, scoured her surroundings, looking for that rotten jewel robber. She could hear scratching from further down the passage, and she crept onwards. She held her hand to the wall for balance as she scaled a thick root, and felt the metallic grains embossed into the subterranean wall.

This is a little odd, she thought, recalling the mostly wooden architecture of Aimore.

The sound of a light percussion instrument reached Neliya's ears. It distracted her from her quest, and she turned around to look at the wreck of a spindly apparatus. Its glass composition drew her attention like a magnet, and she absentmindedly brushed her finger against the material. Her insides lurched as if she were standing on a maglev. Blurs of movement surged about her as the corridor turned into a tower. The particles of dust on the floor leapt up, and assembled themselves into components of the spindly device, which grew more elaborate.

In the blink of an eye, Neliya found herself standing beside the glowing glass device in a tower of blue-green marble. Beneath her feet was a boardwalk suspended over a drop that had to be hundreds of metres down. Before she could move past her surprise to wonder what in the world she was seeing, the entire tower started to shudder. In a panic, she scrambled to the nearby window and saw a gigantic wall of water speeding toward her, a fiery wavefront not far behind. She cowered as it hit, but she felt no pain as the water and fire burst through her harmlessly.

The tower collapsed in slow motion. Neliya looked around, utterly flabbergasted. Aside from the shock of complete immunity to life-threatening cataclysms, she was fine. The same could not be said of the Neiren and Mydians in the tower, who shrieked as the flood consumed them.

Neliya's brain broke.

*Wait, Neiren **and** Mydians?*

A four-fingered, yellow-skinned hand grabbed the railing near her. She reached to help the poor man, but her hand passed through his as if she were a ghost. That startled her, but the sight of the man slipping and screaming as he fell into the torrents mortified her.

Suddenly, it was dark and silent.

Neliya's stomach lurched again. Flashes and blurs of movement flittered around her. When they stopped, she saw a group of Neiren and Mydians huddled around fires. Their clothes, which had been so finely made, were tattered and blackened by dirt from the tower that slowly dissolved around them.

She tried to speak to them, but they ignored her. She tried to touch them and her hands passed through them.

Her stomach lurched again and in a blur the creatures were gone. The tower crumbled even more. Skeletons littered the floor, their races distinguishable only by the number of fingers. Neliya's mind bubbled with desperation to escape what she was seeing. She scrambled over the debris toward the exit. More skeletons smattered the dwellings, covered in makeshift blankets and huddled together for warmth. She covered her mouth to keep from screaming at the sight of several corpses, frozen in poses as they scratched at the wall.

They tried to dig themselves out, she realised.

She looked to the entrance tunnel through which she'd crawled, and saw three skeletons crammed inside. She shrieked as the skeletons broke apart, sending up a wave of dust into the air that covered her tongue in a chalky slime.

Sooner or later, our families end up on our dinner plate.

Neliya's body quaked and she doubled over. Her face scrunched as she fought back against the visions of Gelfri, decomposing flesh, and the resomator burns smeared across Borig's face – scars she helped put there. Grief filled her as her mind conjured the horrific sight of these people trying frantically to escape death.

When would they have given up? Pushing so hard, clawing so desperately to escape. I wonder how many times they thought, 'Just beyond this wall is freedom,' only to find more rock, more wall. Like they're stuck in a mouse wheel … running toward an exit, only to come back to where you started, until you die of exhaustion and spend your last minutes clawing for breath. And even if you reach an exit, what you see outside just makes you want to run back inside!

Neliya blinked repeatedly, hoping to see Sukete or Uenda or Edo. Yet she saw nothing but these effigies, testaments to the angst-ridden fate of these beings. Her head hurt as if the grief threatened to blow her skull out, and she boxed her ears, hoping it would help her escape. Her vision blurred and her breathing quickened until she could bear it no longer, and screamed.

Darkness took her, and she floated aimlessly in it. Her mind blank, the revulsion and terror of that place seemed far away. Then a hand took hers and she opened her eyes. Edo stood before her smiling, a shimmering pendant in his hand.

"I want you to have something to remember me by," he said.

She fixated her gaze on the pendant and its light blew all her pain away. She realized she was lying down in the dirt, gazing at the pendant resting upon a rock nearby. She sat up in a daze, lazily brushed the dirt out of her hair, and looked around. The luminance of the tunnel walls had vanished, and all that remained was a sliver of sunlight creeping through a hole in the ceiling. It struck the pendant perfectly, giving full view of its beauty.

Something to remember you by, thought Neliya as she gazed at the gem. Her mind was so clear, she couldn't believe she had agonised over her decision. She picked up her pendant and thought of Edo and his family.

My family.

She held the pendant to her chest and said, "I won't just remember you."

Needless to say, Neliya's absence from the house perturbed everyone. But her appearance at the door, hours later, covered in dirt and grime, shocked them. She told them what had happened, save for the perplexing vision of a collapsing tower, and then scurried toward the bath. She had to endure a good long chiding from Uenda as the girl washed her back, but she accepted it with a wide smile.

That night, Neliya crept out of the bedroom she shared with Uenda, and sauntered across to Edo's door. She slid it open, and tossed a small book at the sleeping boy to wake him. Then she walked out of the house, forgoing shoes, and stood in the middle of the field. Her feet partially sank into the freshly ploughed soil. Edo approached her, and her smile widened with trepidation.

"Everything all right?" he asked. "No bad dreams, I hope."

"If there were, I don't remember them," replied the Mydian, her eyes returning to the sky above. Edo stood next to her. His urge to put his arm around her was plainly obvious, for she could feel it as if it radiated heat. She shivered, half-pretending, to invite him. He pulled her close, and she let her head fall against his shoulder. It was a moment before Neliya spoke.

"I didn't tell you everything that happened today," she stammered. "I got stuck in that hole and had horrible thoughts of death. Something helped me to pull out of that." She gazed at him. "It was you."

Edo smiled, his heart rising in his chest.

Neliya clutched her pendant and said, "I don't want to just remember you. I want to be with you." Her lips tensed. "I want to stay, and grow old with you."

Edo gazed at her with more emotions than he had words to convey. The enigma of that glimmer in her eyes exchanged itself for fixed determination. She asked, "Do you?"

Neliya's throat was completely parched, and her body trembled as she kept his gaze, knowing his body was responding in the same way. Though their minds had no idea what to do, at the very least their arms and legs had some semblance of will in them.

Edo's hand joined with Neliya's, and they went back to his room.

The bellman tapped the gong with a flourish, and the hall was silent. Foreheads met the floor, and the crowd uttered a prayer. Then Idoru spoke.

"A new life has come to our village. And a fine name is to be bestowed upon it. Even though," he stuttered as his gaze turned to the beautifully dressed yellow-skinned woman before him, "that new life is oftentimes a newborn."

The woman's heart thumped excitedly. She stole a gaze to the little sister who had adopted her, whose own ears fluttered eagerly. Seated next to Uenda, Edo smiled amorously, and it tortured the nameless woman to pull her eyes away.

Idoru continued, "As is tradition, the grandfather of the newborn is to select the name she will carry. Jikyo Sasai, please step forward."

Jikyo shuffled forward, and took a seat part way between the council and their nameless supplicant. He touched his fingers to his lips, then his forehead, before bowing.

"This newborn rode out of the sky on a falling star," he said. "What name could I give to such a woman? I welcome from the family any suggestions."

"Rii-tuan is yellow, like the sun!" exclaimed Uenda, completely ignorant of ceremony. The nameless woman stifled her giggles, but she wasn't the only one trying to maintain her cool.

"She brightens our day," said Sukete, though in a more respectful tone.

"Without her, nothing would grow in our fields, as an eternal night would permit no crop," said Odentii. His lips pursed into a hesitant smile.

Edo's gaze remained glued to the nameless woman. He did not speak, until the woman met his stare.

"She came to us with a name of her own, and I would love her no less if she kept it. But, if she so desires it, then let her have a name that says exactly what she is: a falling star."

Jikyo bowed reverently. "Well then, let me bless you with the name that suits you the most: Riifue."

The woman's eyes closed, her skin crackling with joy as she bowed. "I am honoured. May the Ancestors and the Gods bless me as part of their family." She swivelled on her knees, and bowed to the villagers of Medan. Uenda moved forward, kissed her fingers, tapped her forehead, and then touched them to the woman's shoulder. Edo, Sukete, Odentii, Jikyo, and Arika followed suit. Then so did every other villager within reach, until she was indistinguishable from the community around her.

As she spoke, she felt a pair of eyes bore into the back of her head. A boy from a past she willingly forgot, non-verbally assaulting her with a rage of abandonment of which she washed her hands. The people before her were no longer aliens upon whom she imposed – they were family.

And Fyuren was the alien.

27 | Gone in one big firework

The spring air was fickle: cold one second and warm the next. But huddling under a tree at night was better than the Andou house as far as Fyuren was concerned. He pulled his blanket tighter around him and rubbed his chest, gazing out over the plains where the *Ranegr* shuttle would land. He tried to sleep, though his inner voice screamed with the need to vocalise his rage at Neliya.

Before his frustrated fury could build, a rolled up mass of fabric hit the ground next to him. He looked up and saw Odentii.

"You were missed at naming ceremony," said the man, his rueful smile barely visible in the faint light of his lamp.

"Can't care less about Neliya's new nickname," spat Fyuren. "What stupid name does she have now?"

Odentii only chuckled. "Riifue was chosen name."

"Just so long as it doesn't mean *Femie*," grumbled Fyuren.

Odentii pointed to the roll of fabric. "A tent for you. For weeks maybe you'll camp. Not lonely?"

"Like *Neliya* said, I'm going to have to live without her … at least until she realises how asinine she's being," muttered Fyuren.

The comment, Fyuren expected, would earn him a disapproving glare from the man. Instead, Odentii just laughed. "Asinine … that's funny word."

Fyuren snarled, "So you're making fun of me too. Hold that tone when someone you love abandons you. Hold it when *two* people do it."

"Fyuren-eru, Riifue has made choice she believe will make her happy. Why you happy not?" asked Odentii.

"Because it's crap! She'll change her mind just as the shuttle takes off." He crossed his arms tightly over his chest and added, "Even if she doesn't, she won't be able to give you grandkids ... Sure the mechanics are kinda the same, but not the genetics. And what if those Kehans come looking for a Mydian to dissect?"

Odentii smirked, and sighed tiredly. "True, Riifue may not mother grandchildren of Andou house. And we would always fear Kehandou learning of her. And though Sukete hide it, she think of Neliya's parents also."

Fyuren gazed at the man a moment. His expression was that of someone searching for a way out of an impossible situation. Odentii slumped to the ground beside him with a huff.

"But Edo and she in love," he sighed. "I can stop them not."

Fyuren's eyes fell to the ground in front of him, and then to the inactive tablet beside him. "Well, I've told our friends on the *Ranegr* what's going on. Maybe Gast can help."

Odentii slapped his thighs and said, "Well, a week and then they land. Idoru want to know what need to do."

Oxide-caked fuel cells pushed electricity down the rusted cables into the chugging pump systems of the ancient hangar. The shuttle, with only a few dents and most of its blemishes repaired, sat moored to makeshift berths by umbilical cords. The crew scurried to load it with crates of salvaged foodstuffs and hardware through the mangled hangar entrance.

Kajil walked into the cockpit, where Fenk prepared for launch.

"The shuttle should be able to carry everyone, and the atmospheric landing shouldn't be a problem," said the pilot.

"Good," replied Kajil, a slight trepidation in his voice. "Allo says heat-shield'll whinge a tad on the aft-portside."

"Provided I can manage the controls, we should be fine," said Fenk. "Just need to get my head around this control system."

Kajil gave Fenk a friendly pat on the shoulder. "Ain't ya gonna 'ave some killer yarns back home, eh?" He left the cockpit, negotiated the passages of the shuttle, and emerged on the boarding ramp. Allo noticed his approach and called for silence among the engineers.

"Fenk'll go on the ease and slow," said Kajil. "Shield'll hold?"

"It's gotta," replied Allo, though it was more of a give-up line than a reassurance. It elicited disapproving murmurs from his team.

Kajil marched across the hangar, darting around the Nightshift crew stacking supply crates. He checked his watch and bellowed, "Half an hour, people! Launch in half an hour!" He was answered with an enthused roar. Then he made for the exit.

The corridor changed from a quagmire of jury-rigged bulkheads to the rusted passageways he'd grown up with. Kajil marvelled at the crew's success in reclaiming so much of the ancient ship. Slowing his pace, he ran his hands against the roughened surface of the metal corridor. He thought of Jugga,

Murraloohaa, the gang, teasing Borig, scuffles with the mining crews. A saddening and disturbing realisation came over him.

The Ranegr, the great ship of the Pebhorda, is junk now. 'Em fuel cells kark it, that's it.

Kajil bumped into Deloorie, standing idly by a door. Inside were the upturned remains of bedding that reeked of rust. She had a look that spoke directly to his own troubles.

"Murraloohaa and me," she said, though it was uncertain whether she was speaking to him or to herself. A faint hue rode on her light brown cheeks. Normally that would have earned a few knowing chuckles from the hangar worker. But that joking, cocky guy was long gone.

"Deloorie," he whispered.

"It's alright. I'm tryin' burn it in like it was." She bit her lip, her emaciated hand wandering along her stomach.

Kajil's chuckle started soft and low, growing into a hearty laugh he forgot he could do. That growing ball of emotional cud blew away on the winds that were Deloorie's words, and left him feeling refreshed.

He sobered and wiped away tears of merriment. "Murraloohaa always kicked me in the privies if I'd touch ya, but can I give ya a hug?"

Deloorie hugged him instead. He grunted in surprise by the tightness of her embrace, and he breathlessly asked, "Is this payback for somethin'?"

"Thanks, Kajil," she said into his shoulder before releasing him. He gasped air back into his lungs. "Oh, shut up, I didn't squeeze you *that* hard."

"Yeah, enough reminiscin'" he wheezed, pointing over his shoulder to the hangar. "Use those super muscles 'n' do some liftin'."

Dennie came from behind, scooted around him, and trotted after Deloorie, a box full of data disks in her arms. Gast followed soon after, carrying another box. He stopped beside Kajil.

"Everyone's gone from the aft bridge," said Gast. "All that's left is to go get the kids."

"I ain't sure Fyuren'll s'port the change in plans," Kajil intoned, concern mounting in his voice. "He said he was jitter'd that the TIM device wouldn't jump more than once before it's kark'd."

"It'll be simple to convince him, if it'll get Zeers back," said Gast. He eyed Kajil, recalling that time months ago when he lay at the man's mercy. "And I *will* save him ... It may be harder to convince Neliya, though."

Kajil chuckled, "The oldest yarn 'round the fire-bin: the adventurer in the new world falls in love with a native, 'n' the past ain't matters no more."

"Her past life will have to start mattering again," replied Gast, his tone unequivocal. "I'm not leaving without all three of them."

Kajil grinned just as a slight clanging caught their attention. In the adjacent room, a few of Allo's team hovered around a clutch of the *Ranegr*'s remaining high-yield explosives. The devices seemed benign, huddled together like large bottles of ale. But only a child would not see their death-mongering nature.

"Are you sure they'll work?" asked Gast, his eyebrow raised.

"Jus' one of 'em dust'd a cruiser half our size," said Kajil. "It'll make this bugger disappear."

The two men reached the hangar just as the remaining supplies were secured. The shuttle's drives screeched to life as the power in the fuel cells dwindled to a slow trickle. The hangar lights began to flicker, like a dying soldier clawing for his last breath. Kajil stepped up the ramp, pausing to look around once more. The nostalgia ebbed away.

Good riddance. Hope this place turns to ash, he thought.

The main hatch closed, the crew strapped themselves in, and the shuttle came about at break-neck speed. The purple gas giant came into view, and the large moon floating innocuously above it. It had only begun to grow bigger in the viewport when the sensors console meekly beeped. Fenk checked the readouts, and turned pale.

"Kajil! Get up here!" he bellowed.

Kajil and Gast flew up to the cockpit, and studied the sensor data.

"That's a tunnelling signature," exclaimed Gast.

"I'm reading a ship on intercept course with the *Ranegr*," said Fenk. "Hull configuration and composition consistent with the Pebhasid flagship."

The hearts of everyone in the cockpit froze. Kajil sprinted through the ship toward the rear viewport, knocking over confused crewmen as he went. He gazed out through the wake of the shuttle's thrusters, and saw the *Ranegr*. An equally large, white vessel loomed over it. Kajil recognised it straight away.

Gast and Allo appeared beside him, their jaws ajar with dismay.

"Gelfri really is here," said Allo. Down the corridors, the rest of the crew heard the news. The cabin bubbled with emotions ranging from concern to horror. Before it could devolve into panic, Kajil roared, "We can still take him out! Those bombs are on-board." He turned to Allo and asked, "There a remote on 'em bombs?"

Gast grabbed Kajil by the shoulder, "What's in your head?"

"We blow the *Ranegr* 'n' take him down!" retorted Kajil.

"Zeers is on that ship!" exclaimed the Military Alchemist.

"What do you think then, eh? Let those bombs get nab'd?" asked Kajil.

Gast shook the man by the shoulders. "We go back and save Zeers!"

Kajil swatted him away. "He knows Neliya and Fyuren're on that planet. *Littles* knows. What ya think'll happen if Gelfri decides to go on a jaunt? We blow the *Ranegr*, we save the ones that *ain't* crazy."

In a fit of rage, Gast threw Kajil against the wall. His mechanical palm radiated yellow light.

"Pilot Orthos! Turn this ship around!" he roared into the intercom.

The shuttle cabin fell silent but for the sound of the engines and solar winds against the hull. Fenk licked his lips hesitantly. His throat ran dry as he eyed the planet ahead.

"No," he replied.

"I gave you an order!" bellowed Gast.

"I won't leave my son," Fenk insisted.

"Do it! Or the Drifter's head rolls," spat Gast.

"Well ain't that bonkers, Littles Senior!" exclaimed Kajil. "Is it really an implant what made Zeers nuts?"

Gast's arm fizzled with fury. "And you Drifters? You cut people off because you're too damn cowardly to help them! You stop caring when your own hides are on the line! Uncivilised murderers!"

Gast's head hit the ground with a reverberating clang. He looked up in a daze, and saw Swine standing over him.

"M'lady called us 'uncivilised,'" he muttered. "An' she was right, then. We didn't care. But e'en now, it ain't uncivilised, an' it ain't cowardly, to know when you can't help, no matter how much you care."

Kajil looked down at the soldier, who wrestled with mounting grief and a pointed jab of reality. Out the corner of his eye he saw Deloorie, her fist held tightly to her chest as tears fell down her cheek. Then he looked to Allo. "Gimme the remote."

Allo solemnly cleared his throat, and brandished the device in question. Kajil took the detonator box.

"Please don't," Gast pleaded tearfully. "We're not supposed to kill children."

"Things ain't how you s'pose them," returned Kajil, and he pressed the button.

What began as tiny pockmarks of red across the receding hull of the *Ranegr* gave way to a blinding flash. The crew averted their eyes from the bright explosion. Seconds later, the shuttle shuddered violently, the hull echoing with the dinging sounds of vaporised metal impacting it. They looked out the viewport, and their hearts sank.

The blast threw debris and dust outward from a cloud of shimmering blue and white. Within the cloud, the crew could see the remains of the rear engines, mangled and ruined.

To one side of the explosion, they could see the Pebhasid's flagship. Flames and gasses burst from its hull, and it had begun to pitch. The lights on the flagship started to flicker before going out, and the vessel split apart.

Yet there was little to celebrate in the apparent defeat of Gelfri.

Fizzling out of the dust blanket were indiscernible pieces of derelict, and the crew couldn't help but wonder which parts of the ship had those masses been. Someone's quarters? A piece of the farm? A chair from the old food hall? A bulkhead against which they'd measured their height as they grew up?

Our homes ... all our rememberin's ... gone in one big firework, thought Kajil. He coughed back his tears and tapped the intercom.

"Fenk, how long 'til we hit air?" he asked.

"About two minutes," stammered the pilot.

Before anyone could move toward their seats, a fit of ire burst from Gast's mouth, and he launched himself at Kajil. His face met Swine's fist, and he fell unconscious. Swine and Kajil hoisted him up and put him in a passenger seat. Everyone else returned to their seats. Those who knew the children wore pensive faces, knowing that their grief was soon to catch up to them. Fenk pushed his own guilt aside.

Fyuren is what matters now!

He entered the flight path into the antique console. The centre display lit up with a topographic map of the moon's continents, a path leading through the atmosphere to the isles where Fyuren and Neliya awaited. The ship pitched as Fenk twisted the yoke, and the moon rolled in their view. Wisps of whiteness whisked past the vessel, increasing in frequency and redness as the shuttle's underside met the outer reaches of the atmosphere.

What started like the sound of a tiny insect buzzing around Fenk's left ear was an omen of impending catastrophe. The buzzing quickly escelated into a blast of torn metal. Fenk jerked the yoke back and hard to the right. The shuttle pitched, almost snapping in half as the chassis whined.

"Heat-shield on the aft-portside!" cried the pilot.

The readouts were dead on that part of their underside. An alert klaxon warned of a hull breach. The shuttle was falling apart.

"Extending drag flaps!" barked Fenk. He yanked back on a lever. His internal organs lurched forward, and he growled at the inertia. He breathlessly looked out the viewport. The darkness of an ocean zoomed far beneath them, the glassy firmament of an atmosphere above. Sunlight came from above, illuminating silver reefs below, which resembled a path to the island – to his son.

Riifue sat against a tree in the shade, absentmindedly stroking the fabric of the shawl Arika had made for her. Her eyes locked on Edo, who stood with his father a bit further down the hill.

After today, my life begins, she thought.

Uenda dragged her from her musing.

"Rii-tuan, Grumbleguts needs help," she said, pointing to Fyuren up on the hill.

Riifue looked up, worried that he was having another outburst. Instead, Fyuren was waving ecstatically.

"He says they're on their way," said Riifue. She and Uenda slid down the slope toward Odentii, who then passed on the message and called for the villagers to be ready.

Riifue could hear the voices of the villagers on the wind, discussing and betting on the number of limbs the alien crew would have. She couldn't help but chuckle at the naïve fantasies of even the adults, and wondered why their minds leapt into whimsy when they had a perfectly good example of an alien right in front of them.

"Rii-tuan, I can't see anything," Uenda mumbled.

Riifue looked to the horizon. "They're still too far away."

She swivelled at the sound of Fyuren calling her old name. She walked up the slope to him. He had a very worried look on his face.

"What's the matter?" she asked in Aimorein, before correcting herself.

"I lost contact with them," replied Fyuren.

The field simmered with intrigued banter at the sight of a faint flash on the horizon. It was as if a new star began shining and then stopped just as suddenly.

"That must've been the *Ranegr*," said Fyuren. "It's at the right coordinates. So the bombs must've gone off fine. But I still can't find the shuttle."

Fyuren heard a holler from the hill nearby. He and Riifue looked over to see a group of villagers, their arms outstretched toward the southeast. Fyuren saw a smoking dot and gasped in horror.

"The shuttle's going to crash!" he roared.

Riifue sprinted down the hill, toward Odentii. When he heard her bewildered shrieks and saw the incoming smoke trail, he roared at the top of his lungs. The villagers fled out of the plains and into the trees. Fyuren stood on the hill petrified with dismay.

The dot took the shape of the *Ranegr*'s shuttle. Flames and smoke blew from breaches in its blackened hull as it streaked over the land. The grumbling sounds of its descent preceded it like an ominous thunderclap. Then it hit, and its momentum dragged it along like a knife cleaving Aimore's grassy flesh.

Then it stopped.

Fyuren fell to his knees and screamed.

28 | You sold us out!

Kajil knew he wasn't blind by the sparks punctuating the darkness, and his ears were working fine despite the ringing, which penetrated the cacophony of panicked voices around him. He couldn't blame his crew for panicking, but he could definitely yell at them for it.

"Everybody shut up!" He coughed up a lung-full of smoke. "Everyone stay together."

Though the crash disoriented them, the crew managed to regroup. Someone found an emergency kit, and soon flashlights were passed around. Casualties were few, and due only to the misfortune of a shoddy harness.

"Where's Gast?" he asked.

"He's here," said Deloorie, hovering over the man still unconscious in his seat.

"Must've clonked 'im good, eh?" said Kagoolie. Kajil wondered if the old lady could survive anything as she hobbled toward him, her left arm hanging from the shoulder.

Fenk's voice echoed from the cockpit, his sunlit silhouette barely visible through a blanket of smoke. "Kajil! Is everyone alright?"

"Far's I know," spluttered the captain.

"There's an eject system for the front of the cockpit," said Fenk. "I'm going to blow it and we can get everyone out."

"Hurry up then, air's gettin' toxic!" shouted Allo.

Seconds later, a thunderclap reverberated through the shuttle as the cockpit blew away. Air rushed about the cabin, carrying the smoke with it like a flood that wasn't sure where to go. Sunlight blinded the crew in a way no light ever had. When their eyes adapted to the strange sensation, they looked past the curtain of smoke and saw a green alien landscape, valleys to one side and mountains to the other.

Fenk's feet hit the browning earth, and he scurried away from the burning wreck like a forager from a bushfire. The rest of the crew followed, but no one got far before they saw a front of terrified bipeds advancing on them.

Fenk threw his arms up in surrender. "We mean no harm! Don't attack!"

The Neiren villagers reached the alien arrivals, taking time from being both nervous and mortified to eye the dirtiness and ravaged appearance of yet more Mydians.

"Where is Neliya?" he asked.

Upon hearing the name, every pair of eyes turned to a short woman in their midst, and Fenk blinked in shock. The woman with the brunette hair chirped, "Here, Fenk."

Fenk didn't have time to be amazed or sceptical. Kajil appeared at his side, with the rest of the crew accounted for. "Neliya, skip intros 'til later."

"Water carriages are on their way," said Neliya. "Anyone who needs medicine, we'll help."

An older man, who Kajil assumed was Odentii, stepped up. "Any else, help block fire."

The crew split in two, the injured following the woman who appeared a shadow of the Neliya they knew. Fenk caught up to the woman and asked, "Where's Fyuren?"

Neliya directed Fenk to the northern hilltop, upon which Fyuren sat immobile. He broke into a run that not even his broken ribs could slow. He pulled himself up the hill, ignoring the shaken villagers that withdrew from him. At the top of the hill, the boy he'd longed to see for innumerable months sat blank-faced, eyes unfocused in shock. Fenk fell to the ground in front of his son. He called his name, shook his shoulder, and no response came.

The shuttle's gone. And we're stuck. Trying for years to get back, he just watched the whole thing blow up in his face … Again.

That same realisation grew in Fenk's mind. At first he was empathetic for his son, and knew that with time, it would turn into grief of his own. But for now, he had to comfort his son.

"I'm here, Fyuren," he said firmly. "And even if we can't get off this planet, I'm staying with you."

Deloorie eyed the young woman in alien garb, wrapping bandages and applying ointments. Given Neliya's hair, tattoos, clothing and disposition, it was no wonder Fenk couldn't recognise her. The glances she lent to one of the native men were enough to make Deloorie grin in spite of the desperate situation.

While Deloorie silently marvelled, Dennie openly pitied Fyuren.

"That's the last straw for the poor darl, eh?"

Deloorie glanced away from slinging Kagoolie's broken arm, and eyed the wrecked shuttle. "He's good, but no way he'll be able to fix this,"

Her eyes scanned the scenery. Within the smell of quenched metal and smoke, a nostalgic scent tickled at her senses, though she could not recall the last time she smelled it. The sensations elicited a vision of a savannah, a hue of green outlining a horizon, above which loomed a single moon. "This place isn't all that bad though," she mumbled, trying to name the place in her vision.

"It's not home for them," replied Dennie, whose eyes were still fixated on the father and son on the hill.

None of the Neiren dared touch the Mydian with the metal arm. He proved far scarier awake. Like one possessed, he ignored the aliens and invalids around him and searched the crowd. He found his quarry and forewent his Alchemic abilities for a more satisfying and personal blow to Kajil's cheek. Everyone cleared away as if the two men were diseased. Kajil was quickly matched by the man's pure rage.

"You killed him!" roared Gast, throwing a punch with his metal fist that narrowly missed Kajil's face. "I could have saved him and you killed him! So now I'll kill you."

A few of the more able-bodied survivors grabbed Gast and overpowered him before he could land any more blows, leaving Kajil to catch his breath and nurse a few new wounds.

"I wasn't turnin'," barked Kajil. "How good you are ain't nothin', Military Alchemist. They'd a killed ya. *Littles* woulda killed ya."

"You killed Zeers!" Gast repeated.

"We don't know if Zeers was on that ship," Kajil retorted. "We can go back to the Pebhasid station and find him."

"How d'ya 'spect we do that? The shuttle's a wreck," asked Allo, barking from just within ear-reach as Sukete wrapped his broken arm in a sling.

"Fyuren's smart, he'll think of something," retorted Kajil, though he obviously didn't believe it.

"He must think fast, or no chance," Odentii interjected.

All eyes turned to the approaching Neiren, who wore a grave look with a dash of guilt.

"You are Odentir?" asked Gast.

"My family has been caring for your children," replied Odentii.

"What ya mean, *no chance*?" asked Kajil.

Odentii turned to address the survivors. "Your ship burned hole across the provinces. While just Fyuren and Neliya here, there was chance to keep secret. Now, we can't hide. The Uasaajya sends soldiers. The Kehan will want to know all about you and your ship."

Every Mydian's chest burned cold, as if their hearts had stopped. Before anyone else could react, Gast and Kajil approached Odentii, their earlier quarrel put to the back of their minds.

"You sold us out!" barked Kajil, gripping Odentii by the collar. Edo moved to his father's aid, stopping only when Gast held out his metal hand.

"I tried to keep secret," rasped Odentii, Kajil's grip constricting his speech.

"Who is this *waa-sar-jeea*?" exclaimed Gast.

"He is leader of Aimore," gasped Odentii. "He no want you here too. The Kehan want you."

Edo stole Kajil's chance to ask what *Kehan* meant. He swatted Gast's hand out of the way and reached for Kajil's arms. But both men dwarfed him in size and strength. Kajil shoved the boy off with a jerk of the shoulder, and Gast hoisted him into the air with his mechanical arm.

"Gast!" exclaimed Kajil.

Gast turned to see Kajil, Odentii's shirt collar still held tightly in his hands, a knife to his throat. Neliya's gaze wafted between the both of them, betraying only a hint of hesitation as she edged the knife closer to Kajil's jugular.

"Put them down," she said unequivocally.

Gast gave a sardonic scoff. "I can just whisk that butter-knife out of your hands, Neliya." Then he felt something sharp prickle against the back of his neck. He couldn't see it, but he knew what it was. Edo growled, "Die if not."

Kajil released Odentii, his earlier fear-driven fury drained by Neliya's threat. He breathlessly muttered, "Ya ain't lil' Femie in the tunneller now, eh?"

Neliya turned to Odentii, speaking in Myddish, "Is there some place we can hide them?"

"No, soldiers come from all ways," replied Odentii.

"There's gotta be a place we can go," said Allo, eyeing the participants and hoping for no more outbursts.

The debate continued, more harmonious than before, though as options dwindled the participants became more fervent. Talk had started of fighting back, before a shrill voice bisected the discussion. A babbling Uenda dragged them to the far side of the wreck, and pointed at another dot on the horizon.

The realisation struck Kajil first, but he denied it to himself.

Then Allo caught on. "Maybe a bit stingy on 'em warheads." His tone was flat, as if his voice hadn't caught up to the stream of horror filling him.

Gast, having reached the same conclusion, found himself a little ambivalent about the situation. "That's another shuttle. Gelfri is coming, maybe Zeers too."

"Let's go," snapped Kajil. He and Gast started to move first, the rest in tow.

"I 'sume you cookin' a plan?" asked Allo.

"We need to get the civilians out of here," said Gast, eyeing the triage camp.

"Gelfri'll just pick 'em off," said Kajil. "He'll be droolin' over an 'abitable place."

"He no take village," snapped Odentii. "Army comes."

Both Gast and Kajil sighed with dismay.

A battle on two fronts, and no way out, thought Gast. He heard Edo babble something to Neliya, whose eyes lit up excitedly.

"Edo just said, let's get the Aimoren army to take them out," she said. "You can take the shuttle and go once we knock Gelfri out."

Gast frowned. "And what kind of weapons do they have? Spears and rocks?"

"Have guns," said Odentii.

"Who'll tell 'em who's bad and not?" asked Kajil.

Odentii and Edo raised their hands. "We tell," said Odentii.

Gast saw the shuttle getting closer. He snapped his fingers and drew attention to himself. "Alright, here's what we'll do: get the critically injured out of here. The rest will stay and be decoys to stall Gelfri. Neliya and I will keep a watch on the shuttle until the native army comes and takes Gelfri out. Everyone clear?"

The group nodded in unison.

Odentii, Edo, Neliya, and Uenda took off toward the triage camp. The crew packed up frantically, the trauma of the crash amplified by the imminent appearance of their former captain. As the injured disappeared into the woods, Kajil called the able-bodied crewmen, of which there were few, to his side.

He looked fixedly at Gast. "You bring 'em soldiers here, and we'll save Zeers together!"

Both men locked hands as the group cheered. Their gazes met, they steeled their resolve.

"Don't hold it to my son if he's brutal," he said as he parted from the crowd.

Kajil laughed. "He's always been brutal. It's why we love him."

Gast turned away, allowing himself a rare smile before chasing after the small stream of people disappearing into the woods.

The winds blew in force as the Pebhasid's shuttle loomed over the wreck. Of the same intricate design as the now-wrecked flagship, it came to a graceful halt in the air above. Torrents of air buffeted the survivors, blinding them as they shielded their eyes from ballistic dust. Armoured hands threw them to the ground as the whir of atmospheric drives died down.

Kajil blinked away the agonising dirt trapped in his eyes, cursing whoever cuffed him before he could rub them clean. Then he looked up and saw a face that filled him with rage, dread, and sorrow.

"Gelfri, you're shorter than I 'member," he managed to say. "'N' a lot paler. Been a sickie, eh?"

"Just a few injuries," replied the Pebhasid. "Had a handful of homicidals homing on my heart, I have. None of them managed to destroy my flagship, though … until now. Good job, you ragtag, wriggling ring-worms! If I hadn't had the shuttle prepped for launch before hand, I'd have died in that explosion."

"Oh, that's too bad, eh," retorted Kajil, instilling as much bile into his response as he could muster. "Me crew and me'd just love to hear about all your pain."

"How about we hear about yours, cantankerous Kajil," came a second voice, bearing a dash of familiarity. Closely following was a foot to Kajil's solar plexus, throwing him onto his back.

Littles glared down at the dazed man, exhausted staring eyes radiating a manic aura. He bellowed, "That's for destroying my ship, you babbling back-sloggin' bastard!"

29 | I've been in way worse

The crew fled through the forest. The Neiren helped those who were limping, and carried those who could neither stand nor maintain consciousness long enough to try.

The branches above started to sway. Twigs, leaves, and seeds rained down as the treetops bore the brunt of a sudden gust that could only have come from the second shuttle. Several people panicked as they imagined their homes ransacked by alien marauders. The subsequent sound of mechanical whirring behind them only disturbed them more. A nervous murmur permeated the crowd when Gast appeared behind them.

"What's it like?" asked Fenk, grunting under the weight of Fyuren's comatose body.

"Gelfri took the bait," replied Gast. "I spied a little as they landed, and Zeers *is* with them." He made no effort to hide his relief.

Neliya wasn't so relieved. "Did he bring troops?"

"A whole legion," replied Gast. He saw Edo and Odentii and barked, "Why are you still here? Go and get the troops!"

"Need weapons," said Odentii. He bellowed a few commands to his fellow villagers, who headed for the village proper. Gast followed Neliya and the Neiren family along an up-hill trail, and across a half-tilled field to the house the children had called home for a long while. Idoru stood on the porch.

"Gast, this is Idoru, the village leader," said Neliya. The man mumbled what Gast assumed was a situation report. Odentii replied with a grave tone, and Idoru's face broke with a horrified expression. The conversation turned to an argument, at which point Gast's face crumpled with annoyance and he blurted, "For those who don't speak local?"

Odentii sent Neliya inside with Edo, and then turned to Gast. "Our Saajya hoped you leave with no accident, but accident happened, and more invaders. Idoru and Saajya angry."

"Did you tell him our plan?" asked Gast.

Gast spoke to Idoru a bit more. The village leader pondered a moment, and then spoke up. Odentii translated, "We send runners to tell army. Have they traits different from friends?"

"Enemies are wearing blue uniforms," said Gast.

Idoru nodded, and then mumbled some curt commands to the young men waiting by the house, who then departed for the forest. Gast sighed with relief, and turned to Fenk, "If we can take out the Drifter soldiers, we can steal the shuttle and get out of here."

Fenk grinned and tried to rouse his son, but the boy was unresponsive. Even when Uenda held a bowl of some smelly muck to his nose, he showed no movement besides breathing.

"We can worry about Fyuren later," said Gast. "Orthos, can you fight?"

"With respect, sir, even if I am court martialled, I am staying with my son," said Fenk with an undeterred gaze.

Gast's jaw tightened, recalling the pilot's earlier disobedience, though his annoyance lost out to his empathy. He ordered him away to the centre of town with Sukete and Uenda. He then looked into the alien rural household, and saw Neliya and Edo whispering to each other as they tied elastic strings to long planks of wood.

So much wasted time!

He paced toward the door and prepared a drill sergeant's roar to snap the tardy recruits to attention. He stopped in his tracks when he processed what he saw.

His mind wandered to the looks passed between Neliya and that boy. It elicited nostalgia, and a sensation of warmth that was quickly doused by the realisation of what fulfilling his mission would do to her. He had hoped her feelings had not drifted too deep. Yet, though he had no idea what they were saying, their affectionate gaze told him those feelings went as far as his once had. His heart ached as he read their lips, and accorded one phrase to memory.

Keta sayei.

He quickly realised what he was doing and backed away from the door. His foot bumped against a bowl on the floor, the same bowl Uenda held up to Fyuren's nose to rouse him. Curiosity partially divided his flummoxed daze, and he leaned down to pick it up. In the next instant, he withdrew from it in revulsion.

"What is this muck?" he shrieked.

"Kusin fungus," said Odentii, picking it up as if it were nothing harmful. "It grow on bad crops and we use it for animal feed."

"You can't smell that?" exclaimed the Mydian.

"Seem only Mydians smell it," shrugged Odentii.

Gast's eyebrows shot up. The stench was as potent as the idea it gave him. "Have enough for a distraction?"

Fyuren's back ached from being hunched so long. He rubbed his eyes, wondering how long they'd been open. When they cleared, he looked up, and saw a truly welcome sight.

"Dad," he tried to shout, though his voice his was too hoarse. He pulled himself to his feet, and gingerly moved to hug his father. "How did you get out of the shuttle?"

"You don't know?" asked Fenk, wincing as he spoke. "We escaped through the cockpit eject hatch. Most of us got out with a few scrapes and broken bones, but we're alright. What about you? You were in a daze, like someone hypnotized you."

Fyuren tried to focus, but his mind was full of pleasant blankness and clarity. With a smile he said, "Just got a little lost in my own head." He looked around, and saw the familiar scenery of Medan. People had gathered in the village square near the temple, where some had taken to prayer. Others tended to the *Ranegr* survivors. Sukete and Uenda sat nearby, relieved at his awakening.

"Where're Neliya and the others?" he asked while trying to stifle a yawn.

"Gelfri came in a shuttle of his own," said Fenk. "Kajil and anyone who could fight stayed behind, while the wounded got out. We're waiting here until the native army gets in to beat Gelfri."

Fyuren swallowed. "Neliya is with them?" He gazed over the treetops to the west. The wrecked shuttle still billowed smoke visible from behind the hill. Wheels turned in his head as if greased to perfection. Never had his mind been so clear.

He looked fixedly at Fenk. "I have to go help Neliya and Zeers." Then he leaped to his feet and sprinted down the path.

"Wait, Fyuren! You can't go alone," shouted Fenk.

Fyuren swivelled mid-run, and said with a giddy grin, "Don't worry. I've been in way worse."

Gast carefully pushed back a branch near to the verge of a cliff. A white painted spacecraft stood triumphantly near the miserable hurled-down wreck of the *Ranegr*'s shuttle. Though they were much too far away to see faces, Gast could tell by his prominence that Gelfri was there amongst the legion, pacing in front of a line of subdued prisoners.

"I can't see Zeers," said Neliya, who peered over his shoulder.

"He's probably in the shuttle," replied Gast in a whisper. "Hurry. The soldiers should be in position, if they're as prompt as Odentii made them out to be."

The pair slid down the steep path before pacing along level ground. A twig snap from their far right alerted them, and they scrambled behind some wide trees. Gast silently tapped some controls on his arm while Neliya notched an arrow. Her heart thumped with excitement as she edged around the side of the tree to see some slightly rustling bushes.

Out popped a strange four-legged creature, its vibrant stripped fur slightly dirtied, and a tiny morsel flailing in between its bared teeth. It's jaws clamped down, its eyes seeming to flash with joy as purple liquid dribbled from its mouth. The prey disappeared behind those fangs, and the animal dashed up a nearby tree as fast as Uenda.

Neliya and Gast stayed their weapons with a sigh. They cleared their hiding places and moved further through the trees toward the south clearing.

"We're getting close to the clearing," said Neliya.

"Go over the plan again for me," said Gast.

"When we're in position, we signal Odentii and the others on the east ridge," said Neliya. "They throw your kusin bombs into the valley to distract Gelfri. You go in and free the prisoners."

"Let's hope Edo has reached the advance troops and they're in position as well," added Gast.

"Odentii will signal us if they're not," said Neliya. "And I draw Zeers to the south clearing, and lure him to the field near the river. I hold him 'til you get there."

"I remove that implant, and he should be back to normal," Gast finished.

"We'll have to see," she mumbled. Her voice lacked anything resembling hope or pessimism. He recalled her moment with Edo, and took the chance.

"Does *keta sayei* mean 'I love you?'" he asked.

Neliya tried to move forward, but Gast stopped her. "Boggima told me how Zeers used to look at you. He might recover if he thinks you're waiting for him."

Neliya looked squarely at Gast. "It's said from a wife to her husband." Then she shook him away and walked ahead. With a steeled tone, she said, "I'm not going back. Over the last who-knows-how-many years, I've seen so many people stuck in a rut. The crew of the *Ranegr*, Zeers and Fyuren. I even saw it in a cave underground. Gelfri said once, 'Your family will eventually end up on your plate.' It's like a cycle, like the *Othala*. With Edo, I have a chance to break that cycle, and I'm taking it."

Gast ran his hand through his thinning black hair.

"What about your parents? Your mother and father?" he asked, knowing from the look on her face he was grabbing at straws.

"I can't even remember their names," said Neliya flatly. "I rarely ever saw my planet-side father, and my mother always worked. Here, I have not just a mother and father, but a sister as well. I have someone I love. I'm *happy* here,

Gast."

Gast saw before him a transformation. No longer did he see a schoolgirl drinking in the experiences of a cultural exchange trip. That girl disappeared, and a tattooed woman, indistinguishable from the aliens around her, took her place.

"You're not fighting to save your crew. You're defending your home, aren't you?"

The woman's gaze was unwavering.

"My name is Riifue Andou," she proclaimed.

30 | You make it better every day

Littles strode, his cape wafting behind him, toward the garrison. A wide smirk covered his face, hiding the otherwise obvious fatigue plaguing his eyes. A few scouts followed, carrying a strange apparatus.

Gelfri looked away from interrogating a Nightshift worker with a taser. Littles momentarily wondered whether the creature looked so ugly before the Pebhasid had his way with it. The prisoners winced both at their comrade's pain and their tightening cuffs.

"Did you get anything from this choleric clod?" asked Littles, squatting down to poke the smoking body.

"The clod was surprisingly contrary," replied Gelfri, amusement overshadowing the distress in his voice. "Wouldn't even tell me if there are naïve natives nearby." His turned his gaze to the rest of the crew, rewarding their bloodthirsty glares with an almost bored expression. "Any of you cursed contagions coming cooperative?"

Deloorie, who was nearest the Pebhasid, hawked and spat at him. A simple gesture to express her and her husband's latent rage, it was rewarded with a blow across the face. She fell backward, a red waterfall flowing from her teeth.

Littles shrugged disinterestedly, and said, "Look what we found on the hill nearby." He upended the bag in his hand, and sifted through the contents. He sniffed a shirt, and said with a raised eyebrow, "Wow, Shorts has gotten big. Looks like he's been busy too."

Glad to be rid of the pain in his lower back, the scout lowered the device to the ground. While Gelfri gazed at the machine, stroking his chin in thought, Littles studied the faces of their prisoners. One expression stood out.

"Delicious Dennie," he exclaimed, snatching the taser out of Gelfri's hand and matching toward the trembling woman. He wrapped his free hand around her shoulders and said with a grin, "Dennie, define this dubious device, will ya?"

"Something Fyuren was workin' on," mumbled Dennie as she tried to pull away from him.

"Duh, Dennie! But he must've mentioned something, right?" Dennie was silent, so Littles thrust the dormant taser to her cheek. "Right?"

Dennie devolved into a paroxysm of panicked shrieks. Tears began to dribble down her face. "Yes, yes, we were! He said he'd built a power source for the TIM device. It could replace the *Ranegr*'s tokamak."

Gelfri looked up in amazement. "Another gem from the illustrious intelligence of Shorts! Assuming she's right, of course."

A squishy mass suddenly hit the side of Littles' head with enough force to knock him off balance. The rancid odour of the projectile made him recoil in revulsion. The mass landed on Dennie's stomach, and elicited a screech. She twitched and writhed to get it off her, and crawled away. Littles and Gelfri leaned over the vile mass.

"Is this old resomator run-off?" asked Gelfri.

"No, it's worse," exclaimed Littles.

A platoon of Pebhasid soldiers fled in all directions as if a grenade had been thrown their way. At the epicentre stood a soldier, doubled over and vomiting, his uniform stained by green-white muck. Another platoon jumped away with a shriek when more gunk landed near them.

"Get back in line, you fart-phobic funkmeisters!" bellowed the Pebhasid, his sleeve over his mouth.

Another muck ball hit the ground and destabilised Gelfri's troops even more. The hostages grew restless as the stench hit them as well, several passing out after holding their breath. Another muck ball hit the side of the shuttle, and another landed inside the hatch.

Littles scanned the surrounding hills, and his irritation grew into fury as the realisation hit him. "Gast! Femie! Shorts! Where are you?"

Gelfri turned with raised eyebrows. "Ah, you think this is a prank by those precocious—"

"Shut up, Gelfri," barked Littles. He swivelled and fired blindly. An unlucky soldier took a bullet to the thigh. Littles wailed with irritation louder than his underling. "Look what you made me do, you stupid stinkbugs!"

The barrage of stink bombs persisted. Littles fired aimlessly several more times, narrowly missing hostages and even Gelfri, before his clip emptied.

A boom echoed from the north. The hairs on Gelfri's neck stood up, and he glanced over his shoulder. Behind the northern hill wafted a cloud of dirt. He gazed upwards, and saw Gast hurtling toward him.

Gast's metallic arm buzzed with an orange glow, seeking its target in the

Pebhasid's forehead. Gelfri raised his right hand. An explosion electrified the air around them, sending out beams of blinding light. Gast's stomach lurched as if he'd been thrown out of a tunneller mid-flight. He tumbled along the ground, head over heels, before gaining his footing again. Gelfri gripped his burning sleeve and tore it away with a flourish. Steam flowed from the blue luminescence of the metal arm's inner workings.

"A Megin Limb!" exclaimed Gast.

"Put to much better use than by it's former master, I assure you," said the Pebhasid, clenching his metal hand and savouring the silence of its mechanisms.

Gast eyed the limb, trying to remember the last time he fought another Megin user. His eyes imperceptibly darted south, and he started to chuckle for the first time in his memory.

"Hardly, you third-rate circus magician," he spat between increasingly fervent bursts of laughter. Littles ecstatic grin slowly turned to confusion, then to anger.

"What's so funny, Gast?" asked Gelfri. Gast gave no reply and continued to laugh.

"Answer him, you giggling git!" roared Littles.

Gast pointed to the south. The Pebhasid and his underlings turned, and saw Edo. A horde of the aliens joined him, armed with long-barrelled guns cocked at the ready. Another battalion of alien soldiers appeared from the north, and another from the east. Odentii and Idoru emerged from the forest with a fourth battalion.

"You are surrounded! Surrender now!" bellowed Odentii.

Littles' eyes widened so much only his nerves held them in their sockets. He stammered and babbled, gazing at his troops, incapacitated by the diabolically smelly muck. Calculating an impending loss, he turned his gun on Gast. The gun clicked empty.

"It's over, Zeers," said Gast. "It's time to come home."

The Pebhasid chuckled, "It's far from over, Military Alchemist."

A high-pitched whirr flooded the valley, giving rise to a mighty roar of aerospikes coming to life. Whatever muck stench remained was blown away on the winds of Gelfri's shuttle rising off the ground, turrets on its underside swivelling.

Gast focused his mental strength at the shuttle. The craft pitched and the gunfire ceased. The Military Alchemist turned to the alien army and roared, "What're you waiting for?"

Odentii and Idoru let out a war cry, their swords raised. Bursts of sound and flashes of light exploded from the incoming army, felling several of Gelfri's soldiers. Then, their single shots expired, the soldiers drew long blades and dashed down the hill.

Those that hadn't been maimed by the primitive rifles shook themselves out of their shock and cocked their guns to retaliate. Gelfri, bewildered by the sudden onslaught, forgot about the prisoners. Littles didn't, and turned amidst the brawl to see Gast blast away the shackles binding their hostages. A powerful bloodlust took over his body. He snatched a gun from a soldier protecting Gelfri and took aim. Gast pressed his palm to the ground, and by the force of his telekinesis he hurtled through the air, over a flabbergasted Littles, and into the brawling crowd.

"Gast!" screeched Littles. He ignored Gelfri's calls for him to stop and charged into the fray. At first he thought he saw Gast in amidst a scuffle between a red-uniformed Neiren and a Pebhasid soldier, and he pushed both of them aside. But his quarry was nowhere. "Come and fight me, Gast!" he shouted, his challenge lost in the cacophony of stray bullets and clashing swords.

He glanced to the south and saw between clashing sides an infinitely more stirring prize. Though barely recognisable beneath tattooed arms, darkened hair, and time, Littles had no doubt that it was her. She slunk backward into the forest as if goading him to follow. Nothing else mattered now. Littles slipped his firearm into the back of his pants, scooped up the sword from a nearby alien soldier, and then sprinted after the girl.

His legs seemed imbued with infinite energy as he bounded through the woods, stopping only when he could neither see her tracks nor hear the sounds of the battle behind him. His blade at the ready, he eagerly surveyed his surroundings, his panting radiating a beastly sound through the silent woodland.

I should be able to smell her fear ... Where is it?

He darted around, hopping over a few tree roots and fallen branches and paused again. In a slow, squeaky voice he muttered:

> *Runs away, always away,*
> *Hides from me, cowardly she.*
> *Can still been happy, you and me,*
> *Come on out, it's okay.*

No reply came.

> *Oh, who do I kid?*
> *You I'll still flay!*
> *Haunting my dreams, night and day,*
> *Of her crippling face I'll be rid!*

"Quit trying to be like Borig!" Littles looked up into the air, and saw his personal poltergeist standing on a high branch. "He was way better at it than you, anyway."

"There you are, Femie!" he snapped with villainous glee.

The tormenter promptly notched an arrow and fired. Littles swatted the shaft. He looked up to the branch, and she was gone. His eyes darted between the twigs and branches of the canopy, until she barked, "And quit calling me that too!" Littles turned, barely fast enough to flick another arrow with his blade. The woman moved before he could look again.

"What would you rather I call you? Neliya? Boring name."

"Riifue is my name now," came the voice, from a tree behind him. Littles swivelled on his guard, expecting another projectile. When none came, he looked out from behind his blade.

"Leefooey? What kind of stupid name is that?"

"It means sunshine," retorted the woman, and she pulled on the fistful of branches she held. Littles got the full brunt of the midday sun, and he wailed as his eyes burned. Then a huge weight hit him from above, throwing him onto his back and smacking his head against a protruding root. He opened his eyes to see his hated prey bound away. Casting aside blurred vision, ringing ears and a sore back, Littles scrambled after her.

His quarry stopped in a grass plain, beyond the edge of the forest. A shaft notched in her nauya, she glared back at him. She loosed the projectile, Littles deflecting it as he charged toward her. She fired two more, before drawing her own blade and locking with his.

"Wow, fearless Femie wants to melee?" grumbled Littles. He blatantly sniffed her alien scent. "So you're really leaving Neliya behind, like I left Zeers behind."

Riifue's eyes flashed with trepidation. "I wasn't brainwashed, Zeers."

"Neither was I!" snapped Littles, throwing more blows. "I chose Gelfri! I chose to take the wedge out. I wasn't going back to the wheel, to being miserable."

Riifue tried to gain some ground, but between Littles' rage and his increased muscle mass, she found herself overpowered. Her nauya gone, her blade shattered, she ended up on her back wrestling with Littles for his blade.

"You heinous hypocrite," growled the mad man. "You go ahead and abandon your old self, the world you hate. But then you tell me I'm brainwashed for doing the same thing?"

Riifue pushed back against the advancing sword, growing ever nearer to her neck.

"I made the choice," she grunted. "You had the choice forced on you."

"Did you choose this too?" growled Littles as he pushed all his weight on the blade.

The blade began to pierce her skin, and the pain ignited a crucible of dread as she screamed, "Hurry up, Gast!"

The weight of Littles' body suddenly disappeared. At first Riifue thought Gast had tackled the murderous fiend. Instead, it was Fenk. The pilot disarmed Littles and threw him across the grass like a ragdoll. Another figure appeared and lifted Riifue to her feet.

"Fyuren! You're alright!" she exclaimed.

"I will be soon," he said, fixing his gaze on Littles.

Fenk landed a powerful blow to Littles face and sent him to the ground, then slowly backed away toward his son. Littles climbed onto his feet, rubbing his sore head and stretching with a distinct air of hostility. He glared at Fyuren.

"Shorts, it's been too long," he panted.

"I still go by Fyuren, Zeers," snapped the boy. "And I can still remember fight training. So if you fancy a little three on one …"

Littles grinned, a maniacal gleam in his eyes as he procured his gun, and aimed for Riifue's head. "Track never taught you to run faster than a bullet!"

"No one's shooting anyone," snapped Gast, emerging from behind a bush. Littles almost shrieked in surprise as he turned his weapon on the man. Gast raised his flesh arm in a gentle show of truce, and managed a brief smile.

Littles growled, "You think a smarmy smirk'll make me like you?"

"No," replied Gast. "I'm just glad to see my son again."

"It'll be the last time, you puerile patriarch," spat Littles. He cocked his gun.

Gast opened his arms welcomingly. Littles froze, confused and hesitant.

"C'mon, then, *Littles*," muttered Gast with a dash of Gelfri-esque sarcasm. "Send me to the Hereafter, so I can be with her again." Littles face drained of colour, and the barrel of the gun began to shake. Gast dropped his arms with a chuckle. "That Drifter nut didn't completely rip you out, Zeers."

"Gelfri *did* rip him out," retorted Littles. "He took out the wedge and made me strong. No more Teary-Zeery now. Gone he went!"

"Gelfri did something to you, that I know you hated," said Gast, his tone low and calm despite the nerves firing across his chest. "He took out the best of you, he tried to make you like him."

"He made me strong, so that *she* won't make me forlorn anymore!" screeched the boy, backing away as Gast advanced.

Gast slipped his hands into his pockets, and fiddled with tufts of grass with his feet. "Did I ever tell you about the day you were born? When your mother told me she was pregnant, to say we were over the moons was an understatement. So you can imagine how she felt when the labour started."

"I bet it was, 'Oh no, I've died for a useless waste of oxygen!'" spat Littles.

"She was weak, toward the end," Gast went on, his smile growing. "But strong enough to hold you. And when she saw you, all she said was, 'He's a cutie!' She always had that air about her. It was what made me adore her so. She called you Zeers, the Old Myddish word for 'Jigsaw,' since you were the last piece that made her life complete."

With every word, Littles' hyperventilating grew in severity. His eyes reddened as blood filled his cheeks, and panting was all he could do to keep his heart from melting. "Yeah, I made it so complete she didn't need to live anymore."

"I never blamed you for her death," said the Military Alchemist, the words seemingly stopping time. Littles stood wide-eyed, his gun still cocked, his breathing hitched. He pushed back, and screamed, "She's gone! I took her away."

"No, Zeers," was all Gast gave in reply.

Zeers panted heavily, fighting a losing battle to hold back his weeping. He profusely shook his head, denying whatever voice was screaming in his head to listen.

"I couldn't make it better," he breathlessly wailed. "I wasn't worth her. I tried so hard to be, I wanted so much to be. But I couldn't ..." He wrapped his arms around himself as if in a blizzard, and Littles growled, "Take it away, please. It fries me, burns me cold. I can't make it better!"

Gast drew near enough to touch his son.

"You make it better every day," said the father.

"No I don't!" screamed Zeers, the gun now pressed firmly to his temple. Riifue, Fenk, and Fyuren gasped. Gast kept his cool, even as the boy roared, "It's my fault." Tears dribbled down his cheeks as he repeated the words over and over again. "I'm bad! I hurt people! I just make you miserable! That's why you never want to see me!"

Gast advanced further, and murmured, "I distanced myself because she *is* you. I see her in you, even now."

"Mum wouldn't hurt her friends!" roared Zeers. "Mum wouldn't hurt people. Mum wouldn't pick fights just to be cool. I killed her. I deserve to be miserable and alone! You *should* blame me! You should hate me!" He pushed his father away as hard as he could, but met only a brick wall, against which he threw feeble punches. And he repeated over and over, "Hate me!"

Gast pulled his wailing son into his arms. "I will not hate you. Never. Because you make it better every day. Even when you fail, you somehow make it better." Gast shifted his mechanical hand to the back of Zeers' neck, ever so slowly. And he looked into his son's eyes and he said, "Time to come home."

Zeers flew backwards. A mellow surprise flashed across his face as a red torrent issued from his neck. Fyuren and Riifue dashed forward horrified.

"Bind the wound," Gast commanded, his clenched mechanical hand stained dark with blood. Fyuren quickly tore fabric from his shirt and applied the makeshift dressing around Zeers' neck. Fenk approached Gast, who stood sniffling at the sight of his bloodstained hand.

"Good to see you didn't completely desert us, Orthos," said Gast with a croaky throat.

"My son wanted to help," replied Fenk. He gazed at the mechanical hand. "What did you do?"

Gast opened his hand, revealing a malignant pulsating ball of flesh. Within the mass blinked faint lights that slowly faded until the thing stopped moving. Riifue and Fyuren looked away from the patient a moment to study the thing.

"This is Littles," he proclaimed. "This is what Gelfri did to him during the mutiny on the ship. One of my friends with the intelligence division got drunk with me once, and blabbed about an implant that reordered memories, blotting out some and amplifying others. The idea was to change how the person valued their past, so they'd start to act the way the enemy wanted them to. If the implant wasn't removed soon enough, the change would have been permanent."

"How would Gelfri get something like this?" asked Riifue.

"Same way he got a TIM device," said Fyuren. Then his brain did a double take. "Wait, Zeers had that thing in him for almost a year! Are we sure he still isn't, you know, *Littles?*"

Gast looked up with a confident smile. "He's Zeers." His smile vanished when he looked over to his son, and saw nothing but a bloody stain on the rock where he'd been laid. His sword was gone, and a tuft of bushes ruffled at the edge of the clearing.

31 | What now?

A Neiren soldier roared as he swiped his sword through his alien foe, nicking the calf of the monster with the metal arm. Gelfri growled irately at the sting, and swivelled to blast the wretched annoyance. Edo glanced over in horror at the power of the Megin device.

So this is that Gelfri that haunts my love's nightmares.

Gelfri's preference for guns gave Edo an epiphany. He continued subduing alien soldiers nearby with the hilt of his blade and flesh wounds from his arrows, while listening for the signature ethereal squelch of the Megin device. He heard it, and glanced at the Pebhasid. Gelfri had just felled a half dozen Aimoren soldiers with an invisible blast. Then he went straight back to firing bullets aimlessly. The limb billowed steam that seared his skin.

Edo directed his father's gaze at the Pebhasid.

"Father, he is weak," he yelled. "He uses the machine arm, and then needs a rest."

Odentii looked over his shoulder to Kajil, whose back was pressed to his own, wrestling with a few of the larger Pebhasid brutes. He stole a moment of the man's attention, and drew it to Gelfri.

"He rest after using arm," he said. "After next time, we attack."

Kajil nodded.

Gelfri fell to his knees after his last attack, and they moved. Edo fired an arrow at the Pebhasid's left hand, knocking the gun away. Then he charged at the last two bodyguards and felled them, while Kajil and Odentii assailed Gelfri. Disarmed and his energy rapidly draining, Gelfri could only dodge Kajil's fists and parry Odentii's sword swipes. Alarm mounted in his mind as Swine and Deloorie flew at him with weapons borrowed from downed soldiers.

"For my husband!" shouted the grief-fuelled Earthen woman.

Gelfri roared and swiped his metal arm, issuing forth a translucent blue wavefront that launched his assailants away. Then he gazed to the northwest and grinned at the sight of his shuttle coming about. He slapped the ground beneath him, and rode the recoil of his metal arm's action into the air. When he landed on the shuttle's windshield, he bellowed, "Fire all turrets! Kill them all!"

The shuttle swerved in the air, and sprayed its aerofoils like a bird-of-prey readying to strike. Its turrets veered downward and started to glow menacingly.

"He's gonna carpet the whole area," gasped Kajil.

Swine let out a howl, which drew the attention of some of his Nightshift comrades. They saw the shuttle incoming, and exchanged quick glances. A long-necked creature braced himself as a pair of burly beasts climbed into his shoulders, and he launched them into the air. They flew toward the shuttle, grappling onto the side of the turrets and tearing them off with loud groans.

"We got 'im!" bellowed Swine. He sprinted down the hill to where a few of his Nightshift comrades had bested a platoon, and yelled, "Swing me uppers, and I'll take 'im down."

"I'm up too," Kajil and Deloorie shouted.

Three of the larger beings stepped up. One grabbed Swine by the forearms and began to swing him around. Two others picked up Kajil and Deloorie, and braced themselves. At the last second, Edo leapt up onto Kajil's broad shoulders, and roared, "Go!"

Up they went, the shuttle dropping below them, and then coming toward them as gravity yanked them down onto its surface. Edo fired his last arrow, which glanced off Gelfri's shoulder.

"You ghastly gang of gunk and garbage game to gamble?" he roared with a grin. He fired a telekinetic wave at them, and they scattered, only to come about on the moving surface of the shuttle and charge him.

Swine and Kajil double-teamed him with meteoric punches, which glanced slightly but enough to knock the Pebhasid off balance. Gelfri punched Swine and backhanded Kajil, caught Edo's sword in his metal hand and used it to block Deloorie's blow before knocking them both backward. He caught Swine's arm, then leaped over the beast. He used the momentum to turn Swine into a club with which to knock Kajil over the edge.

Kajil expected a plunge to death. Instead, he found himself hanging from his shirt collar, held by Odentii.

"Thanks, but I figure we done fightin' now," he yelled over the hissing of the engines.

"That not point," returned the man, who twisted the release hatch handle onto which he hung. The door swung open, and they climbed into the shuttle. The shuttle was deserted except for a few Pebhorda officers manning the now-ruined turrets. Kajil and Odentii made short work of them, before climbing to the cockpit and putting cold metal to the pilot's throat.

"Land or die," said Odentii.

Deloorie managed to land a few unbelievably satisfying blows to Gelfri's face before the Pebhasid threw her off him. In a daze, he realised the ground was growing very close. He was so distracted he didn't notice Swine behind him, until the beast lifted him and threw him over the edge.

Gelfri slowed his descent quickly with a spray of his palm, the ground below him flashing cyan in response to his Megin device. And he landed safely.

The battleground was silent but for the dying of the shuttle's engines, and a curtain of smoke obscured much of the horizon. Then Gelfri heard a soft murmur on the winds that slowly turned into a bloodthirsty scream. He turned just in time to parry the savage blow his blade-wielding assailant intended for his heart, and saw eyes wreathed in a flame he thought he'd extinguished.

"Littles?" he asked flabbergasted.

The entity roared and swiped vengefully, blocked only by Gelfri's reflexive use of his Megin limb. Panicked, he threw a kick into the attacker's stomach and sent him flying. When the attacker rolled over to push himself up from the ground, Gelfri saw the bandages on his neck. He clenched his fists angrily.

"Damn it, Littles, I told you to watch your back," he howled. "Specifically your neck's back! Now I'll have to reimplant. Trust me, it's gonna hurt a lot more now."

"You go not!" yelled Odentii. He descended the shuttle's ramp, Kajil in tow, and Swine hopped off the shuttle's top, carrying Deloorie and Edo.

Gelfri stammered through a caustic chuckle. "I don't need a crew to fly that shuttle. Also, your combined quintet couldn't conquer me."

"Not just five," bellowed Gast.

Gelfri swivelled, and saw the Military Alchemist. Fyuren and Fenk stood nearby. Then the curtain of dust cleared, and Gelfri's breath caught in his throat. His troops lay strewn across the field, the alien troops standing over them with bewildered looks. Their swords cocked his way, eyeing his Megin limb warily. Then his eyes fell on someone standing amid them – a woman he recognised too late.

Riifue raised her blade and roared, *"Zaodekka!"*

The Neiren army charged. Gelfri's heart sank, and his Megin limb reacted to his instincts. A tidal wave of kinetic energy sent the incoming army flying, and the air around him crackled with sparks that deflected any incoming bullets or arrows. Neiren troops all around backed away fearfully from the seemingly invincible monster from the skies. But those who knew better continued the assault.

Zeers launched himself mindlessly at the barrier, smashing against it futilely. Kajil and Swine joined him in the assault, but Gelfri's limb threw them back effortlessly. The barrier waned slightly, and Fenk pushed past it and launched his own attack. His boxing blows were dodged, deflected, and met with a crippling blow to his chest. Fyuren then leapt into the air to kick the Pebhasid, who simply caught his flying foot and threw the boy over his shoulder. Deloorie flew at the Pebhasid, her sword shattering on the metallic limb. Riifue and Edo tried their luck, and ended up on their backs. A barrage of gunshots and arrows met the newly erected barrier, and where there were openings, Gelfri retaliated with psychic blasts.

The ground suddenly heaved beneath the Pebhasid, and he went flying. Riifue seized the chance and pierced his hand with her last arrow. Gelfri growled and raised his mechanical arm to her, but sensed an oncoming attack, and swivelled to meet Gast.

Energetic barriers of blue and orange luminance reflected and repelled each other, fuelling eddies in the air throughout the valley. Gast broke off the assault and stepped back to glare at the Pebhasid.

"Arrogant Alchemist, I expected something more from you," spat Gelfri. "I mean, seriously, all that meticulous military training and you can't even—"

Gast pressed his arm to the ground, which split beneath Gelfri. The Pebhasid bounded away from the small fissure, and deflected the clods of earth Gast threw at him.

The remaining fighters fled up out of the valley, away from the clashing titans and their war. The Neiren troops, exhausted from their battle with sky beings, fell to awestruck prayer at the supernatural combat they beheld.

Gast found the biggest boulder he could hew from the ground and launched it at his hated enemy. Gelfri burst it apart, only to see the fire in Gast's eyes as they hurtled toward him in the downwind of the stone projectile. Panicked, Gelfri darted to the left, and swung his own Megin limb down upon Gast's exposed back.

He'd fallen for it.

Gast swivelled, caught Gelfri's wrist, and wrenched it behind his back. The Military Alchemist hissed with ire-fuelled glee as he pressed his foot to Gelfri's back and twisted the Megin limb meticulously. Gelfri's suppressed screech came out as a long grunt.

"The Megin limb is a sacred privilege," he growled. "For what you did to my son, I'm going to rip this stolen weapon off you, one nerve strand at a time, and jam it up your backside, *sideways!*"

Gelfri chuckled, "I didn't steal this, I earned it."

Throughout the valley, jaws dropped in horror at the tendrils of electricity arcing from Gelfri's fingers. They enthralled Gast, seeping into the gaps in the mechanisms of his arm and ripping them apart. He staggered backward in surprise, and Gelfri rose to his feet. A furious roar accompanied arcs of plasma from his arm that went after Gast's body. A final sadistic shriek from the Pebhasid turned into another psychic blast that threw Gast backwards. The ruined man fell to the ground motionless. Gelfri panted only a moment, before throwing back his head and laughing.

"What wonderful will-breaking world-destroying power!" he marvelled in between breathy cackles. "Which one of you whimpering willies want to waltz, eh? *Fizzle and drizzle, sibbledadee,* who's the next war casualty?"

The Neiren soldiers, the *Ranegr* crew, even the Pebhasid's followers could not immediately comprehend the sight of such villainy. Every sane mind on the battlefield turned against the monster that had abandoned comrades and ordered a carpet-bombing of friend and foe, and those few insane minds couldn't imagine opposing him. Everybody was rendered immobile by the rage they felt for the man, and horror of his power.

Zeers' heart stopped in that moment as he saw the faces of friends, crewmates, and strangers, all of them mirroring the same helplessness. Then his gaze turned to his father, lying dead on the ground.

Like your mother. You drove them both to this, didn't you?

A tiny bead of life was hardly visible in Gast's chest.

"No," murmured Zeers.

Then an electrifying surge of strength pulsed through his body. He pushed up from his place in the dirt, and his raucous high-pitched howls overshadowed the Pebhasid's laughter.

Zeers sprinted toward Gelfri. He swiped and kicked and punched, driving the Pebhasid back with as much ferocity as he could muster. Gelfri tried to grasp his foe with his limb, but Zeers was too fast. He nimbly dodged the metal appendage and swiftly drew his sword to sever it. But the Pebhasid saw the attack, and caught the blade before it could touch him. Blood seeped from the flesh of his left hand, gripping the sharp metal as he wrestled with Zeers. A quick twist of the wrist saw the blade shatter in the Pebhasid's hands. Yet enough blade remained for a small knife, and Zeers pressed his attack undeterred.

The two combatants locked eyes. Zeers saw a horrible vision, one he recalled from months of looking in a mirror and loathing what he saw.

Teary-Zeery!

His mind gurgled with a long forgotten voice that caught up as if it had wings on its feet. A thousand more followed, fuelling a cold snap in his chest. Zeers' strength faltered, and Gelfri snatched the blade out of his lethargic hand. Then came punches, the metal blows against his skin much less painful than the anguish that drained his will.

Gelfri's foot launched Zeers screaming through the air. His head and body smashed against the landing gear of the shuttle. Through his heavy eyelids, Zeers watched as Gelfri, his eyes flashing with insane fury and glee, raised the sword. Time slowed as more recent memories surfaced: foremost, an image of Gelfri holding a dessert fork in a likewise fashion.

"My knife is fast and accurate," the Pebhasid had said.

Ah, that was it. That was where he lied to us. We were naïve, though. I was naïve. I'd just made up with my friends, and was starting to think it might be good to go back with them ...

"You've got that right, darl," he remembered Dennie saying. "We gotta stick together out here. You stay alone and don't help each other, you sink."

I sank. I should have gone back with them. Yeah, that's the reason. Things aren't the way we suppose them, because we intentionally stuff them up. I did bad things, just so I could stay miserable. No way I can go back now.

"Really?" said a woman who appeared before him. At first, he thought his poltergeist was haunting him one last time before he met his just desserts in the afterlife. Though this Neliya seemed hardly the sadistic temptress of Littles' deranged mind. She smiled softly, and uttered words he'd heard in a dreamlike memory. "I don't like the idea of being somewhere without you, Zeers."

Then the mirage morphed into a brunette with the kindest, dulcet smile. Gelfri, the shuttle, the crew, and the battle around him faded behind a transparent veil of emotional fuzziness, until all that remained was the woman whose photo he'd seen many times in his father's wallet.

"You're the last piece of my jigsaw, my little cutie," she said, holding out her hand. "Time to come home, with me."

With a grateful smile, Zeers raised his hand to take her offering.

A metal object bounced harmlessly off the ball of his palm. The veil shattered, revealing to Zeers the flabbergasted expressions on the face of everyone around him – especially that of Gelfri.

Zeers caught the deflected knife in mid-air and locked his eyes onto his foe. He dashed forward, the wind on his heels as if his mother, father, Jugga, and Murraloohaa were charging with him.

Gelfri readied to blast his assailant with an electrical burst. But Zeers was already within a metre of him. The man was as nimble as he was strong. He darted around the swing of Gelfri's metal arm, and swiftly drove the blade into the mechanisms of Gelfri's limb and shattered the Megin device it contained. Then, with the elation of blunting the monster's teeth, he wrested the blade from the arm and brought its remains across the Pebhasid's face.

Zeers blocked his opponent's blind jab and threw one with his other hand, followed by a haymaker to the stomach. He pushed against the Pebhasid, and threw punch after punch Gelfri was helpless to deflect. He landed more blows in a second than anyone else the entire battle. Even when Gelfri managed to up-hand him, and even when blows of metal met his arms raised in defence, they did little to overcome his rage. Zeers countered the blows and threw Gelfri off balance, and exacerbated it further with a head-butt that drained strength from the Pebhasid's knees.

Kajil suddenly roared over the crowd, "Get him, Zeers!"

"Bash that bastard!" bellowed Swine.

"For Murraloohaa!" shouted Deloorie.

The *Ranegr* crew and the Neiren soldiers joined in a raucous cheer, as Zeers boxed Gelfri to the ground. Even as Gelfri wailed in pain and frustration, barely recognisable under developing bruises and lacerations, Zeers was not finished – he hadn't even started.

The man stood over his opponent and, at the top of his lungs, he roared, "Get up, you third-rate circus magician! I'll show you just how good we are!"

The crowd roared with overwhelming support.

Gelfri scrambled to his feet and charged blindly, meeting Zeers' meteoric fist. The young man relentlessly advanced, landing savagely focused blows, one after the other. Each strike elicited a terrified squeak from the wretched Pebhasid, until his legs gave out and he fell to his knees sobbing.

Zeers stood before him, his eyes blank with fury, as if looking upon the face of every bully and tormenter in his memory. Then he twirled, and his heel swept away the last of Gelfri's life. The Pebhasid fell, his eyes unfocused.

Zeers heard nothing but the throbbing of blood flowing through his ears, the strident scratching of air through his windpipe, and the dull-pitched whirr of his nerves radiating pain from his extremities. He waited, the last of his dwindling energy holding him up, for some semblance of closure or joy that never came.

Frustration spurred him to his knees over his vanquished enemy, and he wrenched the lifeless mass up by the collar. His desperate pleas for peace of mind, for solitude from his torturers, left him in animalistic roars, unintelligible babble, and bloodstained tears. But the corpse vexed him with silence, like a vindictive classmate sealing his secret behind a smirk.

Zeers threw the dead man back to his undeserved rest and staggered away. His confused stare met the nervous gazes of long-forgotten friends whose faces he could barely make out in the cacophony of strangers. He might as well have been in the middle of an uncharted forest, surrounded by trees that viewed him with as little interest as a worm in the mud.

His mother did not appear again, nor did Neliya. All he felt was misery.

"What now?" he gurgled.

His legs gave out, and he collapsed.

32 | I won't convince her for your sake

The Saajya looked as if he hadn't slept for days, no doubt trying to talk down rival governors and annoying foreign dignitaries demanding to see the site of three consecutive meteorite crashes.

Idoru sat before him, trying not to crumple the dossier in his moist palms. Afterimages of the supernatural battle still loomed fresh in his mind, only exacerbated by the possibility of an alien invasion. He remembered decorum and propriety, however, and made sure to meet the handmaid graciously as she accepted the dossier and rewarded him with tea. He hissed in thanks, and moved to sip the tea. A prompt un-scrolling of paper made him shriek, and the tea went down his shirt. The handmaid quickly went to his aid with a damp cloth, while the irate Saajya scanned the document.

"Be silent, Idoru-eru," rasped the Saajya.

"Yes, Asaajya-idi," exclaimed Idoru, bowing emphatically, his chest still tingling from the burn. He politely dismissed the handmaid, despite the pain, and tried to regain his composure.

The Saajya read the dossier several more times, and then thrust it into the flame before him. Idoru sighed at the blackening paper, and lamented the effort that had gone into producing the handwritten document. But there were more important matters than the desecration of his calligraphy.

"What of our neighbouring provinces?" he asked.

The Saajya harrumphed. "Pago and Fahai still believe it to be a meteorite crash. Eranon will never get close enough to find out. And the visitors will soon leave."

Idoru cleared his throat and mumbled, "Not all, Madokai."

"Ah yes, I understand the Andou family have adopted a deformed girl with yellow skin and a missing digit on each appendage," said the Saajya.

"Young Edo has an affinity for misshapen women, it seems."

"And your thoughts on this matter?" asked Idoru.

The Saajya stifled a yawn. "Who Odentii's wife chooses as bride for her son is no one's business but hers."

"And if the Kehan come looking for a Mydian to study and dissect?" retorted Idoru.

"What business is it of mine where they found *him*?" replied the Saajya nonchalantly. Idoru shot him a very confused expression. "Do you think Aimore is the only place where meteors fall?"

Idoru's confusion slowly melted as he sensed the governor's meaning. He smirked, and gave a slight chuckle.

"Is there another Mydian on our world?" he asked.

"I know only that the Kehan's focus is elsewhere," replied the Saajya. "There need be no concern for Medan, so long as our visitors leave. And the Kehan would hardly be concerned with a misshapen girl, would they?"

"No, Madokai," replied Idoru. An image of the monster with the metal arm flashed through his mind, and he groaned silently. "The aliens may leave, yes. And Riifue Andou may seem hardly un-Neiren. Yet, there are many families whose fathers and brothers will surely return with *memories* of these events."

The Saajya nodded thoughtfully. He added slowly, "Those memories may be the seeds of rumour ... rumour that could one day reach those familiar with Mydian appearance. In such a case, gossip may prove the undoing of a false tale of meteorites."

Idoru's eyes turned pensive, before he glanced back at the Saajya. Beneath the tiredness and the nonchalance, he could see the governor's meaning, and his unspoken orders.

"Such an event would cause great suffering," replied Idoru flatly. "But preventing it may be more painful."

The Saajya only nodded.

"Isn't it interesting," Idoru added, "that our happiness may be affected by people unseen to us."

"And that we may affect the lives of people we cannot see," replied the Saajya.

Idoru saw nothing more to say, and politely bowed. He rose and moved to leave the room.

"My son," said the Saajya, his tone oddly casual. "You did well."

Idoru turned again, this time beaming, and he bowed even lower than before. Then he left the room.

Dim hospital lights pervaded Gast's unconsciousness and pulled him into the waking world. A Mydian doctor waved a pen-light in his eyes. When she was satisfied with his physical state, she said, "Can you remember your name?"

"Gast Indra," he croaked. He sat up and looked about. The infirmary was so rowdy he couldn't make out any of the fast-moving faces in the crowd. Medics moved about between beds that supported the more serious cases, while those with just cuts and bruises were on the floor. Most of the faces were unfamiliar.

"You're one of the Pebhasid officers?" he muttered with a hint of insecurity.

"Don't worry," replied the doctor. "Our loyalty to the last one died with him."

Gast grinned thankfully, breathing in a deep sigh of relief.

So, someone managed to kill that bastard. I can sleep happily.

Then the matter of his son pierced through his peaceful mind. Gast looked around, scanning the rowdy infirmary. His search in vain, he hurriedly hopped off the bed and fell flat on his face. The doctor leaned down to help him up, gingerly avoiding the metallic stump where his prosthetic had been. "Gelfri destroyed your mechanical arm. We don't have a replacement."

"Where's my son, Zeers?" said an ambivalent Gast. The doctor looked confused. He reluctantly added, "You knew him as Littles."

"Oh yes, the one that killed Gelfri with his bare hands," said the doctor.

Gast could have jumped for joy if his body hadn't hurt so much. The doctor led him to the corner of the room, where a body lay with bandaged limbs, and a dozen IVs snaking from his arms. The face was recognisable despite the bruises across it. Gast's mouth fell agape with concern, regarding the patient as he would a priceless treasure tarnished by a robber.

"What happened to him?" he cried.

"He fell unconscious not long after beating Gelfri, and hasn't woken up since," replied the doctor. "The bone fractures are mainly in his hands, forearms, and a few at the base of his skull. The hands and forearms, I'm sure he got those from breaking Gelfri's face. The skull fractures, I'm not so sure."

"They were likely from me," said Gast. His only hand slipped into his pockets, and withdrew the hated talisman. The torn flesh had since dried to rubbery residue upon its metallic surface. The sight fuelled his outrage, and he considered destroying the thing right then and there.

Don't forget the Kulanki. He captured that MCV and subjugated the researchers aboard. That's a capital crime. I bring Zeers home, he goes to the gallows ... Unless I have this.

He closed his hand around the cursed thing, the cold metal burning his skin. Then he picked up his uniform jacket, and found a patch sewn into the inner lining. He tore it apart with his teeth, and eyed the thumb-sized data module that fell out.

Neliya has to come home, too.

Gast pocketed the two items, found a seat, and began his vigil by Zeers' bedside.

Time turned into a blur, during which the infirmary slowly emptied as the seriously injured were treated and restored to health, and beds were freed for the less critical. Kajil, Deloorie, Dennie, and other *Ranegr* crewmen slipped in to visit the invalid Zeers, wondering if he'd improved. Gast remembered them only in slivers of thought, in which he gave involuntary absentminded responses, though there were times in which his autopilot mode let him hear tidbits like, "Fyuren's installed his new reactor and they're setting up the TIM device." His tired mind settled with every scrap of information it gathered. Far more attention went to the heart monitor display, punctuating the seconds with faint beeps that drew out into long dull drumbeats.

A woman sauntered over from outside his vision and sat next to him. Her fingers brushed soothingly over the lattice of his prosthetic interface, and she said, "He'll wake up. Don't worry."

Gast turned to her, and smiled painfully. "I know. But will he be able to move past it?"

The woman shrugged. "You have the implant. What was it called?"

Gast chuckled. "I can't remember. I was so drunk, I can't believe I still remembered that it exists. No, even if he was exonerated, or even given leniency, will *he* be able to move past it?"

The woman caressed his shoulder, eliciting a feeling eerily reminiscent of a drug to which he'd long since beat his addition. His heart raced longingly, and he looked to her. Her smile was just as warm, intoxicating, and uplifting as ever.

"He will, I know it," she said.

"I'd be more confident if you were here, Onne," said Gast, his voice steady despite his glistening eyes.

"But I'm not, Gast, I'm dead," replied the woman curtly.

Gast's expression cracked. "Then stop being so real. Stop appearing in his eyes, speaking in his voice. Let him not be burdened with reminding me of you every day."

Onne gripped his hand tightly, and drew his gaze.

"I'm not in his eyes or his voice. I'm not waiting for you in some afterlife either. I don't exist anymore." She pointed to the boy – now man – on the bed. "He is real. And he won't get better if you can't let go."

Gast's sobs broke past his dam of military discipline. "I can't let you go, Onne. You're a part of me."

The woman gazed fixedly into his eyes and said, "Zeers can't be your Megin limb anymore. He has to live. You both do."

Gast glanced to the bed with stinging eyes, his mind lingering on the data module in his pocket.

"He won't want to live without her," he mumbled.

"He will," said Onne with a chuckle. "A man always remembers his first love, even if he loses her."

Gast turned back to his wife, and cradled her face in his two hands. He savoured the smoothness of her skin in his palms, and brushed her hair out of her face. He kissed her once, the agonising sensation like finding water in a desert.

"I'll see you later?" he muttered hopefully.

Much later.

Gast's eyes opened. The infirmary was empty. His back felt like a rigid elastic band, and crinkled as such as he sat up. He stretched and yawned, shook himself all over, and then looked at the bed. His bladder almost emptied in shock.

"Where's Zeers?" he yelled at the doctors. The attending saw the empty bed and signalled a missing persons alert. Gast ran out the door, and scrambled through the ship. He ran into Kajil at the exit hatch.

"Zeers is missing," he said in response to the captain's inquiring glances.

"He didn't come outside," Kajil replied. "We've been working on the hull the last day and half, and no one saw him."

A crackle through the radio interrupted him, and he listened a moment before uttering, "Security thinks they found him in the aft storage bay."

At Kajil's direction, Gast navigated the shuttle. But his missing arm had shifted his weight off-balance, and he tripped several times before he finally reached the storage bay. Two Pebhorda officers stood at the entrance to the room and, when Gast asked, pointed out a lone coop amongst the stack of empty crates. A shadowy creature sat inside.

Gast approached the cell and opened it, only for a bandaged hand to shakily snake out of the darkness and pull it closed.

"Zeers," he called out.

"Go away," croaked the shut-in.

Gast dismissed the guards with a glance, and then gingerly settled down next to the cage.

"I don't remember much after Gelfri zapped me," he muttered gauchely. "I've got to say, he was a quick study to have mastered Electro-alchemics so quickly. Good thing you took him out when you did … In the way you did. I wish I could have seen it and cheered you on."

"Made no difference," Zeers whispered. "Just made me feel worse."

"I hear Fyuren's almost finished installing the TIM device," said Gast. "As soon as we get back, I'll find you a good rehabilitation service."

"Maximum security prison?" grunted Zeers.

Gast's knee jerked, "No! That won't happen."

"The *Kulanki*'s crew will see to it," Zeers insisted. "I terrorised and enslaved them. And more, I helped kill hundreds of Pebhorda people, subjugated them all for Gelfri. I should at least go to jail for that."

Gast fumbled with his pocket, and held up the device. Its glimmer elicited a hoarse shriek from within the cage.

"I have this," said Gast. "I will call in every expert I have to. They'll examine the device, and your brain, and show you were not the monster who hurt those people. I swear I'll clear your name."

His voice reverberated with every ounce of sincerity and conviction he could muster. As soon as he was finished, he realised he'd never before made such steadfast promises. It felt good, and he smiled to his imagined Onne seated next to him.

"Smile at *him*, you idiot!" she mimed, before disappearing again.

Gast pursed his lips with disappointment, and then gathered his courage and gazed into the cage with the same smile. Glimmering irises of the same light brown colour as his own met his gaze, and held it. They darted between his face and the nightmare-infusing metal talisman resting harmlessly in his palm. Then they closed. Sounds of shuffling trickled past the bars of the cage, until Zeers' back was pressed against his father's.

"She won't forgive me," he muttered.

"She will," said Gast.

"She's not even Neliya anymore. Gone she went." His words carried a dash of ironic humour, at which neither man could help but chuckle.

Gast looked over his shoulder. "Zeers, I'll convince her to come home. And when she does, you can ask her to forgive you."

Zeers sighed and tilted his head back against the bars. "I don't want her to."

Gast frowned. "Come home? Or forgive you?"

"Both," said Zeers. "I hurt her, and I don't want to be forgiven. I saw her fighting alongside one of those Neiren. He had the same style as her. I could see it the moment they looked at each other. She only once looked at me vaguely like that, but with him, it's obvious to even a complete moron."

Gast's jaw tightened, since he couldn't tighten his fist to vent his frustration. He cursed himself for not rescuing Neliya and Fyuren sooner. He cursed Neliya for forgetting Zeers and the people who risked everything to find her.

Once again, he summoned his muse, and he nonverbally asked her what he should do. She just shot him back an annoyed glance, and disappeared.

Focus, Gast. Zeers is the important one now.

"You'd only come home and face trial – which you *would* win – if she loved you instead of Edo?" he asked.

"No, they're two completely separate things," Zeers blurted, his voice finally raising above a murmur. "I have to go home to face the music? Bring it on, the sooner the better! But I don't want to drag her back to the Othala. She hated it there. I want her to forget all about it, and me. I want her to be Riifue."

Gast smiled, and the tingling in his chest drew the smile even wider.

"You love her that much, don't you?" he chuckled.

Zeers grunted in the affirmative, and though Gast couldn't see it, he knew his son's cheeks were crimson.

He touched the data module in his pocket, and shook his head in dismay. A load came off his chest, only to be replaced with another, smaller but denser. He looked up to the ceiling, and said, "Then I won't convince her for your sake."

33 | They'll come looking for you

Riifue held out her arms as Arika measured her girth and length with a strip of fabric. Uenda giddily bounced on the floor next to Sukete, whose face belied an equal excitement. Riifue was clearly the most excited of all, her cheeks a deep crimson as she twirled to let Arika access more of her measurements.

"Rii-tuan's gonna be beautiful!" exclaimed the hyperactive girl when her grandmother finished measuring.

"Are you sure its alright to make a dress from scratch?" asked Riifue, clasping her arms around her waist modestly. "It was so much work to make that dress for Chisafenu."

Arika dismissively raised her hand. "Riifue, it is tradition that the grandmother of the groom make a new dress for the bride. And I am honoured to do so."

"That's it, isn't it," said Uenda. "Mummy picks Big Brother's bride, and Grandma makes the dress." She tugged at Sukete's sleeve. "I wonder what my dress will look like."

"That's up to the grandmother of whoever you marry," chuckled Sukete.

Uenda replied with a pout, "Rii-tuan's so lucky. I want to have a pretty dress. I need to tell all the other mothers that I'm a good bride."

The three women burst into a fit of laughter at her adorable mannerisms, and Sukete said, "There'll be time for that when you grow up."

"If only I had enough time to make the dress before your friends leave," sighed Arika.

Riifue gave an unhindered smile. "It's alright. I'm sure they all want to get back as soon as possible. Especially Fyuren."

"Husband is glad to have his tool shed back, no doubt," said Sukete.

A soft knock foretold Odentii's entry. The father slowly slid the door aside and eyed the four, in particular the measuring tape in Arika's hand.

"I'm about to sneeze. Is someone talking about me?" he mumbled with a smirk.

"Only nice things, dear," replied Sukete. "Is it time?"

"They say the ship isn't ready yet," said Odentii, edging into the room. "It might still be a day or two."

"I bet Idoru-ken won't be happy about that," said Riifue.

"It's his son's problem now," said Arika. In response to the shocked stares, she added, "Idoru stepped aside as chief. Nuto-ken is now the leader."

"Well, he'll have plenty of headaches to keep him busy," said Sukete. "Busy enough to distract him while his mother looks for a wife for him."

"Oh, tell her I'm a good pick!" shouted Uenda.

"No!" barked Odentii, though a tugging at his lips betrayed his jest. "You're too young, and I'll not have Idoru as an in-law."

"But I want to have a pretty dress! Like Rii-tuan!" Uenda protested.

Odentii scooped up his daughter, straining a little under the weight, and said to her, "You're plenty pretty without a bride's dress."

"Daddy's just saying that so I won't complain anymore," pouted Uenda.

"Yes I am," chirped Odentii. "Now go play in the garden. I think I saw some grubs eating the flowers again."

Uenda's eyes lit up with a vengeful flame. She launched herself out of her father's embrace and scrambled out of the house. Odentii breathed in his relief, and then turned to Riifue. "One of them has come to see you."

The women exchanged intrigued glances before following Odentii out of the house. Deloorie stood on the porch. Riifue embraced her old friend. Deloorie gripped her tightly and sniffed back imminent tears as she mumbled, "I'm gonna miss you, ya know?"

"Me too, Deloorie," mumbled Riifue.

Deloorie broke the hug, wiped away her tears, and stepped back to look at the house. "So this is what a Neiren house looks like, eh?" Her eyes scanned the wooden structure. "I can see why you like this place. Much nicer than rusted metal walls and UV lights."

"That's not the only reason," said Riifue, eyeing the figure climbing out of the tractor and crossing the field to meet them. Arika and Odentii stopped Edo, whose eyes were fixed firmly on his bride-to-be. The Earthen woman, anticipating a touching scene, frowned as the two elders unintelligibly chided the young man. She eyed Riifue, who wore a disappointed smirk.

"What's going on?" asked Deloorie.

Odentii shot Riifue a stern glance and explained, "Lovers had together time. Now pledge is announced, and they can't touch until it's done."

"That's silly," murmured Deloorie. "Why let them have their time, then make them wait until their wedding?"

Riifue narrowed her eyes at Arika and Sukete, giggling to each other, and said, "More gossip that way!"

Deloorie burst into laughter, which infected Odentii, then Sukete and finally Arika. When the old lady sobered, she announced, "I've got some work to do," Then she strode down the path to the gate, a visible spring in her step. Riifue beamed excitedly as the old lady disappeared through the gate like a giddy child.

Deloorie turned to Riifue and said, "Gast and Kajil wanted to talk to you. That's why I'm here."

Riifue huffed, "Probably to convince me to go with them."

"I'm not going to do that," said Deloorie, her throat clenching.

Odentii spoke up, "I think should go. At least see friends before they leave."

Riifue sighed and agreed. Odentii beckoned the group to follow, heading down the path to the shuttle. He and Sukete kept their son up front to enforce tradition, allowing Deloorie and Riifue a chance to speak.

"About Murraloohaa," said the younger woman. "There's a saying, *chinne ma kyaunadyo yao taku mona atupposu ze*. It means, *wash away the worries of the past like dirty laundry*."

"That's what I plan to do," Deloorie replied with a smile more happy than sad, though not by much. "Gelfri is dead. All I think of is the happy times now." Riifue slid her arm over Deloorie's shoulder, momentarily wondering if the woman had shrunk. The widow reciprocated the hug with a grateful squeeze, and then, sniffing back the nearing grief, she said, "So, you had your time together …" She shot Riifue an accusatory glare. "Details!"

The giggling that erupted from the back of the line reached Edo's ears and made them ruffle excitedly. His father strengthened the grip on his shoulders, making him wince, and he looked up at the old man.

"Seriously, Father, it's a silly tradition," he exclaimed.

"And one you will carry on, Edo," Odentii returned. His ears twitched at the Myddish words entering them. At that moment, he wished he didn't understand the language, so he wouldn't then be guessing what kind of salacious gossip his son's fiancée was whispering to the dark-skinned alien.

That sight was all Edo needed to know, and he called over his shoulder, "Riifue-ken, stop talking about me behind my back." Odentii promptly twisted his son's head forward, earning a few more chuckles from the women behind.

The forest path gave way to the clearing, where the Pebhasid shuttle still stood. The grass in its shadow withered from days without nourishing sun, which Riifue hoped it would soon get. Odentii and Edo scanned the horizon, knowing the Aimoren military was keeping watch from a distance.

Gast stood at the top of the shuttle's entrance ramp. His missing arm was only slightly less unnerving than the mechanical limb that used to be there.

He eyed Riifue with pursed lips as she ascended the ramp for what she clearly wanted to be the last time.

Gast led the Andou family through the cramped corridors of the shuttle to a small conference room. Fyuren and Fenk sat at the table, while Zeers stood in the corner. He saw Riifue, and a dark look fell over his face. He nodded politely and looked away.

When everyone was seated, Gast looked to Odentii, "Will you translate for your family?"

"Actually," interjected Riifue. "*My* family can understand Myddish."

Gast clenched his jaw and said, "Fine. Neliya, I can't allow you to stay on Undarli."

Riifue groaned irately, while Sukete frowned and Edo growled.

"You have no control over what I do, Gast," retorted Riifue.

"But we *can* stay here until you do as you're told," replied Gast. Fyuren looked horrified at the notion, but kept quiet.

"Unacceptable," said Odentii. "The Saajya wishes you gone."

"I agree," said Gast, his gaze fixed on Riifue. "*All* Mydians should be off this planet … for everyone's good."

"Riifue not want go," intoned Edo, his jaw clenched tightly. "How her good?"

"Because the Dosag family is one of means," said Gast. "They will not accept that their daughter is gone, and will come looking for her. And they will bring the Mydian military. When the Mydians find a world such as Undarli, they annex it. And I know *Neliya* knows what that means."

Riifue's throat ran dry as she imagined Mydian cruisers bombarding her home world from space, countless Neiren survivors rounded into reservations, cities toppled to make room for Mydian dwellings. With a shake of her head, she pushed the visions away and rasped, "Just report that I died. They won't come after me then."

Fyuren slapped the table and roared, "Get over yourself!"

The family backed away from the table, except for Edo who leaned toward the irate boy. He mumbled an Aimorein threat in a low, menacing voice. Odentii and Sukete's faces turned pale at the utterance, and Riifue refused to translate.

Fyuren did not back down.

"If your government learns about Neliya's existence, they will come after her," He looked straight at Edo. "They'll experiment on her, study her, *dissect* her. They might even see if she can breed with a Neiren, one that'll *not* be you!"

Edo clenched his fist, ready to take a swing at the prodigy. At the last instant, he felt a pair of soft hands on his wrist. Riifue looked straight into his eyes as she lowered his fists and mumbled, "Calm." Edo stilled his breathing and stepped away, soothed by his fiancée's touch.

Riifue turned to Fyuren, and steadfastly said, "I'll say I'm just a deformed girl. My husband will protect me."

"Fyuren, let's go over the tunnelling telemetry one more time," said Fenk, rising out of his seat. He had to drag his fuming son out of the room before an argument could start.

Gast gazed to the others in the room, before reaching Odentii. "Can Neliya and I have the room, please?"

Edo growled, "Her name is Riifue! I stay!"

Gast glared imposingly at him. Edo stared right back at him, his pointed ears upright and prominent like a beast baring its claws to attack.

Odentii stood up and walked toward his son.

"Come," he said firmly. Edo would not budge. Odentii leaned close to his ear and whispered, "If you want to be a good husband, know when your wife can stand on her own." Edo's gaze fell, and he glanced at Riifue. Her smile calmed him, and he turned to leave the room with his father. Sukete silently squeezed Riifue's hand before following her husband.

Zeers passed her last. Her ears tickled with the sound of a murmured apology before the door slammed with a mechanical clang.

Gast and Riifue were alone.

"You have to come home, Neliya," he said unequivocally.

"I am home," retorted Riifue.

"Your home is where your mother and father are," Gast said, edging into the seat next to her. "You can't imagine how much they miss you."

"I'd imagine it if I could even remember what they look like," said Riifue with a face halfway between sorrow and indifference. "I hardly ever saw my mother even when I *was* on the *Othala*. And my father was always on Lethanis. The Dosags are strangers to me. *Neliya Dosag* is a stranger. Here, I'm happy. Playing with Uenda, talking with Sukete, learning Haisou with Edo, helping Odentii on the farm, drinking tea with Arika and Jikyo. I have so much here that makes me happy. What's for me on the *Othala*? An isolated world, drinking the same glass of water every day, eating the same piece of kerec every day, eating the same bowl of cookie dough ice cream, *every day!* The best I had was Fyuren and Zeers. But now, I can barely speak to them. They're different people, and so am I. Tell me, Military Alchemist, what's waiting for me on the *Othala*?"

Gast gazed at her, listening quietly to her tirade. Then he plugged a data module into the console on the table. A few screen taps later, a photo appeared before her.

A woman, her glistening face wearing an ecstatic but exhausted smile as if she'd just lifted a tremendous weight. To her left, a man with an equally gleeful grin, a doting look in his eyes as he gazed down on the newborn the woman cradled in her arms.

Gast looked at her. "You stay here, and no matter how much you love him, you'd never be able to do what your mother did for your father. That's a fact. Stay here, and have us lie to the people in this photo, and you will be spitting in their face after what *they* did for you. They'll never accept that you're dead until they see your corpse. They'll come looking for you. And the Mydians *will* come after. What do you think will happen to the Andors then?

"And even if they don't come, what if the natives come looking for a Mydian to dissect? Obviously there are some higher-ups who know what a Mydian looks like, so what if they hear rumours of a man whose wife looks exactly like one? For one, the Andor family would be incarcerated. Imagine that happening to Wenda. I trust Odentii as far as he can throw me, but he says Aimore won't give you up, so these Kehan might end up invading to get their hands on you."

With every sentence, Gast drilled into her, and the images his hypotheticals painted in her mind were as dynamite blowing holes in her resolve. Tears dribbled down her cheeks, and she felt as if she were about to be diagnosed with a deadly disease.

Gast leaned down close to her, and said very sternly, "You risk throwing *their* world into chaos and destroying *their* lives, for your own happiness. You're no better than Gelfri."

Neliya finally cracked, her grieved breaths escaping her in shrill gasps. She looked at Gast pleadingly.

"It won't happen like you say," she stammered in a hoarse whisper.

Gast growled, "You know it will. You knew, even when you were with Edo, this was all just a dream. No different from a cultural exchange trip."

"Please, don't make me go back. I'd die if I left," Neliya wailed.

"And *they* would die if you stay," retorted Gast. "Either you come willingly and dignified, or I drag you back to the *Othala*, kicking and screaming."

Neliya lunged forward, and met a wall. She threw her fists at him, at first enraged, then slowly in desperation. Each and every weakening blow she punctuated with a feebler, "No!" until she fell to her knees clawing at his shirt. Gast looked down at her, a resolved sneer on his face.

Outside, Zeers studied the security feed. Behind him, Sukete sobbed in her husband's arms. Edo growled and punched the bulkhead, startling his parents. He pulled away, his fingers obviously broken, and slumped to the floor. He scrunched his hair in his hands, his body trembling with rage.

"That man is a bastard! Cruel! Despicable!" he growled fiercely.

"He is doing what needs to be done," said Odentii. "Look at his eyes, my son. Only his eyes."

Edo looked closer, and the smallest sliver of his mind uttered, *He looks like he's living a nightmare.*

34 | Please, adopt me

The field was silent save for the greenery ruffling in the wind. Sparse clouds trudged across the night sky, diminishing the luminance of Sikai. There was still enough light for Riifue to find her way as she crept away from the shuttle. She clutched her shawl around her and sprinted through the forest, navigating the dark from memory alone. She emerged from the woods near the outskirts of town, and headed straight for the temple.

Her heart raced with desperation as she entered the building and marched barefoot across its cold wooden floor. She stood motionless a while, gazing up at the idols of the Ancestors – those same idols that once terrified her. Then she dropped to her knees, and made the customary gesture of prayer.

"Oh, Ancestors of the Aimoreka," her voice softly echoed through the unlit hall. "I stand here, an intruder. I am no relative of yours, born of at an infinite distance from your kin. This intruder is a harbinger of calamity. You would sooner order me gone than suffer what is to come. But if I were a true Neiren, then no one would suffer. No one's happiness would be forsaken for my own. So …" Her sobbing grew. "If the gods do really imbue you with power to answer prayer, and if you do see it in your hearts to grant this intruder's one wish … Sharpen my ears, pale my face, give me another finger and toe. Please, adopt me."

Riifue held her breath, anticipating an immediate miracle. As if futility finally broke through her self-delusion, her sobbing evolved into anguished cries like those from an innocent man bound for the gallows. Amid her grief, she felt Edo's presence beside her.

"I thought I could be like Muneuo," she stammered. "I thought if I asked the gods, they'd make me like you … just like for Tashua." Her fists started to grasp at the wooden floor as if it was the last lifeline to her desire, and she wailed, "Why can't I be Riifue?"

"You can be," Edo said, drawing her tear-soaked visage. He took her hand in his. "Let's go. Now, while everyone's asleep. We'll disappear together, and go where no one will find us."

Riifue shook her head furiously. "What about your family? You'd have to give them up."

"You gave up your friends to be with me," replied Edo. "What husband would I be if I weren't prepared to do the same?"

"But you don't want to leave them," said Riifue. "You don't want to leave your mother and father any more than I do. I'd be sad to see those friends go without me, but I wouldn't lose sleep over not seeing the *Othala* again. I don't care about them. I don't lose anything. But you would."

"Fine," snapped Edo. "Then we'll just say you're not leaving, and if that brutish cripple of a magician wants to fight me, let him come! I promise you, Riifue, to take you away would be the end of him."

Riifue smiled, a chuckle bursting past the sorrowful aura about her. Her smile turned rueful, and she looked into his eyes. Her sorrowfully scrunched gaze drained all the energy from his muscles, and she breathed heavily.

"Gast is right," she sobbed. "I can't be Riifue. I have to be Neliya."

Edo's vocal cords froze in place. All he could do was grunt and shake his head. "No! The Ancestors won't answer your prayer, but they might answer mine."

"I have to go, Edo," said Riifue with a resigned shake of her head.

Edo buried his face in his hands, sobbing softly though his body demanded he heave and wail. His inability to control his body gave way to irritation, then anger. The same anguish with which Riifue fought gripped him.

"Fine," he snapped. "Go back to your ship. Don't sully this place, *intruder*."

Riifue threw her arms around him and gripped tightly. "Since I called off the engagement, we don't have to worry about tradition anymore."

"I don't understand," babbled Edo.

"Once I leave, I'll have to live on a ship forever," said Riifue. "I'm not spending a single second of my time left away from you."

She looked up into Edo's eyes, her gaze like that of a dying person hoping for her final wish to be granted. At that, he melted. He slid his arms around her and his floodgates burst.

"Riifue …"

Uenda arose, sleepwalking toward the scent of cooking egg and rice. Absentmindedly, she droned, "Good morning, Mummy. Good morning, Riituan."

When there was no response, she looked again.

"Oh, she slept over," she droned. She yawned again, and then popped down next to her mother, who took two forceful shoves to pull her out of a daze. Sukete resumed stirring the chigua pot, though her face remained blank. She served Uenda, who sampled it with a frown.

"This tastes funny, Mummy," she yelped.

"I must've burned it a little," replied Sukete, yawning harder than her husband who sat across the hearth. "It's still fine. Eat up."

Odentii finished his meal then went out to the fields, though his gaze was empty, like he was on autopilot. Uenda obliviously proceeded to babble about her plans for when Riifue returned from the ship, with ideas ranging from planting new flowers in the garden, to collecting more ingredients for Sukete's motosu recipe. Her light-speed rambling stopped when Riifue and Edo appeared at the door, hand-in-hand. Odentii, Arika, and Jikyo stood behind them.

"Rii-tuan's back!" exclaimed Uenda, throwing her arms around the girl. Riifue took a deep breath, and looked down at Uenda's beaming face. She almost lost confidence, until spurred by Edo tightening his grip around her hand.

"I'm going with them," she said. "If I stay, my family on the *Othala* will pursue me, and bring the Mydians and much worse things with them. I won't let that happen to people I love. When the shuttle leaves tomorrow, I'll be on-board."

Sukete's lips tightened with suppressed grief, mirrored in Arika and Jikyo's sorrowful glances. Riifue forced herself to look down at Uenda, who quickly released her embrace. The girl's face was incomprehensible. She suddenly yanked Edo's hand out of Riifue's. She glared at her, gave a single punch to her stomach, and then ran out of the house.

Of all the wounds Neliya had sustained over her journey, the scars of which were smattered across her body, that feeble blow from a young girl hurt the most, and the deepest.

Kajil visited the house in the morning to give Riifue some Mydian clothes to wear. They felt and smelled terrible, and she put them as far away as she could. Thereafter, she spent every second on the porch, trying to memorise the world around her. After her sixth cup of tea, she closed her eyes and recalled Chisafenu. The scent of the bonfire filled her mental nose, and the koeri music filled her mental ears. The melancholic fog lifted from her mind, the koeri's sound like a child's voice come to banish the winter within her.

A voice brought her back to the present. Arika and Jikyo stood on the front porch, solemness colouring their smiles.

"I'm sorry you have to go, Riifue," said Arika, eyeing a bundle of wrapped cloth in her arms.

Riifue's eyes widened. "You didn't finish the bridal dress already, did you?"

"No, not at all," exclaimed Arika with a smile. "But I did want to show you what it might have looked like."

The group retreated inside and sat around the hearth. Arika unravelled the cloth, revealing a wonderfully vibrant blue and white garment. The cloth, though fine, betrayed the rigidity of age.

"I wore this when I married Jikyo," she said. Her husband's face crinkled into a nostalgic grin. "I was so nervous that day. The dress looked so lovely I was afraid I'd break it just wearing it."

Riifue pressed her fingers to her lips as she drank in the design, running her free hand delicately along its multilayered patterns. She felt like she was touching a cutout of the sky.

Jikyo interjected, "We brought something else you'll like." He handed a bag across the hearth. Inside was a roll of paper, anchored to wooden handles. Riifue unfurled it. The paper was bordered by intricate and colourful hand drawn designs, girdling a large glyph in the centre.

My name ... Riifue.

Jikyo took it from her, and walked to the wall beside the door, where the other name scrolls hung. He screwed a hook into the wall and hung it beside Edo's scroll. Riifue broke down as Arika snaked an arm over her shoulders.

"Even if you go beyond the stars, you'll still know there are people who love you here," said Jikyo, holding his gaze and warm smile.

Riifue breathed deeply again and faced the elderly man with a reverent bow. "Thank you so much, Grandpa Jikyo."

Sukete entered the room to find Riifue sobbing in Arika's arms, and her heart ached. Riifue turned and beamed through her tears.

"Jikyo made a name scroll for me," she exclaimed. Sukete frowned as she looked to the wall. Only four scrolls hung there. Arika and Riifue started to fret, but Jikyo's better hearing sensed the soft closing of wooden cupboards. He strode to the linen cupboards on top of which Riifue used to sleep. He slid the right door open. Nestled between the towels was Uenda, clutching the scroll.

"Uenda! Why are you hiding Riifue's scroll?" exclaimed Sukete.

"Scrolls are for family!" snapped Uenda, holding the scroll as if it were made of gold. "*Neliya* is just a guest!"

"Uenda, how can you say that?" whispered Riifue. "I'm sorry to be going, but that doesn't mean I don't like you or anything."

Uenda bellowed, "I don't care! Get out of here, you intruder!"

Suddenly, Sukete bellowed in a gruff, overbearing growl the likes of which Riifue had never heard. And it terrified her.

"Uenda Andou! Enough with this rudeness!" she roared.

Uenda froze, paralysed with fear and surprise. Clearly it was a first for her as well. Her face began to scrunch and her body shook. With an outburst of, "Stupid Neliya!" she threw the scroll on the floor and then sprinted out of the house. Arika and Sukete, mortified by the scene, tried to give chase.

Jikyo squatted to pick up the scroll, rubbing a mark on the polished wood floor the impact left behind. As he returned the scroll to the wall, Riifue tried to pretend Uenda hadn't just said such things.

I can't leave like this.

The final meal with the Andou family was solemn, and it only grew tenser with every effort people made at conversation. Riifue was even more troubled at Uenda's absence. She eyed the door to the room Sukete had sent her without food. That alone was enough to hamper any hope of leaving Ondyaarii on a positive note.

When the meal was done, Edo pulled her up from the floor and beckoned her to his room.

"Mother and Father gave me permission," he said.

Riifue managed a giggle, though the shrill screams of Uenda's resentment still loomed fresh in her mind. "I have to make up with Uenda. I can't leave with her hating me like that."

"She doesn't hate you, Riifue," said Edo, caressing her brown hair. "She's angry that you're leaving. That's all. Let her sleep, and then talk to her in the morning."

In the morning …

She looked around. The room was small compared to the living room, and when she stretched her memory, she realised it was no bigger than the chamber Allo had given her aboard the *Ranegr*.

She looked up into Edo's eyes, and in them saw a river of stars glimmering over a spotless sea. In that moment, she lived a dozen fantasies all at once: wearing a dress of vivid blue and white, hand-in-hand with Edo; looking down on her hands and seeing five fingers; in those hands, holding a baby with Edo's eyes. Voices reflexively spoke up against her flight of fancy, though they were drowned out by a single overbearing command.

For tonight, I will pretend.

Passionate dreamlike hallucinations peppered her sleep, from which Riifue arose very reluctantly. A sliver of light trickled through a gap in the door, tickling at her sleepy eyes. That glimmer reminded her.

Today is the day.

Her gaze moved to the man sleeping by her side.

But now is not the time.

She snuggled closer to him and fell into a soft snooze.

The time did come eventually. Riifue threw on the Mydian jumpsuit Kajil had given her the day before, and they went out into the living room. Sukete, Odentii, Jikyo, and Arika sat beside the hearth. They all gazed up at her.

"Ready to go, Riifue?" asked Sukete.

She gave an acquiescent nod. Odentii brought the carriage to the front, the mashi irate at being put to work so early.

Riifue stepped onto the carriage, took a seat next to Edo, and clasped her trembling hands around his. Her entire body shook uncontrollably, made only worse when the sound of arguing erupted from the house. Sukete dragged a loudly-protesting Uenda toward the carriage. Riifue cringed at the sight of Sukete harshly scolding her daughter.

"Uenda! Come and sit with me," she called out in the warmest voice she could muster. The girl sneered and sat at the front of the carriage.

Edo tried in vain to comfort her, as did Sukete.

"Don't worry," she whimpered. "We should get going or Kajil will be mad."

Odentii yipped the mashi along the path, leaving Riifue to gaze at the house. Between her longing and tingling remorse, she felt amazement at something she'd never noticed before.

It's so small, that house. No housekeeping staff, no maids or chauffers. Just the house, and the family in it. May it stand forever.

The carriage passed through the farm and into the forest. It rounded a few turns in the path, before passing through another threshold of trees and into the field where the shuttle waited – along with the entirety of Medan Village.

Idoru stepped forward with a sorrowful smile and said, "We all want to bid you farewell."

The woman was far too flabbergasted to respond, or even move. Edo and Sukete had to rouse her from her shock-induced stupor, though she was hardly responsive as she hopped off the carriage and paced cautiously into the crowd. The villagers parted as she walked, and each kissed their fingers, tapped their foreheads, and then touched her reverently. Those who couldn't reach held out their hands anyway, though they didn't crowd her as she moved unhindered toward the shuttle's ramp. With every touch to her shoulders and arms, Riifue felt a wave of joy ripple through her. It filled her to the brim and overflowed in the form of tears and hiccups. She reached the edge of the crowd. Fyuren and Zeers waited at the shuttle's ramp. She turned to see a collage of sweetly sorrowful faces.

She hugged Arika and Jikyo first. "I am sorry I could not be your granddaughter-in-law."

"You were a wonderful granddaughter," said Arika.

"Be safe," said Jikyo.

Then she bade Odentii and Sukete farewell, exerting all her will to restrain her emotion. She looked down at Uenda, and almost lost control when the girl turned her shoulder.

"Good bye, my little sister, Uenda," she stammered.

Then she looked into Edo's eyes. All control went out the window, and her lips were on his. The perturbed murmurs of the crowd fell on deaf ears. She threw all her thought into memorising the sensation, before finally breaking it and saying, "Goodbye, Edo."

"Goodbye, Riifue," Edo whispered.

No sooner had she left his embrace did another pair of arms grip her.

Oh, thank you, Ancestors, Goddess … What ever you are!

"Thank you, Uenda," she said, returning the hug. But the girl didn't let go.

"Rii-tuan's not going," snapped Uenda. She looked up at her with great big overflowing eyes. "You're not going! You're staying here. You marry my brother and stay!"

Riifue choked with dismay. "I have to go, Uenda. If I stay, it will only be bad for everyone."

Uenda only gripped harder and bellowed, "I don't care if those ugly aliens come! I'll beat them up!"

"Uenda, let go," said Edo.

"No," grunted Uenda.

"Uenda, you're being silly," chided Sukete, trying not to choke on the same emotions in which her daughter's heart was soaked.

"No!" yelled Uenda.

"I have to go," said Riifue.

"NO!" screamed Uenda. The shrill echoes died down, leaving behind only her distressed sobs. "Rii-tuan doesn't have any family in space! *We're* her family! She's *my* sister! She's *my* brother's wife! You aren't taking her!"

Riifue pulled her arms away and knelt down to look at her.

"You have no idea how happy that makes me," she said, barely able to hold back her grief. "But I *do* have family in space. And they're waiting for me. You have family here. You have your brother, your mother and father, your grandparents. You have all your brothers and sisters of Medan."

Uenda's breathing laboured through her gritted teeth, until she broke down. "But Rii-tuan won't be here!" She desperately gripped the hand that caressed her moistening cheek, digging her nails into Riifue's skin. "Stay with us, please."

Riifue cupped Uenda's cheeks and kissed her. "I love you, Uenda."

The girl frantically screamed in protest as Edo prised her away. Stealing one last look at the world she loved, and the distraught sister flailing for her, Riifue turned her back. She looked up to the hatch, where Zeers and Fyuren waited. The hum of the engines, the mechanical clang of her feet on the metal ramp, and the painful hiccups of her own grief were completely drowned out by the little girl screaming her name.

The hatch whirred closed behind her.

Don't turn around!

A horrific surge coursed through her chest, slowly sneaking up on her like an unknown infectious illness. From the time she had climbed into that tokamak coolant pipe it languidly gnawed at the tether to her life on the *Othala*. Even as she crashed onto this terra incognita, that bond held her by only a fraying thread.

But as that hatch cut off the last rays of Ondyaarii's morning sunlight, another bond broke, and it did so abruptly and callously. When it snapped, the sensation of loss she had come to know well fell upon her like a boulder, the weight of which was only magnified by the last words Uenda screamed, "Sister Riifue!"

In that instant, she reached out to stop the hatch, but her hands met cold metal. Its unforgiving clang reverberated through her body. She turned to her friends, who wore faces of concern and worry.

"Zeers! Fyuren! Open the door," she snapped. "I've changed my mind. I can't leave."

They gave no response.

"Open the door! I changed my mind!"

The shuttle's chassis began to rumble, amplifying her dread.

"I changed my mind!" she repeated, and continued to repeat as Zeers caught her. She thrashed in his arms, repeating the same words over and over and over, until she collapsed long after the shuttle had cleared the atmosphere of a world she could not live without.

35 | Don't think! Just talk!

Flurried wisps of cloud zipped past the viewport, melding into a bright blue haze on its way to the callous blackness of space. Neither Fyuren nor Zeers noticed the glimmering marble shrinking behind them as they hoisted a babbling, barely conscious Neliya onto the small cot. Kagoolie wiped her wrinkled cheeks dry.

"Go to sleep," Zeers cooed, though he did so reluctantly. He eyed the sobbing woman warily, as a convicted yet repentant murderer would gaze awkwardly at one of his victims. When Kagoolie and Fyuren moved to exit the room, he mumbled, "Wait, someone should stay with her."

"How 'bout you do it?" said Kagoolie. Her smile carried with it some of that same cheekiness for which Zeers knew her.

"I don't think I should," he returned. "I haven't really spoken to her since before, and I … *my* face shouldn't be the one she sees when she wakes up. How about you, Fyuren?"

"No," snapped Fyuren in a whisper. "I've gotta check the polywell."

"Kagoolie?" Zeers question was loaded with pleading.

"Oooh, space travel makes an old lady tired," said Kagoolie, and quitted the room with a fake cough. Fyuren shot him a smirk that seemed to say, "Make up with her," and closed the door.

Save for the hum of the engines and the whirring of the life support system, Zeers heard nothing other than the Aimorein babble of Neliya's grief-fuelled delirium. He found a small stool nestled into the corner of the cramped quarters, and sat quietly.

At first he stared at Neliya, whose sobs' ferocity steadily diminished. When she showed signs of drifting off to sleep, scraps of Littles' inane, malicious thoughts sprung to mind: ideas of heinous acts, which brought Zeers' bile close to his throat. He shuddered with fear and wrapped his arms around himself. His skin crackled as if a thousand poisonous bugs were gnawing their way through it.

A soft voice scraped against his eardrum.

"Edo?"

Zeers jumped in fright when she said it, and he looked up to see the sleeping woman. Her eyes were partially open, but sightless. Her chest slowly rose and fell and her breath left her in sonorous strokes.

Sleeping?

"Edo, *orou-ken*," muttered the woman.

Even in old age, Zeers might never know why he took her hand, but he did. And he spoke to her.

"Speak Myddish," he whispered.

"Why, husband? You don't speak Myddish," droned Neliya.

I should I call you Riifue now.

"I want to practice, Riifue," replied Zeers.

Don't think! Just talk!

"Alright, husband, but when we make our pledge, we'll do it in Aimorein, just like the Ancestors want," said Riifue through gently upturned lips.

I'm not Edo. I shouldn't be doing this. Shut up and talk!

"Yes, wife, when we marry," stammered Zeers. "I've forgotten. What will we say?"

Riifue giggled, "Have you been drinking sahi again with Nuto and Idoru? Kajil and Jugga forgot entire days when they drank too much." She giggled again, more fervently. "But that's just fine, husband. I'll remind you.

"You'll wait before the Ancestors, with Sukete. And I'll appear at the temple and ask your mother to be married to you. Of course she's already decided. She'll have fantasised about this day since you and I met. She'll grant me permission to be her daughter-in-law, and then we'll sit next to each other. I know Uenda won't be able to sit still through the whole thing. Idoru will give us *shesosuke* and *zuen ne katton* – you know, blessed water and the matrimonial knife.

"It'll be the one part I won't like, but I've born with worse. As I bleed myself into the cup, I say, 'To you, my husband, give I the blood of my kin. From the Ancestors' roots, my vine has followed a path through the walls of time, and henceforth is entwined with yours. With this blood, half my soul to make yours whole, my life to double yours. Take it graciously, and I will love you forever.' Then you do the same, and say the same. Though, maybe you could change it up a little. Odentii might be bothered by that.

"Once we have drunk from the cup, our blood will be one, won't it? Maybe then, the Ancestors might answer my prayer."

Zeers was sure he was as dazed as Riifue, or at the very least hypnotised by her semi-conscious rambling. Though he trembled as he stroked her hand, he would later marvel that those moments were the most peace he'd had in years.

"What prayer?" he asked.

Riifue's brow furrowed. "Don't you remember? That night, I snuck away to the temple?"

"Lots has happened," replied Zeers. "Remind me again."

Riifue's quivering lips widened into a smile, accompanied by forlorn tears. "I asked them to adopt me. Sharpen my ears and give me another finger and toe … So that the baby in my dreams could be yours."

Zeers heart and lungs turned to rock. His mind was completely gone to oblivion, and what remained had only the presence of thought to say, "I'm certain they'll answer it, Riifue. They'll definitely adopt you. And you and I can be together."

Riifue sighed contently, and gently kissed his hand.

"Husband, come hold me?" she implored.

I draw the line here.

"Soon, wife. I have to help father with some things," Zeers blurted. "You sleep, and dream of our child."

Riifue drifted off, and Zeers pulled his hand out of her grip. He buried his flushed face in his hands. His laboured breathing was hardly audible over the boiling blood pulsing through his head. The sight of the brown-haired woman, clothed in alien garb, tattooed with symbols he couldn't begin to understand, singed his retinas.

Why did I let him do this? Why did I agree to this? I'm helping to drag her back to a world she hates. I might as well have let Littles assault her to his heart's content!

Realising he could no longer internalise his sobs, Zeers fled the room and sprinted down the corridor. He ran, bumping into crewmen and dodging others, until he found a corner of the shuttle where he heard nothing. He slumped against the wall and let his sorrow out in slow, controlled bursts of air. His self-directed rage left him in swift painful elbow blows to the bulkhead behind him, and furious punches to the wall in front of him.

"Zeers?" a dreadful voice echoed down the corridor. Neliya appeared before him, though he was in such a daze he thought it was another hallucination.

"Come to torment me again, Mum?" he groaned. "Or Neliya? Whichever."

"I'm not going to torment you, Zeers," said Neliya. "Why would I do that?"

Zeers thrust his hands into his armpits and rasped, "You did it to Littles all the time, even when he was asleep, so why not do it to me."

Neliya knelt down before him and placed a hand on his shoulder. "I'm really here."

Zeers flashed white with rage and slapped the suspected ghost. When his hand struck real skin, his heart jumped into his chest, and he launched to his feet. "Riifue! I didn't mean to … I'm so sorry!"

"And after I worried about you," growled Riifue.

"I thought I was hallucinating!" Zeers exclaimed. "Whenever I had a dream about Neliya, she'd always attack me! I thought it was happening again, and I didn't want it to. I'm sorry, Riifue."

The woman sighed, "Why would you be hallucinating? Why would you think I'd want to hurt you?"

The mood settled slightly enough for Zeers to recollect his earlier thoughts, and he shuffled.

"Because I dragged you away from him," he muttered. "I didn't want you to come back to the *Othala* with us, because I knew you were already home. And I pulled you away from that."

Riifue pushed downward on his shoulders, pressing him against the bulkhead to steady him.

"I'm not so vindictive as to hurt you for that," she said forcefully. "Of course I'm upset, but Gast was right."

"But you prayed to be adopted by them," returned Zeers, his grief mounting. "You wanted to have kids with him, and I helped take that away from you."

"Even if that future is gone, it doesn't mean there isn't a future for me elsewhere," said Riifue. She caressed his cheek. "Who knows? Maybe we can be together now." Zeers shook his head furiously, clearly disgusted by the idea. She didn't let him respond. "But whatever. What I mean is, the future's still open for us. Still open for you."

The frantic man's breathing slowed to a series of long, drawn out pants. The tears eventually stopped, and he met Riifue's gaze. "How can I enjoy that future, given what's behind me? Even if Dad can convince the courts that I was brainwashed, how can I forgive myself?"

Riifue smiled, and leaned forward to peck his lips with hers. The shock of her act lit his every nerve alight with a cooling flame, and he stared back at her. She gave him a grin, and said, "You just do it."

Zeers fell off the stool and on to the floor, his hand still tightly gripped in Riifue's as she dozed quietly on the bed. He pulled himself up and looked around. He hadn't left the quarters, and the clock on the wall told him an hour had passed since he sat down. With a mind too confused to remember his earlier angst, he weaselled his hand out of Riifue's and ran his hands through his hair.

My dreams are too damn vivid.

He exited the quarters with the intention of going for a walk, but found Gast waiting beside the door.

"Is she alright?" asked his father.

"She's sleeping," said Zeers shakily. "I don't think she'll be waking up any time soon."

Gast pursed his lips and said, "She'll have to. Fyuren says they're ready to try a jump and we need to strap in."

Zeers mouth said, "I'll leave that up to you then," but his eyes said, "I'm not going back in there."

Gast pretended he didn't notice his son's discomfort and said, "Go strap in. I'll wake her up."

Zeers marched away from the door with odd purpose, his mind filled with a soothing sensation he couldn't yet identify. He reached one of the shuttle's seating bays and buckled down into a chair. Around him sat other Pebhorda soldiers, some of whom were still nursing battle wounds, others who regarded him with either contempt for killing the Pebhasid, or admiration for killing the Pebhasid. Kajil and Swine entered the room and strapped into the chairs opposite him, and any compunction the surrounding officers had to speak up was extinguished.

Fyuren soon followed, and sat to Zeers' left.

"The polywell is running fine, I hope," he said with a shaky sigh. "The TIM device should have one more go in it, but I'd say that's it."

"We're goin' to the Pebhasid station first," said Kajil. "We'll free the *Kulanki* crew, then send ya on ya way."

"Thanks," murmured Fyuren, his voice supressing the giddy gratitude of being granted a long-unsated desire. Then he turned to Zeers, "Let's just hope they're in a forgiving mood when they see you."

Zeers' eyes kept their gaze directed to the floor as he intoned, "That's already handled."

"What did you do?" asked Kajil.

"You'll see when we get there," replied Zeers.

The shuttle's intercom crackled with electricity, which parted to let Fenk's voice filter through.

"Ladies and gentlemen, we're almost ready to make our CTN jump. We just need to pass a debris field on our starboard side, then we'll be under way."

"Oi, that's the wreck of the flagship!" exclaimed a soldier seated next to the window. Driven by morbid curiosity, every passenger moved to the windows to catch a glimpse of the derelict. The mess resembled two droplets of water contaminated with different coloured mud, seeping into each other while the sun's gravity gradually edged it inwards. Tendrils of ripped metal and fried biomass trickled downward into the star's well, soon to be devoured and lost forever in that celestial resomator. The tiniest particles of dust harmlessly dinged against the hull of the shuttle. To Zeers, it sounded eerily like rain.

Zeers straightened up and decided he'd seen enough. He looked over to the window at the back of the cabin, where Neliya stood lethargically against the windowpane. She regarded the derelict cloud with a vacant expression, as if she was sleepwalking. Zeers could not find an excuse to approach her, or even what he would say if he did.

"Everybody, we've almost cleared the field, so strap yourselves in," said Fenk. The passengers fell into line, and the cabin momentarily simmered with the clacking of seatbelts. Fyuren plopped into his seat, grinning nervously. Neliya sat in her chair as a condemned prisoner willing falls into a gas chamber.

Between them, the most battle-scarred of all, Zeers just felt ambivalent.

36 | What future is there for me on the *Othala*?

With what little time the *Kulanki* crew had off from studying the baffling tunnelling solution developed by a child, they had steadily rebuilt the habitat within their dome world. Crops trampled by Drifter pirates were re-sown; houses marred by gunfire were repaired; and, once that teenaged murderer and his insane master had their tunnelling solution, there was time to at least rebuild the children's playground.

Thereafter there was little sight of the Drifter soldiers. Though if one looked up, out of the dome, during the night cycle, anyone could see the hostile sentries patiently guarding their lord's prize. Also, when there was maintenance to be done on the life support systems, one learned very quickly the vigilance of the enemy soldiers who stood just beyond the metal doors of the habitat.

At night, the prisoners in their own home would gather in the village square. Contributions of food and drink from every house would be shared amongst all of them. One particular night, as they celebrated the repaired bioplant's third consecutive week of operation, the mayor raised a glass in thanks.

"Let us be grateful to the gods and goddesses of the world, for though we have met with unexpected hardship, we know now that together we can rise to the challenge."

"Hear, hear!" bellowed a few of the diners.

"Excuse me!" roared a man from the edge of the village. Everyone snapped to attention before their cups hit the table. People gasped in a unified chorus of dread, as Littles appeared with an armed contingent in tow. Most of them were too fearful or outraged to notice the barely healed battle scars, the bandaged fingers, and a very clear change in the man's eyes. There was at least some light in them now.

The man stammered nervously, "The Pebhasid is dead. I killed him. Which, I s'pose, makes me the new leader." The man they knew as Littles gazed around the stalled banquet, and studied the uncertain faces of his captors. A loud hissing of silence in everyone's ears eventually prompted Littles to say, "I'm releasing you. Effective immediately."

"Releasing us? Why?" asked the startled mayor.

"I have no need for you now," returned Littles. "I'll have your communications repaired as soon as possible, so that you can contact the Commonwealth and have support crews brought in."

"Wait!" shouted one of the scientists, whose face Littles barely recognised. "You capture us, kill our crew and our associates, and even one of our families! You force us to work for you, and then you decide, 'Nup, we're done! Have a nice day?'"

The protestor's sentiments spread through the crowd like wild fire.

"That's total nonsense!" snapped one.

"To the gallows with you!" snarled another.

Littles drew his sidearm and fired into the air. He stopped short of emptying his clip, and the banquet was silent.

"I am sorry for what I did to your support crew," he muttered. "But as for your associate ... Will the town mayor please come with me?"

The mayor went pale and would have profusely refused the invitation had Littles' subordinates not dragged her away with him. The distraught villagers charged forward with pleading eyes, but met a wall of Drifter soldiers.

The soldiers almost carried the mayor while remaining hot on Littles' heels, taking a few twists and turns through the ship, until they reached the starboard airlock. The hatch gave way to a docked vessel. The sounds of complaining children trickled through the passageway, reaching the mayor's ears long before Littles passed into a seating cabin.

The mayor's jaw dropped at the sight of a man and woman, surrounded by their litter of restless children. The mayor thought the family dead, having been Littles' example to the rest of her colleagues.

"Professor Elska!" exclaimed the man.

The children launched off their seats and embraced the mayor. "Auntie Elska! Please take us off this shuttle! We're so bored!"

The mayor's voice was scared away into a hole by the sight in front of her. She finally found the sense to ask, "What is going on here?"

"It seems this such and such used only sleeping gas." Obviously the man wanted to use more colourful words to describe Littles, but censored himself for the sake of his children. "My family woke up an hour later. Ever since, we've worked in the farms aboard their station." He turned to his wife and added, "Now that we're home, maybe you could take the kids along."

"My subordinates will show you the way," Littles intoned.

The woman took her children, curtly nodding to him as she guided them down the corridor. Her husband stayed behind and fixed his eyes on Littles.

"I should rightly be outraged with you," he said with a voice that faltered like an unsteady acrobat on a trapeze. "But given your experience, I suppose the best thing to do is move on with life. I wish you a speedy recovery." He bowed, and then left.

Littles turned to the mayor, threw off his jacket with a grateful shudder, and exposed his still bandaged neck to the her.

"The Pebhasid, Gelfri, embedded an implant in my neck," he explained. "It turned me into the monster you know as Littles. My name is Zeers Indra, a citizen of the *Othala*."

The mayor stepped back in shock, her shoulders raised as a chill of recognition went up her spine. "I know you! It was all over the news for months: lost children from the *Othala*. We couldn't use the CTN for weeks after that. You're the one who was lost?"

"I was, and two others," replied Zeers. He beckoned the mayor to follow him down the corridor to a meeting room near the cockpit, where several other individuals waited. He introduced Gast, Fenk, Neliya, and Fyuren.

The mayor's eyes widened. "Fyuren Orthos? You're the one who designed that tunnelling solution?"

"Something I really regret in hindsight," returned Fyuren.

The mayor shook her head with amazement. "I knew there were gifted kids, but nothing of this magnitude."

"I had a little help from people around me," said Fyuren. "But that's nothing now. Zeers has transferred leadership of the Pebhasid to Kajil, a friend of ours, who will help you get back on your feet."

Gast stepped forward. "In exchange, we must ask a few things of you."

"Ask of us?" exclaimed the mayor. "Given the circumstances, I don't think there's much more you *can* ask. You attacked us, so if you're trying to make amends, getting us back on our feet is the least you can do. Why then should we have to do anything for you?"

"You don't," said Zeers. "You can just say, 'Out the airlock, your corpses soar!' That's fine by me. But Fyuren just wants to go home."

The mayor's face melted when she looked at the boy before her, on whose shoulder his father rested a supportive hand.

Pointing at Gast, Zeers went on, "And he needs to take me home so I can face trial for what I did here. He was sent to apprehend me. He lost his Megin limb to catch me. So if you help us out, your lost crew might see justice."

"If you were brainwashed, you'd never see trial," returned the mayor. She knowingly added with a glance Gast's way, "And no father would put his son through that, would he?" Her eyes fell on the mute Neliya seated a fair distance from anyone, and asked, "How about Madam Talkative over there?"

Neliya snapped to attention after the third call of her name. She shrugged, "I'm just tired from a really, really long trip."

The mayor harrumphed, and shuffled backward a little. With every nervous twitch of her body her vengefulness declined.

"I'll explain this to my crew," she acquiesced. "The fact that you left that family alive should go a long way to convincing them that we have more important things on the agenda. As soon as a tunneller is available, you'll go."

Fyuren leapt out of his chair and threw his arms around her with enough force to knock her on her back. Everyone in the room moved forward to help the woman up, save for Neliya, who gave a caustic chuckle.

The five travellers stood beside the hatch in the *Kulanki* tunneller bay, their spacesuits donned. As their tunneller was slotted onto the launch tray, the five travellers turned to their companions. Kajil moved forward and held out his hand to Gast.

"Hope they give you a new arm, Mister Military Alchemist," he said, before turning to Fenk and shaking his hand as well. "Be good, Shorts Senior."

"Thanks for looking after the kids, Drifter," returned Gast with a smile no one had seen him wear.

Dennie and Deloorie threw their arms around Fyuren and Zeers, only slightly disappointed that they could no longer reach all the way around their broadened shoulders.

"Don't fight anymore, you two," said Deloorie. "You have to look after Neliya as well. Look after each other, like always."

"We will," replied the boys.

Allo stepped forward and shook Fyuren's hand. "Glad to work with you, Shorts. And I'm sure Malse would've felt the same."

"Don't link the tokamak to the sewer system again," said Fyuren with an acerbic point of his finger.

"Yes sir!" snapped the engineer.

Neliya still hadn't let go of Kagoolie by the time Swine and his men stepped up to bid her farewell. The surviving Nightshift of the *Ranegr* stood at attention. Swine roared, "For our lady, who cared for us!" Then the rabble of creatures bellowed, "Farewell, M'lady!"

Neliya only smiled and bowed in return. Then she turned to Kagoolie. "I hate goodbyes."

"Who doesn't?" returned the kindly old lady.

"We should hop on," said Fenk. He and Gast edged toward the tunneller.

"Wait!" yelled Kajil. The three friends turned to see the new Pebhasid coming at them. He scooped them up and squeezed them in one go, surprising and winding them in the process.

"From Jugga and Murraloohaa, and everyone else," he whispered. Then he let them go. "Now go on, the lot of you! Enough with the sappy moments."

"Or what?" returned Zeers with a grin. "You'll cry?"

"I ain't cryin'," barked Kajil. "Go home before I boot ya into the resomators!"

The children – no longer children by any stretch of the imagination – laughed in return, and waved their friends goodbye. Fyuren and Zeers went in first, leaving Neliya to look at the people she'd called her crew for so long. In that instant, she froze.

Lost Edo and Uenda, lost Ondyarii. Now I'm about to lose them.

Without realising it, she had climbed into the tunneller, and the hatch sealed behind her.

In front of her, Fyuren mumbled, "Faster, faster, faster, faster, faster!"

Behind her, Zeers chuckled, "Want to double-check the TIM device's alignment one more time?"

On the intercom, the tracking officer's voice echoed with a countdown.

The tunneller lurched forward and gravity suddenly disappeared. They were floating free, but thanks to her harness, Neliya was stuck.

Why not stay with the Pebhorda? She mused. *They're all people I know and trust. How about it?*

The countdown reached three.

One goodbye is enough for a lifetime, isn't it?

The countdown hit two.

Isn't it enough to lose one family?

The countdown hit one.

What future is there for me on the Othala?

37 | The future's open for us

The bed sheets were cold and scratchy, the hazmat-clad nurses and doctors callous and terse. One nurse regarded her patient as a dangerous artefact as she read the name from the tablet. "Subject: Dosag, Neliya, Decontamination day four. System has been purged of pathogens, and final cultures awaiting analysis. Project release in two days."

Neliya pulled herself out of the bed and rubbed her head. Ever since she'd been thrown into this prison cell of a decontamination chamber, a migraine had mounted in her head. Fyuren said it would happen, since they'd been away for so long and been exposed to different environments. Also, the *Othala* had imposed much more restrictive guidelines for environmental protection after the Bioplant Crisis.

She gazed to her left, drawn by the sound of curtains opening. Fyuren had just been given a change of bed sheets, and a new gown. Neliya just got an unwelcome glimpse of his bare backside. A barrier of soundproof glass prevented the dismayed chiding she'd have let out, were she so inclined.

To her right, Zeers stood near the glass barrier of his cell, speaking with a few officers on the other side of the threshold.

They've been interrogating him since he got here, she thought. *Didn't the doctors even give a report and a brain scan?*

The officers wrapped up their discussion and left. Zeers returned to his bed, scratching the faded scars on his left eye where Gelfri's brand had been. He nodded to her with a smile. Then her nurse drew the curtains and hid her friends from view.

"Bedding needs to be changed, and you need to be cleaned again," she said curtly. With a sigh, Neliya crawled off the bed and threw off the gown. The nurse pulled away the bedding and tossed it down a chute, replacing it with new sheets. Then she beckoned the patient into the middle of the room. Neliya nonchalantly eyed the doctors ogling her like a laboratory specimen.

Seriously, I don't know why I ever bothered with embarrassment. If it'd get me out of here, I'd walk around naked forever!

The nurse procured a tank of whatever disinfectant they'd adopted, and began to cover her with the odourless chemical. She turned on the spot. The doctors, obviously lacking in every department other than objective medicine, offered raised eyebrows at the sight of her scars and marvelled at what kind of battles she'd endured.

There! I gave you a twirl, now let me out of here.

Clothed, new bedding, and disinfected *again*, Neliya popped back onto the bed and tried to sleep. However, she'd done nothing but sleep for days, so she gazed at the observation portal – the closest thing there was to a book or television. The doctors had gone, and two faces replaced them.

What? Here to gawk at victims of the disinfectant brigade?

The figures just stared back at her, though their faces wore far more emotion than hers. The woman pressed her hand against the glass, the other she used to cover her mouth in astonishment. The man beside her looked as if he had seen someone come back from the dead. Then the voices came through the intercom.

"Neliya?" said the man.

"That's one name I go by," she said sardonically. "Not my favourite name, not my most hated one either."

The woman exchanged a borderline mortified glance with the man.

"Neliya? Sweetheart, it's us!" she rasped.

Neliya readied another snide quip, until she looked closer. Then she rose out of the bed and drew near to the portal. She touched her hand against the glass, over where the woman's pressed.

"You're home, Neliya," said the man.

Neliya only stared back at them. She tried to match their hesitant but overjoyed expressions, but nothing came.

I don't know you.

She bit her tongue.

Zeers wrung his fingers as if to squeeze trepidation out of them. While it gave his fingers something to do other than scratch at the tattoo removal scars around his left eye, it did nothing to relieve his nerves. The maglev coasted along the tracks, with every smooth stop bringing him closer to his destination.

The maglev ground to a halt at the Sector Twenty station, and he hopped out with the torrent of late afternoon commuters. For neither the first nor the last time did he wonder if the whole place had shrunk since their tunneller mishap. The whole place seemed so small.

He boarded the escalator for the surface, and gazed around. A sensation of déjà vu began to itch as Zeers' eyes fell upon the skinny man behind him. The man met his gaze and expressed the same bout of slippery memories, until it hit both of them. Zeers didn't know which of those old bullies he was looking at, but it didn't matter. He just nodded politely, and upon receiving the same non-verbal response, he turned and walked up the escalator.

Zeers exited the station and jogged across the road to the café at the intersection. He wet his dry lips as he peered inside and looked for a familiar face. He saw the long auburn braid hanging from Neliya's head. With trembling hands, he tapped her shoulder and stammered, "Sorry I'm late. Proceedings took a long time."

Neliya just shook her head, clearly lost in her own thoughts. He sat opposite her, and clenched his hands together. He tried to focus on the woman before him, but the shimmering pendant around her neck repelled his gaze.

Another figure yanked a chair over and plonked down excitedly. Fyuren's gaze darted between the pair, a big grin on his face.

"This is great!" he exclaimed. "Finally, we can hang out again!" Zeers managed a half-hearted smile, while Neliya just cocked her head and sipped her tea. Fyuren continued, "And the faculty is amazing. Though my tunnelling solution wasn't fully effective, they were so impressed by my polywell design they gave me tenure. I'll get to teach classes and run my own research team. Oh, by the Gods, I'm so glad to be home!" Out of breath, he turned to Zeers and asked, "So, your sentence came back?"

"The *Kulanki* crew testified, so did Dad, and the judge was convinced," Zeers mumbled. "I've got to spend a year in a psychiatric ward, so that they can be sure I'm not still … *Littles*."

Fyuren growled, "But the judge was convinced, wasn't he?"

"They want to assess my mental state," said Zeers. "If I check out after a year, I get a suspended sentence."

"But you're fine now," Fyuren protested.

"Fyuren, seriously, this is a slap on the wrist compared to what I deserve," Zeers insisted.

"You want to be punished more?" asked Fyuren.

Zeers shrugged, "Just so I can feel as if I had a *little* control over Littles. So I can at least own some of my actions."

"Why?" exclaimed Fyuren. "Who would want to claim responsibility for something they were brainwashed to do?"

Growing aggravated, Zeers ran his hand through his hair.

"Did no one ever wonder why I started doing those alliteration spiels?" he asked.

"Gast said it was because of the implant," said Fyuren.

Zeers looked fixedly at him. "Did no one ever wonder why Gelfri did it too?"

There was a brief pause, in which Fyuren made the realisation, and then wondered why it hadn't dawned on him before. "Gelfri had the same implant."

Zeers nodded. "If I'm not responsible for the bad Littles did, then ... whoever he was before ... *he* isn't responsible for the bad Gelfri did. But if I wanna continue hating that bastard, I should face at least a few tunes." His piece spoken, Zeers caught the waiter's attention and ordered a sandwich.

"Well then, we'll visit," said Fyuren. He eyed the mute Neliya. "Right?"

Neliya grimaced and nodded. The jovial boy added, "And after that, you'll probably be going to school again. Right? Maybe even the university, and we'll be able to hang all the time."

Zeers shook his head, "Nope."

"Why not?" said Fyuren.

Zeers hoed into his sandwich. He mumbled, "My Dad's calling a few people, so when I get out of the cuckoo house, I can start my cadetship at the academy."

Fyuren fell silent, his jaw ajar, while Neliya finally spoke, "You're planning to join the Guild?"

Zeers cracked a wide smile at the woman, which he couldn't hold for long as he said, "Wrong again. I like having both my arms. But there's no reason I can't be a regular soldier. I've got plenty of experience, even in a command position. Though I'll be better at it than Littles."

Fyuren scratched his head. "Wait a tick, there's no military academy on the *Othala*."

"I'm going to the one on Khayns," said Zeers. "There's a psych facility there too, so I'll be able to take some of the preliminary courses while undergoing my evaluation."

"Oh, so you're leaving the *Othala* too?" asked Neliya.

Zeers nodded. "I'm tired of space."

Fyuren's knuckles turned white and he glared at Neliya. "What do you mean, 'too?'"

Neliya took a long sip of her tea and said, "I've spoken to my parents. They've decided to post a regional manager to the *Othala*, and we're moving to Lethanis. They want to spend more time with me, and I suppose they want to get to know me better."

Zeers smiled, though he couldn't keep his gaze on the woman as she stroked her pendant. He managed to say, "So, you'll get to be on a planet, like you wanted."

"Not the planet I wanted to be on," said Neliya, her voice trembling. "But it's a start."

"You didn't tell your parents about Edo?" asked Zeers. "I'm sure they can keep a secret."

"Yeah, I tell them that I'd forgotten about them, and they'd contemplate suicide," spat Neliya. "I just don't want to deal with that. I just want to get on with my life."

The table shuddered as Fyuren launched to his feet and roared, "We just got home!" The whole café fell silent, but the boy paid it no mind. "We just got back home after years! Years! I spent all that energy turning a cruiser into a tunneller, then hacking together a communicator – I built a fusion reactor *in a barn!* With a box of scraps!" Tears streamed down his cheeks as he screamed, "Now, you're leaving me!"

Zeers and Neliya looked right at each other for the first time since Littles nearly cut Riifue's throat. They nodded resolutely, and turned to the distraught boy between them.

"Fyuren, we want to move on," said Zeers. "Before Gelfri got me, I was ready to come back to the *Othala*, but I wasn't going to stay here. Even if we hadn't gotten lost, I still planned to enrol in the military, and I'd've left anyway."

Neliya spoke up, "And I was going to leave eventually too, since I'd have to take over the bioplant business. Now, I don't think I'll do that. But I definitely want a solid ground beneath my feet."

Fyuren stomped the ground beneath him. "Not solid enough for you? Breathe in that air that those trees outside exhaled! There are bioplants on Lethanis too, ya know? Or is this just payback for dragging you away from your precious hyper beanbag?"

Neliya's empty teacup came down upon its saucer hard. Then she stood, ignoring the shocked gazes of the other patrons. She looked down at Fyuren and snarled, "You're not a child like Uenda, so you should be able to deal with someone leaving. Get over yourself, Shorts, and grow up."

Zeers intoned, "Aren't you supposed to be smart?"

"I got you back here, so you're supposed to stay for me!" roared Fyuren as he punched the table. "To hell with Kagoolie! Things'll damn well be the way I want them!" With that, the boy stormed out of the café. A few coughs permeated the awkward silence, before conversations resumed. Neliya and Zeers sat back down, and sighed at the sight of the proverbial bridge burning beside them.

"Too harsh?" asked Zeers.

"I don't care anymore," said Neliya.

Zeers chuckled, "What do you care about, Riifue?"

Neliya's lips pursed at the name, and she mumbled, "I don't want to go into the family business." Her mind churned with a mix of Myddish and Aimorein thoughts. "To be honest, I wish I'd paid more attention in language class. Learning Aimorein really was fun."

"Why don't you study that, then?" asked Zeers excitedly. "Become a linguist or something."

Neliya's eyes brightened at the idea, and she chuckled. It allowed Zeers a moment of happiness and he laughed too.

"That really would be a different path from the family business," she said. "I don't know what'd happen if I did, but I like that idea."

"Who cares what'll happen?" exclaimed Zeers. "We didn't know that tunneller would stuff up, and while we had a lot of bad, you at least had some good time with Edo and Uenda. Who knows what good stuff'll happen from now on? The future's open for us." He eyed the café exit. "Fyuren doesn't want to admit it, but he'll definitely make some new friends in his tenure-thingie."

Neliya chortled, "And drive them insane with his rambles."

When they sobered, Zeers raised his finger, his eyes fixed on Neliya.

"Let's promise," he stated. "In four years, no matter what happens in the future, we'll meet up here, and have a bunch of new stories to tell."

Neliya pondered the idea a moment, and it forced a grin out of her. She offered her hand and said, "Promise!"

They finished their food, paid their bill, and walked outside. Before they could part, Zeers noted Fyuren lurking in a park nearby. Neliya saw the upset boy, and recalled every moment she'd spoken with him. She remembered how his eyes ignited every time he talked to her about his work, and how he fell into her arms when he was upset.

I'm taking that away, she realised.

They approached him, somewhat reluctantly, and tapped his shoulder. He jumped three feet in the air and growled, "What now? Come to tell me you never liked me to begin with?"

"No," replied Zeers.

Neliya allowed her expression to soften, and she said, "I'm sorry, Fyuren. Thanks for working so hard to bring us home." Tears dribbled down Fyuren's cheeks. Neliya went on, "I know how much we mean to you. And I'm grateful that you cared so much about us."

"Then why leave?" growled Fyuren.

"Because life has to go on," said Zeers. "I have to decide what I want in life, and so does Neliya."

"You get to choose that, so why not us?" asked Neliya.

The question made Fyuren flush, and his body trembled with increasing ferocity. He wiped away his tears, but his scowl remained. He whispered, "And you just have to run off to have that choice?"

Zeers grimaced, "If we stayed in a place we don't like for you, we'd just end up resenting you. Trust me, I know that really well. Do you really want that?"

Fyuren swallowed a very solid lump in his throat and croaked, "No."

"There you have it," said Neliya. She added with a bright chirp, "And there's no reason we can't stay in touch. Zeers and I just made a promise to meet here in four years with a bunch of fun stories to tell. And we'd want to meet you here too."

Fyuren smiled weakly. He sniffed back his tears and said, "Just let me know when you're leaving so I can see you off, okay?"

Both Neliya and Zeers grinned, "Definitely." And they pulled him into a tight embrace.

Fyuren didn't stop crying.

Neliya ruminated over a bowl of soup in her parents' favourite restaurant. The view of the harbour it offered felt, in a way, like another lookout. It gave her comfort as she pondered. She couldn't remember the last time she'd considered the future before she left the *Othala*. Of course, it didn't help that she remembered very little of her life before that event either.

Maybe that's a good thing. Since I barely remember the past, the future is there for me.

A polite waiter bussed her empty plate, and after ordering some tea, she eyed the folder again.

From Lethanis, I can see the sky whenever I want. And I can get Fyuren to tell me exactly what star to look for when I want to think of Edo. And if Ondyaarii was such a wonderful place, who knows what else waits outside this mouse wheel? The universe is infinite, after all.

Her tea came. She waited for the waiter to leave, before sipping the drink and hissing. The second-nature custom reminded her of Ondyaarii, and the words she'd embedded in her memory from long ago.

Chinne ma kyaunadyo yao taku mona atupposu ze!

She uncapped her pen, and opened the folder. The paper read, "Lethanis University, Linguistics Faculty, Enrolment form." She filled the name field, "Neliya Dosag," and in the preferred name field, she wrote, "Riifue."

Wash the worries of the past with the dirty laundry. That's damn right.

• • •

A soft wind blew through the stone-paved courtyard, loosened technicolour petals skimming the polished floor. The breeze wafted about the pillars and statues that adorned the countryside mansion, carrying pollen, leaves, and dust, imbuing a crisp spring smell into an atmosphere crowned by three moons. The mansion stood like a stone isle in a sea of wild flowers, and an old man stared lazily at them.

Though he seemed to be enjoying his final days in peace, he was deep in thought, meditating upon machinations far removed from him in space and time. So too were those seated at his table. Each individual wore pensive, disconcerted, or irritated expressions – or combinations of the three.

His eyes stole from the scenery to glance at the man seated three places away to his left. Much younger, though old enough to be called regal, he appeared to listen to the conversation just as intently as the others, though his mind was elsewhere, and the old man knew it.

The woman to the old man's immediate right, a tall, slender being, brushed her long unrestrained hair out of her face, and adjusted her spectacles. She tapped her tablet, and reached the final page of her report.

"Thus, business concerning Khageh and Teldi is reaching a conclusion," she said briskly, though there was a growing frustration in her voice. "The dense veins of compatible resources make them possible candidates. However, Liadri remains elusive. The Evelyns continue to interfere."

"Can we be sure they do not suspect our objective?" asked the younger Mydian.

"Zis odjectibe haz been enbijioned for generazions! And yet zey habe not made a moobe agains uz," gurgled an Aquilan, tapping its damp fingers on the table as it gazed fixedly toward the Mydian through a watery shield. The mechanisms in its sleek environmental suit spiked in pitch as it reached for the teacup and drew some of the cooling liquid through a straw in its helmet.

"I agree," said a dark faced Earthen woman. Her eyes were as sharp and focused as the speaker. She wore far less than her Mydian counterpart, and her skin was bedizened with tattoos and tribal piercings, not even slightly diminishing her standing amongst the group. "Liadri *is* most certainly in their territory. We have been held at bay for so long because they will not be brought into the fold."

The reptilian creature to the Earthen's right gurgled its throat clear, and raised its hands. Like its Aquilan counterpart, this Ranian wore an environmental suit, which billowed steam and warmth as the creature made a sequence of gestures with its six-fingered claws. A synthesised voice uttered from a translator on its wrists, "Perhaps the time is near for more drastic action."

"You mean war?" asked the Aquilan. "I theem to rebember a war not too long ago. Imbazience iz imbrudence, Ranian."

"Let us not go down old paths, companions," said the Earthen, glad to be quelling the argument before it started. Yet irritability hung over the table like a blanket of bad weather, shooing away the calming breeze.

At his age, the old man expected his hearing to fail him. And yet he could hear the clenching of teeth around the room. He made no effort to suppress a grin.

These young'uns! To feel such anticipation, such passion ... such frustration.

"Let us leave Liadri to hereafter," he mumbled. "If the Evelyns have it, they will keep it until we have it. It is not going anywhere beyond where we cannot get it." His eye opened a crack, ignoring the expectant glances in his direction, and looked to the perspiring object of his interest.

"Berikas," he intoned, the silent man snapping to attention. "Surely you have lost your animosity for the Evelyns. Did they not recently help find something you lost?"

"That something lost itself," replied Berikas. "But yes, the Evelyns did help to recover it. In so doing," he began, but uncertainty gagged him. He gazed around the table before clearing his throat. "In so doing, this unexpected excursion may have borne fruit, which, at the very least, may put the Evelyns and Liadri to the back of our minds."

Berikas picked up his own tablet and called up the information.

"Fyuren Orthos, my nineteenth son, born to my fourth concubine," he began. "I am sure you know him as Progenitor Nine?"

The title elicited a few surprised glances.

"Sinkrel's living progeny," the old man intoned. "After eight failures ..."

Berikas went on, "While the Evelyns did succeed in locating him and his companions due to a CTN malfunction, it was in fact Progenitor Nine who returned home. He successfully extended the tunnelling equations to larger vessels, extending our potential reach much further."

"Much further?" asked the Mydian woman. "Such a feat would make obsolete our mass colonisation fleet."

Berikas waved his hand dismissively. "His invention is nought without its flaws, as further review of CTN telemetry shows a high rate of failure with increasing size and distance. Perhaps the problems are fixable, perhaps not. Whether to suppress this information or not is at our discretion. However, the knowledge lives on in his mind, over which we have free reign. Further, he has implemented a new power source design heretofore considered purely theoretical. All of these prove the success of Sinkrel's progeny."

"Then we can perhaps move forward with the covenant ahead of schedule," said the Earthen excitedly. The Ranian signed a fervent agreement, while the Aquilan pressed its palm to the table and countered their suggestion. Before a debate could break out, Berikas raised his voice, "Perhaps our decision of what to do with this knowledge should be made at a later time."

"Have you more to say?" asked the old man.

"Nerosmin has come to us," said Berikas curtly.

The participants almost exploded.

"You lie!" barked the Ranian and the Aquilan, almost damaging their suits.

Berikas reached into his breast pocket and cast a small animal-skin sack into the middle of the table. It hung open lazily, revealing a shimmering sapphire, cut into a perfect polyhedral shape. The group beheld it in awe, before their gazes turned to Berikas, who allowed himself a brief smirk.

"Where had it been hidden?" asked the Mydian woman.

"As Progenitor Nine searched for materials to implement his solution to return to his mother, he found a rogue planet. The coordinates have been secured from his memory. He described the symbol of Nerosmin, as a mural within a tomb buried in igneous rock."

The meeting was silent. A strange blanket of tension fell over the table, buffeting the participants. The old man smiled, as if someone were playing a melody on a favourite instrument he'd long lost the ability to play.

"There is more," said Berikas. "I believe an important element has surfaced."

The old man said in a tired rasp, "Another?"

Berikas breathed shakily and said, "Progenitor Nine took refuge on a habitable moon the natives call Undarli. If his memory of the night sky is accurate, it is the home world."

Not a muscle moved. A sudden gust swept across the table as if some omnipotent being was expressing shock in their stead. Berikas gazed around the table, trying to gauge their reactions. Perhaps the news overwhelmed them and they had lost consciousness.

"As I said, my friends, make what you will of this," Berikas went on. "I have only presented the facts. And I said, 'If his memory is accurate.' Perhaps Progenitor Nine was mistaken. Yet this coalition has little issue with reordering the entire Commonwealth for the sake of an 'if'. Move mountains, crush glaciers, destroy worlds, to unearth a diamond. That is how our ancestors operated. *If* it is accurate, we have not just found the home world of the Orda, but the resting place of Baumei. The progeny of Sinkrel gave us Nerosmin, which will lead us to Baumei. At that, Liadri and Aers will come to us. The time for teeth gritting is done, my friends. The time of the covenant may very well be at hand within the lifetime of at least one of us." He punctuated that phrase with a smile more sly than sincere.

The covenant with Espavel, thought the old man with a grin. *The end of transience.*

The group turned to the old man, who eyed the flowers again. Savouring the wind beating across his wrinkled, leathery face, he proclaimed, "We shall observe Progenitor Nine as we always have done. Perhaps he has much more to show us. Nerosmin will be with us, as with Sinkrel. The search for the others shall continue. See it done."

"Yes, Lord," droned the group in an obedient bow.

"Progenitor Nine's family has, I must say, given us some trouble with the Evelyns. Their assistance may undermine our plans in the foreseeable future. Especially if the Mydians' reliance on them exacerbates." He paused to gaze at the flowers, and pondered a little longer. "Too much uncertainty at present. We will monitor, but always be aware of the actions to take."

The old man eyed the sapphire, momentarily mesmerised by the mysteries it withheld, the destiny it promised, the horror it foreshadowed. The old man was ancient, and no stranger to decisions of great consequence. And yet never before had he felt as if he were about to change the course of events to an outcome he couldn't predict.

I feel young, he thought giddily.

Then he looked to the group and said, "Target Undarli for Annexation."

About the Author

Craig Stephen Cooper grew up in Wollongong, New South Wales, Australia. At a young age, he quickly developed a flare for the dramatic, an obsession with various video games, and an aptitude for expressiveness.

In response to his desire to develop video games, his parents allowed him to study software engineering under a tutor while still in primary school. At the same time, he took dance lessons after school. He later decided drama was a path better suited to his love of storytelling, and studied speech and drama during high school.

While completing a Bachelor of Computer Engineering, he underwent practical and theory examinations for an Associate Diploma of Performance Art. During his Doctor of Philosophy in Telecommunications, he taught speech and drama to primary school children. As a member of the Fellowship of Australian Writers, he has presented workshops on storytelling and poetry, drawing on his speech and drama studies.

Final Flight of the Ranegr is a mixture of his boyhood experiences and inspiration from various science fiction epics and Japanese anime, of which he is a fan.

He also dabbles in video game and mobile app development.

About the Illustrator

Tessa Eden grew up upon the shores of Australia's sunny beaches, frolicking in the sand and exploring the beautiful underwater world. Her father being a software engineer, and mother an illustrator, it was natural that she would grow to combine the two, becoming a digital artist. She now spends her days painting digitally, and creating 3D animations and CGI for animation studios in Sydney.

www.ingramcontent.com/pod-product-compliance
Lightning Source LLC
Chambersburg PA
CBHW030630110726
47901CB00002B/393